WINTERMIND

WINTERMIND

Marvin Kaye and Parke Godwin

DOUBLEDAY & COMPANY, INC.
GARDEN CITY, NEW YORK
1982

All of the characters in this book are fictitious, and any resemblance to actual persons, living or dead, is purely coincidental.

Library of Congress Cataloging in Publication Data

Kaye, Marvin.
  Wintermind.

  Sequel to: The masters of solitude.
  I. Godwin, Parke. II. Title.
PS3561.A886W5   1982   813'.54

ISBN: 0-385-14891-7   AACR2
Library of Congress Catalog Card Number 81-43111
Copyright © 1982 by Marvin Kaye and Parke Godwin
All Rights Reserved
Printed in the United States of America
First Edition

CONTENTS

INTRODUCTORY

While individual effort is greatly prized in our City, purely personal sacrifice is little regarded (a fact that alienates older coven-bred hospitants). So students who appreciate our necessary emotional priorities may justly wonder that I, chief administrator, devote precious time editing and introducing Spitt's account of the so-called Wintermind horror.

I do so because its aftermath can't—mustn't—be ignored. Before extinction, certain prehistoric mammals wrought great havoc with the same rampant attributes that doomed them. To study the fate of the mammoth or the sabertooth tiger is to heed the warning of the Wintermind tragedy.

Those unfamiliar with early City-coven history may not fully grasp the unique sociopsychological status of our world at the beginning of the cooperative era. To rectify this and save precious research hours via synergizer, I've encapsulated the essential facts below and also include a revealing prologue from Spitt's unedited diaries.

Randall Singer, when lecturing, once held that "after the fall of the old western empire, only the City preserved ancient technology." I always suspected this, like all generalizations, to be misleading. Today we know it's false.

The fault is it implies a world largely sunk in barbarism—which existed, to be sure, though it's illogical to suppose a culture whose automated craft probed as far as Pluto (and might've put people on other planets) would revert to bearskins and battleaxes. Lack of written record doesn't mean lack of culture.

Those who didn't or couldn't become part of the City had many hard options. Some survivors of the ancient "Jing" invasion and occupation evidently became less concerned with *what's left?* and more with questions of personal and collective identity. From this admittedly hypothetical base emerged the covens and, with them, the unwritten Uhian dialect composed of fragments of English (coveners call it Old Language), slang and accretions too numerous to catalog here. (Synergizer referent: 952/129—877(8)-0294/270.)

As covens formed political and ethnic entities, there arose a faith and way of life so interwound that coveners neither had nor required a separate word for religion in the Uhian tongue. Everything spiritual—"everything good," they'd say—came to be known simply as Circle.

Circle was based on antique witchcraft. Not the dark, persecuted protest of devil worshipers, but the older, purer celebration of earth and the joyous aspects of life itself. That coveners reverted to this system of belief isn't surprising. Witchcraft was the prevalent religion of western Europe before and during much of the Christian era. Between the last of its active adherents, arguably in the late 17th Century A.D. and the end of the American empire, there stretch barely four centuries—almost an instant of time to a citizen.

A clue to the coven value system is lack of a calendar. They developed a deceptively simple spiritual culture in a simple forest setting. Their year became a wheel always returning to summer, evenly divided into precise seasons by religious festivals (fire days), with no need for numbered revolutions. This important fact was first noted by my late daughter, Judith, in a vital passage from one of her notebooks:

The timelessness of Circle ultimately brought coveners to cultural stasis, but initially it provided strength in the guise of group identity. Circle means freedom from the forging pressures of solitude, whether spiritual or merely physical. Unlike City people who prefer personal isolation for work and thought, coveners fear loss of familial oneness. Circle worship strives for merging of identity through dance, song, ritual and symbolic magic (via their "lep").

So it isn't surprising that a covener totally separated from his fellows might well go insane or die.

Predictably, Circle ceremonies grew more elaborate as history eventually caught up with the unchanging covens; as this people grew more sophisticated, they increasingly needed grander rituals to achieve the oneness so sought in any religious communion. In my daughter's words: *the painful price of mind.*

Ironically, Uhian geography shows individual covens remote from one another. Except for chance meetings during trading expeditions, or maybe on a youthful trek to a close neighbor, a Shando rarely encountered a Karli or south Wengen, while the possibility of laying eyes on a Suffec or Fleeter remained distant in an entire lifetime.

Yet—and this is crucially important—covens weren't as isolated as this fact seems to indicate. During long centuries of unrecorded history, coveners practiced much inbreeding to their advantage . . . and detriment.

The advantage: emergence of the unique trait my daughter described above as *lep.*

Lep (te*lep*athy of an intensity and sensitivity unknown till recently in the City) is the identifying mark of the covens. If we see the human mind as an overlaying of abilities from primitive to complex, then lep properly belongs to the most primitive underlayer, one of the last vestiges of an early stage probably well before the development of systematic speech, when *genus homo* still needed more reliance on herd instinct than intellect. Its re-emergence as a dominant trait among coveners was the result of inbreeding and natural selection. Those possessing it in greatest degree become priests of their people: *masters,* such as Arin and his wife Shalane.

While mastership confers rank and some power, mainly it demands rigorous mental training and bodily discipline, subordinating each master to the community's needs and safety.

The full cultural significance of lep to coveners can only be guessed at by pure-born City people. Certainly lep permits coveners to share subtle, elusive emotions. It allows small groups of hunters to remain in reassuring touch with their home coven. But most impor tant, it enables these people to link minds and share emotively, even hallucinogenically, during ceremonial worship.

Life was never the idyll prompted by the static, insular existence of coveners. Marauding nomads, wild dog packs, mercenary (merk) raids, plague threatened forest life. But the deadliest enemy lay within—the disadvantage of countless centuries of inbreeding: an inelasticity of bone that made childbirth difficult and dangerous. In the

last century before Garick's battle of Dannyline, coveners were a
failing people with a steadily declining birthrate.

Dating pre-Dannyline coven history is still next to impossible.
To limn their beginnings requires the combined skills of an archae-
ologist, historian, etymologist, musicologist—and considerable guess-
work. But with the birth of Garick, master and god of the Shando,
the covens move abruptly into the light of recorded fact.

At that time, our City was impregnably girded (so we thought)
by an electronic barrier surrounding our approximately 1,500-mile
border. Essentially, it analyzed brain patterns of trespassers and
beamed back a complementary negative set—waves that burned away
every trace of cognition and personality. Coveners called it the Self-
Gate because it reputedly shreds the person defying it with unrelent-
ing self-analysis. This theory was mere speculation. Until Garick's
war, no one survived the barrier to describe its subjective effect.

Then, 28 years before Dannyline, my daughter Judith left the
City, though I pleaded with her to remain. Her subsequent researches
among the coveners had far-ranging consequences, but the details are
chronicled elsewhere. For now, we need only note that she finished
her work and applied for re-entry. But the sensors reported incipient
biological breakdown and the presence of bacteria for which we had
no immunity.

I simply couldn't risk endangering our entire populace. So I denied my Judith the right to return, though expulsion from the City, I
knew, meant a tragically early death for her.

Exiled, she married Garick and bore him a son, the historically
elusive Singer, who disappeared shortly after we opened the City to
coveners. Singer's half brother Arin (Garick's son by the late Shando
goddess Jenna), I suspect, knew more about his brother's motives
and whereabouts than he ever told.

Judith's influence on Garick was galvanic, crucial. She taught
him to read and write, directed his eyes to the world beyond Circle.
My daughter conceived a need for open coven-City relationships,
partly because she knew the covens, if they remained unchanged,
would die. Garick's mind was ready tinder wanting only a spark;
Judith fired him with purpose and over the years he accreted wealth
and power till, long after Judith's death, Garick united nearly all
Uhian covens—Shando, Karli, south Wengen, Suffec—in a war to
force the City to recognize Uhian needs.

Garick's councillors regarded his plan as quixotic. Even if the
united covens defeated the well-drilled mercenary armies maintained

throughout Uhia, how were they to breach the Self-Gate? Mere numbers meant nothing to it. Communication by message seemed useless since we'd remained silent behind the gate for more than 2,000 years.

In truth, we only supported merks as border patrol to turn away possible gate suicides, but the divisions grew without our awareness. Garick actually petitioned us for help before deciding to fight, but subversive elements in the merks prevented his pleas from being transmitted to us via the phone connections we then maintained with border posts. We would've willingly sent Garick medical supplies against the then-rampant plague, if we'd known about the danger to coveners. But his plea didn't get through, and he mounted an offensive that would've rolled right up to the Self-Gate, only to be effectively stopped by it. Nothing but a major breakdown in our defenses could've opened the City to Garick. (I don't defend this fact, merely point to the dead weight of tradition even in advanced social institutions.)

In a larger sense, contemporary opinion may condemn the original cultural exclusivism of the City, but those few residents who recall the days of the "Jing" withdrawal know there was no other course. Society was rapidly disintegrating and intellectualism became gravely suspect. To achieve our ultimately humanistic aims first required that we personally and institutionally *survive*. So the gate was built and activated—at great cost and pain. (Researchers interested in the Great Schism may trace this skein of City history under that heading in the synergizer. Also: consult coven legends of the Myudans. As a matter of fact, they are briefly alluded to in the Wintermind tale.)

Garick ultimately learned it wasn't the City that was his enemy but Uriah, leader of the Kriss, and his son Jeremiah. These two commanded a community of militant Christians dedicated to destroying or subjugating the covens.

Uriah nearly murdered Garick's son Arin, but he escaped with news of the Kriss' true intent. A subsequent slaughter took place in the Kriss settlement, Salvation; Uriah is believed to have died then. Jeremiah perished at Dannyline, his forces crushed by the covens.

Garick—now uncrowned ruler of all Uhia, including Mrika—marched into the border town of Lorl. Meanwhile, Arin successfully "ran" the Self-Gate, found and persuaded me to enter Lorl and parley with his father. The incentive was adaptation of lep (via immediate employment of coven minds and eventual breeding of the trait into a new generation of City-educated coven children) for the acceleration of the City's immediate purpose: programming the synergizer with all analyzable knowledge so that phase 2 of our work may be undertaken.

It was a hard decision for me. Garick's people were already dying, but slowly. To confront the coveners with the sheer size, let alone technological sophistication of the City would be to subject its members to a shock that might sever them from their deepest spiritual roots. Had I the right to commit them to a cruel experiment whose chief benefit was City-directed? A dreadful dilemma. But Garick's son urged me to ask the synergizer, just as I did when Judith petitioned for re-entry.

Five of us, led by Arin, went to Lorl, spoke with Garick and at last agreed to shut off the gate.

It was the beginning of a new era.

The contemporary source for this period is the City-circulated work and personal journals of the Mrikan, Spitt. Already 50 when the coven war began, he was Garick's Mrikan sales agent for sida (fermented apple liquor) and secretly his invaluable spy. Spitt operated for a year in Mrika under Jeremiah's nose, never suspected. On the one occasion their paths converged, Jeremiah didn't even know who Spitt was.

As a spy Spitt had the double advantage of being both inconspicuous and unlikely. According to Garick "a round, popular little man, bald as a melon, with a perpetual expression of childlike surprise. He looked like he ought to live in a basket."

Much of this was protective pose. Careless spies don't live to write memoirs. Garick taught him to write. Spitt learned fast. In 3 years, he was fluent. In 10, he had a narrative style that distinguishes his journals and translations of ancient works.

As Garick's minister-at-large, Spitt showed a singular lack of greed or vanity. Garick made him rich enough, but to the end of his brief life Spitt remained as unstylish as Garick himself. Neither clothes nor house reflected Spitt's wealth. Invariably he entertained visitors amidst clutter, wearing a robe that Corian Trevanni bluntly described as "stained with ink, snot and his most recent meal."

Out of Garick's war Spitt gleaned the MacCauley diaries, early writings that became his obsession to his dying day. In translating these lay Spitt's genius: he listened to thousands of hours of City tapes, reviewed newsreels, read and collected texts unopened by City technicians for hundreds of years. He re-mined the language, its color and idiom; his distillation produced a subtly complex, seemingly artless style that perfectly reflected the author himself.

His literary detractors claim he lacked detachment, novelized history, was too close to his subjects for dispassionate analysis. All true—yet irrelevant. Spitt can't be avoided. His 130-year span bridged old and new times. He saw and reported a decisive turn in human history. Any student of Garick's or Arin's life must consult Spitt. Literary historians researching lyric poets need Spitt on their shelves; in his memoirs appears Corian Trevanni when he was just a grubby medic hobnobbing with whores on Lorl's Crib Street, his first poems still years in the future.

Corian's role in the Wintermind tale is as crucial as the keystone of an arch, but Spitt spends little time describing him. Instead, characteristically assuming every reader shares contemporary knowledge (a trait which dated Spitt's work quickly), Spitt introduces him without description other than the indirectly communicated information that nine years earlier, Corian had a clubfoot and walked with a crutch. This is insufficient for any reader who hasn't studied the poet Trevanni.

Partially to rectify this, I've added an opening section of pertinent notes transcribed directly, though not always chronologically, from Spitt's personal journals, as well as a brief epilogue from the same source.

Here, then, in slightly expanded form, is Spitt's account of WINTERMIND.

> —MARIAN SINGER
> Chief administrator, City

WINTERMIND

Don't you feel old Goddess
Turned year-wheel all too fast?
Don't you guess the Shando
Seen just about the last
    Of Goddess bringing summer round
    In Sinjin green and flower crown?

                    —late Shando folksong

CORIAN

(Prologue from Spitt's Diary)

Got to talking not long ago with Jay Kriss about Christianity and its peculiarly stylized concept of an afterlife. In the middle of a thought, Jay broke off, laughing. I asked him what was funny.

"Just thinking about Corian," he chuckled. "I wonder what he'd do in Heaven."

Without hesitation, I said, "Change the rules."

I knew Corian by sight as a familiar figure in Korbin's or Crib Street long before Garick told me of their meeting at Dannyline.

The last of Jeremiah's soldiers got caught on a ridge surrounded by thousands of coveners. After Jeremiah died and they surrendered, Garick allowed them to walk home provided they march single-file past a huge basket and drop in ten krets apiece—Garick's price for letting them leave the ridge.

Coveners buried their dead at Dannyline, but the dead merks rotted where they fell. Dannyline was a sickening place. Corpses bloated in late summer heat; the air was barely breathable; gorged buzzards lurched back and forth among swollen bodies, more wheeled in the white sky.

In the middle of the carnage on the ridge, Garick noticed a single man hopping about on a crutch, shooing the scavenger birds furiously, cursing as they settled again and again only to flap off in frustration as the frantic little man lunged at them. But there were too many for him. In sheer desperation he flailed his crutch at them, fell down, struggled grimly up and waved away the buzzards once more.

Bowdeen, constantly at Garick's side, recognized the distant figure. "That's Corian."

Garick was mystified. "Why's he still up there? Doesn't he want to go home?"

Bowdeen sighed. "Already asked. Said he ain't about to."

Garick winced with the pain of the battle-burned arm strapped across his chest. "Wait here, Bow. Be right back."

Curious, Garick cantered his horse up the slope to the ridge saddle where he found a space cleared of bodies and ten men alive but too badly wounded to be moved, all filthy under their fresh bandages.

Hovering over them like a worried brood hen was an undersized boy no more than eighteen, naked except for a blood-spattered white apron, leaning on a crutch to compensate for the right leg that ended in a blunt knob at the ankle. Deftly tying off a dressing, he barely acknowledged the champion of the battle, Garick, god of the Shando coven.

"Come to collect?" he snarled over his shoulder. "Forget it. These are *my* patients, master Garick. You don't make no ten krets off us."

Garick recognized the rapid Wengen lilt. "Bow says they call you Corian."

The boy swung his free arm at a low-swooping buzzard. *"Hi!* Geddouda here, you motherless— That's right: Corian, medical sweep, southern division."

"There's no more division, sweep. All you have to do is walk home."

One of the men stirred feebly and groaned. Corian went to him at once. "Jon, a man would think you was hurt bad." He put brown fingers to the man's throat, counting the pulse. In a few practiced movements, Corian swabbed the wounded man's arm with alcohol, stripped the covering from a needle ampule and administered the shot.

"These mofos can't be moved yet, Garick. And them birds up there, they ain't gonna be choosy between live and dead unless I stay to keep 'em off."

In the shattered men Garick saw the look of coming death. It registered on his keen coven senses like a sound plucked from an arrow-string. Dull-eyed, unmoving, few had even turned their heads when he first rode among them.

The birds waited overhead.

"Better go home, boy."

Corian was already working on another man. "No."

"I know how you feel, Corian. I've buried my own here."

"Hey, man, we'll cry all the way home."

"Home? They won't make it," said Garick.

Corian's head jerked up. "Won't make it?" The words seemed to ignite something in him. He pulled himself up, quivering with anger. "Won't make it? You men hear what Garick says? Shando god says you're birdmeat, man. Good as dead." He wheeled on Garick, bent over the crutch. "Listen, goddammit, these are *my* patients, Corian's, and we got all we need to get back: antitet, antibio, dressings, City pain-killer, even food stripped off mofos who died before I could help 'em. But nobody dies on *me*, Garick, not when I say they don't. Hey, you people hear that? Nobody dies! That's a goddam order. We're gonna make it!"

Looking back, I can understand the violence of his reaction. What Garick said put a torch to something that smoldered in Corian all his life. He struggled to be born, killed his mother in the attempt, fell into the world without a foot, limped on a crutch through a starved childhood, never knowing health or a full meal before he came to Lorl. Death was his personal enemy.

Corian pawed a wad of sweat-soggy bills from a pocket of his bloody apron. "You're a long-chance man, Garick. A cool-as-ice, roll-the-dice gambler, that's what I heard. Now, I ain't paying no ten krets to no Shando to walk off no hill, not'n leave men too sick to walk. But I'll just bet you the ten we make it to Lorl."

Insects buzzed in the sick-sweet air. Garick felt his stomach heave. He had to get off that ridge fast, but if betting would keep Corian's men alive, he'd cover it.

"How can I collect?" he asked.

The boy pegged over to Garick's stirrup and thrust out the money. "You hold it till I get there."

Garick had to grin. "Just to stay honest, you'll find me at Korbin's."

"Figured to be there myself. We got a bet or you all mouth?"

Garick took the bills. "If that's how you want it."

"That's how. Fair bet." Corian swabbed his sweaty neck, squinting at the sun. "Now if you'll haul ass out of my hospital, I got patients to feed."

As he cantered down the hill, Garick heard the raucous clang of a heavy spoon against an iron bucket and Corian's strident voice.

"Awright, awright. I'm talking to the sick, lame and lazy. Suppertime. Hey, c'mon, suppertime! You can't just lie there, you make it too easy for the birds, man. We're going home, and you know what I mean. Crib Street full of lonesome girls ain't been done right since we been gone. Heyhey, sit up! C'mon now, I got ten krets on you mofos. Gonna have to walk soon, start by sitting up. Everybody spoons for himself. I'm your mother, I should feed you? Hey, what are you waiting, let's go, let's movemove*move*. Suppertime . . ."

No one beyond Lorl knew who Corian was then. Years later, when it was hard to find anyone in a thousand miles who didn't, I remarked to Garick that if Corian had been born with two feet, he might have made the rank of sub in the southern division, perhaps even commander.

Garick snorted. "Commander, hell. One more foot and that little bastard would've won the war."

♯

When Marian Singer first emerged from the Self-Gate, she was accompanied by four other City residents. One was Dr. Theodore Rashevsky, who, several years later, replaced my old heart. A slight man with a neat dark beard that never changes length, color or style, he is as youthful and ageless as all City folk. I first found it unnerving to discover he's well over 700 years old. Later, though, he became a good friend of mine.

Rashevsky introduced me to the incredible resources of City libraries, especially the newsreels, drama and music tapes preserved from pre-Jing times, an era that fascinates me.

Though chiefly a surgeon-researcher and occasional psychological advisor, Ted also used to be the main medical contact for the merks in the years before the battle of Dannyline.

Ted and I visit rarely now, but write often—pure courtesy on his part since, in his tape messages, he employs Old Language, a tedious medium for City people used to a bewilderingly compacted mode of communication consisting of isolated sounds and rapid finger motions. Incomprehensible to an outsider—the coveners call it *shortmind,* a term now in general usage—it's a system which saves City dwellers a great deal of time exchanging ideas. (When it comes to keeping an eye on the clock, City folk are worse than Sidele managing her crib girls.)

In one of Ted Rashevsky's letters, I find the following reference to Corian, probably the first time City took any real notice of anyone beyond the Gate:

Before Dannyline, medical stations at Lorl and Filsberg required only a few simple supplies, little time. Usual problem: venereal infections. We sent out oral and mechanical contraceptives plus instructions to treat the women before the men. Apparently no one listened. I was constantly pestered for ichthammol for burns, thimerosal, alcohol, salve for bruises, apc's, antitet and morphine derivs for field use. Plus plenty of penicillin. Must've lost a few allergic merks. Otherwise, only other supplies I remember sending were solar-powered recorder/players and instruction tapes couched in primer language.

Then—a few years before the coven war—I suddenly became deluged with phone-ins from the Lorl checkpoint. That was surprising in itself. Direct voice communication was rare, mostly messages came on tape. But one morning the phone rang. I jumped. I picked it up, heard somebody who sounded very young telling me to send this, send that. More tapes, more sulfa derivs, local and general anesthetic, forceps, scalpels, sponges, retractors, the list went on and on, all interspersed with the most colorfully obscene language I'd heard in—never mind, you don't want to know how long.

It was hard enough even to understand what he was saying. You know how difficult it is to follow that southern Wengen dialect: half-sung, half-swallowed, all of it almost as fast as a tape played at double speed. He finally communicated his name, Corian, and he'd memorized every tape ever sent by us to Lorl. He wanted more instruction, especially on antiseptic abortion, normal and Caesarian birth methods, whole blood and plasma techniques. I was stunned. Like many City residents, I was tacitly convinced only barbarians lived outside.

Corian raved to me that "crib girls"(?) were too stupid or careless to use contraceptives correctly. A lot of them got pregnant. Later he told me he delivered six children during his stay at Lorl, three of them by section. Five lived—astounding for the conditions he worked under. Even a minor opera-

tion with basically primitive equipment like sponge, retractor,
clamp and scalpel is hard without qualified assistance and
months of drill. The most amazing circumstance of all was,
Corian wasn't yet nineteen—essentially an embryo to a City
resident!

Was Corian a good doctor? Probably not. He was too emotional, too involved with each case. Far too much empathy.
(And yes, Spitt, I had to look up that last word. Haven't had
need of it for centuries—the word or, for that matter, the
emotion.) Yet we can't dismiss certain aspects of Corian's nature which any physician might envy. He had an instinct, an
insight rare even in the most expert diagnostician. He's a borderline case, you know. Not exactly a non-telepath, but too
low a potential to measure or control effectively. He can't
transmit, but he sometimes receives and definitely is able to
"share"—that wordless emotional commǐuning that coveners
manage. Corian can "read" coveners without words . . . and
that, Spitt, is the only true way to understand a people whose
basic cultural concepts are totally non-verbal.

The crib girls were loyal to Corian as to no one else. He loved
them all—enthusiastically—in a kind of barter arrangement. When a
girl checked out clean, her first favors usually went to Corian. Bowdeen and Sidele hadn't yet organized them into a profitable family.
They were independent and competitive as hell, and nobody rode
free. The money went on the bed before the girl; if not, she was a
fool. But any girl who tried to charge Corian so much as a half-kret
was outcast, and no one would drink with her at Korbin's.

"That last baby, the one that died, that was Sayna's."

I still have the tape on my recorder, a little fuzzy with age and
replaying. The speaker was a crib girl before she went to live with
one of the survivors of Dannyline. She told me the story one day
over dinner and a jug.
     "Sayna and Corian were the same kind," she said, "both of
them close-in Wengens from around the iron works, you know what
kind of life that is. Both of them scrawny and undersized, grew up
sick and hungry all the time. Only difference, Corian was smart and
Sayna was dumb as a Shando horse. She'd let half the goddam divi-

sion ride on credit. Some paid, most didn't. If she liked a man, she couldn't do enough for him. Like one time the zone guards found this silly little bastard who tried to jump the Self-Gate into City. I met him the night before, that stupid mofo asked *me* to go along for company. Well, the guards hauled him out of the zone, and they were really surprised to find he wasn't dead. They dumped him in a pigsty near Sayna's crib. She found him, nursed him three days, didn't turn no money the whole time. Said she stole some off him, probably not enough.

"Sayna never slept in a real bed on a wood floor till she came to Lorl. Ate with her fingers, wiped her hands on her clothes, you'd think she was deepwoods. Couldn't keep clean, always clapped up to the ears. Corian'd get so mad: 'Sayna, didn't you wash yourself? Didn't you take your pills? Didn't you make 'em wear conts? Goddam stupid woman, I gotta follow you around with a needle up your ass to keep you clean?'

"And Sayna'd just pull her head in like he was gonna hit her, but he never did. He couldn't hurt anything, just yell and fuss and hop up and down, he got so mad, and Sayna'd cry a little and ask him please come home with her because she felt lonesome, and when Cory said yes, she'd be happy as a little girl just because he wasn't mad at her no more. Dumb. She never saved nothing. She died bust.

"Well, she got pregnant. Maybe Cory's, maybe not, but you never saw anyone fuss over a birthin' like those two. Corian had the back room of the med station all ready for her, clean as could be, one of the girls to help. Hell, none of us worried, we figured she'd just spit it out like a seed.

"Except she couldn't. The baby was turned wrong way around, and Cory had to cut in to take it out of her. She started to bleed heavy. He couldn't stop it. He lost them both.

"He showed up at my place that night, my private room behind the crib. Oh, Spitt, that was one pitiful sight. Corian was crazy drunk on potato gin. Couldn't make him lie down or even sit, just limped around and around, going on about—I don't know, how Wengen women, coven women were different, all kinds of problems no one knew about. Crying most of the time, his voice all hoarse and raggedy, he was so far gone. He'd took Sayna and her baby out west of town and buried them together. Came back crazy and feeling like he killed 'em both, crying and stomping around, but mostly he was some kind of mad like you never saw before. Mad at something, I never knew what.

"Finally got him in bed, thought he'd sleep, but he just hung on to me, shiverin' like a scared little boy. He couldn't settle down, and I said to myself, shit, there's only one thing I can do for him. Had to love him like a man and hold him like a hurt baby, he was both, he needed it."

The woman measured herself another drink and turned the memory in her mind, a recollection not devoid of pleasure.

"Spitt, I've had some wild rides in my time, but that old bed was never the same after. Corian just bucked and ripped and tore at me like he was out to kill something, just on and on till he plain collapsed on top of me and I had to roll him off to get some sleep.

"Just a skinny little kid, but every girl on the row loved him. He was the only man ever cared about them. And look at him now, will you? Remember the day he came home from Dannyline? Weren't we all fine that day?"

Garick ran me ragged those first weeks after Dannyline, but he drove himself harder than anyone else, one arm burned off and sealing inside himself the grief of the wife lost in battle.* He kept me at hand during those initial conferences with Marian Singer held at Korbin's. When he finally collapsed and Rashevsky stepped in to prescribe bed rest, I felt downright grateful.

One afternoon while Garick was recuperating, I sat alone with old Korbin, finishing some conference notes, when two crib girls bustled in, chattering excitedly, each with an armload of blankets. While we watched, one of them began laying out makeshift beds on the plank floor. The other marched straight to Korbin at the bar with a nod to me.

"Morning, Spitt. Korbin, Corian's back and hungry as hell'n he wants food for eleven."

Korbin just stared at her and then at the other girl who went on swooshing down blankets, humming to herself and very domestic. "What's she doing?" he demanded.

"Get the food," the bedmaker yelled across the room. "Corian *says*."

Korbin had no time to argue. More girls streamed through the door, the gay advance element for a jubilant parade, all bearing blankets and medical supplies. The last of them entered with a definite flourish and held the door wide.

* The Shando goddess, Jenna, Garick's 2nd wife. —M.S.

Pegging on his dark-worn crutch, Corian staggered through the door, sun-blistered, black hair brambled like a bird's nest, the smallest dirtiest merk I'd ever seen. He'd cut the sleeves off his leather tunic and what was left was stiff with blood and dirt. I remembered Garick's story of his bet and reflected how glad he'd be to lose this one. Corian lurched to the bar and fell against it, head hanging down as if it were too heavy for his thin shoulders.

Korbin leaned over the bar toward him, half curious, half in concern. The boy looked as if he'd collapse any minute. "Corian, what the hell you doing?"

"Collecting a bet," Corian croaked out of a dry throat. "Gimme a pan of water, hottest you got. Bossy girl, open that disinfectant."

Then through Korbin's open door came ten filthy, bedraggled merks, leaning on each other or supported by more girls; men sweated out and reddened with sun-scorch, eyes glazed with exhaustion, but ten living men. Corian's patients. He said he'd bring them home and he goddam well did.

"Man, I am covered with *shmutz* one end to the other," Corian groaned. He scrubbed his hands in the washpan and doused them again in disinfectant. "Lay them men out soft and easy, girls. Doctor Corian is about to consult."

He swayed a little, hanging onto the bar for support. "They need food, Korbin, all you got. Dish it up." Uninvited, he helped himself to an open jug, swigged deeply and wheezed. "Charge it to Garick. The son of a bitch owes me ten krets."

Korbin retrieved the jug and stoppered it. "Prices gone up. That won't hardly cover all you want."

The girl called Bossy hooted at him. "Hell it won't! Ain't you mean talking to Corian like that when he's the best man in the division and just about all that's left of it? Now you dish up for these poor, hurt men or we ain't never gonna buy from you again." She turned to the rest of the crib girls. "Are we?"

"NO!"

Korbin protested. "You know food is way up since the war."

One young merk, bandaged from shoulder to stomach, raised his head from the blankets. "Hey, tell us about the war. I hear it was bad."

"Don't even know if I got food for eleven around," Korbin said. "Or where I can get it."

That's when I got into it. Somehow, seeing Corian, a memory came to me: standing by a chicken coop watching new-hatched

chicks wobble down the chute to start life. We culled out the lame
and half-formed before they ever reached grain or water. Last out of
the coop came a chick whose legs didn't work at all, just splayed out
under the fuzzy ounce of body like two spindly oars on a boat, and
that's how the determined chick used them, rowing grimly to catch
up with the others and cheep-cheeping sassy as they come. I figured
something that tough deserved to live. That's why I picked it up and
set it by the feedpan—and poured Corian another drink.

"Dish up, Korbin," I said. "All you've got, all you can find.
Garick's got the bill."

Any customer nosing down Crib Street that hot summer day
went home un-had. Every girl from the row was feeding the
wounded, washing them, or crawling all over Corian. It was a kind of
convalescent celebration and very—the ancient word fits well—very
gallant in its way.

By now, Corian was much sicker than his patients. His exhaustion was far beyond the stage where he could relax normally. He
couldn't sleep, refused even to lie down on the bed the girls made for
him, just drifted like a tired wasp from one patient to another, still
running on the will that served to bring his men home. He ate a little
and drank a lot, hanging over the bar in a dull stupor, unable to let
go.

Some of that stubbornness stayed with him always. Like a child,
he was afraid to miss something. Sleep took him away from touching
people, sleep left him alone. During sleep people could leave him
and he'd never know it, could die like his mother or like Sayna who
slipped away with her baby despite his desperate efforts to save her.
He had to watch every minute because asleep he was out of control.

It seemed the only way anyone would get him to lie down
would be to grab his crutch and knock him out. Korbin was really
considering this when I noticed a young woman just inside the door,
eyeing the crib girls with a mixture of curiosity and distaste.

At that time I only knew her by sight: Shalane, a master of the
Karli, one of the most traditional and conservative of all the forest
covens. She was married to Arin, Garick's younger son.

She wore a new white cotton robe that contrasted richly with
her deep-tanned skin. Coven-fashion, she'd slit it up both sides to the
hip for easy riding, belted with a knotted six-foot cord, the only
badge of her rank. Even without white tabard and thammay-knife,
you still know a master by their stance and gliding, silent tread. The

stamp of their discipline is on them like a brand. Shalane was not a beautiful woman. Her features, like Arin's, were too inbred and extreme for handsomeness. Just under six feet, she was rather short by coven standards; still there was that indefinable wild-deer grace about her that deepwoods women have.

Her nostrils dilated in her thin face, rejecting what she'd call the *cowan*-smell† of Korbin's store and the other women. Shalane was bewildered, out of place in Mrika. Her people, the Karli, bore the first brunt of Garick's war. In a single year Shalane was wrenched from a happy marriage with Arin through the nightmare of the slaughter of the Kriss at Salvation, trekked twice across the killing Blue Mountains, followed Garick to Dannyline, where her mother and more than a few friends were buried. Like the rest of her folk, Shalane had no clear idea of what actually had been accomplished at Dannyline, what enormous changes would follow.

She moved silently to my table and spoke to me as her kind addressed all cowans, as if from a great distance.

"God Garick says when he's slept some—tomorrow—he wants more talk with City folk. Says you fetch him about late sun." She dropped a folded paper on the table. "Sent some writing, too. Wants an answer."

I read the note and began to scribble a reply. Hanging on the bar, bleary with liquor and fatigue, Corian rubbed his eyes and stared at Shalane.

"I know you," he rasped. "You'zat Dannyline."

Shalane paid him no attention, but you ignored Corian easily as a toothache.

"Korbin, this girl is some kind of bad. I saw her at Dannyline, come up that hill with one of our throwers on her back and just about fried our whole first line." Corian saluted her with grudging respect. "Woman, you are one tough box."

Her green eyes went cold. Familiar with coven ways, I understood the unintended insult that froze Shalane with embarrassment and hostility. The word *box*—merk slang for women and their sex organs alike—could hardly offend a girl who worshiped naked in Circle all her life. It was Corian's mention of violence and the ending of life that shamed her. (Much later, I found an expression of this in an ancient book in the City's library: a swordfighter meets a race of people who wear model male sex organs around their waists. The

† *Cowan*—coven term, meaning an outsider, someone not of Circle. —M.S.

swordfighter sneers at them, but one citizen replies, "See how corrupt you are. You wear a sword at your belt, a symbol of death—whereas we wear a symbol of life.")

There in Korbin's bar, Corian grinned up at Shalane, trying to bring her into some kind of focus. One of the crib girls sang out: "If she's so bad, Cory, how come she missed you?"

"I don't fight, I fix."

The girl draped her arms around him. "Well, fix yourself some sleep, huh? Come on, Cory, we made you a real nice bed over there."

He pushed her away. "Lemme 'lone."

I handed Shalane my note to Garick, speaking in a low tone. "See these men? He brought them back from Dannyline, saved them all. Now he's too tired to sleep and too stubborn to try."

Shalane seemed to look at Corian, really examine him for the first time.

"I mean that's one tough woman there," Corian slurred. "Come up that hill behind a line of bowmen that laid down a spread covered the whole motherless ridge, 'n' while we're still ducking and running, up comes—hey, what's your name?—and she points that goddam thrower and—"

It hissed out of Shalane. She shook with fury. "Cowan, be *still!*"

Corian wobbled away from the bar to confront her. Shalane had a good six inches on him, but he glared up at her, indignant. "I ain't no cowan! My name is Corian, my father is Trevanni, my gramma was fullblood west Wengen Circle. Don't you never call me no—"

Corian seemed to freeze in his tracks, his gaze locked to Shalane's. The drawn, angry young face went suddenly blank as the last energy drained out of it. "I can read what you're feeling," he mumbled vaguely. "I can read you Circle sometimes."

Shalane's expression changed too, no longer hostile, merely concentrated and remote. She held his eyes. "Go to sleep."

He blinked, weaving. "Why?"

"Because now you want to."

All of us watching saw him nod, docile as a child. The crutch fell out of his hand; Corian tottered a little like a tree about to fall—"Where'zat ol' bed?"—and dropped forward into Shalane's arms. She scooped him up almost tenderly and carried him to the waiting blankets. Corian feebly tried to kiss her.

"You come back when I'm rested."

Shalane knelt beside him, placing both hands on his temples. "What I do with you, carry you in my pocket?"

"It ain't the size of the gift," Corian sighed, closing his eyes, "it's the love behind it. You come back."

"Just I'm gonna rub your head a little. You'll be asleep before I finish."

I realized then she was using master's magic on Corian. He yawned and sighed deeply.

"One tough box," he murmured. "When I wake up . . ."

But that was a full day later. Shalane was long gone.

Life was easy for me till the end of the war. I only had to stay alert and avoid Uriah's son, Jeremiah. After Dannyline, events and Garick himself moved so fast, it strained my ball-of-fat frame to keep up.

Garick briefly entered City while Ted Rashevsky studied the arm nearly burned off in battle. It was past saving, but City replaced it. Rashevsky told me that they actually grew another. I found it hard to believe even when I saw it and couldn't tell the difference except for the slight marks at the juncture of the old and new tissue. (Later, they did practically the same thing for my heart and I began to understand the process. Ted says City's been doing it for well over a thousand years. Talking with City people makes you feel a child sometimes.)

Once Garick was repaired, rested and comparatively at peace inside, he returned to Lorl to forge the first policies of his new Uhia. He used to headquarter in Charzen, center of Shando covenstead, but no more. He left a trade representative there, as in Karli and other circles. For the next few years his base was as mobile as his Dannyline army. He was riding much of the time and stayed connected to each coven by lep, to me by a rain of written directives arriving almost daily by fast rider.

HAVE GIVEN UP SHANDO CROWN, REASONS POLICY.
MEET ME AT—

His decision to step down as god was politically shrewd and deeply personal. Since he controlled most of the money in Charzen, he hardly needed the antler crown. Or a title among the Karli, holding more than fifty per cent of the investor-block that bought their wool in Lorl and Filsberg and Towzen. Half of the coal wagoned into the Wengen iron works was his. All commerce, the lifeblood of money and change pumping slowly and surely into the waking forest nation was in Garick's hands. He *was* the economy.

But there's this, too. Garick was near fifty. Except for his first few years married to Judith Singer, his life had never been personally happy. He mentioned his wives only rarely and never his elder son, Singer. Others, including myself, learned not to allude to them. All his love went now to Arin, Shalane and their daughter, Mady. They sufficed. To remain god of the Shando would require a new goddess by his side, but Garick's heart had no place for anyone else. More, he knew he could bring change much easier to the clannish covens if he was no longer identified with a particular covenstead. Out of wisdom and personal choice, Garick now rode alone.

There were a lot of things for Garick to set in motion. First and most valuable: sending a chosen group of young masters for psychological testing in City over an extended period of time. These people were to be schooled in return, with emphasis placed on eventual development of lep by City dwellers.

Arin headed the list, Garick's unofficial ambassador to Marian Singer. At his side was Shalane, just starting to carry the first coven child to be born, raised and educated within City.

Marian Singer stipulated she must have a control group of intelligent young no-lep Wengens and Mrikans forming a separate student class. When Garick rounded up a body of volunteers, I persuaded him to include a certain personal candidate.

> TO: DIANE RADCLIF, CITY
> SENDING YOU, GARICK'S AUTHORITY, ONE ADDITIONAL NO-LEP
> WENGEN FOR CONTROL GROUP. NAME: CORIAN TREVANNI. SAYS
> HE'LL TOLERATE NORMAL ROUTINE IF HE CAN ALSO STUDY MEDI-
> CINE WITH DR. RASHEVSKY. THEY'RE SLIGHTLY ACQUAINTED.
> SPITT

So Corian entered City. He became their most valuable student. Within a few years, he was deeply involved in Garick's medical missions, carrying cytotoxin to stamp out the chronic bone disease in coven women. The birthrate shot up, infant mortality sank.

At twenty, still arrogant and largely ignorant, Corian joined the force that cleaned out Lishin.‡ I've kept his letters (below, edited for

‡ A long-dead vermin-infested city. —M.S.

spelling. For years his feel for words far outran his command of them). It was at Lishin that the arrogance began to wear off.

. . . went up the Skanna with thirty boats, 30,000 pounds of fish that I bought from the Fleeters. All packed in City freezers, full of the strongest poison Rashevsky could provide. We dammed the one stream, let the river run acid, killed some fish, sprayed them with cyanide. Not enough. We had to do it over and over. Spitt, I can't put in words what it was like. One day I stood in that closet where Arin hid, and there's enough coven in me to feel what he felt. Some memories stay with you. If I were Arin, I don't think I'd ever want to sleep. I'd be afraid to dream.

A sensitive man, Corian found his own Lishin all too soon.

After Dannyline, the northern division of mercenaries were at Filsberg without pay and effectively without purpose. Garick wrote them a new contract, cut up the division into training units and scattered them through the nation as the Uhian Constabulary. Each nucleus of Mrikan officers and sweeps was augmented with young coven riders, men and women from every compass point. They began to move outward from Uhia on planned missions, scouting and mapping, meeting new people and ideas, bringing them home to Garick while extending his influence. It was another subtle move toward consolidation. A boy or girl who rode one or two years with the constab discovered that distant covens weren't merely names but familiar faces, shared customs, friends, frequently places to meet future husbands and wives.

Soon after Lishin was cleaned out, Garick ordered Corian far west with a constab company. When they reached commune country, Corian (following secret instructions) got lost for three years: Garick had picked up some information in City about a pre-Jing cache of gold, and it was Cory's job to track it down.

He finally did, but almost died along the way. Tough as he was, Corian contracted a strange sickness on an island off the far southern coast. Rashevsky eventually diagnosed malaria, but that was only part of it. Corian's disease did things to his mind as dark and frightening as what Arin must've experienced while hiding in that closet in Lishin. The details are still largely unknown, but there's a hint of it in this letter Corian sent me much later.

Not so much a fever as an acute, violent depression. I was never so totally alone, so alienated. Hallucinations altered with rationality, till I couldn't tell which was which. It was all the worse because each of them came out of me, out of deep places I didn't know I had, didn't want to know. Nobody really knows himself, Spitt, nobody should, not that far down.

Interesting to note how his writing improved after Garick's gold quest. His sensitivity was widening, the poet was stirring.

♯

Corian wastes less life experience than anyone I've ever known except City folk. Everything's grist for his mill. He began writing during his earliest days as a City student. His first major effort, a five-section horror, dealt with the battle of Dannyline. Two lines will more than suffice:

> *Now comes Garick with his coven force!*
> *Shoot the mofo off his goddam horse!*

Mercifully, this was never completed. There *was* a poet in Corian, though it was a long time birthing. The "Dutchman" pages in my translation of MacCauley's journal are almost entirely Corian's work. His native Wengen has been called the graveyard of English because it retains so much of the ancient color, the musical, metaphorical, hyperbolic, splintered and heady language of a long-gone but vital people, full of their remembered restless energy, laughter and national spirit. Corian distilled it in his soul, reinvigorated our own language with a ghost of long-dead times.

Corian has been called a genius, whatever that is. Mainly, I think, he bends close to scrutinize what others ignored. He can't bear to miss anything, probably because of all he lost merely being born. Life fascinates Corian; all of it. His letters contain remarkable insights:

There are two natural fears deep in all humans, maybe in all primates, according to Rashevsky: fear of the dark and fear of falling. But not one of the coveners in City's test group has ever had either, not even as infants. Not one, man!

It's a little thing, but strange. . . .

Not a little thing at all; rather, the turn of a wheel larger than history itself.

This completes the Corian passages from Spitt's notebooks. Below is a final excerpt from the same source. It's essential to the Wintermind history.

—M.S.

Garick's constabulary force drew another unpleasant mission besides cleaning up Lishin. Once and for all, they had to exterminate or drive out of Uhia the roving bands of cowan hunters who were a danger to life and property. Always a hazard to coven trade routes, they simply had no place left to hide in Uhia.

The campaign was brief, bloody and one-sided. The constab used a coven tactic developed against the merks in the battle of Karli Forest, early in Garick's war. Female riders let themselves be seen on foot, alone and unarmed. Cowans naturally pursued them. The women fled in convincing terror, eventually allowing themselves to be caught and surrounded by the cowan hunters—who then had a life expectancy of a minute or less.

Some people, cowan and coven alike, called this cold-blooded. Not all cowan hunters committed crimes against Circle folk. Some were men who just preferred a solitary forest life, much like the Suffec.

But others like Santee's gang were dangerous as packdogs. When Garick's constab all but wiped out Ben Santee's large band, the only national regret was that Santee and a few others escaped.

Santee's origins are obscure, though Fleeters say he came from the Shortree part of the Fist (their name for the cape they live on far up in the Wengen northeast). Santee could write a little and was extremely proud of his accomplishment—he may have been taught by the Kriss leader, Uriah. Now and then, Santee sent Garick taunting, misspelled notes. Rashevsky judged him to be some kind of psychotic.

Whatever he was, Santee was slippery. The trap that sprang on his band didn't catch him or a handful of his closest friends. But the boy he loved was massacred by the constab.

A week later a constab rider found a message to Garick written on a peel of birch bark and nailed to a tree.

YOUR NOT SMART ENUF TO CATCH ME GARIK. YOU KILL MORE THAN I EVER DID. ILL GET YOU FOR THIS WERE IT HURTS.

BEN SANTEE

And he meant it.

SINJIN GREEN

Shalane stirred in the depths of the night, disturbed by Arin's muted moan. Though still asleep, he thrashed fitfully.

Again.

Even after ten years, it wouldn't fade. A master long before Arin, Shalane could read it easily in her husband's mind, the dark nightmare of the first time he had to kill: the boy Holder, potentially infected with plague, a threat to his own people. But Holder was a Shando, and no one ever ended life within Circle. It was bad enough killing a cowan when you had to, but among your own kind it was unthinkable. Arin was the first, and the price was that the bad dream never went away. Sometimes the Holder-memory left him alone for months at a time, but eventually it returned. Arin was never really quit of it, the same invariable scene flickering through his dormant, captive mind like one of those City-magic newsreels—the arrow slamming Holder back and back against the tree as his eyes sought Arin's, staring in pain and shock, unable to believe the act or the coming of death like a swift shadow over the sun.

Arin groaned and writhed slightly under the light covers. Shalane caressed him with her mind and hands, feeling the cold sweat that stood out on his hard shoulder. Gently, as she'd done once with Corian, Shalane enfolded Arin's mind in her own to nudge him not away from life but only deeper into dreamless sleep. The nightmare ebbed, left him limp. His clenched jaw relaxed, leaving only those lines on his face that had been deep-cut there by another ordeal than Holder's death.

Shalane read his mind now; it was at rest, the way a silent room sounds to the ear. She lay back to recapture her own sleep, but it was a long time coming.

She woke with the first cautious birds, opening her eyes in the familiar warm hollow of Arin's shoulder, and for a little while, the agony and bitter memories were gone. His hand brushed lightly over her cheek, aware of her even in sleep. She eased up on one elbow; Arin sighed and turned over. Shalane watched her husband, studying him for perhaps the millionth time, yet always somehow just like the first: at the great, slender length of his body, the reddish hair like his mother Jenna's, the awkward set of the arm broken so long ago by command of the dead Kriss leader, Uriah.

Shalane put the thought away. She had her own memory of the Kriss, and even after ten years, she could not forget the death-smell and the blood-sticky touch of her own hands.

She watched Arin sleep. It was one of her secret pleasures. She knew Arin did it, too, and both knew the other was aware, a loving game to share and keep secret at the same time.

Her mind went out to read her small daughter in the next room, opening to grasp at energies delicate as flower scents. Mady was still asleep: Shalane's family was safe at rest. That much at least contented her, though it was little enough.

She slid out of bed, reaching for the red robe on the nearby chair, then frowned at the garment. *Getting bad as a City woman,* she thought, putting clothes between herself and the sun first thing out of bed. Shalane draped the robe over one arm and moved out of the white room to a door, pressed a button—*no end to City junk*—and heard a faint hum as the panel slid back. *Like I'm too helpless to open it myself.* She looked in on her child.

Mady lay curled around her pillow, her little white nightgown covering all but her head and feet. A few of her toys lay on the floor, logic-toys, Arin called them, games for solving certain kinds of problems. Some of them Mady brought home from school, but most were presents from Marian Singer and many of them (Marian said) very old, once belonging to some other City child. Once Shalane asked Arin, "What's a logic?" and wondered why he laughed.

Watching Mady asleep in bed, a smile whispered over Shalane's lips. Awake, her daughter never sat still for long, but now—there was a word Shalane's old friend Jay Kriss once used when smiling down on Mady. *Angelic.*

Shalane thought about her own girlhood in Karli. *Did I sleep that good when I was nine?* She figured she must've, but couldn't remember. Sure as frost didn't ball herself up in a nightgown, but Mady didn't have her mother's feel for going bare, partly because weather gets sharp in the northern parts of City, but that wasn't the real reason.

Mady isn't deepwoods. As simple as that. And it hurt Shalane. Ever since City opened and she and Arin settled inside its endless borders, she'd lost so much and couldn't even share her memories with her child. Shalane, practically born riding, used to break horses, but Mady never rode, and Mady never hog-greased in winter, and Mady didn't know the deep good taste of coven food home-cooked before it was a half a day out of the ground. The one fire day she'd spent at home, Mady was too young to remember.

Mady isn't deepwoods. And it wasn't just being far away from Karli or Charzen, it was deeper, it was Arin letting Mady learn from City folk who stuffed their heads and stuffed that damn box with everything but the gifts that only come from Goddess Earth. And mostly it was Marian Singer, supposed to be busy running City but stealing time every day to personally teach Mady City ways.

Mady isn't deepwoods. City teaching turned Shalane's baby into a cool, self-possessed girl. Yet her lep was as strong as any at home. It would reach as far as Shalane's someday, a formidable weapon if needed, but the other half, the *sharing,* was not there. Mady didn't share, didn't pass feelings back and forth and wouldn't allow either her mother or father to touch her mind without permission. She simply shut them out when they tried. Thus Shalane found a small, tender joy in feeling lightly at the edges of Mady's essence in those few moments before her child woke.

Shalane pressed the button again and the panel slid shut. She continued down the hall through the main living room and into the kitchen beyond, a room that represented City's attempt to compromise between the constrictive local dietary regimen and the simple yet varied food of the coveners.

No matter how Shalane tried, City words kept creeping in. She was thinking about breakfast and what it might be. Powdered eggs? Fish soo-flay? C-concentrate? The last for sure; Marian Singer always nagged her to include it in all their morning meals, and it wasn't bad.

She stared without love at the electronic wall oven, the range, the mixers and blenders, the cutters and shapers that timed and weighed and cooked and spiced and sauced and stirred and poured

and served, and the result still lacked something for Shalane. Everything in the kitchen was powered like the rest of the house from a
central box that caught and saved up sunrays, turning them into energy. Shalane's mother, Maysa, was so proud when Moss brought her
a wood-burning stove from Lorl, and it was the only one in Karli.
How Maysa would have loved a City kitchen!

Or would she? City people ate like masters, dab of this, bitty
hunk of that, sip of something else, all of it tasting like it was cooked
last Grannog, and maybe it was. And you couldn't bring home-food
into City past the decon stations. All the coveners tried; it was a kind
of game after going home to come back with real coven food to share
around. The merk guards caught most of it, but Shalane could usually get through with a taste of coon or enough horsemint or gold-
enrod hidden under her hair to go one or two pots of tea.

Shalane smiled. Corian was the one to see if you craved home-
food. He was always running back and forth, in and out of City, carrying doctor things that the guards never tried to search, and—

And *yes.* Shalane opened the refrigerator. She'd forgotten: one
dozen fresh-laid eggs from a chicken still clucking around Lorl somewhere. A sly present from little Spitt.

She poured distilled water into a pan and set it to boil on the
solar stove. When it was ready, she dropped the eggs in, disdaining
the timer bell that could measure the desired four minutes precisely.
Shalane didn't need a bell, she could *feel* four minutes. But City people always let *things* work for them, like the screen over the stove
that changed each day to tell the new date and exact time. But as
easy as a Karli woman could tell the right days for starting babies,
any covener knew what day it was now: eighteen more before Sinjin.
Why give them all names?

Shalane spooned up her eggs, ate them moodily with a glass of
C-concentrate. Diane Radclif said the tart liquid prevented colds.
Shalane had to ask what a cold was, but the stuff did wake up her
mouth all right.

5:25. City people lived almost forever, and they had a saying
that *forever is in the future,* but even though they had more time
than anyone ought to want, they still acted like they never had
enough. Shalane couldn't ever figure them out. They pushed themselves and wrote and studied and thought up ways to gain more time.
They named the centuries and individual years and months and days
'n' even the goddam minutes. This one was 5:25-turning-over-now-
to-5:26, and who cared? The sun slanted early green shadows over

the wooded park around their house, and it would be a lovely spring day, but Shalane doubted Marian Singer's people would notice.

Ten years in City. Ten years in a tiny joke of a manmade forest, a park with trees and green and water but with City towering all around it like grownups around a baby's pen. Not as many buildings as down by Marian Singer's work-room, but no matter which way you looked you could still see one or more of them.

Why do we have to live here? Why can't we go home?

Because Arin was his father's voice inside City, and like always, Shalane reflected bitterly, *Garick wants and Arin does.* In the days before Dannyline, Garick's needs cost Arin the proper use of his arm and almost got him born again. Worse, Garick's mission to the Kriss nearly drove Arin mad, and the smell of that journey still haunted Shalane's husband. There were days, especially when the rains of spring fell, when Arin closed himself off and nobody could reach him, not even Mady.

Shalane stopped by the mirror wall in the living room. She didn't often stand there long, but today, maybe because of her mood, she dropped the robe and subjected her image to a minute scrutiny without knowing truly what she looked for.

Twenty-nine.

Arin says I'm not a day older. He just don't know where to look. Time left its track on her like everyone else. In the mirror, her lip curled. Marian Singer seemed younger, but there were probably full-grown trees in Karli not half as old as her. Shalane moved closer to the glass. The planes of her face flowed more smoothly into each other now, softer compared with ten years ago, and her mouth fit better around those big front chipmunk teeth. Her hair was not dulled at all, still corn-yellow and uncut since Dannyline, covering her small breasts and falling over her flat stomach. *Well . . . not so flat since Mady.* Little pale stretch marks from birthing the child crept up her loins. The knees didn't knob out or the elbows jut so bony-sharp as when she was young. She didn't smell of horse any more, either.

At least the mirror gave her back a subtle curve where once there were mostly angles. Shalane smiled thinly at the image. In an hour or so, she'd choose a clean robe, cover it carefully with a tabard, wind the cord belt around it and set the antler crown on her head. Around her neck she'd wear the moon-sigil passed on to her from Jenna, taken by Garick from the dead goddess' throat at Dannyline. Shalane's lips twisted momentarily. *We won, but what?* The question was bitter ash in her memory.

Putting away the thought, she conjured the mental picture of the morning's coming work when she sat beside Arin as goddess of this strange little City-locked coven made up solely of masters. Her duties were all religious now. *Religious. Religion.* More City words. All the masters would be fresh from baths like herself. Not one would smell of rawhide or earth, not one would show a smidge of paint from hunting, a trace of forest-color missed by the hasty wash with fat-soap. . . .

Sometimes Shalane felt like a fool for her home-yearnings; things weren't all that good back there. There were lean years and sickness and children that wouldn't come painlessly or whole like Mady. And after all, Arin still loved her just as much as ever, only— *Only no more children. Not in this place.*

High above the rest of the City, Marian rose even earlier than usual that morning and clad herself in her customary pale gray robe. Once she confined most of her workdays to her pale gray office and adjacent apartment, communicating when necessary with other City people via synergizer, but the advent of the cooperative era changed things for everyone, even the chief administrator.

Today was her morning with the infants, she thought with uncustomary sarcasm. Ten years earlier, her former cohabitor, Randall Singer, and Dr. Rashevsky pressured her into conducting all initial orientation sessions of coven student samples. She tried to put the duty on a rotating basis amongst half a dozen top City officials, but Randall objected because Garick expected Marian to do it personally. It was politically advisable.

Speaking in shortmind, Marian proposed to videotape her remarks, thereby limiting her lost time to one unavoidable occasion, but Rashevsky gravely shook his head.

"Technology," the doctor warned, "never used to be anything more complex to a covener than, say, a new farming tool. But now Garick's forcefeeding change to them, and some can't cope. Most are devastated by the mere size of our buildings. Marian, don't subject those children to meeting you electronically on their first day here."

Swiftly evaluating his position and her objections, she reluctantly capitulated.

But two years later, to Rashevsky's astonishment, she broached the matter again. It was totally uncharacteristic of her; once Marian chose a course of action, she never wavered, not even that tragic time she had to exile her own daughter Judith. Why, then, did her face appear on Rashevsky's scanner screen the day before commencement of the third year of coven testing? She never wasted time on settled issues.

She explained in shortmind that she refused to deliver the prefatory remarks unless two conditions were fulfilled.

Rashevsky's eyebrows rose at her peremptory tone. "First?"

"Newsreel."

"Same rationale," he chided in shortmind.

"Necessary," she insisted, jaw set tight. "They don't grasp concept."

"But the film process will upset—"

"I'll prepare them," she interrupted—which was considered a rudeness by City residents.

"How?"

"By explaining photography."

"*How?*"

She replied in English, practically an insult. "Like a primer, Ted."

After an icy pause, he stiffly asked her what the second condition might be.

"Mady."

Anticlimactic, he thought. She'd shown concern recently that the goddess Shalane was conservative on the question of a City education for her daughter. But he'd heard news from Diane that morning.

"No problem," he told Marian. "Arin's already enrolled Mady. She's assigned to Levitt."

Marian shook her head, then pointed to herself. "Under my personal supervision."

"Why?"

"Ask Randall." And she switched off.

He didn't bother to call his colleague, he was sure he'd cite some political reason. Rashevsky was equally certain nothing Randall could say would induce Marian to give up unrecapturable hours training an infant when capable personnel already were assigned to that function. She'd already complained that her once-a-year speech wasted too much time.

Rashevsky didn't like paradox when it concerned Marian

Singer. He decided he'd better silently monitor her relationship with the daughter of Arin and Shalane.

But the cooperative era kept all the City's top officials busy, and during the next seven years, Rashevsky noted no further unusual behavior on the part of the chief administrator.

Their house sat in a cool nook of the park, five minutes' walk from the main coven dormitory. The Mrikan control group was housed in a structure built in the middle of a wide meadow. At first, there was no mixing between the two peoples, but ten years can rub off a lot of difference, Shalane admitted.

The Mrikan students were young, all smart and curious like Arin and her friend Bern, and they included one or two no-lep Wengens like Corian. In the initial testing by Diane Radclif, both groups began with hostile competition, but soon gentled down to a friendlier rivalry and a gradual realization among the coveners that, in some ways, Mrikans weren't so different from Circle. They could be happy, they felt pain, they cared about their parents and children, could even be kind and helpful. Some of them still believed in an old dead god like the Kriss, but Mrikans didn't kill folks over it. Arin, who was always reading now, said their name came down from a time way behind yesterday when it was a pride to be *American* in a land ruled by Jings.

"We were all Mrikans way back then," Arin surmised. "No difference at all."

Arin said too many Circle folk couldn't see an inch beyond their own covenstead. "And you too, Lane. You're the thickest deepwoods that ever was. I tell you, it's hard to hate someone once you get to know him."

Shalane didn't know about that. Mrikans weren't all that bad, but there was still something inside her that wouldn't bend. The line was drawn thousands of year-wheels back and stamped on a covener at birth. You were Circle or cowan, one or the other. And cowans were different, Shalane knew. She had her own nightmares from time to time, and when she saw her husband's arm flung over the blanket in that twisted way because it never set right after the Kriss broke it, she remembered the deep difference. And some of it was counted in all those shallow graves dug by her people between Karli Forest and Dannyline.

Climbing nimbly up the side of a long boulder, Shalane slipped off her robe once more so she could bathe in the early sun. Out in the meadow, no Mrikans stirred outside their big, square house, it was still too early. She laid down the robe for a blanket and stretched out, listening to the toy forest around her. Flowers swaying in the morning breeze, opening to the sun. Squirrels rustling branches. Birds chattering, the snap of a twig—

Her eyes opened when she heard the twig break. Shalane's senses probed toward the newcomer, brushing aside the familiar sounds to feel at the approaching presence. She fixed on him, identified him at once, long before he bobbed through the trees with his rapid, unbalanced gait.

Shalane turned her head and watched him come. Near nine years he'd been walking on the new foot Rashevsky gave him, yet he still threw his weight to one side as if leaning on the long-gone crutch.

In spite of Arin's position, Corian was the real link between Circle and cowans, welcome at both tables. In City, he was always bounding after Rashevsky for more medical supplies or knowledge, bickering with or propositioning Diane Radclif, getting in Marian Singer's hair. He was one of the first cowans Shalane ever really liked. Sometimes it puzzled her why Corian never settled down with one woman, didn't even stay in one bed long enough to get the blankets warm. Arin said Corian plain didn't trust women, and when she argued and said Corian loved women, Arin said Corian didn't trust them to stay, to be real. To be something he could hold onto.

She waved lazily at the small figure. "Hey."

His head swiveled up to find her.

"Up here on the rock."

He nodded. "Goddess Shalane, I was on the way to your house."

"Arin and Mady are still asleep. Stop and sit."

He clambered up the side of the long rock, thrusting his black medical bag before him. No telling where he'd been for the past two weeks, but his bag was always with him. His narrow face was shadowed with beard, but the green hospital suit was fresh, probably put on at the checkpoint decon station when Corian came in.

Shalane slipped into her robe, more for Corian's sake than her own. There was enough cowan in him not to accept a bare woman with Circle ease. Some part of him always had to do something about it right then and there, like loving the crib girls he doctored.

Corian flopped down beside her with a grunt.

"Where you been so long?" she asked.

"Karli, giving shots, couple of babies."

Her eyes brightened. "You were home? Sure as frost? How is it, how's Moss?"

"Your father's fine," Corian assured her. "Sends his love. I didn't have much time there. Lep came through from Garick right in the middle of a tough delivery. Shouldn't have been so hard. Third child, but the uterus prolapsed. Was I busy? *Dunesk.* Garick wants me to take a med mission up to the Fleeters." Corian grinned at Shalane. "You'd like the Fleeters, goddess. Real old-time Circle, like the Karli. I've lived with them. Sea folk, sell a lot of fish to City."

Shalane made a face. "So that's where they get all that fish."

"Fleeters live out on a hook of land not far from the north end of City. It looks like an arm." He crooked his arm and made a fist. "See that? That's what they call it. The Fist."

But Shalane wanted to hear about Karli. "Tell about home. They all getting ready for Sinjin?"

"Nobody talks about anything else, goddess. Lot more people coming and going now. Ass-deep in kids, but Sinjin's the same."

"Eighteen days from now," Shalane dreamed wistfully, chin on her knees. "Folks coming in from all over, boys and girls picking each other out for the hill, just like me and Arin once. Cooking, meat hanging in the springhouse." Shalane breathed deep. "I can almost taste it."

Corian chuckled. "So, would I forget?" He opened his black bag. "I tell those checkpoint mofos this bag's so full of disease they could die just looking inside. So they don't bother me. Here we are." He lifted out a transparent pouch. Through the clear material Shalane saw the leaf-and-cornhusk wrapping.

"*Oh!*" She clapped her hands like a delighted child. "Cory, you're so good." She hugged him impulsively. "Open, quickquick, let me smell."

"Moss sent it." Corian tore open the plastic. "Just some greens and corn, a little cooked pork."

But it was more than that to her, he knew. "It's *home,* you can smell it." Shalane put the corn to her nose, inhaling deeply. "Nothing in City got any smell. City people forgot how. They see something like this and all they think is it's something they got to keep out or some dumb bitty germ they can't see anyway is gonna get 'em. But I can *read* this corn and where it's been."

Corian liked the way the excitement lit her face. "Tell me."

"I can smell the field they grew it in: fallow last year, sown with clover and turned under, nothing like clover to fresh up tired earth. And there's the block salt they crushed up into springwater when they cooked it." She ran her tongue over the ear. "Spooned possum dripping on it. Mmm. And look! Someone was baking pone in mama's old iron stove, 'n' Moss or somebody grabbed a piece to eat and dropped these crumbs, and—"

Shalane choked off, full of more feeling than she could speak. Corian sensed the conflicting emotions that welled in her. She said in a low voice, "You were good to bring it."

"Goddess?" Corian hovered over her awkwardly. Sensitive to pain, it tore him up to see anyone suffer. He touched her arm tentatively. Sometimes Shalane wondered about his shyness toward her, a physical reticence that extended to no other woman. Perversely it irritated her now. She needed to be touched and held and left alone at the same time and she wanted, she wanted—

"Goddess, what is it?"

"Nothing."

Corian sat down next to her, rummaging his bag for nothing in particular. "You ought to go home," he said after a long silence. "For a little while at least. It's been so long, and you . . ."

Shalane read the thought he left unfinished. "I don't fit in here, never did."

Corian ducked his head in agreement. "Then why do you stay?"

"Oh, Cory." As if she hadn't tortured herself with the same question for so long, as if there were an answer. She shrugged, defeated. "Arin's so different now, sometimes I think he'd be happy never going home. Always reading, always off in his head somewhere. But he stays, and I'm with Arin. You know *with,* Corian, how deep it goes. I smile with his happiness, I can hurt with his pain. And I want my little girl."

Abruptly Shalane picked up the food and rose. "Have to get home."

Corian stood up with her, lightly grasped her arm. "Listen to the doctor, Shalane. Go home for Sinjin. Take Mady, she's old enough to understand it now."

Shalane vented a short, sardonic laugh. "Old Singer woman would love to see me go, but taking Mady would be a fight."

Corian knew the disturbing truth of that. To any rational observer, Marian was much too possessive of a child not her own. He considered the problem, wondering what shrewd old horse traders like Garick or Spitt would do. Shalane couldn't handle Marian, neither could he, but perhaps it could be managed through the back door.

"Let me try something, goddess. Maybe I can get you and Mady home for Sinjin."

Her old chipmunk smile widened her mouth in a flash. "Real? You could?"

He spread his hands. "Who else? I know how things are run around here. Promise."

Or he hoped it could be. In this city of miracles, Corian knew someone who knew someone else who might just work a big one.

On the occasion of Marian's historic first meeting with Garick in Lorl, she was accompanied by three chief technicians: Randall Singer, archivist/historian; Dr. Theodore Rashevsky, and a philologist/educator, Jakov Levitt. Marian didn't invite Diane Radclif, but she came, anyway.

A psychologist/art historian, Diane was the youngest resident of the City, born some fifty years later than Marian's Judith. Her youthful exuberance taxed the chief administrator almost as much as Marian's own volatile daughter once did. While discussing the City's attitude toward emotion in a letter to Spitt, Rashevsky used Diane as an example:

> **Diane's vigor—what you called in your last letter an un-City-like freshness—is merely the residue of her adolescence. At any given time, there are few children in the City, so their proper development is crucial. We guide them carefully through all the necessary emotional stages. Each, so far as I know, delights in the novelty of Experience and the potential of the human body. But the simpler senses become overly familiar through the endless repetitions of greatly extended life-spans; little by little, they give way to the subtler fascinations of mental endeavor. (Cf. Shavian testament in the gospel of our defunct Church of the Irrelevation.) Please note that we don't legislate emotion out of our children. It is a natural process, it simply evolves. Of course, we don't all achieve the same extreme dedication and singularity of purpose that Marian has attained, but we're more alike than different.**

Truly anomalous personalities are extremely rare, at least since the Great Schism and Myudan migration. Judith Singer is the only recent one who comes to mind.

On first consideration, you might think Diane Radclif to be one of those solitary spirits, but I don't think so. Remember, few children are born in the City, and the last ones in centuries (not counting Mady and other coven offspring in the compound) were Diane and her elder, Judith Singer. Isn't it natural, therefore, that some of Judith's creative rebelliousness has loomed as an attractive model for Diane?

But it's just posturing on her part. She's already grown more subdued since Marian appointed her supervisor of telepathic testing—which, by the way, was one of Marian's more calculated actions. She probably foresaw the position as a chance to calm Diane's youthful hyperboles. In the beginning, of course, Diane was also better equipped emotionally than the rest of us to deal with the coveners' incessant tendency to touch. Also I suspect that Diane, barely out of school herself, was exhilarated by the idea of becoming teacher and manipulator of people perhaps six to ten times younger than she. (Cf. Nietzschean testaments, ibid.) However, Marian tends to plan long-range, and I can't imagine the changes of the past decade in Diane's character happened by sheer chance.

I expect the time is near when Diane will completely set aside the playthings of emotional adolescence for those addictive pleasures of her approaching mental maturity.

That morning, Diane remained at home collating and comparing the latest battery of psychological profiles she'd run on the new Mrikan and coven pupils. She used to perform this task swiftly on her office console, but the preceding year Marian suddenly decided Diane needed drill in rapid statistical analysis and therefore refused to clear further synergizer time for evaluation of student tests.

Diane thought it a poor reason for putting a piece of her life at lower priority than available power, but did not say so. Her rank as supervisor of telepathic testing represented the biggest responsibility she'd ever had entrusted to her, and she didn't want to disappoint Marian, so Diane kept her opinions to herself.

At least it was a consolation working once in a while at her private apartment. She never hung any of her pictures in her austere office, lest Marian notice. Not that she'd disapprove, but the chief administrator would probably tacitly regret that Diane still felt the need for a recreational activity other than work.

The irony was there was hardly any time left for her hobby anyway. Long before the beginning of the cooperative era, Diane put away her brushes and cultivated an interest in photography, mainly because it was a less time-consuming pursuit. But now her duties as head of the "lep" study program rarely permitted her to touch her camera. The last occasion it was used was a few years back when she loaned it to Corian so he could take some pictures of his friends up in Wellfleet.

Tall for City, tiny by coven standards, Diane Radclif had short dark hair framing a long face that might have been plain except for alert, deep-set eyes whose darting curiosity animated all her features. Her lips were small and well formed in a line frequently spoiled by a habit she had of thrusting out her tongue to wet them—a result of the uncustomary amount of talking required by her official capacity.

"Before the Gate opened," she once confessed to Corian, "I don't think I uttered as much in seventy years as in these last few."

Corian: more of a distraction than Diane spared time to admit. Surprising he paid her so much sexual attention. Her slight, angular build contrasted sharply with the full hips and bosoms of his prized Crib Street women. Diane was hardly envious. Her body was efficient and functional. More weight and curves would be irrelevant to her work.

Corian: she thought of his small, vital body, teased as by faint music, ghost of a pleasure long ago worn thin. She'd spent—how long?—nearly forty years exploring the needs and diversions of her body. Arousal, climax, the delicate nuances and jealousies and demands of desire, domination games of lovers stumbling over their own egos. The joy of possession and of being completely possessed, the poetry of unselfish love, the steadier flame of companionate pairing. Curiosity, satisfaction, satiety, eventual ennui as the loop described yet another revolution. Perfection, pleasure, heartbreak, happiness, all at last became muted gradations of something ultimately academic.

And the growing need for something beyond: the discovery that nothing is more mutable or enduring than the human mind. Not sensual disillusionment at last, merely the loss of the capacity for illusion. Corian was still a child in a toy shop, grabbing at every bright object that caught his eye, including her. She was unimpressed, for she had lost the need to touch or hold, although now and then, like Goethe, she might have lingered here or there in examining love. Some small things were fair enough. Perhaps she *was* still a child; Marian certainly thought so, yet Diane did not yet entirely reject the possibility of sex with Corian: like an old, familiar book with a passage or two she might read again sometime if she could remember the pages.

After all, Judith did.

Diane paused over her work, thinking of her old friend. She wondered what she could have found with Garick that wasn't already familiar. How could it be relevant?

But now she really was idling away too much time. Marian was waiting for her report.

Rapid statistical analysis.

Diane didn't hear Corian enter the room, but when she bent over to retrieve a dropped pencil, he patted her gently on the bottom.

She stiffened, straightened, turned.

"Hello, Raddy."

"Child." She stared at him. "This is *my* apartment."

"Right. But you weren't in your office. How come?"

"Irrelevant. Please go, I'm busy."

Corian grinned. "Radclif, if I didn't know you better, I'd swear you're mad at me."

She began to reply, stopped, ran her tongue over her lips, then sat. "Anger is inefficient," she continued, calmly. "But you touched. In *my* home. Uninvited."

"Sorry. I had to see you. It's important."

The apology agreeably surprised Diane. Usually, Corian wanted to flirt, to touch her, but now his tone was serious and he kept his distance, hovering near one of her paintings, studying it in preoccupation, hands thrust in the pockets of his green hospital jumper.

"What is it?"

"Business." He still contemplated the picture. "And a favor."

"State."

But the painting arrested his gaze, especially one detail of it. It was a stylized rendering of a volcanic mountain executed with grace and economy in three strokes of black, one of white, to imply the even slopes of the great hill. But the perfect proportion was spoiled by a totally unbalancing slash of red along one side of the canvas.

"So you paint as well as take photos," he murmured. "Never saw your stuff before."

"You never barged in here before," she replied impatiently. "*State,* Corian. I'm in a hurry."

He nodded. "Tell Marian the weather's fine, but it can't always be trusted to hold up on the Fist. Soon I'll need those medkits for the Fleeters."

"Noted," Diane said. "Else?"

"Raddy"—he seemed to be using the painting to focus his thoughts—"how well do you know Arin's wife?"

"Shalane? Not well. Why?"

"She's hurting."

Diane swallowed. Though she grudged Corian the time he took, there was one emotion that never paled in the City: compassion. Every City resident had a deep concern for human welfare; it was the underlying rationale for their system of personal sacrifice.

"What happened to her?" Diane worried. "Does she need medical aid?"

(Reflexive question, Corian thought. City always worried about those "statistically inevitable" accidents that canceled lives and their accumulated acumen.)

He replied, "Shalane's homesick."

"How am I relevant?"

"She wants to go home for Sinjin."

"Let her. My permission's unnecessary."

Corian finally turned to her, holding her eyes. "But she wants to take Mady with her."

"Oh," Diane said after a significant silence. "Oh. I *see.*"

"It's serious, Raddy. I wouldn't waste your time. Shalane thinks of Mady as a fish being forced to walk on dry land. She wants her back in the water. And I don't think a little would hurt. Will you help?"

"*Me?*" Diane shrugged. "Think I'd convince Marian?"

"You could try Ted." And he bent over the painting again, absorbed.

Diane thought swiftly, reached her decision. "All right. Request noted."

"When did you do this?" Corian asked. "Why?"

"I haven't painted since a long time back. What do you mean 'why?' "

"This red blotch. Looks like a goddam wound. Spoils the whole thing."

"Wrong. It belongs."

"It doesn't."

"Entropic, perhaps, but . . . part of it."

"*M'shugah,*" he muttered in Wengen, then faced her again. "You'll call Ted quick?"

She nodded, picking up papers. "If that's all—"

"I know, I know." Corian flashed a sunburst of a white grin. "You're busy. I appreciate this, Raddy. If you make the right moves you could have me."

She was really tired of speech now. "If you make the right moves you can leave without tripping over a chair."

Corian stumped toward the door with his lunging walk. "All right, I'm going. But call Ted—"

"Go."

"—today, Raddy."

"Shut the door."

It slammed sharply behind him. She heard his voice boom from the other side.

"I LOVE YOU, TOO!"

Arin was awake when Shalane got back to the bedroom from her talk outside with Corian. Arms behind his head, red hair tousled from sleep, he grinned up at her and Shalane smiled and dropped the silly robe on a chair. She shared a silent greeting with Arin. They still had that.

Hey.

Without his beard, he looked even more like his mother, Jenna. None of her hardness, though, Arin was never that way. Shalane remembered Jenna as a great sleek cat of a woman, and time lent the same suppleness to Arin's body, giving contour and smoothness to what had once been drawn too taut and fine. A big, lazy cat like his mother, but gentle in contrast to the old goddess' iron, and more content than Jenna, whose heart hid a secret pain all her life.

Yet for a long time after Dannyline, there were things in Arin that Shalane couldn't read, and even now sometimes she caught that faintly remote quality that reminded her of Garick and perhaps more of Arin's strange half brother, Singer. Arin rarely mentioned him and never in Garick's presence.

Like her own father Moss, Arin grew moody when the rain carried a fetid smell from the flats crossriver. Then her husband would close up in himself, apart, untouchable. When Arin was that way, Shalane could only wait till he came back and took what solace he could in his family. She knew she and Mady filled at least one of the empty places in him, and yet . . .

And yet things were not as good as ten years ago when their minds and bodies were like one. There were rifts now, petty hidings, tiny turnings away, spaces to be filled but left empty. Shalane didn't know how to hide things or be so alone, but more and more she had to. They loved each other as much as ever, but the spaces kept getting bigger. A lot of little stones added up to a landslide in enough time, and she and Arin were on boats drifting apart while they reached and strained for each other.

She slid into bed with him. "Hey."

"Hey, Lane."

They lay close together, legs intertwined. She wanted him to love her and pushed his head urgently down to her breasts, but Arin hesitated as the small lep whispered into their minds, gentle but insistent.

Mamadad.

Arin sought his wife's mind. *Mady's up.*

Her hands kneaded his hair, moved down his stomach to grasp his penis. *Don't care. Love me.*

She'll come in.

"Let her!" Shalane said too sharply. "I used to see Moss and Maysa all the time. What's wrong with that?"

Arin hauled himself up on one elbow. "Mady's not deepwoods, Lane. She was born in City, not used to seeing people loving. She can't handle it yet."

Shalane stiffened. "Can't 'handle' it? What kind of goddam City talk is that, Arin? You learn that from Singer-woman?"

He didn't answer.

"Maybe," she protested, "just maybe if Mady went back home and saw how good it is, what she *is*, where she came from, she'd be able to 'handle' it better." She expected an argument, but when Arin encouraged her with a kiss, she went on. "Saw Corian this morning. He's been to Karli. Says they all getting ready for Sinjin. Corian thinks I should take Mady back to see it."

She chilled with the realization: *there, it happened again. I said it, and Arin knows.* Close as they were, each caught the determined *I* that used to be *we.* And like in the sleepwatching game, each knew and pretended not to notice.

"It might be a good thing," Arin agreed.

Mamadad.

The door panel hummed open. Mady trailed into the room, rubbing her eyes with two small fists. "H'lo."

Arin held out his arms. "Housebuilding time, punkin, let's go."

Almost every morning they had this short time together, the three of them. Mady would climb into bed with her parents, hiding under the covers while they looked everywhere for her, grabbing at their toes or making a house out of both of them and snuggling underneath.

The nightgown hiked up over her long skinny legs as she clambered onto the bed. *So pretty,* Shalane thought. *More'n I ever was.* Whatever City put into Mady's head, her body was pure coven, all the signs were there, the thin torso like a tube, legs and elbows like a new-foaled horse, outsized hands and feet that the rest of her wouldn't catch up with for years. From the length of her thigh, they guessed Mady would grow tall as Jenna, well over six feet. The child's hips and tiny bottom were almost nonexistent now; like her kind, she wouldn't round much until she birthed a baby herself.

Mady took Garick's coloring, much darker than Arin or herself. The short chestnut hair sprang into curls that could be waves if Mady wore it longer, but she cut it short like City women. Her eyes were pure Maysa, but bright and sharp where Shalane's mother's were deep and warm. There was a coolness about Mady that disconcerted Shalane, a self-possession you could hear in her clipped, clear speech. No softness, not the sun-warmed lazy Shando drawl or Karli twang. And even when she wasn't a year old, Mady knew how to say no.

Shalane smoothed the crisp sheets over the little body. "Mady, know what's coming in eighteen days?"

Playing with Arin's hair, Mady puckered her brow. "June twenty-first."

"No, what else? You know. What do we do on that day every year?"

"Summer solstice, and the masters form a circle," the thin voice piped without much interest. She snuggled up to her father. He tickled her ribs and she giggled.

Shalane doggedly pursued the subject. "Maybe that's all we do here, punkin, but at home, they dance and sing and—oh, all kind of good things. And I want to take you back to see it this year."

Mady bit off the words with cool precision. "Marian won't let me go."

Shalane besought Arin over Mady's head, and he put his arms around the child.

"Look, punkin. Marian's head of City, but your mama is a goddess, and there's nothing higher."

"Even grampa Garick?"

"Well even he listens when a goddess talks. So if your mother says go—"

Mady flung up her hands in comic surrender. "We go!"

Arin nodded. "That's all the say you need."

Suddenly anxious to please her mother, Mady twisted around. "I was in Karli before, mama."

Shalane laughed at the typical child-trick, telling well-known information to a forgetful grownup. "Oh yes, yes, yes, baby, but you were so little you couldn't remember." She buried her face in Mady's fragrant hair, rubbing her nose affectionately over the clean scalp. "I'll take you to see the new goddess of the Karli. She'll want to meet the pretty girl—oh, the real pretty girl who just might wear my moonsign someday, just like gramma Jenna left it to me."

And Jenna had it from her own mother who was a master of Shando, killed defending a wagon train from packdogs. The masters gave Jenna the sign and her mother's thammay, and what did Mady know about how it was? Mady would kneel to the Karli goddess and know in her bright head why the goddess wore an antler crown sometimes and a wreath of candles others, but she wouldn't know it in the deep, wordless way Shalane did. Maybe in Karli, when Mady saw the dancing done on the rutted earth, saw the loving and touching, heard the music . . .

"It's gonna be real Sinjin, Mady. People getting ready right now, coming in from all over Karli, cooking all kind of good things, you never *saw* such food. You'll clean bust with all of it. It's a special time for girls, too. Sinjin's smack in the middle of Goddess Earth's best time, and old Loomin-winter's far off as he can get. It's a growing time. Just like a woman, the earth's never so pretty as when it's getting ready to birth. It's a happy time. The young folks—not you this year, but soon, Mady, soon—they'll be out for the loving on the hill, and if it's first time, it'll be sweet and funny, too, because the first time always is, and—"

Shalane stopped, suddenly aware of the leak from her daughter's thoughts. Mady hadn't heard a word she said. Instead, she was silently prattling away to Arin with the fingers of both small hands flying, talking to him in City language. Shalane felt herself go cold with a growing anger.

That anger swelled as the oblivious silent dialogue went on. With great difficulty, she suppressed a desire to grab Mady's wrists and twist them hard.

MADY!

The child froze, stunned by the brutal force of the lep that slammed into her mind. The color drained from her face, her lower lip began to tremble. She stared up at her mother, frightened.

Rapt in the digital word-game, Arin looked up, too, startled, but Shalane didn't even spare him a glance.

Mady—

Timidly her daughter responded. *?*

Don't do that when I'm talking to you.

"She's only playing, Lane." Arin's voice held a reproof that shamed her even more while it increased the anger she didn't understand herself.

"I don't care!" she snapped, her hands shaking.

"But I *have* to practice, mama," Mady started to whine. "Marian—"

"Not around me." Shalane's voice trembled suddenly. She was begging. *Please.*

Ben Santee tested the black knife against his left thumb and smiled when a drop of blood welled up at the contact. The secret of coven blades was very old. Wengens learned from the Jings how to make one thin strip and sharpen it, then another and another, up to five or six, and hot-forge them together so there was maybe half a dozen cutting surfaces in one. He'd always wanted a witch-knife, so he made sure to take it from the coven woman they surprised when they stole into the stable to steal the horses.

He glanced coldly at her, struggling unsuccessfully with the ropes that bound her to the log. There was a gag in her mouth.

A little way off, Ritt squatted by the horses. Fat Gosset whittled at a piece of kindling, and the tow-haired boy, Billy Lee, stared with vacant eyes and empty smile at the woman, both brown hands pushed down on his crotch, rubbing it the way he did in front of a fire or any time his hands weren't in use, spitting now and then, rocking back and forth. Rub-rub; Ritt sometimes wondered aloud how Billy Lee didn't wear his cock clean off.

Gosset nudged the boy. "Like redheads, Billy Lee? Maybe she's one of Red Jenna's kin."

The yellow-haired youth wrinkled his face in unaccustomed concentration. "Red Jenna? Do I know her?" He turned to Ben for information.

"She's long dead," Santee said, remembering Garick's second wife. "Uriah's son stuck her at Dannyline."

Ben Santee was an old-fashioned man. But then Fist people, whether Shortree like him, or Fleeter, weren't much on change. They kept family names, proudly conscious of being descended in an unbroken line from Americans who fished the same waters long before the Jings came.

Most Shortree Kriss got along with the coven Fleeters out of mutual advantage. They fished the same banks and must be helped in time of trouble, because you might need them in kind next day. There were some Shortrees, though, who had Scripture-based reservations about mingling with witch people. The Santees were of that hard persuasion.

Never can tell about Fleeters, Ben mused. Shando or Karli, you got to where you could pretty well figure them out, but a Fleeter was different. He might talk to you, he might not. When he did, you still felt that weird riptide sometimes under the calm surface. This was the Devil in them, Santee knew: made them look human while laughing at you underneath. So when he got drunk that time and killed the Fleeter in a flash of anger, Santee had to run south clear of the Fist. Not even his own people would shelter him.

But though he couldn't go home, he never forgot who he was or where he came from. He spent some time in the merks, wandered as far west as Salvation where he met the most important man in his life, the God-driven force named Uriah.

Santee respected Uriah as no one else. Uriah had an iron mission and a hard soul fit for it, and someday he would rise up to crush the covens like bugs, as easily as Santee pushed the knife into the Fleeter. It wasn't like they were people.

But he didn't like Salvation, its crampy houses or working in a dark mine or hard-eyed elders telling him what to do and how and when to pray. Not Ben Santee, who was used to the open sea with nothing between him and God.

So one day, when he was on a coal train to the Wengen iron works, he met a squat, silent man named Ritt. They deserted the wagons after a few days and drifted south into Shando country, living well off the land. Ritt knew the forest. He never said much, least of all where he came from, but Santee recognized Ritt as a man who made his own law.

They attracted others like them, men who couldn't settle down or get attached to one person or place before the restlessness set in. Coveners avoided them or shooed them off when they got too close. Once in a while, they robbed a coven wagon train to Lorl, now and then they took a woman. Or each other. Santee discovered early that when the urge was on him, it didn't matter much. Man or woman, it was just a fever, a fury that needed to spend itself on another body.

And then he was thirty, and if he realized anywhere in his soul that his life was hardening in this mold, he accepted it and went on drifting.

Then suddenly a gale wind named Garick swept across his aimless course. Stomping all over the forest covens, shaking them awake, dragging them to war. Garick the Anti-Christ. If you had any doubt about the evil in Garick or Red Jenna, you only had to re-member what they did to Salvation. Their people murdered all the Kriss there, and Red Jenna personally stabbed Uriah to death. It was God's justice that the red-haired witch met her end at the hands of Uriah's son—though he, too, was killed at Dannyline. Garick reput-edly did it with the help of his son's woman, Shalane. Another name to remember and hate.

In the glade, tow-headed Billy Lee rubbed his crotch and stared at the tethered coven woman. Ritt squinted at the last of the sun fad-ing through the tangle of forest to the west. He was worried.

But Ben Santee just stared at his hands and thought about his enemy, Garick.

By the end of Garick's war, Santee's band numbered about twenty-five men living a fairly easy life: south in the winter, north in the summer, hunting always good. But now the covens were all mixed together and riding with Mrikan merks, *did you ever hear such a thing?* and wiping out his kind like packdogs. A Christian had no chance against that dirty lep of theirs. And now they used their women, stuck them out like bear-bait, and he told Rack and he *told* him about that trick.

Rack was just a boy, a sweet boy, maybe a little Suffec in him, but raised in Towzen. Smooth skin and a soft way of talking. It was the danger, not jealousy, that made Santee warn Rack off coven women, but the boy never listened.

Rack was with the main body of Santee's men when the constab sprang their trap. Santee found him among the others, throat cut, a great dark patch soaking into the leaves under his head. The con-stabs wouldn't even bury him. They only did that for their own. *Not even human.*

He buried Rack two days back. It surprised Santee and trebled his unfamiliar grief that he couldn't leave, that he lingered hour after hour by the low mound.

"Ben . . . Ben?"

It was Ritt. Santee looked up.

"What?"

"One day here's smart. They wouldn't figure us to stay where it happened. But it's two days now. We got to move."

Santee paid no attention. "Get him for this," he said to himself. "Ent never heard a commandment so clear in my soul."

"We gotta move, Ben."

"Like the trumpet of the Lord hisself." Santee stood up. Tall and stringy, he might pass for coven, except for the eyes that judged the world with the hard, unforgiving scrutiny of one who never doubted his reason or his right. "Been thinking on that," he finally answered Ritt. "Billy Lee, Gosset, get over here."

Gosset, who'd just squatted next to the woman, reluctantly heaved his fat frame off the log. Billy Lee stopped rubbing. They drifted to join Santee and Ritt.

"We moving, Ben?" Billy Lee grinned.

"Good idea," Gosset ventured. "Coven all around."

Ritt nodded, prying a thumbnail between his teeth. "Can't go south, they'll be waiting. West, might's well dig our own graves, we too close to Karli now. Just more riders east."

He let the thought trail off, watching Santee scuff a clear patch in the earth. They all knew the truth, even dim Billy Lee. Nothing to stay in the forest for, except to get caught. The pickings weren't worth shit now, and they didn't have a chance against constab in any numbers. They watched Santee draw in the earth with his new knife.

"I'm going home," he said.

They just stared at him. Santee never said that word before; they never thought of Ben as having a home to go to any more than they themselves did.

The knife went on moving in the dirt.

"You heard of the Fist? Summer's heaven, winter ent bad at all." The shape in the dirt looked like a bent arm with a small fist at the top. Santee poked a dot at the very top of the hand where the knuckles would be. "Where *I* come from. Shortree people; named after the way the trees get bent over by the wind and sand."

"Heard of 'em," Gosset allowed. "Fish folks."

"Best fishing in the world, Gossy. Used to run my own boat, sell catch to City. Long time ago," Ben mused. "Way long time ago. Guess I could go back now, no one remembers me." He looked up at the others. "Y'all don't have to come."

They shuffled, silent. Then Gosset spat. "Never *had* to do nothing, Ben. I'll come."

"Gonna be hard," Santee warned, doubtfully looking at Gosset's belly. "North through Karli Forest."

Billy Lee laughed his goatish bleat. "Shee-it, I'll go. You the best, Ben."

Santee smiled, a thin contour that didn't soften his colorless eyes. "You're a good boy, Billy Lee. Always said so. Ritt?"

The squat man glanced around at the engulfing woods. One place was much like another to him. "North is best," he agreed. "Rough country, but it'll slow the constabs as much as us."

So it was decided. Gosset and Billy Lee walked back to the trussed woman, but Santee and Ritt moved to care for their scrawny, worn-out horses.

Ritt shook his head. "These animals won't make it over Blue Mountains. We'll be eating horse before we get to Wengen territory."

"We'll get more," Santee said surely, tightening a cinch.

Ritt put an arm around Ben's shoulder. "North to the Fist. It's good sense, Ben. Thought for a bit you gonna let Garick spook you with what happened to Rack."

Santee stared oddly at Ritt. Before he could answer him, Gosset interrupted.

"Hey, Ben, me 'n' Billy Lee got time to do her proper?"

Santee approached the log and disinterestedly calculated how long he should permit Gosset and the boy to dawdle with the woman before they rode out. Making up his mind, he bent and plunged his black knife just below her right breast and ripped her open, slicing diagonally to a point a few inches above her left hip.

"Get her while she's warm."

Ritt watched numbly as Ben cleaned his knife and walked back over to him while Billy Lee mounted the dying woman.

"I ain't gonna forget Garick," Santee said, gently stroking his horse's mane. "Where we pass, Garick's gonna know."

Rashevsky's fingers deftly punched the call. Seconds later, he was reviewing monthly production figures for the southern hospital near the Balmer passage.

The City was remarkably free of red tape. Sector supervisors generally acted on their own counsel, feeding official activity into the common communication/data storage/postulator system that was the synergizer, an electronic network which reviewed all input and, when necessary, reported anomalies to top-level authority. This seldom occurred.

With the Self-Gate deactivated, only two programs were centrally controlled: food distribution and allocation of medical supplies. The latter was Rashevsky's responsibility. Each citizen had the right to ask details of any decision he made, though, by custom, such queries only came from Marian Singer, and then but rarely. Until—

The ghost of a grin twitched at his lips. *Until that gadfly Corian started browbeating Diane into challenging me regularly.*

As if by lep, his personal-contact bulb lit.

Rashevsky sighed. Before the cooperative era, aud-vid converse between citizens took place infrequently, seldom more than once or twice a month. *Now it's practically every day.* Older City people found it physically distressing; it fragmented their concentration.

Placing the production figures in storage/quick recall, he pressed the line key and, as he half expected, Diane's face flashed on the screen. He immediately discerned that she was mildly agitated.

But there was something else. Some odd detail, he couldn't isolate it yet, but it was wrong.

Rashevsky raised his brows, signaling question.

Diane, nervously shuffling a sheaf of papers, launched into an extensive shortmind report on her latest coven/control group test series.

The doctor noticed she was still unfamiliar with the advanced techniques of shortmind; she restricted herself to the basic method of uttering vowels in conjunction with finger-coded consonants. But even simple shortmind took years to master—except that, with lep, Arin and a few other coveners had come a long way toward learning it. *But then,* Rashevsky thought, *the coven mind has incredible potential. Ten years of study barely scratches the surface. The ramifications of—*

He checked the irrelevant thought. Rashevsky was shocked at himself for permitting his mind to wander off on a tangent. It was inexcusably rude not to pay attention to a colleague, a disgrace to have to ask someone to repeat what they'd said.

Fortunately, Diane hadn't noticed. She rattled on obliviously. The physician listened carefully to her, and began to realize why he'd lost interest: her report contained no significant new data, it was a waste of his time. She ought to have just entered it directly into the synergizer without disturbing him.

He tugged absently at his beard, wondering. Marian wouldn't tolerate her behavior, she would have swiftly switched off. But Rashevsky, professionally habituated to observing and analyzing signs of stress, waited patiently. Something was evidently bothering Diane, and he meant to find out what it was.

Suddenly, his eyes narrowed. He recognized the red-slashed painting—the peculiar detail that had been bothering him since her face first appeared on his scanner.

She finished her report.

"Yes?" Rashevsky gently urged.

"Corian needs medkits for Fleeters."

"Noted. Else?"

Her lips compressed. Diane put out her tongue to moisten them. Rashevsky was amazed at how much unreclaimable time she was taking to get to the point.

At last she spoke: "Shalane's going to Karli for religious rites."

He shrugged. Goddesses were always free to do as they wished, provided they didn't smuggle contraband through the checkpoints. "Else?"

Another maddening hesitation. "She . . . she wants to take Mady."

His mind raced to consider all aspects of the problem. Mady: first City-born covener; intellectually gifted. Karli journey risky; no bacterial immunities. Inoculable. Worthwhile? Randall would urge it: "No goddess ever gainsaid by City. Dangerous precedent, might seriously disrupt lep study." *Conclusion inevitable.*

He nodded to Diane. "Granted. Provided Mady inoculated."

"Will you tell Marian?"

So that's it. She'd asked a bit too eagerly, considering her recent reticence. Abruptly, the doctor demanded to know whether Diane felt sick.

"No," she said, surprised.

"Then why are you at home?"

"Working."

"Without synergizer?"

"No need."

His eyes widened. "Diane," he said sternly, *"state."*

Reluctantly, she revealed how Marian refused her console time for test evaluation.

After Diane switched off, the troubled physician transferred the hospital production figures to secondary standby mode and ordered transcripts of Marian's daily sessions with Mady.

He read them quickly, stunned. Why was Marian cramming the child so full of facts? It reminded him uncomfortably of the Shando story he'd once heard of how Judith force-trained her son, the enigmatic Singer.

Combined with the evidence of Diane's arbitrarily curtailed synergizer time, Rashevsky's findings pointed to an action which he found repugnant. But there was no alternative.

Swiveling to a bank of buttons on the outer curve of his console, he pushed in a demand. The screen immediately flashed—

91057!
64382/727!
91057!

—which signified the synergizer would not release classified documents to him. Rashevsky reluctantly entered his personal identification number and employed emergency medical override code, knowing he'd have to justify his action to the full Executive Council.

The scanner lit.

342/0294–92572(7)81/2100 . . .

He glanced at the first eight-page spread of transcript of Marian's confidential analytic sessions with the synergizer. Then he pressed a fast-forward button and waited for the film to advance to the proper time period he wished to scrutinize.

In the past, the synergizer occasionally brought isolated psychological problems to Rashevsky's attention, but never anything pertaining to Marian. The difficulty was that though the system could receive Datum A and Datum B and from them extrapolate Datum C, it still was incapable of requesting additional information if the human agency hadn't thought to enter (or deliberately withheld) statements from which the existence of, say, Datum D might be inferred.

For that matter, even with a switchbank capable of postulating up to twelve gradations of terms (making the synergizer able to manage both denotation and connotation), the screen would not display potentially vital facts unless the query was precisely phrased. (The exception was a purely electrical or mechanical crisis, such as power loss for the hospitals, or, in the old days, an overload at the Self-Gate. But the subtleties of a human crisis were beyond the synergizer's present capacity; such a thing still required human induction.)

In the case of Marian's analytic sessions, the machine could not equal the diagnostic skills of a qualified professional like Rashevsky, partly because the doctor had not yet deciphered all of the synergizer's own "thought patterns." For example, a term like *neurosis* might imply a certain mental distress or even illness to a psychiatrist, but as near as Rashevsky could hypothesize, it merely suggested to the synergizer a logical extension of certain mental propensities toward self-defense in given circumstances: analogous, perhaps, to the human body's ability to create antibodies to fight infection.

Marian's mind, Rashevsky reasoned, being a subtle and complex entity, might well devise subtle and complex weaponry to protect itself from unwelcome psychological probing.

Rashevsky finished the dossier. Despite the smokescreen, he perceived the problem's nature. *Still not too serious.* But it would only worsen.

He must confront Marian, but needed support. He disliked broaching it to the only logical person, inasmuch as he figured importantly in Marian's file, but there was no other choice, so Rashevsky punched in a personal call to Randall Singer.

Marian Singer stepped out of the elevator and strode briskly past the new students. The "lecture hall" was a corner of one vaulting ground-level corridor fitted with a knocked-together wooden platform with podium, folding chairs, projection equipment and a large screen hung on the wall to the right and rear of the dais. Though constructed a decade earlier, the place looked temporary to Marian, for whom ten years was both a mere flicker of time and an eternity.

There were fifteen students. All selected by Diane, all with notebooks, alphabets and instruction sheets, the latter graphically rendered. They were of both sexes, mostly in their teens and twenties, which roughly corresponded with the first 40–60 years of a City child's life. (But there were no City children at that time.) All stared curiously at Marian. Her pale ivory complexion and large, liquid brown eyes gave her a fragile, girlish appearance, yet they heard she was so old there was no way of calculating, and who'd want to bother?

Slouching carelessly, the coveners half reclined or else sat cross-legged on the floor, avoiding the hard metal chairs. No one spoke or rustled papers, but Marian knew this silence did not necessarily indicate respect, merely that the class was busy sharing a telepathic exchange of opinions about her. She didn't mind.

She mounted the platform, checked the video equipment, then poured a glass of water. It was enough strain speaking English, but on this occasion she had to use Uhian. Marian found that dialect wearyingly imprecise and wordy.

"Good morning. I'm Marian Singer, the City's chief administrator." She paused till the inevitable giggling died down. Though she'd pronounced each word carefully, Marian learned Uhian from

Arin, and thus spoke with a marked Shando drawl. This delighted each new student body. Eight years earlier, Diane found out from Corian what produced the mirth, then distressfully reported it to Marian, but she shrugged it off. She had no intention of devoting further time to relearning her memorized speech. Besides, Dr. Rashevsky said the familiar Shando accent, coming from such an unexpected source, was psychologically desirable; it amused and reassured the new pupils.

The coveners returned her greeting and Marian continued.

"You're here to help us master lep. In return, I've promised Garick to educate you. To benefit, you needn't understand or approve our ways. But since coveners wonder what City's been doing in seclusion for thousands of your year-wheels, today I'll briefly explain. Those desiring further information should request special studies from Diane Radclif."

She paused to sip water. The only pupils she recalled who'd asked Diane to tell them more about City philosophy were Arin . . . *and that irritating ex-merk.*

"Like the covens," said Marian, "the City's rooted in the distant past. Our forerunner was an ancient humanistic doctrine, the Church of the Irrelevation, itself formed from ex-members of several older sects which had been gradually drifting together. These were the names of some of them in 'old language.' "

She touched a button and several words glowed on the screen.

AGNOSTICISM
ETHICAL CULTURE
REFORM JUDAISM
UNITARIANISM

The coveners murmured in surprise. Marian knew the long words meant nothing to them, but they were a device for gently preparing them for the newsreel to come. When the muttering changed to nervous laughter, Marian artfully misinterpreted: "Yes, aren't those words funny-looking? Incidentally, shall I tell you the secret of how they jumped onto the wall?"

Mostly eager assent. Marian removed the slide, handed it down so they could pass it around and see the miniature "painted" words. Then she put her hands in the light-beam and created familiar illusions—old wolf, a flying eagle, a swan—shadow-pictures they could

all make if they stuck their hands between the sun and a tree trunk
or at night you could use a candle or maybe firelight.

"The words on the glass square work the same way, see?"
Marian asked, smiling.

And they all understood. It was a small but vital chink in their
coven breeding.

"Now you'll see and hear the founder of irrelevationism." The
whisper was half-lepped, half-aloud, but she shook her head. "No,
not even City folk live that long, not yet. It's more City 'magic,' but
I'll explain it, too." Then she spoke of echoes in the mountains, comparing them to echoes made long ago that could be caught and
saved. She said that under certain circumstances shadow-pictures
might produce "visual echoes," and before they could protest,
Marian constructed analogies between the shadow-wolf and light and
dark reflecting a real wolf on specially treated paper; she explained
microdots and chemicals and negatives and promised they all could
try the process with Diane's aid.

Not everyone understood, Marian could tell, but the prospect of
Diane's photography demonstration intrigued them, and that was
something. At least they were beginning to imagine some of the good
things a City education might bring.

The lights dimmed. Marian pushed a second button, and the
image of two men filled the screen. One was thin and intense, wore
glasses and sat in an upholstered chair. The other, seated behind an
adjacent desk, had gray hair and looked pleasant; he held a pencil
poised just above the desktop. Behind the two stretched a view of
some seashore.

The coveners laughed once more, louder than before. If asked,
they'd probably cite the unfamiliar clothing on the men in the picture, but the probable real reason once was accurately stated by
Corian (in characteristically colorful fashion): "Man, you tell a
bunch of deepwoods they're gonna see and hear dead people moving
and talking, you're gonna spook 'em so bad, either they'll piss or
pass out. If they didn't laugh, their brains might blow a circuit."

When it was quiet, Marian pressed a third button. The men
moved; the gray-haired one aimlessly tapped his pencil and addressed
his guest in Uhian.

"—true you never admitted who you are?"

"That's right," the thin man said.

"Though thousands came halfway across the country to hear you speak?"

"That's *why*. I claimed to be filling in till 'I' showed up, so they'd listen without a lot of irrelevant emotionalism, cheering and so on. People want messiahs, but they need common sense."

The man behind the desk held up a book. "Your philosophy is called 'The Gospel of the Church of the Irrelevation.' Why? If you don't believe in God, how come *church* and *gospel*?"

The thin man smiled. "Sarcasm and commercialism. Sell people what they think they want, then change their minds. But let me correct you—I never said I don't believe in God. It's religion I distrust."

"You mean you *do* believe in God?"

"I didn't say that, either." (A titter of laughter from the loudspeaker. Marian quickly said that a group of people had watched the debate "off camera.") "Russell wrote that religion has fomented suffering and hatred throughout history. *I* dislike its tendency to uphold the status quo and discourage rationalistic humanism. As for God, he's not dead, just irrelevant." (A shocked murmur from the loudspeaker.) "Practically speaking, it's irrelevant to argue about an unprovable theory when we have more pressing needs—feeding the hungry, educating the ignorant, housing the poor, cleaning the environment. Deity, the soul, survival beyond death, all are wastes of time or worse when they result in persecution and war."

The gray-haired man put down his pencil. "Yet if there were no religion, what would happen to morality? Without an afterlife, would it matter whether one is good or evil?"

"Absolutely!" his guest emphatically stated. "It matters to me, it matters to you, it ought to matter to all the people we share our living space with. Isn't it enough to care for one another because that makes more sense than ignorant hatred? Shouldn't we work to solve this world's problems because this is the only game we know for sure we're in?"

The film ended. The lights came up.

Marian surveyed the students. Some still seemed scared, one or two appeared bored, most looked moderately interested.

"Does anyone have a question?"

Silence. A general shifting to get more comfortable on the cool marble floor. She was looking for the rare pupil, the one mind in 40 or 50 endowed with a special kind of inquisitive wonder. Just as she thought no one had picked it up, Marian noticed a tentative half-raised hand in the rear. She motioned for the covener to rise.

A dark-haired boy of perhaps twenty got to his feet, blushing. "Something strange," he murmured.

"Yes? You were struck by an oddity in the film?"

He nodded. "How come they talked *our* language?"

"What you heard were echoes recorded seven years ago by City technicians. The language they actually used would've been incomprehensible to you."

Stammering thanks, he sat, not fully understanding. Marian made a mental note to schedule him for special testing.

She continued the lecture, much as she would have preferred returning upstairs for her daily session with Mady. But she said it all without skimping on time: how the irrelevationist viewpoint was a natural compounding and extension of many philosophical hypotheses, how technological advances contributed materially to the spiritual scheme of life without myth, especially when it was convincingly shown that death and aging were conquerable phenomena.

"Whether it's desirable to live without foreseeable end is another issue entirely," Marian stated. "The City stabilized its citizens' metabolisms at an early, productive stage, but minds continue to grow. The hardest thing for coveners to understand is that we tend to pass beyond emotionalism; we derive far greater satisfaction from mental pleasures than physical ones. Not at first; it evolves slowly over many centuries, but eventually City folk come to prefer solitude and devotion to our common work."

The youth in back, heartened by his first success, again stuck up his hand, higher this time.

"Yes?" Marian encouraged him.

"Isn't City's work just feeding the synergizer?"

"No. It's a machine, not a god. Another ancient writer conceived an elaborate mental exercise for gathering, systematizing and cross-referencing all existing knowledge. In essence, that's what we're doing with the synergizer. It's hard. We still need many centuries before we finish."

"Then what?" the boy asked.

Marian shook her head. "You may pursue the topic with Diane Radclif." He sat down, dissatisfied. Marian regretted it, but phase 2 might really disturb some of the new students and she'd never discussed it with any outsider save Garick, Spitt, Arin and—of course —his half brother Singer.

The lecture was over. The coveners were as worn out as Marian, maybe more so. Her throat hurt, and they were tired of being talked at, their heads ached from new things crammed inside. Thanking them for their attentiveness, she left the platform and hurried to the elevator. It was a moment Marian dreaded, ever since Corian once stopped her on the way and wasted time with irrelevant questions and cocksure opinions rendered with constant touching of her arm for emphasis. She always feared a repetition someday of the distasteful incident.

She reached the elevator unchecked, summoned it, stepped in. It rose swiftly, bearing Marian upward to her anticipated rendezvous with Mady. Marian mentally organized her lesson: she would show the child a few shortcuts in synergizer keyboard technique. True, she *was* teaching Mady programming at an unheard-of age, but she was so incredibly precocious that—

The elevator door opened. Marian stopped and paused in mid-thought.

At the far end of the foyer, Mady waited. Standing on either side of her were Randall and Rashevsky.

Randall looked the same. His sandy hair was neither shorter nor longer. His pale eyes shone as smugly and serene as ever. But Rashevsky's face looked uncustomarily concerned.

She approached them, her eyebrows raised in surprise, and to signal *question*. Randall started to reply by pointing to Mady, but Rashevsky forestalled him with a brittle tap on the historian's outstretched hand.

The gesture shocked Marian. Randall's back stiffened, but the physician ignored him.

"Mady," Rashevsky said in Uhian, "wait here for us, we won't be long."

Marian's lips compressed. Rashevsky should have spoken in shortmind, or at least English. She began to protest, but both men cast their worried gaze on her, and she faltered to silence. Lightning-swift, for the first time in ten years, Marian's mind turned far inward, questioning, arguing, synthesizing.

Her shoulders sagged. An old familiar chill crept over her as Rashevsky suggested they meet in her office. As she and Randall followed the doctor, Marian felt colder and colder and there might never be any more warmth, but each unwilling footstep carried her closer to the door that would shut her off from Mady.

"EEEEEAA-HI!"

Shalane never knew how Corian did it, but there wasn't a boo out of Marian about taking Mady home. She felt wonderful. She shouted for pure glee. The weather, sunny and not too humid, accented her spirits. The park around their house was deep in green and flowers.

In the heady days before they left, Shalane packed and unpacked twice for herself and her bewildered daughter. Riding a swell of happiness, she promised her masters a trove of home food that three couldn't carry, let alone hide. Her fingers flew; she made a green Sinjin robe for herself, and another for Mady, humming as she fitted the material to her little shoulders.

"Gonna be a fine robe. Just wish your hair was longer."

Mady rubbed her snub nose. "Don't need it."

"Look like a picked chicken," Shalane grumbled through a mouthful of pins.

Lounging on a couch, Arin already missed them. He had no desire to see Karli again, though he wished he might spend more time together with his wife, there was an indefinable rift growing between them. They no longer shared without thinking. Arin supposed she needed time alone with Mady, away in the open where City didn't stifle her.

Corian came to give Mady and Shalane the shots required for the trip. "You first, punkin," he told the child.

Shalane blanched, terrified of the small hollow pin that forced City magic through the pores of her skin. But Mady turned insufferably brave.

"Oh, mama, it doesn't hurt. Watch *me*."

Shalane shivered. "I don't need that thing, Cory."

"Yes, you do." He took her arm. "Don't tense."

Shalane squeezed her eyes tight shut. "Say when you're done."

"What do you want, music?" Winking at Mady, Corian sang, "It's done." He released Shalane's arm. "I want you to take one of these capsules each morning starting tomorrow. Just a mild antibio to supplement the shot."

"Could they get sick in Karli?" Arin asked, concerned.

"No. But their stomachs aren't used to raw food any more or the organisms they carry. The worst, I'd guess, might be a belly-ache."

Don't feel good, Arin. Shalane shared that much with her husband. With a glance at Corian, Arin led his wife into their bedroom and slid the panel shut.

Mady felt idly for her parents' minds, but they were closed off. Meanwhile, Corian took hold of her arm.

"You get a tetanus besides the antibio, punkin. It'll ache a little, so work your arm around. There."

Mady flexed her small arm. "Mama's so silly, isn't she? Frightened of a little needle!"

Corian pulled Mady close and poked her belly-button. "Now you listen, punkin, how many goddesses are there?"

"Eight," Mady guessed. "Maybe nine."

"At the most, nine."

"Why, Cory?"

"It's not a title you get free or easy. Your mama's faced a lot worse things than a needle and didn't get the least bit scared, so don't you ever say anything about it again, hear?" Corian bent forward to kiss Shalane's child. "Don't forget your pills."

Thinking about Mady, Marian stared at the youthful contours of her own face in the mirror and wondered when in the silent arch of the centuries she'd lost the capacity to cry. A line from an old play occurred to her and her lips softly formed the words:

"The tears of the world are a constant quantity."

Abruptly turning from the glass, Marian walked past rows and rows of books, so many she'd forgotten, so many remembered, so many yet to be digested, reduced, programmed. She sought some tangent to divert her troubled mind.

Something caught her eye. She stopped.

On a high shelf, brittle with age, Marian recognized a black-and-white dappled composition book that once belonged to her dead daughter, Judith.

She plucked it down and turned the pages, breath catching as she saw once more that precise yet graceful script.

For a full minute, she skimmed through it. Then Marian stopped at one of her daughter's earliest attempts at poetry—an elaborate conceit in sonnet form on personified Death. In those remote days, Judith spent a few months researching an old form of popular entertainment known as *circus*. The sonnet, which reflected that study, struck Randall and Marian as unintentionally rather funny.

It no longer amused Marian.

> *Sir Clown has cracked his joke; the crowd's enthralled;*
> *To pace his act, attempts to twang a tune*
> *Through tortured teeth that grit a grinning sneer*
> *Behind a patched, a shrivelled, motley hand*

Which, deathlike, crooks in gesture of a jest
Bestowed upon a throng that would not laugh
But chaffs to catch a pratfall in the dust.

He strives to knock 'em dead, his only lust
(Except what praise he wrests on his behalf);
But once this claque-ing mob has come to rest,
The jokester, mirthless, renders them unmanned,
Exacts a tax his auditors still fear.

He pleats his paunch, but no one cheers his rune,
And those who craved his punchline are appalled.

Marian examined it a second time, noting, as she had centuries earlier, that it was a mirror-imaged sonnet, the first line rhyming with the last, the second with the thirteenth, and so on. *Too elaborate, overly clever,* Marian thought, recalling her late daughter's tendency to take a simple idea and twist it into such convoluted forms that the original meaning was hopelessly lost. And yet, that *was* Judith as a young student, and the rediscovered poem was a foolish, dear souvenir of that time.

Marian scanned it again, and as she did, a truth she'd denied for ten years finally, inarguably declared itself: Mady, no matter how brilliant, would never develop along similar lines to Judith; she was separate, distinct, more City than coven, yet a part of each.

Closing the notebook, Marian hugged it to her breast and, for the first time in arid centuries, her eyes filled with tears.

Corian was there to see them off, along with Arin and eleven masters. Each of the latter embraced Mady, cach knelt to Shalane before their personal farewell hugs.

"You come back, goddess."

Arin whispered against her ear, "You come back, Lane."

"I will," she said, trying to quell the mouse-thought nibbling at her peace: that Arin hadn't wanted to come, hadn't even wanted to talk about it. Strange, now when they needed so much to share, how little of it they did.

Mady hopped into the power boat. Corian handed down their packs. Shalane stepped into the craft, followed by Bern, who would pilot them crossriver. As the boat pulled away, Shalane stood in the stern, both arms raised to her tiny circle. The air was sharp and sweet, and old sun never shone so warm. It was going to be real Sinjin.

On the dock, Corian tapped Arin's arm. "Still want to go to the Fist with me?"

Arin nodded. "More than ever."

"Did you tell the goddess?"

"No. It'll be a surprise."

The Wengen observed him shrewdly. "Why in hell didn't you go with them to Karli?"

Arin waited till the boat was a tiny chip in the middle of the river before turning away up the jetty and replying. "I couldn't, Cory."

"Why not?" Corian demanded, stumping along at his side. "Nothing here you're wild about."

"Nothing there either." Arin dropped a long arm over Corian's shoulders. "In Karli you have to believe a lot of things. Goddess, earth, sun, what happens in the circle. I've lost all that."

Corian nodded. He had his own Lishin.

"Still, Arin, might be good for you and Lane up there on the Fist."

Mother and daughter stepped onto the first slow highway ramp, skipped lightly to faster lanes until they flew through the sunlit morning. Shalane felt freer with every breath. She sat down, loosed her hair from strip and pin, shook it out and let the wind take it.

"Wheeee, mama!" Squinting against the warm breeze, Mady laughed excitedly. "You look like a flag!"

Shalane joined her daughter in laughter. She even felt like a flag, too long furled, glad to wave at last. Throwing back her head, she let the winds of summer burn her face. It felt like food after hunger, love after loneliness. Pulling Mady close, she sang.

Spitt arranged for Shalane and Mady to travel from Filsberg with a wagon train of farming implements. Two horses were supposed to be waiting for them crossriver. Shalane spent an impatient half-day on the dock while the heavy wagons creaked and clattered onto barges and ornery stock was rounded up and herded to the jetty.

Ten years wrought a lot of change in Filsberg. Business and people moved and mixed faster, but it was still the frontier. Beyond the river was coven country. The wagon traders were Mrikan, friendly enough in their way, but though some of Shalane's stiff prejudice wore off in City, she still kept a little apart from them.

Their barge pushed off at last. When the Karli bank neared, she pointed ahead to the woody shore and identified it to Mady. The child was not particularly impressed.

More confusion on the Karli quay as the wagons rumbled ashore and teams were bawled and cursed into line. Shalane prowled the beach restlessly, looking for the promised horses. Mady sometimes hopped, sometimes skipped to keep up with her mother's long-legged stride.

"Damn your fat ass, Spitt!" Shalane swore. "Where's our horses?"

Here, goddess.

The subtle lep nudged at her mind. Back from the bank at the tree line, a lanky young woman in constab leather waited with two saddled mounts. At Shalane's signal, the girl led the horses forward. Mady watched her approach, a loose-jointed, raw-boned young woman in deerskin trousers smeared grayish brown with leaf paint. She wore a sheddy sword and black knife belted over thin hips; a full quiver was slung over one shoulder.

She awed and repelled Mady. The child had never seen anyone so picturesquely filthy or potentially dangerous.

The constab girl looked down at Shalane with feral eyes slanted over cheekbones streaked with dirt and traces of camo paint. Her teeth were stained and uneven. Meat grease and crumbs clung to the corners of her thin, unhumorous mouth.

I looked that way ten years ago, Shalane thought with an odd pang. *Wonder what Mady thinks of her?*

The constab handed the two pairs of reins to Shalane, communicating entirely by lep.

Ride with us? Shalane asked courteously.

The girl shook her head, scratching hair chopped within an inch of her scalp. *Going north.*

?

After cowan hunters. Crossed trail a day west. Bad.

Without a spoken word, she faded back into the trees.

"What coven does she belong to, mama?"

"Suffec, Mady. Swamp folks. Don't see many of them." They were always shy, Shalane reflected, but Dannyline really thinned Suffec ranks. They were the first to ride against Jeremiah's merks. No one could stop them, not even Garick, and few survived.

Shalane sized up the small quarterhorse mare she planned to let Mady ride. "This old woman's little and smart like you, hon. Won't have no trouble with her. But that one there . . ."

A small-headed, coal-black beast that dwarfed Mady's mount at the shoulder; nervous, skittish, rolling its eyes, suspicious even of its placid four-footed neighbor.

"That's a Suffec horse," Shalane said. "Been ten years since I sat one like her."

Mady murmured appreciatively at the muscles rippling under the shimmering coat. "It's beautiful, mama."

"It?" Shalane laughed. "*She,* and don't you forget! How'd you like to be called a it? Up now—put your foot in the stirrup, that's it— and don't fret this old woman with too much rein. Knows more about riding than you do."

Downshore, the wagon men were shouting and waving to them, ready to move out. Hands on hips, feeling marvelous, Shalane sized up the quivering, overbred mare.

Shalane chuckled low in her throat. "Old woman horse giving your mama the bad eye, Mady. She thinking: 'What's this dumb Karli want, trouble? I got it for her.'" She moved upwind of the trembling mare, crooning softly. "Horse, don't make it hard on yourself."

She gave the horse time to find no fear in her own scent, then Shalane flowed into the saddle like a shadow. The mare shied suddenly and reared high, whinnying. Mady gasped. But Shalane gathered the reins tight, bringing the rebellious head up. Gradually, the mare subsided, movements less random, responding quicker to the rein, until Shalane brought her to a full halt.

Flushed with an excitement her daughter barely understood, Shalane said, "Now let's ride to Karli!"

To Karli they went, far ahead of the wagons. Shalane pointed out trees and birds to Mady with the pride of personal ownership. When the child grew chafed with riding, they dismounted and lazed along, leading the horses.

Shalane reveled in the green around them, doubly glad because ten years earlier they could not have traveled so carelessly through Karli Forest. Most of the danger was gone now, and the beauty might vary and fade, but always came back.

She chattered on, unaware that Mady's interest and spirits were drooping fast. ". . . and that's sugar maple, must be a farm close by. Grampa Garick brought 'em from north Wengen. When I was little, we tasted sugar maybe once a year. Look, see that young beech over there where the bark's torn away? Old whitetail been at it, they just love to nibble."

"Yes, mama," Mady repeated.

Once, Shalane moved off the trail to pick a double handful of a broadleaf plant with faint reddish streaks down the stems. "What all them Mrikans call dinner, we'll cook this up with it. Poke, Mady. Grows up in a bush taller'n you with poison berries. But this time of year it's young, you boil a mess of this with pork and no one ever ate better."

"Yes, mama."

Next day, Mady's feet were sore and her bottom raw from riding. But neither discomfort matched the pains in her stomach. For the third time, she told her mother plaintively that she had to go.

Shalane nodded, gazing up the trail with narrowed eyes. "Go ahead. I'll be up a bit."

Mady went into the bushes and relieved herself, repulsed at the crudity of having to do so outdoors. Never in her life had she been without a bathroom. Ashamed, disgusted, she stumbled back to the road and saw, some yards ahead, her mother on one knee studying the ground.

When Mady joined her, Shalane pointed to a patch of churned earth that cut across the wheel-rutted trail. "Remember what the Suffec girl told us?" she asked in a no-nonsense tone that meant there was something important to be remembered.

"No, mama, what is it?"

"Cowan hunters rode here. We always have to watch for that, Mady. There's not many of them left, grampa Garick's seen to that, but I guess there's still a few loose, and they're bad trouble."

Dutifully, Mady scrutinized the hoof-marks, but they were just a jumble to her, they told her nothing.

"Four horses heading north," Shalane said softly. "Probably stolen, goddam cowans. One horse lame, he's dropping back. The constab'll get that one, sure. Only cowans ride this close together." She didn't tell Mady why that was so, that once merks hunted coveners for money, so spreading out meant less death. She and Arin didn't talk of it between themselves, let alone to the child. There were better memories to share, memories like old treasures, polished with much retelling.

Like: "Your dad was still growing when I met him, Mady, all hands and feet and legs like you. And three years later he came back a master. Oh, you would've liked to see him the day he rode into Karli again with Kon'n Magill and the rest. We all ran out to meet them, and they lined up and bowed to the god and goddess. . . ." But that was the old god Hoban, who got born again seven years past. Tilda was still alive, the last Shalane heard, but she was no longer goddess. She was in her seventies when she rode with Hoban to Dannyline; now she lived someplace with her grand- and great-grandchildren.

The war took a heavy toll of Karli masters. The new ones were mostly young. At Karli, god Darin and goddess Turi were only just pledged to the inner circle when Shalane followed Arin to City.

Another old memory to share: "When Arin first come with his people, we knew it days ahead 'cause we read the Shando lep every night. Later, when everybody else thought your father had got born again, I still read him, clear across Blue Mountains!"

Shalane stopped short with a sudden, impish grin. "Hey, wanna try tonight? I bet Karli could hear us now." Her voice trembled. "Sure as frost they could."

"Do we *have* to, mama?" Mady was exhausted. Her feet hurt, her sunburn itched where it didn't ache, and bugs were exploring her underpants. She was hungry, too, but Shalane insisted on lepping first.

"And we can't eat till we do," she admonished. "Need a clear head to lep. That's why masters eat just enough and never more."

Mady capitulated without argument. Seated by their fire, they prepared to lep to Karli. Mady opened her mind and her mother joined it. She always loved her mother's lep, the power under her own like a strong arm, or the pedal tone on one of Corian's organ tapes, not so much heard as felt.

They concentrated.

ShalaneMady. Coming in tomorrow.

No reply.

ShalaneMady. Coming in tomorrow. They sent again and again.

"It's too far, mama, they won't read us."

"Twenty miles? A master can hoot that far. It'll take 'em a bit to gather in, but they hear us, sure as frost."

Shalane read it first, then Mady detected the answering power that grew steadily.

Who?

Goddess Shalane and Mady.

The Karli lep altered, not massed minds now, but one alone, warm and friendly. *Mady?*

"It's goddess Turi," Shalane whispered. "Say hey to her."

Across the silent forest night, the child's lep was a tiny flute-tone, tentative but clear. *Hello, goddess.*

You're tired, child. The answer was like a warm smile. *Meet tomorrow. When?*

After high sun.

The power faded from their minds. Mother and daughter relaxed. Shalane spooned the greens from the small pot.

They ate slowly. "Her lep's so strong, mama," Mady said. "Strong as you."

Shalane smiled, savoring her food. "I guess old Singer woman couldn't do that, could she?"

Mady gravely shook her head. "Marian would just use the phone."

Turi moved the synth-oil lamp closer and opened the leather bag, spilling a few of the bright coins on the table. New money in gold, stamped with Garick's profile on one side; on the other there was a simple circle with tiny cups at the four compass points .

The coins were of varying sizes for different amounts: one, two, five, ten and twenty krets. Some older Karli looked fish-eyed at the gold and other innovations, but none of them criticized the better life that came with them. Hard money gave Karli muscle in trading. This year, it made up an imbalance with the Wengens due to a bad year for Karli sheep. Soon, the gold would be indispensable.

Corian found the gold for Garick, tons of it in neat bars, hidden when the Jings came, useless and forgotten until he and Spitt broke the ancient code that guarded its locations. They could have gone another thousand years without it, Turi guessed, but others broke the code, too, and were using gold in the west.

A light tap at the half-closed door. Darin put in his shaggy head.

"Hey," he greeted her. "Hear Shalane's coming."

She nodded. "Tomorrow."

Darin came in and closed the door. A big man with bulky shoulders, he still trod the plank floor without a sound to sit down opposite Turi. He looked grim.

?

"Some of the masters picked up a weak lep," he replied.

"Who?"

"Constab, north near Wengen. They couldn't read much. It's Santee."

Turi protested. "They cleaned him out."

"All but Ben and a few others. They jumped a farm near the border." Darin dropped his head into his big brown hands. He and Turi had dealt with it for years, were heartily sick of it.

"How bad?"

"Stole some horses, slaughtered the stock."

"Karli farm?"

"Yes."

And the folk?

He opened his mind for the goddess to read.

All?

He nodded. "Burned inside the farmhouse."

It was sickening, but Turi sensed something worse behind. "What is it, Darin?"

"The constab were close behind. They just missed Santee, but they caught one of the others." He raised his eyes to Turi. "They're bringing him back."

Turi knew what it meant. She pinched her tired eyes. "That patrol's mostly Suffec. They never take prisoners."

"It's a Karli bringing him in, the one that caught him."

The god and goddess shared a glance of understanding. They sickened at the execution of cowan hunters. The few passed back by patrols were put to sleep and painlessly despatched, but ending any life was dreadful to coveners, and Darin and Turi despised the necessity.

The Karli rider who captured Santee's man might feel some compunction about killing, but more likely he also needed a rest. If you brought a criminal to Karli or Charzen, you could count on a night's sleep in a bed and three good meals. This particular patrol, Turi and Darin knew, had been riding before Belten, over seven weeks. That wouldn't bother a Suffec, but Karli and Shando liked to get home now and then.

Privately, Darin and Turi wished they could make an explicit order of summary execution. It happened, anyway, nine times out of ten, but to officially legislate it involved a precedent no Circle god wanted to set. So killing the cowan had to be their own dirty job.

Turi sighed, heavy with the knowledge. "When will they be in?"

"Maybe two days," Darin replied. He reached across to take her hands. "I can do it alone this time."

She lifted his hands and kissed them. "No, it's a misery for you, too. Together."

The meadows and fields Shalane once knew were dotted now with many more farms than she remembered. Beyond, the unchanged stockade still circled the masters' hall, where she pledged at sixteen. She shaded her eyes. Past the stockade to the southeast, Shalane marked the wood where oak, beech and walnut trees, never touched by axe or saw, enclosed an ancient clearing, its circle trench worn deep from countless fire days, ages of Sammans, Beltens and Sinjins. There the ground was hard-packed from centuries of dancing feet, gray-white with the ash of innumerable sacred fires. The earliest memory of Shalane's life, and its center.

She was home.

Something welled out of her chest, stung her eyes, squeezed her tight, exploded with joy. She yanked her mare about; at a flick of the reins, the animal leaped forward, plunged recklessly down the slope. Mady followed slowly.

A bowshot ahead, Shalane reined in at a small brook, dismounted and took off her clothes. When Mady caught up, she stripped her down to skin and shivering dignity and scrubbed both herself and the long-suffering little girl to pink freshness.

"Only one color for Sinjin, and that's green," said Shalane, slipping the new robe she'd made over Mady's head, smoothing and tugging it till it hung right.

She prepared herself with less urgency, her movements more controlled, as in a ritual. The green robe rustled down over Shalane's shoulders and breasts, hook-fastened tight at her waist, fuller as its slit skirts fell to her ankles.

Shalane donned a new white tabard, belted it precisely with the knotted cord, and attached the white thammay. Then she swung up onto the mare and Mady passed her the antler crown and moon-sigil.

Time for last-minute reminders. "Now, Mady, when you speak to a master, call 'em that. Kneel to Darin and Turi like I showed you, and just stand still when the masters kneel to me. We get kind of loose in City, but Karli'll 'spect you to have some manners."

"Yes, mama. But is it all right if I walk?"

"Walk?" Shalane wondered whether she'd heard right. "Walk into Karli?"

"Mama, I'm all sore behind and inside my legs. Please let me walk."

"Well, I 'spect not! No girl of mine's gonna walk into Karli like a sheep. Get up now, you don't hurt that much. "

"Please, mama," Mady begged, but Shalane's robed arm shot out, pointing like fate to the quarterhorse.

"UP!"

No reprieve. Mady struggled painfully into the hated saddle, forlornly wishing she were home with Marian and her daddy.

Long before they entered the stockade gate, Shalane saw the changes ten years made in Karli. The new houses began as far as a mile from the masters' hall, each with three or four acres under plow. Familiar paths over the sheep-cropped hills were almost like streets now, and there was no more than a bowshot between houses. The old coven signs—sun, moon and earth—were still daubed over doorways, but rendered now in bright weatherproof paint, sold by Mrikans who learned how to make it from City.

No sheep ambled about the stockade yard, no longer did hogs root or hens cluck in the clean-swept space, but people by the dozen hurried about their business with energetic strides, scarcely nodding to the goddess as she and Mady rode by.

Awful lot of Mrikans, Shalane noticed. *And don't folks know what's right any more?* When she was a girl, visitors were a rare event, and nearly everybody turned out to meet them, but now some people gave her a courteous greeting, but most didn't. And meanwhile there were children, children, children everywhere squealing and tussling, skipping and running, darting in and out of Shalane's path, not even mannerly enough to bob their heads as they passed.

But she was glad there were so many children. Coveners lost few at birth any longer, men like Corian and Ted Rashevsky changed all that. Though change made more change; more children needed more houses and more food. Twice as many sheep grazed the hills, half as much raw forest still girdled Karli, the new-bared land under plow, its timber disappearing into the hungry maw of a new sawmill.

The old, weathered masters' hall, she noted gratefully, was the same. But there was a smaller building with a lettered sign over its entrance next to the hall. Shalane never expected to see a sign with writing in Karli, it seemed an intrusion.

"Mady, what's that damfool thing say?"

The child told her: UHIAN CONSTABULARY AND COMMERCIAL.

One thing at least would never change: the masters waiting on the steps of the hall in a grave arc around the tall figures of Darin and Turi.

Shalane reined in before the formal group and dismounted. Mady floundered clumsily out of the saddle to edge in close to her mother as the eleven Karli masters came forward and knelt to Shalane's crown, then stood aside to let her pass.

Shalane mounted the steps, bending smoothly to the Karli crowns, Mady in awkward imitation. Then Shalane removed her own headdress and passed it to her daughter in the ancient protocol that recognized the god's and goddess' authority on their own covenstead.

Darin gave her a ritual kiss. "Karli's own should come home for Sinjin," he said.

Shalane received another embrace from Turi, who said, "Goddess Earth is green again," and then the ceremony was done. The masters broke ranks, crowding in on the visitors with warm greetings.

One master had a chain of wildflowers woven into a crown for Mady. She blushed and stammered her thanks.

Darin and Turi stood a little aside while Shalane engulfed old friends in her arms.

"Remember Jenna?" Turi murmured to her husband. "Bet this Mady grows as big. Six foot before she's sixteen, just wait."

"Easy," Darin nodded. "She's got the bones."

The god and goddess of Karli were a little younger than Arin and Shalane, coming to mastership in the middle of war, to the crowns in the wake of revolutionary change. Big, blond Darin had a body scarred with merk arrows and seared by the thrower-weapons Jeremiah used at Dannyline. Freckled, energetic, homely Turi had a luxury of fine brown hair that fell behind to her hips, but the hairline under her crown was deeply furrowed where a merk cut her in the battle of Karli Forest.

From the beginning their leadership was more political than religious. They dealt in hard money and harder choices—like having to kill cowans like Santee's man about to be brought into Karli. The two could read and write, and they used those gifts to conduct business their predecessors Hoban and Tilda never dreamed of. But Darin and Turi knew that the covens were no longer an island; like it or not, they were part of a larger world waking from a long slumber.

"Try to hold back time, it'll roll right over you," Turi whispered to Darin. She was quoting Corian, cocky, arrogant Corian who came back from his gold search a skeleton, regaining health but never quite his ignorant boy's superiority. He drank less now, and much more carefully. And never alone. Passionate, lonely, complex Corian, not quite cowan, not quite Circle, but knowing Circle mind better than any outsider Turi could name.

He's Shalane's friend, Darin thought. *He could help her.*

Turi squeezed his hand and twisted her own mouth at the notion, hoping Shalane hadn't read Darin by accident. But it was true. The woman certainly needed help, you could read pain all over her.

"It's her own fault," Turi muttered.

Partly anyway. Ten years in City with one of the best men of their time, with a daughter so smart and lep-strong the child was scary, almost—and yet the damfool wouldn't even learn to read. Not couldn't: *wouldn't.* Shalane once asserted it with a pride that embarrassed Turi to admit she could. But you almost had to be able to read nowadays, how else could you deal with Garick and so many distant peoples? It was actually faster to write a few pages—and the hell with the spelling—than to gather in masters and spend time and energy on a lep that other masters might or might not read.

Poor Shalane, Turi sighed, sharing the feeling with Darin. She'd be happy as old fox chasing rabbits in a coven that never heard of City or Garick, breaking horses and birthing children. *Born too late.*

Shalane spotted the white-haired, bearded man coming from the constab house. She hurried through the crowd toward him, dragging Mady along.

"Moss!"

He turned and his face lit with pleasure. Shalane threw her arms around her father, face buried in his frost-streaked beard.

"Oh, *dad,*" Shalane exclaimed, "lemme hug you!" She laughed but with moist eyes. "Mady, this is your grampa. Last time you were too little to remember, but here he is!"

Moss picked up Mady as easily as a flower, kissing her, holding her without strain. Fifty-eight, content with a new wife, he seemed to his daughter as young and strong as ever.

Taking Betta home to live was a good idea, Shalane thought. With her mother Maysa buried at Dannyline, Moss spent two disconsolate years rattling around, lonely, in their big house. *And he's not the sort to live alone like Ar—*

Shalane's breath caught. Now why did she almost think that?

"This my girl?" Moss chuckled, tickling Mady's chin with his beard. "Hey, Mady, y'all come home. Betta's waiting and there's some kind of supper."

"Fresh corn?" Shalane asked, tempted.

"Early corn, a little. But just about anything else, Lane. Come on."

"Lookit you," Shalane whistled. "Moss, when'd you start wearing Lorlcloth?"

Her father preened a bit. The shirt and pants were new and fit well. "Since it got so cheap and you can buy it over there in the commercial-house. Heck, old skins too hot for Sinjin, anyway."

Shalane turned slowly about the busy stockade court. "It's all so different, dad. Where'd all these folks come from?"

"All over. Wengen, Shando, some Mrikans."

Her mouth turned down. "Cowans."

Moss admitted there'd been many changes. "It dizzies me, too, sometimes, Lane, but we never lived so good."

She bridled. "We did all right before!"

"Maybe," Moss shrugged. "Ready to come home, Lane?"

"Not just yet."

Her father studied her, worried, but he understood. "Want me to take Mady on ahead?"

"Thanks," she nodded. "I'll be along soon. Just want to look some."

As Moss set her down, Mady asked in a small voice, "Grampa, may we walk? Please?"

"Sure," he smiled, giving her his big hand. "Maybe we'll do some berry-picking 'long the way, but don't let's get that pretty new robe stained. Likely you'll be the best-looking little girl at the fire. But who the hell cut your hair?"

Gosset's horse stumbled, righted itself. Wheezing, he asked his captor to stop a few minutes, but the taciturn rider shook his head.

The fat man was sweating, unused to such a long stretch of fast riding. He felt sore and a little sick from the continual jogging. He attempted to adjust the rope where it chafed, but the constab yanked it tight and warned Gosset to keep his hands off.

The exertion of being forced to sit a horse too long was bad enough, but what really scared Gosset was what they might do to him in Karli. All right, he admitted to himself, pale with terror, we all burned out the farm sure enough, and he and Billy Lee stuck the box before she got ripped apart, but since when did deepwoods mofos make a fuss about just taking a woman? The killing didn't involve him, that was only Ben and Billy Lee, and like he'd heard Ritt mumble, Billy Lee was born crazy and Ben was getting there fast.

Hell, Gosset thought, *all I did was set a fire and take a horse. They shouldn't no way kill me for that.*

The silent constab flicked the reins and quickened the pace to Karli.

The man in deerskin walked out of the constab house and strode across the court toward the gate. Even after ten years, he was still unused to the verve and color and bustle of the place.

A hunter by his look, with a month's growth of black beard and a bow slung over his shoulder, he stepped along lightly, thinking about the changes a decade had wrought in Karli. All through the war, you could always tell a Karli by the buff-colored skins they wore; Shando dressed in green with brown streaks; Suffec, sort of gray-brown; Wengen, dark brown with sooty streaks. Not all that different, but each an identifying mark, a badge. Deepwoods folk used to know who they were, but now most people he saw had on light cotton clothes or cut-off shorts; only a few wore green in honor of their coming fire day, and he was the only cowan in buff deerskin. An outsider might mistake the Karli stockade for Lorl, and not only because of the garments, but the two came close to matching in noise as well. Once, you could stand in this courtyard and hear the wind sighing through the forest like being alone in church on a hushed summer morning, but it was all changed now.

He noticed a familiar-looking woman dressed in traditional green. His eyes narrowed; he glanced at her a second time. Then a broad smile swept over his face.

"Lane!" he shouted.

She whirled, saw him, and then they both ran to collide in a clumsy tangle of arms and kisses.

"Jay!" she squealed her delight. "You old Jay, I'm so damn glad to—"

"How long has it been?" Jay Kriss held her out to look at. "Five years?"

"All that much. More."

"My God, but you look wonderful! How long are you here for? Arin and Mady with you?"

"Uh-huh, Mady is. What're you doing in Karli, Jay? Thought you lived in Charzen."

"I do, but there's a house here I use when I ride for Garick."

She took his arm and they walked out through the gate. "Things changed here, sure as frost."

"And more coming," he nodded; "it's the way of things. I've been mapping a route between here and Lorl. Garick's running a phone line into Karli next summer."

"A *phone?*" She snorted her contempt. "Place already full of cowans, next our kids'll go to bed with—" She stopped herself, instantly sorry for her words. She pulled Jay to a halt. "Oh, no, Jay, I don't mean you! Why, you know what—you know what I mean."

"It's all right. I don't feel very cowan any more. My wife says I'm just like folks."

"You are. I love you special, Jay." Shalane touched her lips to his. "You were there in Salvation when I needed you."

"It's all right, Lane. You were there for me, too."

"Spitt says you got babies."

"Boy and a girl."

"How are they?"

Jay laughed. "You know Shando, think the world was created in Charzen. How's Arin?"

"He's good," she said. Jay noticed the hesitation. "Filled out some, ain't such a stringbean."

"And you're happy?"

She watched two mail riders trot toward the stockade with their bags. "Yes."

She didn't sound or look it, Jay thought.

Turning back to him, Shalane asked seriously, "Jay, you ever miss what you were? In Salvation?"

He shook his head, slowing his pace to the rhythm of his thoughts. "There's nothing to miss. Nothing I want to remember."

"But I hear you went back."

"Yes, for Garick. Just to get the mines working. Those shafts can be dangerous if you don't know them."

Not sure she should ask it, Shalane murmured, "Did you go into the town itself?"

"Yes. It's falling down, all grown over. Nobody comes near it any more." Except he had to, some beliefs die hard. He wrapped his parents' bodies in coal sacks and gave them Christian burial, reciting the service from memory.

Jay looked at Shalane with a curious expression. "I went to Uriah's house, Lane. I was going to bury the elder."

"He died in his bedroom." It was one bloody memory she permitted herself to bask in. "Jenna got him good."

Jay pursed his lips. "I wonder."

"What?"

"He wasn't there, Lane. Wife and daughter, yes. But not Uriah. I saw some stains that might've been an old blood trail, hard to tell, the black dust was so thick on everything. I traced it into the street, went to the church, thought he must've crawled in there to die. Nothing."

"Most like he bled to death in the woods." She said it with fervent hope.

"There was a lot of good in Uriah," Jay asserted, knowing he could never make her see it. "He could've been important to Garick."

Why not? she thought bitterly, *Garick uses everybody else.*

Jay paused by the side of a house that seemed new-built. "Lane, sometimes I look at my children and feel that the best of my faith and the best of yours aren't that far apart." It was his perennial philosophic obsession, and he might have expanded on it, but he saw unhappy bafflement clouding her eyes and he moved close to hold and comfort her.

Shalane was grateful for Jay's arms around her and his whiskery mouth against her cheek. She loved him once and never regretted it. She didn't want him that way now, it was just that Jay understood so much.

"I been wanting to come home, Jay." But what *was* home? Was it Karli, a place that no longer resembled where she'd grown up, or was it the memory of Karli as it used to be? Was home a way of doing things unchanging as the year-wheel? Or maybe it was really people—her father Moss, only he lived so far off now and had a new wife; or maybe home was Mady and Arin, she was with them, except being with someone meant never losing them, and yet without moving an inch, Shalane forced herself to realize, she seemed to be drifting away from both.

"I wanted to come home, Jay. Just I can't find it anywhere."

Long after supper, Turi sat hunched over the cleared wooden table working on the daily records. Darin entered the room, bent down and kissed her cheek.

"Hey," he greeted, "Shalane's come."

Turi sighed and scooped the coins back into the bag, tying it. She jostled the papers into a neat pile. "Some good news for her," she said to her husband. "Rider from Filsberg brought Shalane a letter."

"From Arin?"

She nodded. "Ought to cheer her some."

Darin straightened his long body. "Well, you see her then. I'll get the kids to bed."

He ushered in their guest and left. Turi lifted an eyebrow when she saw Shalane. Her own light shirt and pants were almost too much for the humid summer evening, but Shalane was in full robe and wool tabard. It made no sense. As a young master, Shalane used to go naked most of the time when it was warm, and when she did dress, her clothes looked like somebody threw them at her.

Turi motioned her to a chair. "Sit down, Lane."

But she hovered diffidently before her. "Favor, goddess."

"Since you helped teach me my mastership, can't you call me Turi? What can I do?"

"At Sinjin tomorrow. I'd like to be in the circle."

"Of course." Hardly a favor, Turi thought. It was the usual courtesy to let visiting masters share a ceremony if they so desired. "Well, how do you like being home, Lane?"

Shalane's eyes roved the room, not resting on anything. Turi supposed she remembered it the way it was when Tilda was goddess, when the place was dark and always smelled musty, but now it was bright-painted and decorated with fresh flowers.

"It's good to be back," Shalane said without much conviction.

"I guess Moss' house changed some."

Shalane shrugged. "Oh, he and Betta just love Mady. Don't guess she ever ate so much at one sitting."

"Food all right for her?" Turi wondered. "She looks real City to me."

"She's not." The correction was a little too firm. "Just no chance to learn anything else."

Turi appraised her shrewdly, but held her tongue. Rising, she took a small packet off a nearby shelf. "This letter just came for you, Lane. Must be from Arin."

Shalane glowed like a lamp suddenly lit in a dark room. "Real? Oh, my! Let me see." Turi gave it to her, and Shalane turned the envelope over in her hands. "First time in my life someone ever sent me writing."

The flood of emotion leaking from Shalane almost made Turi wince, but she forced herself to stay open, sharing. With painful certainty, Turi read the other's sorrow, that compounded sense of love and loss which Arin signified.

Shalane shyly passed the letter back. "Please tell me what he says."

"But this is family," Turi demurred. "Why not ask Mady to read it to you?"

"Because it's *my* letter. I'll tell her what's in it if I want. Go on."

The sharpness surprised Turi, but again she kept her opinions to herself. She opened the letter and read it aloud.

Lane,

I hope Mady won't have trouble reading this to you, I'm trying to print clearly. Hope you're both having a good time together. Corian wants you and me to help him with the Fleeters on the Fist. I think we should. We don't get much time alone, Lane, and I miss you. You'll love it, don't even have to sleep in a house if you don't want, and Cory is eager to show you the ocean, so you can see how big it is, you never believed me when I told you. Get Mady home after Sinjin and fastramp to north med center. We'll meet you there,

and we can go out by the Whitestone passage. Punkin, I miss
you and your mama,

with you both,

ARIN

"You know," Turi said, after she'd repeated the letter to Shalane twice, "that would be some kind of summer up there. You'd like
it, Lane. Real old-time folks." She folded the letter carefully and
placed it in front of her guest.

Shalane said nothing. Her head was bent over the letter, fingers
spread over its surface to touch what he'd touched.

Turi patted her shoulder. "Will you go?"

Shalane smiled so broadly that her chipmunk teeth stuck out
and she looked nineteen again. "Sure as frost I will. Arin and me,
we'll show them Fleeters how it's done."

Because Shalane felt happy for the first time in she couldn't
remember how long, she suddenly sensed that the Karli goddess was
not. The woman held some private anguish. With a sure, gentle
power, Shalane probed.

Turi, what? Share.

Reluctantly, Turi lepped the news of the farm sacked by Santee,
of the murders, of the prisoner being brought in and what must be
done with him. "Me and Darin, we hate it. Damn it, Lane, it just
never ends."

"Always you and Darin alone? Why not the masters?"

Turi didn't answer right away, thinking out her reasons. "Lane,
do you ever talk to Mady about the war?"

"No. Never."

Turi nodded. "Course not, you keep that locked up where it belongs. Darin and I do the same. We spare them that."

Shalane understood, but she shrugged. "Shit, it's just a cowan."

Turi stiffened. "And we just have a notion that life is sacred. Or
had it once. Seems to've got lost."

"Yes. It's not all that did."

Turi rose and stretched to ease her tired back. "Well, tomorrow
I'll see you're in the circle at the fire. Good night, goddess."

Mady woke again, terrified. If she could only sleep, maybe tomorrow might not be so bad, but she kept having upsetting dreams, and she didn't think it was the rich food, though Betta's fried possum and poke made her burp for an hour after dinner, and she had to get up twice during the night, but at least grampa Moss had a bathroom.

In her nightmares something prowled, ready to leap at her, and only music or words, words, words staved it off, set up a barrier. And so the syllables pattered on and there were Bach fugues like a fortress of notes barricading her against the unseen thing that lurked in the dark.

Mady missed her father, but now she especially wanted Marian because always, at home, when Mady had a bad dream, Marian would calmly and patiently explain what it meant, discussing each dream-image till Mady saw them as the harmless symbols they were.

The child was tormented by a sense of guilty shame. Of course she loved her mother, and grampa Moss and Betta couldn't do enough for her, but all she wanted was to go home. For the first time in her young life, Mady was frightened of sleep.

And then it was Sinjin.

The fire both excited and scared Mady, she couldn't handle it all at once, though she believed she knew what the holiday meant. Her mother had said it over and over: that Sinjin was Goddess Earth at her most beautiful, the sun at his closest and most powerful. (But why give thanks for something that happened every year, did coveners *really* worry it might not?)

At the fire, Turi would be the symbol of the earth. She'd be poised by the piled fruits of their crop and, in her dance, would become earth in its three phases: young girl in spring waiting to be kissed by the sun; midsummer wife heavy with life inside her; old woman in autumn and winter, her promise kept, waiting to be born again in the eternal year-wheel

. . . which represents a stage in religious ideation older than monotheistic or personal god/man relationship; odd echoes occur in Nietzschean "eternal recurrence." [Q.V., + vide. 877(8)-0294/270 . . .]

Fire days in the City were clean and neat, indoors in bad weather, sometimes with Diane taking notes, but in Karli it was something wild burst out of a cage and so intense that the lep-sharing hurt, and mama always was beautiful, but when she dropped her robe to go into the circle naked, she changed, grew, shone with terrible energy.

With Darin as the odd thirteenth, the sun, each of the six couples in the circle danced to the music chanted by the people outside. Turi danced as if she had no bones. Must be strong to move like that, Mady reflected, strong as mama and that was saying a good deal because on the trip from Filsberg, Shalane staymagicked a rabbit for supper, her mind a tight fist clamped around its tiny will, but the animal never suffered—one quick chop across its neck, and only fur held the long-eared head to the body.

How mama can dance! The sight of her and the other masters was both beautiful and a torment. Their intensity built with the throbbing chant till, seduced by the pulsing surge and ebb, Mady could not resist opening her locked mind to share.

She reeled and almost fell. Mady, panic-stricken, shut down again quickly. Dark, sweet, bitter and brilliant. Simultaneously joyful and threatening. A deluge of emotion mysteriously connected with the glistening forms of the male masters in the circle. Mady knew how and why their bodies differed from hers, but now they were subtly unlike the way she'd studied them, and she couldn't understand why the change should be so scary.

Yet she was tempted to open her mind a second time, just a little, but if she did the prowling presence might jump inside. Mady wanted to run away and yearned to stay.

She tried to divert her attention by focusing solely on the singing. She'd never heard it from so many throats before. It was a very old kind of music, related to pre-Jing varieties she'd listened to on Corian's tapes, except his most intricate recordings paled beside coven rhythms which went in four tempi at once and still managed to come out together.

Once, Mady tried to tell her mother about the music.

"Mama, that's seven-four."

"Hell, that's just Loomin-song."

"But Cory says the time works out to seven-four. And Belten music is *real* hard, it's eleven-four at the beginning and—you know the part, mama, where you come in '*dum*-dum-da-dum'?—that's three-four over four-four—"

"*Will* you stop talking at me, baby?"

"Well, I heard it on Cory's tape and he said—"

"Cory don't know everything, and you, bitty girl, don't know nothing!"

Oh, mama.

. . . dance in primitive culture is ecstatic, it effects the release from self into group consciousness, and may actually merge into the hypnotic. . . .

But Corian also says you have to be there, that's all, the numbers don't mean much, you can beat out the time, but when you hear it and see the dancing and how your mother whirls in the firelight, body gleaming with perspiration, all you can do is swallow and wonder.

The voices now sang only a few beats in each measure. Shalane danced the rest and it had to come out just right, too; a master who lost the beat in implied time must be out of tune with Goddess Earth who never lost or wasted anything.

Studying her mother, Mady decided she just wasn't ready to attempt to imitate such power, she couldn't move anywhere near as well, and even though she still wanted to share, she had a greater need to run from all of it. The mounting fear was not unmixed with sweet excitement, but the sharing was too frightening, she couldn't take so much of it at once, overloaded with emotions only dimly comprehended—smells of anger, love, fright, each possessing its own special scent that played havoc with her mind.

He smells bad, daddy.

No, he's just scared. If you ever got very frightened, you'd smell it on yourself.

Like one time in the park when she almost fell off the big rock. There was a sick-hollow sensation in her stomach and then the fear-smell came.

But the odor of the masters in the circle was new, a raw, pungent tang like ammonia and pepper. It smothered all other scents.

At last the rite ended. A rush of the younger coveners filling the cleared space to dance. Eager-shy, hitting and tugging each other, kicking like colts, clumsy as rag dolls after the smooth control of the masters, they lost and found the rhythm and lost it again, but it didn't matter. They touched one another more than the adults, grasping and petting, tickling and pulling with a shy, fierce need that Mady didn't like. Yet the laughter of the watching adults was warm and happy as they remembered this poignant awkwardness.

The young couples didn't dance long. Two by two, they dropped out of the circle and disappeared into the woods, nervous, jerky laughter trailing after them like bird-cries.

Consumed with curiosity, Mady considered following them, but she put the thought aside, she didn't know why; after all, she'd seen enough bio-function tapes. The penis entered the woman, and a baby might grow, but it was all foggy and disconnected and a little silly, too. Certainly not of any concern to her, but the tapes could not evoke what she now smelled and sensed till it ached.

Mady squirmed through the milling crowd of coveners until she found her mother, still naked, leaning against the feast-laden table, her green robe draped over her sweaty neck, drinking a cup of sida.

"Mama, you never drink!"

Shalane took her daughter's hand. "Honey, tonight I do. You just bet tonight I do."

"Why?"

"Why not?"

"Drinking hurts the body."

"Who says?" Shalane waved away the question. "Never mind, you can just bet I know."

Mady withdrew her hand. "Mama, I want to go home."

"Mady!" Shalane's eyes widened. "Oh, baby, oh, *no!* This is why we came, what I wanted you to see. Why don't you dance?"

"I don't know how."

"Oh, that don't matter," Shalane scoffed, reaching out to grasp the hem of her daughter's robe. "Come on, lemme help you off with this and—"

"Mama!" The child skipped back, grabbing her clothes tightly about her. "Don't!"

"Looklook, see? There's a bitty boy like you, punkin. Bet you could dance him blue."

"I don't want to dance, mama, I want to go home!"

Her mother glared at her, then emptied her cup and set it on the table. She gathered her daughter close. Mady smelled the pungent odor she couldn't name. It made her stiffen, her instincts roused like raised hairs.

"First night I was with Arin, Mady, we ran all the way home from Samman fire 'cause we couldn't wait to be together." Shalane paused, brooding. Mady felt the change in her mother like sunlight suddenly shrouded by a stormcloud. "Arin had to be so goddam smarty-dumb like Garick and change everything."

"Daddy's not stupid!" Mady was outraged. "He's intelligent, Marian says so."

At mention of Marian's name, Shalane pulled away. She reached for the jug and refilled her cup. "If your daddy was so smart, he'd be here with us." She took another long pull of sida.

Mady swallowed, aware that she was daring much. "Daddy says Sinjin's old-fashioned."

The cup slammed on the table. Liquid slopped over the brim. "Let me tell you something, bitty girl, some things are better the old way. Some things should never change." She grasped her daughter's wrist. "Come on now, you're going in the circle."

"No!" Paralyzed, Mady dug in her heels. Shalane tried to lift her, but the child was dead weight. "Mama, *no!*"

A few heads turned toward them. Angry and embarrassed, Shalane lowered her voice to a tense whisper. "What's the matter with you?"

"I don't want to, mama," Mady whined.

"How you gonna learn how things are? Come on!"

"I already learned!"

"Learned *what?*"

"About sex! Don't pull me, *please,* mama, don't pull me. . . ."

Shalane loosed her hold, but did not let go completely. Suddenly struck with sympathy for her daughter, she thought she finally understood what frightened her.

"Oh, baby, nothing'll happen, you're too young. Just this is so you'll be ready when you're older."

"But I already know what happens then," Mady objected, writhing to get free. "Marian—"

Shalane went white at the repetition of the hated name. "Marian? What's she know about men? She give you talk-boxes to listen to, newsreel to watch? When you're with a man, Mady, you *feel* it, and that's one thing that old bitch can't do, she ain't had a man since they built Karli."

"Mama, you're hurting my wrist. *Let go!*"

"If I do, will you go into the circle?"

"NO!"

Shalane released her daughter, but it was too late. The scream shattered the festivities. Voices hushed, people stared and even Shalane couldn't catch a trace of lep. Then everyone tried to be polite and not pay attention to the goddess and her livid, trembling child. The revelers took up Sinjin again, but just a little too loud at first.

Shalane threw her robe on the table. "All right, Mady, you go home if you want, you're smart enough to find it. Go away, I'm sick of looking at you." She strode off toward the circle.

Her mother's anger hurt Mady. She clenched her fists and teeth to keep control of her emotions. For a moment she stood alone, feeling abandoned, watching her mother seek a partner. Darin stepped into the circle and invited Shalane to dance.

Mady miserably wormed her way through knots of people, left the firelight and started down the path to her grandfather's house, choking back tears.

Shalane almost never drank. It did nothing for her and made her feel rotten afterwards. But tonight, an urge pulled at her soul, impelling her to another and yet another cup of sida, *yes more now hurry* and maybe she'd explode with yearning, so she danced furiously with Darin and other men without really wanting to go out on the hill with them. Vaguely, she hoped to find Jay in the crowd, but he wasn't there.

Finally, she gave it up, there was no joy for her this Sinjin. With the consuming ache still in her breast, Shalane stepped heavily from the circle and found her robe. Her father and Betta were still at the fire, but she decided to walk home to Moss' house.

As she moved away from the firelit grove, she draped the robe about her shoulders because the night air was cool. Her feet felt like they had iron chains wrapped around them, and there was a tight knot in her stomach, but as she walked through the quiet forest, the bracing night air chased off some of her sida-dizziness and her head didn't throb so much. The silence all around calmed her, but she was in no hurry to get home and maybe face Mady again, so Shalane picked a roundabout path that brought her close to the masters' hall.

There she dawdled, thinking about the letter Arin sent her. Remembering it, she started to feel a little bad for the way she'd talked in front of Mady. The journey to the Fist was going to be real good, she and Arin would be with each other, they'd start sharing again, and this time she would not allow anything to come between them and change it. The sweetness of the resolution eased the dull sorrow in her chest.

Just then, she heard the sound of approaching horses, two riders coming on fast. Shalane stepped into the stockade clearing, curious to find out who was on the roads Sinjin night instead of at the fire. Then she sourly recalled that Karli nowadays was crawling with cowans. *Probably some fat-ass Mrikans.*

Two men rode into the open space and reined in alongside the squat building next to the hall, the one whose sign read UHIAN CONSTABULARY AND COMMERCIAL. The first to dismount was a Karli constab. The other rider was fat, soaked in sweat and tightly bound with ropes.

Knowing who the prisoner must be, Shalane turned away and started walking again. The cowan's fear-smell disgusted her.

Her father's house was dark. Shalane opened the door to the room she shared with Mady—her own old room—and peered into the gloom.

"Mady?"

Silence.

Feeling for a box of City matches, she lit the synth-oil lamp. Its light spread across the room.

Shalane's breath caught.

Mady lay across the bed, shoulders heaving convulsively, though she made no noise as she sobbed. The child was dirty, and her arms and legs were covered with cuts and scratches.

"Baby . . . *what happened?*"

Mady knew her way to grampa's well enough. The houses along the path shimmered silvery in the moonlight, and the sap-smell of their new-cut planks mixed with the heady perfume of summer night. It was something like the park at home, rich with flowers and grass and the acrid reek of bird droppings and damp earth, only now it was overpowering, out of control. She needed to detach part of herself from it, pull away from the profusion of sensory stimuli.

Her path now led through a murky patch of woods. Mady had no fear of the dark, never did, but she was sharply aware of furtive movement and sounds all around. Off to her left, the high, light yapping of a fox; closer, in answer, the same kind of bark, but in a boy's poor imitation, ending in an exaggerated howl, followed by the thin, tinkly laughter of a girl.

The night was heavy with stealthy sounds: whispers and giggles; footsteps sliding stealthily through the trees; sibilant murmurs and agitated thrashing in the leaves and underbrush, and somewhere to her right a high voice uttered a soft gasp that suddenly rose to a smothered cry.

Over it, Mady's sensitive nose detected the same scent which both drew her to and drove her away from the dancers' circle, that ammonia-and-pepper thing which assaulted her nostrils like skunk musk.

She reached the edge of the woods and stepped out into a moon-washed meadow. A slight rustle of movement to one side caught her attention; she turned that way, and froze.

On a dark square of blanket, two gangly bodies squirmed and tossed, locked together. Though in the shadow of the trees, the light was bright enough so their whiteness stood out sharply.

Mady watched their last final twitchings in fascination, fear and shame. Sighing deeply, the boy rolled off the girl, reached for a jug stolen from the feast tables, tilted it to his mouth. It sloshed faintly.

Lorn's sharp forest senses, returning from satisfaction, picked her up like a clean, cool breeze threading through springtime grass. He waved to her.

"Hey," he hiccuped, "who you? What y'all doing out, little girl?"

His companion, fourteen like himself, shifted on the blanket and smiled at the trembling child in the green robe. "Hell, Lorn," the blonde tittered, "she just a baby, too little."

"Not on Sinjin night," the boy laughed, rolling indolently onto his back. "C'mere, baby."

Mady gulped, heart pounding as she stared at the dark nipples of the leggy girl's half-budded breasts and the boy's still-moist, semi-stiff penis. "I'm going home."

"Aww, don't go yet," Lorn drawled. "Just might give you a drink."

"Don't want any."

The lithe blonde suddenly jumped up and took Mady's arm gently but firmly. She pulled the reluctant child down on the blanket, running her fingers through Mady's cropped hair.

Breathing rapidly, Mady glanced from one to the other. She wanted to wrest free and run, but her legs were like rubber.

"I know who this is," he said. "Bitty City gal."

"Sure as frost! She come with the goddess."

"Leave me alone," Mady insisted, wriggling to release herself from the girl's grip. "I have to go."

"Baby wants to go home, Lorn."

"Your ma won't mind," he laughed easily, "she's back dancing. C'mon, baby, let's play."

And they did; Mady was their rag doll, they ruffled her short hair and flopped her this way and that, they rolled her over and hiked her robe so they could pat and tease and lightly stroke and slap her bare bottom; she begged them to stop, but they wouldn't. Neither had any thought to hurt Mady, there was no malice or bullying in them, but they were both euphoric with the thrill of their first time, and their intoxication spilled over into a kind of rough, sensual affection which Mady didn't understand and couldn't tolerate.

"Stop, please stop!" The terror worsened as Lorn got up on top of her. The girl held Mady while Lorn pretended to love her with a flurry of grunts and moans, and he took care not to put his weight on the child, but the sense of nightmare grew as Mady shrilly protested, "You stop, you stop, mama says I'm too little!"

"It's Sinjin, baby girl. Ain't gonna hurt you."

But Mady didn't know that at all. It was just play to Lorn, mainly to amuse his girlfriend, but the child was frightened and out-raged and *City people don't touch* so Marian accorded her respect and distance from the very first, and even mamadad playing house-building in bed never poked around her private parts with stinky fingers, and the boy's half-erect penis pressed its sticky tip between her legs and he rubbed it back and forth till her loathing and fear and rage swelled and she shrieked and struck him with her fists and mind.

"You too rough, Lorn, she's scared," the girl said, but he was already rolling away, head clutched in his hands where Mady's angry lep slashed him with the pain of a sudden sharp headache. He tried to tell her he didn't mean to hurt her, but now Mady couldn't stop herself as she screamed and lunged at him, clawing at his face.

Lorn stumbled to his feet and tried to keep the kicking, biting savage at arm's length. "Baby, baby," he crooned, "I didn't mean nothing bad, just it's Sinjin."

The blonde put her arm around Mady's shoulders to comfort her, but twisting free, she staggered off a few steps, choking, mouth dry, throat raw.

Clutching her robe to yank it down over her legs, Mady was horrified to discover her own body had shamed her. *Mama's pretty robe!* Her fists bunched and knotted, and the boy worried she was about to attack him again, but then deep embarrassment overcame Mady and she ran away, her sobs trailing behind like torn flesh.

"Honest, he didn't mean it, baby!" the girl called, concerned for the child and also scared for herself and Lorn because, after all, the City girl was the daughter of an important goddess. "He was just fooling—real!"

Mady hardly heard her. Ragged breath tearing her lungs, she churned her legs fast till she saw a copse and dashed into it to escape the naked moonlight. She did not slacken pace amid the concealing trees though twigs whipped and cut her arms and brambles scratched her legs.

She emerged near her grandfather's house. Crumpling to her knees, Mady vomited in the long grass.

"Baby . . . *what happened?*"

Sullen silence.

Shalane felt for Mady's mind, but she locked it tight behind her will—though not before her mother read the revulsion and resentment.

"Mady!" Dropping across the bed, she took her in her arms. Mady's breathing was spasmodic and her cheeks were damp with tears. *Open up, let me share.*

"N-no, mama."

"Come on, you need help."

"No. I just want to go home."

Her mother tried to soothe her. "But this is your home, baby."

"It is not. I hate it here." Mady shook off her mother and flung herself face down on the bed.

Feeling numb and useless, Shalane hovered close, smoothing her daughter's short, tangled hair, trying to caress her violently trembling body to calm it. "Tell mama, honey, please tell mama, please."

Sniffling, voice jerky with greater emotion than she had sufficient words to tell it with, Mady reluctantly attempted to explain. "I . . . I was c-coming home through the woods, mama, and . . . and there was this . . . this boy and girl and they . . . p-pulled me down on a blanket. . . ."

The bald facts could not communicate Mady's complex shame and anger, but Shalane thought she understood. This sort of thing happened often at Sinjin, she'd gone through it herself, sometimes it was a little rough but only just fooling, she couldn't imagine the boy actually hurting Mady. Abruptly, Shalane rolled her child over and yanked the dirtied, rumpled robe above her hips.

"Don't, mama!"

"Hush, baby, I got to look." She pulled her daughter's thighs apart and spread the inner lips, unaware she was making Mady feel newly violated.

"I told him . . . to st-stop, mama . . . but he wou-wouldn't. . . ."

"It's all right," Shalane said, relieved. Mady was red from the saddle-chafing, but otherwise hadn't been touched. She cuddled the child close, Mady's damp weepy face against her own. She wished her daughter would let herself open up so she could help. Sure, once she got a bit roughed up, too, at Sinjin, and maybe it made her a little mad, but not hysterical like Mady. Hell, that was how to learn loving, you were ready for it when it really came. If only Mady would share, then Shalane could pass the gift down that her own mama Maysa once shared with her, and then Mady would understand that what took place with the boy and the girl on the blanket was just part of being alive.

She tried to say it in words that stammered and halted, but it all got mixed up with how it never hurt because what with her breaking horses and her own self-curious tickling experiments, Shalane didn't have anything left for a boy to force, and her first time on the hill was with a boy so excited and clumsy that he finished before he was half in her, but it was sort of fun trying and it sure wasn't scary and children always messed around together like that.

Her mother rambled on. Mady's anger cooled and condensed into a small, tight knot in her chest. When Shalane faltered to a stop, Mady stared at her and spoke as if from a great distance. "No, mama, most of that's irrelevant, there's more than just the sex."

"What then? Lep, Mady. You know I'm not any good at dumb words."

"No." The cold syllable dropped like a stone. "I want to go home, mama."

Her unexpected self-possession disturbed Shalane. She groped at her daughter's mind, but Mady kept it resolutely shut.

"Mama, I said I want to go home."

"In a few days."

"Now! I want my daddy. I hate Karli."

Shalane gasped. "Well, I never thought a girl of mine—"

"Mama," Mady interrupted, "I want to go back to school."

"To *Marian?*"

"Yes."

"Damn that woman, what's she turned you into?"

Mady glared at her.

"Baby, if you'll only just share with me, I promise it'll make everything all right."

She realized her mother meant it, but Mady couldn't. Before she opened her feelings to others again, she wanted first to know them herself. They were too frightening: the lack of sleep, the prowling nightmare, the total assault on her senses of sight and smell and sound, and the ultimate outrage to her body, her *self.* She distrusted the engulfing coven sharing that wrought havoc with her mind like an idiot turned loose with red paint in a white room, it was too much power because she felt inadequate to control or channel the flow, maybe she had to be older.

"Baby," Shalane pleaded, "you're hurting, I know. Tell mama, I want to make it all better, please let me."

Part of Mady really wanted to respond to the love and concern, but Shalane only spoke Uhian and that wasn't subtle enough, and even English had its limitations, which left only one way the child could express herself without lep. Half out of longing and need for her mother and half out of spite, she decided to try.

When Shalane saw her daughter's small hands begin to move, anger and frustration welled up within her. "I asked you once not to do that," she warned.

But Mady's fingers flew, snapping and curling and shaping, each movement cluster representing ideas ten times faster and more complicated than she could ever manage orally.

"Stop it!" Shalane snapped. "Don't do that to me. I can't understand that fool shortmind, Mady, you know that."

"That's not *my* fault, mama."

"What you doing, anyhow?"

"You asked me to tell, so I am, the best way I can."

"Not like that," Shalane spat. "Tell. Or lep."

"But words are *insufficient,* mama," Mady taunted, deliberately employing an unfamiliar English term.

"Huh?"

"That means words aren't enough, mama. Neither's lep."

"All right. Then share."

"No!"

Shalane shook her fiercely. "Goddam you, Mady. You're a Karli. You share."

"I am *not* a Karli!" Mady twisted away. "I'm CITY!"

The blood rushed from Shalane's face. She felt suddenly dizzy, thought she might faint. But she answered Mady, each word pronounced with extreme precision.

"Bitty girl, you sure as hell ain't."

Surging to her feet, little fists clenched, eyes blazing, Mady bellowed, "City, mama, *CityCityCity!*" She hit out at her mother's reaching arms. It was too late now, Mady's fury pushed her beyond love or kindness or even caution as the hurtful words spilled from her contemptuously curled lips. "You leave me alone, mama, I can't talk to you, nobody can 'cause you don't know anything and you don't want to know anything and you don't even want anyone else ever to know anything! You won't learn, you can't even read like Turi."

Tears started in Shalane's eyes. *No, baby, don't, you're all I've got left, don't do this—*

"You're IGNORANT, mama!" Mady was out of control, she couldn't stop. "And keep away from my mind, I hate that! You—"

"Mady, stop." Shalane's hands twisted spastically.

"—don't know how I feel, don't care how *I* feel!"

"Mady, stop!"

"You're just as bad as that boy. First thing you do, you roll me over and grab and look up my legs without asking. How can I share, you don't even know I don't want to be touched, not like that? You don't know anything about me, mama . . ."

"Mady, *stop!*"

". . . and you don't even know what *daddy* thinks any more!"

"SHUT UP!"

Shalane's hand shot out when she shrieked, striking her daughter so hard she fell. Howling with pain, Mady scrambled to her feet, hands against her nose, blood trickling through her fingers.

Shalane was instantly horrified. She'd never struck her little girl since she came out of her body. "Oh, baby, oh, I'm sorry! Let me fix it."

But Moss and Betta came in from outside and his gruff voice sounded from the kitchen. "Hey, what the hell's the matter in there?"

Mady ran out of the room, bawling. She flew into her grandfather's comforting arms.

Shalane stared at her hand as if it belonged to somebody else. Turning down the lamp, she closed the door and sat on her old bed in the dark, her mouth buried in the sleeve of her Sinjin green robe so Mady and Moss and Betta wouldn't hear her crying.

The morning after Sinjin, the stockade court was quiet and empty. Darin and Turi stood in front of the masters' hall, grave and still, watching Shalane and Mady walk their horses through the gate. Moss was behind them leading a pack horse.

In the middle of the calm, sunny morning, the silence was oddly tense. There was something heavy in the air, a lowering gloom.

Shalane noticed it at once. She thought it was just her own mood, but Mady's small bandaged face tilted up suddenly, and she knew the child read it, too.

"Stay with grampa," Shalane ordered curtly. "I'll say goodbye for both of us." No need for Turi to read more than she already was picking up.

Shalane approached the god and goddess, bowed to their crowns and sensed the tautness in both even as they tried to mask it.

"Be careful on the road to Filsberg," Darin advised. "It's clear, but the patrol in that sector's way north now, probably trying to catch up with Santee. Watch yourself, you never know."

"Moss will ride a spell with us," Shalane said shortly.

"You feel bad, Lane?" Turi asked solicitously.

"Bad as you. You two read like sore teeth. What's the matter?"

They lepped, a painful intertwining of reluctant thoughts. *The cowan's inside. It's today.*

"We wanted to say goodbye first," said Darin, trying hard to smile. "Ride with the sun, goddess."

"And be born again to the Karli." Turi kissed Shalane, then she and Darin re-entered the hall.

Shalane started back across the court. Tension festered in the air like summer heat just before the explosion of a rainstorm. She halted, stroked her mare's neck, looked back toward the masters' hall.

Inside, Gosset sat motionless with the constab rider standing over him. He still didn't know what they had in store. Here, at least, he was allowed to sit in a comfortable chair, and the woman even gave him a mug of hot tea before she and her tall mate went outside.

Gosset was clammy with fright when they first led him into the large room. Ben said they weren't really human, but somehow he felt less afraid now, even relaxed, maybe because they asked him to sit down to tea like neighbors. But he still didn't hope much, either.

The tea was good, though. His shaking stopped, he wasn't piss-scared any more.

And then the man and woman returned. The look in their eyes seemed far away, like they were watching him from the moon.

The man broke the silence. "How do you feel?"

"Kinda tired." Gosset's mouth was dry despite the pungent tea. "What happens to me?"

No answer, just that distant moon-look.

"Well, what? I ain't afraid of you, what you gonna do, kill me?"

He couldn't understand these people, they just turned away like he hurt *their* feelings.

"Yes," the woman said finally. "When you're asleep. There's no pain."

Gosset tried to laugh, but it came out flat and false. "You think I'll just lay down and go to sleep for you?"

"Yes." Darin stated it like an accomplished fact. "You're on the way now."

Shit! Gosset swore to himself. *The tea!* That's why he was so drowsy.

"Hell I will!" Gosset lumbered to his feet, shaking off the restraining hand of the constab rider behind him. It was an effort, but the fat man intended to fight it all the way, they wouldn't finish him so easy, not for something he didn't do.

"Look," he protested, "wasn't me or Ritt killed those folks. Ben did it, you know how crazy Santee is. I tried to stop him, I said, 'Ben, leave 'em be, we got the horses, let's—' "

But his legs would no longer hold his great weight. Gosset floundered into the chair, fought to stand again, but a ton of softness pressed him down.

For a moment he wheezed noisily. Then, with a kind of pathetic pride, he said, "All right, I don't wanna wait. Kill me now. If I go to sleep, how'll I know?"

The coven pair didn't move. Their hesitation agonized Gosset, he couldn't take it. He started to curse them, but midway his voice quavered into pleading, and then, unexpectedly, he yawned. It surprised him. It sure seemed weird at such a time.

"Don't fight it," the woman begged. Gosset wondered why she felt so bad when he was the one going to die.

Gosset pulled himself together with a grunt. "Goddam you big sonsabitches, look at me straight and do it!"

But they still turned away, and then the room grew hazy with dots dancing wherever his eyes darted, along the floors, the walls, dots jiggling near the door.

The door.

Someone standing in the door who didn't turn away but held his failing sight in a steel will. The beginnings of a pulsing heat like fever flared in his skull. The fat man put numb fingers to his forehead, then all feeling ceased. His face went slack. Gosset collapsed like a sack of potatoes, whitebrained, his mind a vegetable.

The will that burned his brain closed like a vise around his heart and stopped it.

Shocked, angry and relieved all at once, the Karli god and goddess gaped at Shalane. Turi felt for her old friend's mind, but touched a surface as hard and unreadable as her sister goddess' green eyes.

"You were sick with it," Shalane told her. "Now it's done."

"It was our responsibility," Darin said, gravely reproving her, "not yours."

Shalane said nothing.

"We have to live with these things," Turi said levelly, conscious of the embarrassed constab rider who'd stood silent behind Gosset during the whole business. "You don't have to, Lane."

An offhanded shrug. "It was easy. Like stepping on a bug."

Without sparing a single glance for the dead cowan or another word to the god and goddess, Shalane slipped out the door and left Karli.

Ben Santee lay on his back by the tiny fire and gazed with blissful contentment at the thick oak limbs silhouetted against the muted colors of a calm sunset.

"That is an *in*spiring sight," he decided with conviction. Shaved, dressed in clean cotton, he felt like new. There was no need now to hurry or hide, the danger was gone.

Their camp lay in the high, lush hills just north of a Wengen iron town where Ben had felt the urge to socialize. No one up this way knew his name very well and iron towns don't much care who a man is, anyhow, so he rode down alone into the village, had a bath, bought some clean clothes and hefted a few drinks with the workers. Gratifying what a man could learn if he just drank quietly and listened.

Ben spun out his news for Ritt and Billy Lee.

"The iron works shipped out some special freezer boxes today. You heard of Corian?"

Billy Lee's memory never stretched beyond yesterday. "Who?"

"Doctor," Ritt remarked. "Goes all over for Garick."

With a nod, Santee took a slug of potato gin from a new jug and passed it to Ritt. "Heard in town that old Corian's going up the Fist to the Fleeters."

Billy Lee stopped fingering his crotch. He recognized that name, Ben mentioned it a lot, it must be important. "Fleeters?"

"Now, goddammit, Billy Lee, I told you six times who Fleeters is, I ent gonna tell you again. Just listen."

Ben said that while he was in the iron-town tavern he heard a worker black as Bowdeen talk about how the new freezer boxes were built special to lug medicine and had just been picked up by Garick's own son.

Santee bought the iron worker a drink in a friendly way. "That right? Garick's boy?"

The black man nodded, guzzling gin. "Now what the hell was his name?"

Santee refreshed his memory. "Arin?"

"That's him. Big red-haired mofo, chilly around the eyes, but soft-spoke. Says he never been up on the Fist before."

"Oh?" Ben was politely curious. "He traveling with Corian?"

The worker swallowed another mouthful. "Said so. Him and his wife going 'long with Cory just for the fun."

Ben smiled at the tree branches etched in stark relief against the scarlet flush of a dying day. What with Rack and Gosset gone, he deserved some luck. "You heard of Arin, Ritt?"

Busy with his own thoughts, Ritt grunted. "Who ain't?"

"You, Billy Lee? Hey!" Ben kicked the boy's foot. "You heard of Shalane?"

Billy Lee swallowed fiery gin and belched. "She pretty?"

"If you like deepwoods, and you do. She's a goddess, Billy Lee. One of the Devil's own chosen daughters, that's the truth. Gotta go in the circle and get down on a man for that. Right down on him, you know what I mean? There ent nothing you can do a bitch like that ent been done to her before. She was one of them that cleaned out Salvation."

Billy Lee remembered Salvation because Ben talked about it all the time. "That was bad," he nodded sympathetically.

"Babies and all," Ben said darkly. "Cattle, horses, chickens. Nothing left alive. Choked the working shift down in the mines, buried 'em alive."

Billy Lee reached inside his hide shirt to scratch, puzzled by an inconsistency. It took him a while to get it straight, but it seemed worth the effort. "That why we doing it back to them, Ben, right?"

"That's why."

The small fire snapped and sputtered. Santee savored his gin. "Arin and Shalane up on the Fist," he repeated. "Just never know what you'll learn by listening."

Sunset was almost over. The light had faded and the bent oak limbs were dim against the sky's subtler reds and deeper blues.

"Guess those two are all Garick's got for family," Ben said softly.

Ritt emerged from his own worries when he caught his leader's drift and heard the unpleasant softness in Santee's voice which Ritt had grown to hate more and more over the years. The hate stemmed from a fear: Ben had no bottom to what he might do when somebody crossed him. That worried Ritt. At least Gosset could think straight now and then, though Billy Lee never could think at all. But Ben—the old shrewd brain in the man just rotted away a little more each day.

"Jee-zus shit," Ritt grumbled, "ain't you had enough?" He said it low, not sure he wanted Ben to hear.

The jug lowered from Santee's mouth, untasted. "Enough what, man?"

Ritt jerked a thumb at the tree. "That. We're taking too many chances. There's no need."

"Ent there?" Ben whispered. "We ain't done yet, Ritt, not yet. Maybe not never."

Wind stirred the wooded hilltop. The ropes that stretched over the tree limbs creaked with the weight of the hacked bodies swaying slightly in the dawn breeze.

Santee learned a lot by listening in the tavern. The Filsberg constab chased Ben till he caught them.

WELLFLEET GREEN

Taking Arin's hand, Shalane stepped aboard, fretting that the craft was too frail.

"Goddess," Corian tried to reassure her, "Fleeters range hundreds of miles out to sea most of the year in ships just like this one, and we aren't even leaving the Sound. Looky." Beckoning her to the three-sided wheelhouse, he spread out the chart of their route and ran his finger along the blue line that indicated the waterway the boat rocked on at that very moment. "Here we go, out the passage, up the Sound to Buzzards Bay, through the canal and into the inner bay of the Fist, then straight across to Wellfleet Harbor. We'll see the ocean, but you won't be out on it."

Shalane was not reassured. Bending over the unfolded map, she frowned and said she couldn't find any place where the water left off being ocean to become Sound, it was all one big blue splash on the paper.

Corian held both hands palm up in a typical Wengen gesture. "What can I tell you? When we get there, you'll see."

The ship's high prow swept back in a lower beam, barnacled and salt-bleached. It was an old Fleeter fifty-footer modified to carry a sun-powered battery engine aft beneath the wheelhouse. The unsteppable mast seated midship shadowed new hatches forward; the Fleeters were old-fashioned most ways, but not when it came to fishing. The City, which bought most of their catch for food and medicine, offered them modern freezer units that were gladly installed in the ancient hatches by the Fist men.

Shalane and Arin sat side by side, saying little, but when Corian, at the helm, pointed over the bow at the narrowing banks ahead and said they were the start of a channel that would soon widen into the Sound, Arin put his hand over hers, and she was grateful for the contact. In the past, when her husband tried to tell her how big the sea was, Shalane didn't believe, but now with the surf whispering far-off and gulls shrilling overhead in the salt-smacked air, she knew with dismay that he hadn't lied.

Corian tried to cheer her by singing one of the lustier songs he liked to collect on his travels. It didn't help; there wasn't anything Corian could say or do now, short of turning the ship around, that would make her feel better. She saw the shore receding again, and knew they were almost past the channel, nearly there.

The river widened into an estuary enclosed within the seaward curve of a brake-fringed headland. The vessel plowed across the bay, following the gentle cupping of the shoreline. Shalane's panic mounted as they neared the last lip of the natural harbor.

Then they entered the peaceful waters of the Sound. For the first time in her life, Shalane saw the sea and despite her people's landlocked history, something older stirred her blood and her pulse slowed in sympathy to the rhythm of the tide.

"See that line, goddess?" Corian gestured eastward to a wall of surf that cut the calm water like an incision. "That's the Atlantic. If I'd told you that you can see where it begins, would you have believed?"

Shalane did not reply. Eyes wide and glassy, she stared where the glimmering sun flecked the ocean crests with streaks of silver.

For the past several minutes, Arin had read her growing fright, but now her silence worried him more. Many coveners experienced profound emotional shock upon first glimpsing the unending skyline of City, and Shalane, who'd never set eyes on a body of water bigger than a forest lake or river, had to be undergoing a similar thing. Holding her hand tight, Arin put his other arm around her shoulders.

It's all right, Lane. I'm with you.

Their minds linked. They shared. It was a sweet pang to Arin, like finding something precious he'd undervalued till it was lost. He kissed her, saw that her eyes were misted with tears.

Lane?

She shook her head. *Nothing. Just I'm glad.*

But even as her spirit folded gently into his, Arin noted the small corner of her mind she was keeping locked off from him.

At the wheel, Corian watched the sea. In spite of the blazing sun, he felt a little cold.

That night, Shalane and Arin slept by the forward hatch in a large, comfortable sleeping bag that muffled but barely contained their lovemaking. Time after time they would peak only to have the need flare once more, as if they hadn't loved at all. Breathing hard from their latest climax, they would start all over again.

Next morning, a yawning Corian saw the ripped sleeping bag and the scratches on Arin's brown back and whistled appreciatively.

"Gonna have to hit Lorl one of these days," he told himself, taking the wheel to bring the craft around north. The weather held good. He kept close in to the shoreline, and now there was land on either side, which vastly relieved Shalane.

The trip was taking longer than it had to, but Corian allowed the engines to loll them up the coast, figuring his friends needed as much time together as they could get.

Their laughter sparkled like sun in their wake, like the cheery rocking of the boat beneath them. Arin lay on deck, Shalane's head pillowed on his stomach. She was telling about her journey north from Karli.

Corian leaned against the side of the wheelhouse and wondered why she avoided mentioning Mady in her narrative.

"So I come to the Filsberg decon point," Shalane continued, "and old horse was just loaded with home-food." She twisted round to bite Arin's stomach. "You listening or what?"

"Listening," he grinned.

"So what did you work?" Corian asked.

"Sort of a staymagic. Got about a bowshot from the guard, 'n' he wasn't sure he saw a horse or not. By the time I come 'longside, he didn't see any horse *at* all. Old cowan looks dumb at me, says, 'Didn't you have a horse?' And I said, 'Y'all don't see a horse, do you?' Just 'bout then, old guard starts to get real sleepy, like he might close his eyes a bit."

Corian chuckled. "That's cruel."

"Shouldn't play with power like that, it's risky," Arin said. Then, because Cory was there, he continued in lep. *It's dangerous, Lane, laying hold of folks' minds, that was Singer's kind of game.*

Singer. Garick's first son by Judith, daughter of Marian. As always, whenever Arin thought of his long-lost brother, he wondered where the hell the hardhead little bastard disappeared to—a peculiarly apt way of putting it because the last time Arin had read him, Singer was walking north wearing an invisibility shield known as the Girdle of Solitude.

Arin's thoughts returned to Shalane. Willful or not, he was glad
to have her close again. He stroked her breast lightly, kissing her
caressing fingertips while Shalane purred with drowsy pleasure.

"Hey, goddess," Corian prompted her, "don't leave us hanging.
How'd you manage the fastramps?"

She grinned. "Old horse didn't like them ramps one bit. Had to
cover her head with my robe. When Bern met me, I was bare as a
skinned deer. You know Bern with his new City talk, well, he just
stands there laughing and says, 'Goddess, you're a natural wonder.'
Arin, what *is* a natural wonder?"

"You, Lane."

Wriggling with pleasure, Shalane pressed his hand tight against
her breast. "So that's how our City masters got some kind of supper
for a couple nights, anyhow."

Now that she and Arin were with one another again, Shalane
felt exhilarated. Even Corian's presence comforted her. True, she
missed Mady, but at the heart of her daughter's absence was anger
and an ache that had been growing since Karli. Her child rejected
her. For the first time, Shalane had a lot less love than she needed,
and she turned to Arin with a sharp hunger.

Later that day, Arin bent over the taffrail and watched the fish
leaping high off the stern.

He needed the loving as much as Lane, it was always good between them, even after ten years. But the undertone of her desperation troubled him. They shared so much during loving that a lot
leaked from one mind to the other and even though she tried to shut
it away, Arin read her anger and knew they must soon turn it to the
light. Loving her was complicated and mysterious, but he supposed
all really close ties between people were like that.

"Hey, Cory," he said suddenly, "how come you're not with
someone?"

The other tossed a reply over his shoulder. "Got too many
women now."

"Sure, but you're not with them. You never met someone you
wanted to stay with?"

Instead of replying, Corian jerked his head toward the shore.
"Hey, look. Moster dock up ahead."

"Moster?"

"They're Mrikan, but Fleeters call them Mosters because they're almost on the Fist. We could stop and get some fresh oysters. Goddess Shalane?"

Crouched over the prow, she eyed the land suspiciously, as if it might vanish if she didn't keep close watch over it. "What, Cory?"

"Wanna put in to eat?"

"YAY!"

"I think she's for it," Arin remarked wryly.

"All right," Corian called, "watch the sail, she's coming about."

Arin followed him to the wheelhouse. The Wengen spoke softly, almost to himself. "Well, I guess there was one woman."

"Who?"

Corian shrugged. "Doesn't matter. She was with someone else."

Catching a color that leaked from Cory, Arin decided not to pursue it. The knowledge didn't surprise him, though. Corian was so open, he was closed. You could know everything and nothing about him.

Corian gave and took a spoke on the wheel, cutting the throttle. "Just as well," he murmured. "I get too close to people."

Hearing a tentative tap at her office door, Diane switched off power, swiveled away from her console and bade Mady enter. The child, looking both perplexed and a bit apprehensive, stepped in and immediately asked to see Marian.

"Unavailable," Diane signaled.

Mady's right hand framed a question. "Where?"

"Balmer."

"How long?"

"Indefinite."

Surprised and dismayed, Mady looked inquiringly toward the telephone, but the woman shook her head.

"Impermissible."

"Why?" Mady demanded aloud, her lower lip trembling. "Doesn't Marian *want* to see me?"

"That's not it, child," Diane replied, instantly switching to oral communication. She interpreted Mady's lapse into Uhian as a sign of psychological upset. In moments of emotional stress, Rashevsky once hypothesized, coveners appear to derive some degree of comfort from the pure sonority of articulated speech. *As now.* Diane lowered her hands and spoke in what she hoped was a soothing timbre. "Marian got very tired. Dr. Rashevsky sent her south to rest."

Mady couldn't accept her explanation. "But Marian wouldn't violate her own CWC,"* she protested with absurd child-logic. "And even if she did, she'd just go on home to bed."

---

* CWC = Computed work capacity: catchall for synergizer predication of minimal systemic needs for any given citizen. —M.S.

Diane did not comment, mainly because she, too, wondered about her superior's unprecedented departure. She couldn't conceive of Marian enduring the enforced inactivity of a fastramp ride all the way down to the Balmer sector . . . let alone the ensuing hospital confinement. Presumably Ted knew the answers, but he positively refused to discuss it.

"Mady," Diane said, "Marian left you instructions."

The nine-year-old's face lit up. She raised her eyebrows, signaling question.

"Tomorrow you'll enter Levitt's fifth-level class."

Her face fell again, though she did not argue. There was no point; neither she nor Diane could ignore a direct order from Marian. Mady raised a hand and returned to shortmind. "Else?"

"Sleeping," Diane gestured. "Your option. Home? Dormitory?"

"Home," said Mady, deciding she wanted her own things about her on her first night back from Karli.

Nodding, the woman signaled that the interview was at an end.

The park seemed larger, even a bit mysterious, but that was because the firstlings of a sea-fog cloaked it, misting its modest boundaries. Even though Arin and Shalane were far away, Mady knew she was perfectly safe amongst the familiar trees and shrubs cradling her parents' house, and yet, as she made her way homeward, the child felt unaccountably nervous.

The feeling worsened when she walked through the front door and was met by a strange silence in a place always filled with small cheerful noises of her family's daily routine: the sizzle of eggs on the stove, shower-water sprinkle-tapping in the bathroom, Shalane humming at her sewing-table. Any second she thought her mother might walk into the living-room with a glass of milk and a hug for her baby.

Like all coveners, Mady had no innate fear of the dark, but when she went to sleep that night in her own small bed, she left the light on.

The fog deepened, smothering the City. In the middle of the night Mady woke screaming.

Arin!

He came awake in a blink, alert, poking his head out of the sleeping bag into dismal morning to see Shalane rigid at the rail. She spun to him, terrified.

Arin, it's gone.

?

"The earth," she wailed. "It's gone!"

He stumbled to the rail, already infected with her fear. His mouth fell open. Their ship drifted in a white wilderness of fog and limitless gray water. Shalane clutched his arm in panic, her world vanished.

"Arin, where's the earth?"

In the wheelhouse, Corian stopped humming to himself. Hunched over his tea, he said, "Too many small rocks and islands in the bay. Battery's low, so we're running under sail, only there's too much fog for safe visibility. Had to take her out a bit."

"Out?" Shalane echoed numbly. "Into . . . ?"

"Yes, goddess," Corian nodded. "Sorry."

Arin took her hand and stared silently into the bleak expanse. After a while, he whispered, "Thought it looked big on the maps. But even seeing it from the Sound . . ."

In a voice smothered as his, Shalane managed, "How big, Arin?"

"Three thousand miles that way," he pointed.

"That's more miles than ever was." Shalane shivered. "What's on the other side?"

"Who knows? Like to find out someday."

But the white wool fog and dark water filled him with awe, and at the moment Arin wasn't all that curious. *Next year, maybe.* Right now, like Shalane, he yearned for earth underfoot. The sea was eerie, its loneliness echoed in the spaces hollowed out of his soul at Lishin.

Shalane remained at the rail when Arin went back for their tea. She didn't like this water or its strange salt smell or the sobbing wind that shook their sail like the rattle of muffled bones. No magic would work in such a place, nothing was normal here. She knew Goddess Earth never wasted anything, but could find no reason for this desolation. *You can't drink the water or cook with it or even wash in it much.* It wasn't natural, it was a thing apart from the Goddess, like Lishin and the Kriss. Shalane wanted none of it.

"Arin," she decided, "that's more water than anyone needs."

Well, it *was,* so why was Cory laughing?

The wind fell off around high sun, though in the fog they wouldn't have known the time at all but for the quartz-locked chronometer next to the wheelhouse compass.

With the dying of the wind, the fog closed in until visibility was no more than a few yards, but Corian, still humming under his breath, carefully navigated the craft back into bay waters.

Tense at the rail, Shalane wondered yet again, "Where's the earth, Cory?"

"Only a few miles. You'll see it when it clears."

He watched his coven friends restlessly prowl the foredeck, silent, close together. He knew they were sharing, binding together for comfort in this place that was no part of any cosmos they knew. Corian checked his compass and veered off a point to port, softly intoning the same three-word phrase again and again.

Arin couldn't make out the words, but he wished Corian would hum something else already, the little tune rubbed at his nerves. Cory had been singing it interminably, but Arin doubted his friend was even aware of it.

It was a simple enough melody, just three identical tones with a higher one stuck in between the second and the third, but it made Arin think of some animal lost in the night, crying to be found. The thing was vaguely depressing.

There. This time, Arin saw Cory's lips absently shape the syllables. He strained to catch the words.

In the fog,
In the fog.

"What in hell *is* that?" Arin abruptly demanded.

"Huh?" Corian's head jerked up. "What?"

Arin repeated the four-note tune. It puzzled Corian briefly until he realized he must have been muttering it to himself all morning.

"That?" Corian mused. "Piece of an old Fleeter ballad I heard last time I was on the Fist. Guess the fog brought it back to me." He hummed it once more.

Arin made a face. "Can't say I like it much."

"Funny thing, but neither do the Fleeters. They consider it bad luck to sing it just before setting out on a fishing trip, or even in town when the weather's foggy like today."

"What's supposed to happen if you do?"

"Hard to say," Corian shrugged, "you can't get them to talk about it. I think they're afraid that singing about the Wintermind is like inviting it to come."

"The—what?"

Corian repeated the strange word. "Dam'f I know how they picked a name like that, but it's what Fleeters call a kind of sea-death." He shook his head. "Inconsistent. Every other Fleeter song I know refers to the ocean or to death as *he*. But the Wintermind is always *it*."

"What's a Wintermind?" Arin asked.

"*The* Wintermind," Corian corrected, "there's only one. The words of the ballad are vague, but they give the impression that the Wintermind's a kind of killer, and you know it's coming when you hear it howling—"

"Stray packdog, maybe."

He eyed Arin curiously. "From the sea? The Wintermind Ballad actually doesn't describe the thing much," he explained, "but it says just where it comes from. 'The East, from the sea.' And always 'in the fog' . . ."

Where it cries in the dark like a losted child,
A baby that y' better not find,
Cos its claws run red and its eyes are wild,
And it cries, how it cries like a losted child,
That thing called the Wintermind,
That thing called the Wintermind

In the fog,
In the fog.

His voice described a kind of wail on the last repetition of the word "cries." It disturbed Arin, it called up deep-buried memories that were better off left alone.

"That the whole song, Cory?" Arin hoped.

"Just the chorus. There's lots of verses. I can only recall the first two . . ."

> *When the Fleeters come back to their daddies' home*
> *   In the summer o' thirty-three,*
> *They kissed the sand and they blessed the foam*
> *As they swore no more they would have to roam,*
> *   But the mist on the Fist hid the sea,*
> *   Yes, the mist on the Fist hid the sea. . . .*

"Sounds old." Arin read about the Fleeters before setting out with Corian. "Numbering years like that, must go back to Jing times."

"A little after," Corian judged. "Fist people were deported out to commune country, but once the Jing armies withdrew, they swore they'd get home again no matter how long it took. And that's quite a story, Arin. You can hear it from any Fleeter, they like to tell about their early history, except for the Wintermind story. The second verse goes—"

> *Now us Fleeters ent scared when the smoke hangs thick*
> *   Or a noreaster wind starts t' blow,*
> *But a cry in the fog like a child that's sick*
> *Makes a man ship oars and crowd sail quick*
> *   And we take up our nets and we go,*
> *   Yes, we take up our nets and we go*
>
> > *In the fog,*
> > *In the fog. . . .*

"Then the chorus comes in," said Corian with a slight frown, "but I'd rather not sing it again."

"No," Arin nodded. "Once is enough."

Diane felt an unfamiliar shame as she punched the code into her console. Marian alone had the authority to monitor high-echelon citizens at work, though she'd never exercise her option before making her intentions known to them. Spying was so alien an act in the City that the word had all but disappeared from shortmind usage, yet Diane still intended to observe Levitt's class without his knowledge or permission.

Citizens were so seldom disciplined that Diane had absolutely no idea what might happen to her if caught. Loss of rank and concomitant curtailment of synergizer time? Transfer to a remote outlying sector? That would be a great disgrace.

But though she feared the consequences, personal risk was of less weight than her concern for Mady. The look of silent misery that she'd last seen on the child's face still haunted her. *Absurd that a mere embryo should be so unhappy.* But her pain was unmistakable, and Diane felt compelled to identify its source so she could help rid Mady of it.

But assignment to Levitt's advanced study group was unlikely to improve matters. Not that Diane questioned Marian's assessment of Mady's academic attainment level (though her new instructor certainly did), but she had grave misgivings about the choice of Levitt himself.

Jakov Levitt was an anomaly, both physically and emotionally. Most citizens grew toward inner serenity, but Levitt seemed to become more petulant and crossgrained as the centuries stole on. Essentially humorless, he was one of the oldest men alive in the City, dating back to shortly before the Great Schism. According to rumor, he'd actually been one of its prime instigators, but, in characteristically perverse fashion, elected to remain behind when the rest left.

Other residents appeared to be in their late teens or early twenties, but Levitt's sparse dark hair was shot with gray, his cheeks slashed by deepening frown-lines. His students whispered he was so mean he didn't even like himself, so he skimped on his daily *metabs*. Corian once asked Rashevsky why Levitt wanted to look middle-aged, but the doctor called the question an invasion of privacy and refused to answer.

Levitt was outraged at Marian's directive to add Mady's name to his advanced section roster. Diane tried to enlist sympathy by speaking of the child's emotional distress.

"Irrelevant," he brusquely judged. "Refer to Ted. I won't slow pace to babysit a coven brat."

Her temper flared. "Marian's decision, *not* mine!"

He nodded, sourly amused how easily he'd provoked her into showing her real feelings towards himself.

Well aware that he'd never consent now to let her audit the class, Diane avoided the formality of a foredoomed request lest it put him on his guard.

Nervously licking her lips, she tuned in her viewscreen and turned up the gain.

"—example is the quest for a prime number succession formula," Levitt lectured. "One amateur labeled 2 the 'anchor prime' because it supposedly rooted all succeeding primes, each factored by 2 so that, after all earlier non-primes had been eliminated, only one position on the positive integer line appeared for each next highest prime. Unfortunately the system quickly ceased to prove valid—as early as 11 and 13. *Child, are you listening?*"

The shrill question startled Mady. Marian never raised her voice.

"Well?" he demanded.

"Yes."

"And understand everything?"

Mady nodded.

"Really? Then prove."

Her lips tightened. Levitt was calling her either a liar or an imbecile, possibly both. She got to her feet and tried to reply as concisely as she could.

"Example points to danger of inductive method, reasoning from insufficient evidence." Her fingers flew. "But science depends on educated guesses. Early cosmology hypothesized stable universe and Big Bang theories, then sought support—"

"Yes," he snapped impatiently, "elementary. Are you unable to extrapolate?"

The child faltered. "How?"

"Synergistically."

Diane watched him bait Mady with growing pique. How *dare* he put her on the spot like that? Synergistic extrapolation was an intellectual game, hardly of value to anyone who hadn't studied programming technique. Mady couldn't be expected to know anything about it yet, but then, neither would any of Levitt's pupils. *Thoroughly unfair demand.*

"Come, child," Levitt taunted, "no need for encyclopedic response. Any aspect. Music, philology, mathemat—"

"Socio-scientific philosophy," Mady interrupted, crisply pronouncing each spoken syllable. "Cosmology advances, human nature lags. Spiritual void—"

Levitt clapped his hands once to show his annoyance, but Mady ignored the single sharp report.

"—brought pre-Jing spate of charlatanism, decline of church and state . . ."

"Shortmind!" he gestured angrily. A few students laughed.

". . . parent-child gap, countermovement of filial pity till old ideas dead vs. Nietzschean stance re pity, timeliness ultimately untimely, Novak—"

"Sufficient!" Levitt said aloud.

"—premise of disposable myth, Katz puzzle-box cosmic-molecular analogy leading to irrelevationism . . ."

"SIT DOWN!"

She did so amidst the laughter of her classmates.

Levitt ignored her for the rest of the period.

Diane gaped at the screen, stunned at how much data Marian must have crammed into that small head. Stories inevitably came to mind how Marian's daughter, Judith, spent her dying days assailing her young son Singer with more information than any child could hope to assimilate. *Except they say he did.* Not that anyone had any idea what use he ever made of all that knowledge. Strange, too, how

Marian always seemed to sidestep any discussion concerning her grandson.

Diane turned off her console and thought of her late friend, Judy. She still missed her, still wished that someday she might meet her mysterious son.

One of the first to leave the classroom, Mady saw Diane a little ways up the corridor and ran to meet her. At the last minute, she checked her impulse to hug the woman, *City people don't touch,* though she sometimes thought Diane wouldn't mind too much, at least not like Marian might.

Diane asked about her new class, but Mady skirted the subject. She had a question of her own.

"Diane, is it all right if I change my mind and sleep in the student dormitory?"

"Of course. Any special reason?"

"Oh . . . just it's too quiet at home," Mady said, looking away.

Corian cut the sun engine to save the batteries. There was enough breeze to dawdle along at four or five knots, safer with the fog closing in again.

Suddenly, ahead of them, they heard a guttural wail that climbed swiftly to a deafening roar, then died in groaning menace. It sounded a second time, and a third. It curdled Arin; Shalane cringed.

"Nothing to fear," Corian laughed. "Just the canal foghorn. Goes on automatic when there's fog and a ship comes close." But labeling it wasn't enough, he had to tell them just what it looked like, why it made such an awful noise.

"Means we're almost to the canal," Corian instructed. "Practically in Wellfleet, goddess."

Shalane and Arin both felt better when the foghorn shut down after they entered the canal.

"Just like a river, see?" Corian tried to reassure Shalane. "Only eight miles to the inside bay."

"*More* water, Cory?" came the pathetic reply.

"Hardly a swallow, Lane. Harbor's straight across, but we'll follow the shore even if it takes a bit longer. You'll have land to look at the rest of the trip, and no way we can get lost in the fog."

His last words reminded Arin of the old ballad, but now he realized the reiterated tag wasn't meant to sound like an animal at all, but the mournful call of a foghorn.

At the end of the canal, Corian headed the ship toward starboard and, true to his word, they drifted along the coast.

"Close enough to meet some Fleeters, I bet." He vented a long blast on the boat horn.

An immediate chorus of answers, three of them very close. Trying to gauge the distance, Corian hit the horn again. Once more, the invisible trio brayed in response off the port bow.

Arin and Shalane listened gratefully to the bleak music, glad there was something else alive in the white nothingness. Then Shalane caught Arin's hand. A strange lep abruptly intruded on their senses.

Who?

"Getting a lep, Cory."

"They're Fleeters, then. Send my name, they know me."

Once more they received the peremptory lep, aloof as a stranger looking them up and down before venturing a real greeting.

Who?

They linked and sent: *Corian.*

An answer shot back, crisp and cool, perhaps a bit impatient. *Corian's no-lep. Who?*

A little put off by the bristly demand, Arin and Shalane lepped once more, using extra power for emphasis: *GOD Arin. GODDESS Shalane. Who?*

No reply. Corian hit the horn once more.

Silence. They rocked on the calm, fog-smothered water and waited.

Two prows slipped out of the fog, then a third. Engines purring softly, they moved dead slow across the visitors' bow less than a hundred yards ahead. Now Shalane made out the men and women moving about decks hung fore and aft with nets. Each craft was rigged with two small dories hung from stern and starboard.

A man in the lead boat, dressed in a long black coat and floppy hat of the same shiny material, put a hand to his mouth and hailed.

"That you, Cah-ree?"

"Me all right," Corian bellowed cheerily. "Who's that?"

"Nathan Brew-stuh heah. Ent seen you in a sight. Didn't hear your engine. Trouble?"

"Just giving the batteries a rest. Wind'll take us in."

"What there is," Brewster noted laconically. "God Pettibone's wait-in' for you at Meeting Beach."

Arin and Shalane had to strain to make out the queer fall of the Fleeter dialect. They knew the sound of west Wengen, but this man talked through his nose, with odd splits in the middle of words like Meet-ing, and all the accents hit the wrong places.

The ships inched across their prow, making for the mouth of the canal. Corian waved his farewell. "Going out, Nathan?"

"Damfool, you can see that."

"Good luck."

"Thanks."

"Morning, Nathan."

"Mawnin, Cah-ree."

Not another whisper of lep or any further greeting as the three craft slipped off into the fog again. They might not have passed at all.

Shalane was furious at the slight. "Well, if that ain't some kind of rude! We have to wear the crowns to get a Hey out of them?"

"No, Lane, they're friendly enough, but they were headed out to sea," Corian explained, keeping his eye on the compass and steering closer to shore. "They've got their own ways."

She sniffed. "Just saw their ways."

"Did you really, goddess? Think about how the big water scares you."

"What's that got to do with it?"

"Soon they're going to be out in the middle, maybe a hundred miles from land, more if they have to. They expect to come back, sure, but anything can happen. Storms come, ships get lost or they sink. Death and the sea are one and the same to them, it takes some of the warm out of Fleeters."

"Well . . . maybe," Shalane grudgingly allowed.

"Death and the sea," Corian repeated. "You'll see how it's always a part of them."

She shrugged. "Still don't think one Hey would've hurt that Brewster. Who is he?"

"Same as most Fleeters, a fisherman."

"Seems to know you fairly well," Arin observed.

"Ought to. Last time I was on the Fist, I delivered his son." He smiled at the memory. "Celebrated with Nat over a bucket of oysters and a jug, but I didn't really get on his warm-water side till halfway through the second jug when I asked him about the Coming Home. . . ."

Corian snapped the last picture of the roll and put down the borrowed camera. Nathan Brewster settled back and tamped bearberry tobacco into the bowl of a clay pipe with one salt-cracked finger of his left hand.

"Now if you ent truly interested, Cah-ree, don't ask just to be polite."

"I'm interested, or I wouldn't've said."

"If it pleasures you, Cah-ree," Brewster said, still doubtful. He paused to open another oyster and pop it in his mouth. "Now take these, for instance. Wellfleet oysters, the best. Man's gotta know what's important, what's good. You can talk all you want about bluepoints, chinc'teeks, or your pearls, but let one o' these romp over your gullet and the rest can go home."

Corian waited patiently, knowing better than to rush a Fleeter about to make a point.

"That's how we are, Cah-ree, particular. Fleeters got long traditions, just any life wasn't good enough, still ent. Others got sent west, too, but most weren't particular enough to return." He puffed on his pipe and eyed Corian curiously. "Heard that Deepwoods never numbered their year-wheels, so they only recollect fire days and the last few generations. That true?"

Corian admitted it.

Brewster shook his head. "Well, Fleeters always counted, ever since we come home. That was a long time ago, Cah-ree, but you stop at Town Hall and see if you don't read about Brewsters way back at the start. And Hopkins, too, and Wilkses and Putnams and even Pettibones, they were the ancestors of our present god, and they leaned toward Wicca, that's what they called Circle in those days. . . ."

"But what's the Coming Home?" Shalane wondered.

"One helluva story, goddess. You ask Abby Pettibone. Now you'd best get ready. We're almost at Meeting Beach."

The fog cleared and the sun came out, blinding in its intensity. They saw the long sand beach stretching in a gentle curve for several miles to either side of town. Away from the harbor, it rose slightly to low hills and scrub brush. Now and then they spied a distant fisherman casting the surf.

Corian pointed out a straight stone arm thrusting easily two hundred feet into the bay. A silent group waited at the end of the quay, watching their boat.

Still a bit bothered about their perfunctory greeting from Nathan Brewster, Shalane and Arin were heartened that the inner circle of Wellfleet had dressed formally to receive them, though none wore green under their tabards.

"They don't wear green until Lams," Corian told them.

"Well, I do," Shalane declared. "All the trouble making that robe, might as well."

"Don't, goddess." Corian was serious. "You either, Arin. For you it means Sinjin, but it's not a happy color for them. It's the sea and the Wintermind and death. I wouldn't."

Corian smiled at their deepwoods pride as they chose traditional deerskin to wear under their tabards. There seemed a vast incongruity in home-cut skins dry-cleaned by a City process.

Quickly he reviewed the protocol they could expect on the quay. "Fleeters have lots of old ceremonies and some leftovers from Christian tradition, like the way they number their years."

Shalane lowered darkly. "They got Kriss here?"

"Not like the ones in Salvation," Corian soothed. "Here the Christians live in peace with Circle." He hardly expected to convince her, not after what Arin suffered at Uriah's hands. "Most of their customs come down from Wicca tradition. So you'll see that the god will greet Shalane first, the goddess will greet Arin. Male to female. Sun to moon."

The ship gently bumped the stone causeway. Corian heaved the bow line to one of the masters, then calloused hands helped them up the rocky step and Arin and Shalane faced the power of Wellfleet.

Despite their use of City equipment, the Fleeters were old-time coven untouched by and unconcerned with Garick's war or new Uhia. Most of the masters looked over forty, the god and goddess well beyond that. Tall, with weather-darkened faces, contained and aloof. In the sharing demanded by courtesy, Arin and Shalane read formidable power and a carefully qualified, extremely tentative acceptance of themselves: we know your accomplishments and honor your rank, but we'll like you when we're ready.

As if to demonstrate this reserve, the masters did not kneel, merely bowed their heads to the visitors. Jon Pettibone stepped forward, lanky as Arin, cheeks ruddy with tiny burst veins, black hair salt-and-peppered under his crown. He embraced Shalane formally.

"Moon sister," said Pettibone, "we're right glad you came."

Abby Pettibone was as tall as the god and as wind-burned, with tight steel-gray curls and a long, sharp-featured face, eyes the color of sword metal.

"Brother sun," she greeted Arin. "Stay with us for Lams."

When Arin and Shalane removed their crowns, the sparse ceremony was done. The masters went to help Corian unload his medical supplies with "Howdo's" and "Hey there's" and no protocol whatever. Corian was known everywhere, welcomed by gods and crib girls alike.

"Met Nathan Brewster on the way in," Corian remarked, passing a box to one of the masters. "How's that boy I birthed for him?"

"Nathan took him to Doane graveyard last month, Cah-ree."

Corian stopped working. "What happened?"

The master reached for another box. "Don't matter now."

"Cory," Jon Pettibone invited. "Come up t'home and take some tea."

Abby Pettibone surveyed Shalane up and down.

"Seen deepwoods before," she allowed in a tone that indicated less than impressive memories. "You ent big as some or old as others. How long you worn the crown?"

"Nine years, sister."

"Nine years," Abby snorted. "Hell, child, I got a boy your age. 'Pear you're a sight young for it."

It was Shalane's lifelong misfortune to be short by Karli standards, not quite six feet. She gathered all of it into a ramrod of dignity to answer Abby Pettibone.

"Sister moon, I was never too young or too little for anything."

Abby's hard mouth broke suddenly into a grin. "By damn, that's how to talk, no sass from *no*body." She put an arm around the younger woman's shoulder. "Goddess, you come t'home, and we'll put on the ket-tle."

The gods walked behind the women. Jon Pettibone studied the tall redheaded young man by his side, then decided, "He didn't look like you, not by a long shout."

"Who?" Arin asked.

"Said he was your brother."

Arin stopped short. "Singer?"

"That was the name. Said Garick was his father. Don't know Garick, don't hold with all I heard. Around Leddy fire, 'twas, two years gone now. Just passing through."

"To where?" Arin urged. "Please, it's important."

Pettibone shook his head. "Can't say. Like skates and sharks, always passing through, always looking. But that don't mean they find."

Ten years, Arin thought. *Ten years without a home.* "Where'd he go, which way? Do you have any idea?"

Pettibone swept his long arm north where the bay waters met the endless rim of the sea. "Out there."

Pettibone's house had an upper story, which would have been un-usual in Karli. Deepwoods dwellings tended to be built on one level, and the older ones all were hewn from rough timber. But the Fist boasted an unusual number of excellent carpenters, and since there wasn't all that much room to spread out on, two and even three floors were quite common in Fleeter homes.

Tea stretched out till dinnertime. Afterwards, they all sat on the porch and discussed the similarities and differences of deepwoods and Fleeter ways. Shalane related easily to Abby, and the two women were learning that though their covens were far removed in distance and custom, some things didn't change all that much if you were a goddess.

Abby went inside to fetch a fresh pot of tea. Corian grasped the opportunity to whisper a diplomatic suggestion to Shalane. She nod-ded. When her new friend came back, Shalane accepted more tea and a hard biscuit and asked Abby about the Coming Home.

The question sat well with the Pettibones. Both liked to tell Fleeter history to anyone who asked, but since it was Abby who'd been spoken to, it was her right to spin the story. With a nod to her husband, she sat down and started to speak.

"Not sure how much you've heard about Jing times. There was a big war, and they won, but it didn't have much to do with ideas or anything except land. There was this crop blight, and just too many people didn't have enough food, so they come over here to get fed."

She paused to raise her cup, and Jon Pettibone filled the gap.

"Jings emptied the whole east part of the country and sent the people out to giant farms in the Midwest."

Corian stared into his cup as if reading the leaves like old Sidele. "Went out there once for Garick. They still call it commune country."

"They?" Jon Pettibone asked. "Folk still live out there?"

Corian said they did.

"Shows us Fleeters kept good track of the past."

"Now, Jon: who's telling this story?" And Abby Pettibone took up her tale. . . .

"Wellfleeters found themselves in dry flat country called Kansas, farming under Jing guards. Cruel sun in summer, mean prairie winters. You could lose a cow in a snowdrift and find it there in the spring, stiff as a board and the meat still fresh, and if you don't believe, just go t' Town Hall and read all about it."

Seasons and years passed, Abby said, and then one day the Jings were gone, most of them, anyhow, and there was no more forced farming. A lot of families stayed, said they broke their backs on that Kansas ground, they'd stay and take some profit from it. But Fleeters didn't hold with mingling, and especially when so many Jings were settling down to be part of whatever was left.

"Weren't just Fleeters then, Lane, there was a bunch of Shortree from up north of here, maybe twenty, thirty families from Chatham, Barnstable, Yarmouth." Abby pronounced the old names with the careful pride of preservation. "Mostly, though, it was Fleeters: Brewsters and Pettibones and Baileys. Some Baileys still among the Shortree. Good fishermen, decent folk for Christian, all but a few trash clans duneside. Well, the Fist folk up and said they were by damn going home. So four hundred started out on foot, carrying what food they could and heavy clothes for when the snows came.

"They steered for towns at first, thinking they'd get help and extra supplies along the way. They found out quick that was a mistake. Packs of starved dogs, looters, Jing deserters who shot first and took women afterwards. And not just trash like those, but plain folks, too, just trying to protect what little they had. The country was finished, nothing left you could put a name or a flag to, and the Fleeters had no friends anywhere they went."

Abby crunched a hard biscuit with her horsey front teeth. "Fall came. The walking got harder and colder. Children were born in abandoned houses if stopping wasn't too dangerous, in the woods otherwise. Lot of newborn died, mothers too. Some names got wiped out of everything but memory. Like Edwards," she reflected. "Not an Edwards left after that."

Three hundred of them straggled into Missouri. By then, the leaders knew they couldn't keep even Fleeters alive without enough food or clothing, unless there was something to draw them on, a picture in their hearts. So by the time they reached Illinois, where wind sliced sleet into their chapped faces, the Brewsters and Pettibones and Hopkinses started organizing the night fires into times when you talked about home in a special way, magnifying for cold children the tolerable summers, the mild winters, the different moods of the sea and the salt smell of the marshes and the gulls calling by Nauset light. The *tastes*—oh, the tastes of home—lobster out of the shell and drowning in melted butter; chowder made with scalded milk and potatoes and onions and big, chewy quahogs and a little salt pork thrown in for goodness; bog cranberries so tart they turned your mouth inside out with a sweet-bitter memory. Beach plum jelly preserves and corn meal pudding with frozen flavored cream in the middle.

"You see what I'm saying?" Abby Pettibone asked her guests. "It was a dream they needed, something better to remember and reach for. Something like the thought of clean sand and dusty miller growing all over. Smells and sounds and sights and tastes to stick with a person and make him downright ashamed to lay down and die in Illinois snow. That's when the saying came about that you can still hear on the Fist, 'When we see the miller and smell the sea.'"

The Fleeters inched across Indiana and Ohio, Abby went on, and the lake wind was a scythe and the powdery snow stung like a billion whips. But they were a people again, a changed people, leaner and harder, with a new awareness not all good. But the miller and the sea drew them on.

Their shoes were falling apart, but the wild dogs who followed their blood-trail in the snow ended up fresh meat. Small armed parties scouted when a town was near, and when they came back with food, no one asked any questions. Even the children were delighted now to find the occasional frozen body because it meant better shoes and maybe a coat or even a rifle and ammunition if they were lucky. Supplies were rationed according to need, the decision of the leaders inflexible. Only once did someone question their authority, but Abby's memory failed on the name.

"Who was that, Jon? You know the story."

"Forgot the name," the god confessed. "One less mouth to feed, that's who it was."

"Birth customs started then," Abby remarked. "You have children, goddess?"

"We have a girl," Shalane volunteered without elaboration.

"Children were scarce and precious then. Right up to today, women fish and sail as good as a man, but once we're carrying a child, it's off the decks and into the circle with the protecting masters, and that began on the Coming Home."

Two hundred made it to the western foothills of the Appalachians by early spring. The mountains were a hard climb, chilly and wet and always another hill in front of them. "Call 'em Blue Mountains now," Abby recalled. "Rough country. Break the heart out of anyone."

"We know," said Arin. "We've been there."

The last of the journey was the worst. A hundred and fifty left Blue Mountains and rafted over the Delaware, then it was more miles of nightmare with too many towns to go through and every one of them bristling with hard-eyed people who'd learned to shoot strangers on sight. "They might warn you off," Abby said, "they might ambush you for what you were carrying. Sometimes it was the Fleeters themselves that had to make that choice. You had to live."

By July they were close enough to Hartford to smell the unburied bodies and burning buildings. In the late summer, almost a year after they left Kansas, ninety-five Wellfleet and a few Shortree straggled up the last hill past Doane Rock and across the marsh bridge to Nauset light.

They walked in twos and threes down to the beach and just stared at the ocean for a long time. Some of them took up handfuls of sand and kissed it before letting it sift through their fingers. Then Sam Pettibone, one of the leaders, spoke to Matty Wilkes.

"And you know what he said?" Abby's eye gleamed pridefully. " 'Matty,' he said, 'we come a long shout.' They did that, Matty allowed.

" 'Ought to do some fishing,' says Sam. 'Just might,' says Matty Wilkes, and they did. And all that day, they say the seagulls sang like larks, but that's probably stretching it some. But all the rest is true.

"And that," said Abby Pettibone, "is how the Fleeters came on home."

The story was done. Jon Pettibone pointed out—Corian knew he always postscripted it this way—that he was a direct descendant of Sam who sired Paul and Parker, and it was Parker, the younger son, who begat three children in a line that came down to himself.

Corian interjected suddenly, "Was that the Sam Pettibone in the Wintermind ballad?"

To Arin, it seemed that Jon Pettibone's genial host-smile froze for a moment. Corian had strained coven courtesy by naming something normally left silent. That much leaked to the Shando from the Fleeter god and goddess.

"No," Jon stated, his lack of emphasis itself a comment on Corian's lapse of manners. "That was a long time later, a thousand years or more."

"Nathan Brewster sang it for me once, but I only remember the beginning. Jon, would you—"

Pettibone began shaking his head before Corian was finished. "Not when there's fog. Never at night. Except for Lams." He exchanged a meaningful glance with Abby, then rose. Corian had the feeling that their social evening was concluded.

"I'll get a light, show you where you're staying." The god stalked out of the room without another word.

"Never you mind," Abby smoothed things over. "Wait till Lams, Cory. You'll hear it then. Often enough."

Arin stared at the distant gap of sea. "Out there, Jon said. Just out there on that big water. Why, Lane? Where could Singer go?"

"Don't know."

Ranging along at her husband's side, Shalane only half listened and cared less, not in the middle of such bright summer peace. They were walking on the long spit of tidal marsh and pine hills called Great Island. All sound was hushed. She couldn't hear the ocean or the people digging back at the clam run, not even a bird. Above them on the heights, both red and pitch pine bent to earth in graceful, serpentine curves as they shrank back from the salt air to touch the ground and sometimes take new root.

Shalane found to her delight that she loved the place and the people. Fleeters weren't rude at all, just forthright. A master passing by might give you no more than a nod, but they'd stop in almost every day with little gifts of food or a waterproof for wet weather, and they'd brush away any thanks with a "Guessed you needed it. Mawnin' now."

Their cottage sat on the bay side of the Fist, right on the water. On cool evenings, she burned a bundle of seaweed and cattail in the fireplace, and she and Arin would fall asleep in each other's arms, lulled by the gentle surf. Some nights were so dark it seemed the world went away, while others were so clear that she could count every star that ever was and watch the tiny sparkling creatures that danced upon the crest of the incoming tide.

The house was trim and cozy, and she liked it. Fleeters built tidy and spare as the way they spoke, and nearly every place they lived in had a name: Abby's Pride, Brewster's Fancy, Wilkes Rest, and one she especially liked, Where Jenny Smiled. In the quaint names she felt the warmth of the Fleeters.

She grew more and more to like Abby, with her weathered, leathered face, her hands laced with fish hook scars and the gaunt body taut as a strained hawser. Now and then when they talked, Abby would share with her, and Shalane began to know the music of the Wellfleet soul. Spare and self-sufficient, yet underscored with an odd minor strain that one didn't find in deepwoods.

Abby was all coven, though; she knew her manners. She served an abundant meal and took it as natural when you only ate a little as a master should. She might ask about Karli ways, but never where you got your own scars. Real Circle, Abby Pettibone, and well brought up.

On the Fist, Shalane said to herself, you fall into a rhythm like a dance at home, a beat made out of days and what filled them. Tide came in, tide went out, and the days danced slowly toward Lams. Skies went gray and blue and sometimes impossible red, and maybe even four different kinds of sky at once, depending on where you looked. She felt more relaxed than she had in years, and she slept better than she could remember, soothed by the tide and the wind.

I love it here. It's a place I could stay.

"Mady would like it here, I just know she would, wouldn't she, Arin?"

Arin kept his answer to himself. A sudden, undeniable truth struck him. *When the fight comes, it's going to be over Mady.* He knew Lane still loved him as deeply as he did her, but now they had to bend to meet over the reality of their child. Ironic that his wife was one of the strongest masters of her time, yet lacked the power to know herself or her daughter.

Mady's her own person, more than we ever were. Why must she be another you, Lane? But as they both did more and more, he kept the thought to himself.

For a long while, he'd told himself it was the newness of City that made Lane slow to adjust to the changing times, but now he admitted bleakly that it was much more serious, she could not accept progress, she pushed it off, blocked it out and refused to see him growing away from her because everything had to keep on becoming or else die.

It wasn't just that he'd lost Circle from his heart, but something kept crying to replace it, and who cared if it had no name yet? Arin lived with confusion and temporarily accepted it, though there were moments in the midst of all the questions when an amorphous answer whispered to him, usually when he gazed with wonder and more than a trace of fear at the vast flat dish of the sea.

Out there, out there where Singer went . . .

Corian nibbled at the moist cake that dripped blackberry preserves from its middle. He put it back down on his plate, licked his fingers, and pushed the recorder start button.

Corian to Rashevsky, tape number one, Wellfleet, duplicate for Garick through Spitt.

Hey, Ted. I've done the med survey, Fleeters are in fine condition. Nothing chronic, no dietary deficiencies. I shot them with tet and typhoid, but cytotoxin is wasted because the bone condition of deepwoods women seems totally absent here. Most serious problem is that erythro-fetalis condition noted last time. Usual symptoms, swelling of the infant's liver, spleen and kidneys. It passes, mortality is very low on this, but there's gotta be something we can do. It's just tissue that won't stay put in the bone marrow.

He stopped the recorder and studied the tranquil lagoon beyond his window. Mortality low, sure, but one baby was too much to lose anywhere. Life was hard to come by and, among Fleeters, hard to keep. He should have been there, maybe he could have saved Nathan Brewster's little boy, and now Nathan's boats were long overdue, his woman down on the beach every day, looking and waiting. So at least a baby ought to have the chance to grow up.

Corian finished the cake and pushed away the plate. He'd have to quit, he'd stuffed down a ton in the past week.

If I don't stop eating cake, I'm gonna have to come back sideways into City. These people eat very well, though they could use a little more beef and pork for variety. No problem on vegetables, they freeze enough in summer to last the cold months. They do eat a lot of bread and cake and noodles, especially this time of year. Ritual or not, Fleeters get fifty times more carbohydrate than any other coven.

I set up an aid station for light stuff, like my place at Bowdeen's. Teaching them how to handle exposure, cuts, lacerations, contusions, even a plasma routine and sterile delivery methods, but nothing much else. Kid fell off a roof, broke some ribs and went into shock. I set him, taped him, administered a glucose i.v. and that was that. All for now, Ted. I hope you can do some work on the fetalis thing. Tell Mady that mamadad miss her, and I do, too. Tell Raddy I still want her ass.

The maddening thing about research was that most answers just meant more questions, especially when he tried to get something viable from the synergizer. Not an official member of City, he wasn't authorized syn/time and had to beg or steal snippets of it as the opportunity allowed. He was permitted to work with Diane Radclif on Project Enclave, her coven lep and intelligence studies, but his own theories languished for lack of solid work. When he could get at the computer, it took its good time warming up to him. His mind raced ahead of his ability to phrase questions properly, so the synergizer just kept absorbing what he fed into it and rarely correlated independently, but if he asked it to, it'd probably just reply ∼. He swore to Raddy it had a personality of its own and didn't like him much.

The Fleeter phys/med profile was practically identical to other covens, even to their lack of the primate fears of falling and darkness, though Corian deduced that they must have developed hereditary lep way ahead of other coveners or the normal pace of evolution. *And they import a lot of their flour from people that make it but barely use it.* Why so much carbohydrate in their diet, especially between Lams and Samman when, logically, they really needed more C and iron?

His mind was tired of wrestling with the problem for the moment. It sought for a diversion, and leaped to the puzzle of the Wintermind ballad. Folk song was a hobby of his, but he'd never encountered anything like the Fleeter legend anyplace else. He knew Fleeters were superstitious about the song, but that didn't account for old Pettibone walking out of the room when Corian brought it up. He thought back to when Nathan Brewster reluctantly sang it to him, and vaguely thought he understood why Jon behaved that way. *Guess I rattled some family skeletons.*

Corian hadn't meant to tread on his host's sensitivities, but it was hard to figure Fleeters, what they considered bad manners to ask. The carbohydrate problem, for instance, he couldn't just bring it up, it was too basic to their way of life, they'd probably regard his inquiring as a crude violation of visitor's privileges.

And he kept wanting to ask Pettibone about Nathan Brewster's chances, the later it got, but there was something peculiar about the way Jon veered off the subject.

Of course, there was more than one way to gather information, but it was more than rude, it was downright spying. Still, Corian never had been applauded for his manners, and if he didn't hear something soon about Nathan, he might just go ahead and do it.

If Arin'll help.

A few days before Lams, Arin and Shalane walked into Wellfleet town and saw everyone wearing the forbidden green. Green shirts, pants, masters' robes. Not the bright green of Sinjin, but darker, subtler, like the sea.

Fleeters ate a deal of bread year round, but at Lams the most expensive flour was broken out and consumed in an orgy of baking. Children combed high moors and low bogs for beach plum, blackberries and cranberries. Kitchens were blizzarded with white dust as flour was sifted, mixed with milk and water, pounded into mountains of dough, flattened out, cut into strips for noodles or baked into butter-soaked loaves and huge sweet cakes.

Arin and Shalane, who grew up without much bread at all, sampled it politely when pressed, but neither was accustomed to sweets. They couldn't understand how the Fleeters could gorge so much of it day after day.

"Sticks in my throat," Shalane choked.

Deepwoods grew no wheat, bought just enough in Mrika for fire days when bread was associated with happy festivals. But Lams in Wellfleet was not a joyous time. The Fleeters wore their sea green and chanted songs darkened with somber strains. There was one they heard over and over among the clam diggers and along the beach where Nathan Brewster's wife waited for his overdue ships.

"Yes, it's sad," Arin admitted to Shalane, "but there's something else, hear it?"

She did, but had no word for what she sensed. "Something not right about that song, Arin."

Bottom's leakin', got to bail,
Got to reef that raggy sail.
Woman's cryin', times are lean,
Guess she'll wear that Wellfleet green.

Gather round her,
Gather warm.
Goddess, keep my girl from harm.
Tell her when she
Bears my chi-yuld,
Raise it where the winter's mild.

Couldn't make it, sailed too far,
Couldn't find a guiding star,
So tell my gal I won't be seen,
And wrap my bones in Wellfleet green.

Arin asked Corian about it later.

"Sure I noticed," the physician nodded. "It's the word 'child,' Arin."

"That's *it*."

"Uh-huh. 'Chi-yuld.' The notes don't go with the rest of the song, like they broke loose. No sense to it."

But deep within, the illogical sounds brushed the top of memory Corian couldn't quite place. More like a feeling, a fear.

"No sense at all," he decided.

Wellfleet had more than one location for sacred fires. Lams was held on the moor above the salt pond, traditionally the path followed by the Kansas survivors on their way to Nauset Beach.

There were many Shortree guests from up around Truro. It was an old custom on fire days, since many of their own holidays fell so close to the same time. The lives of the two peoples were closely intertwined and friendships were common. Shortrees knew Circle ritual as well as their hosts and Fleeters knew the prayers for the Thanksgiving and Christmas feasts to which they were always invited.

Arin found it delightful. "Beats hell out of killing each other."

Shalane did not comment. As far as she was concerned, they were still Kriss and she could never forgive Uriah's people for what they did to Arin.

Shalane was not in the best of moods. She was put out that neither she nor Arin would be allowed in the circle on Lams night.

"Sister moon," Abby explained, "it's a sight different here. You wouldn't know what to do."

The refusal hurt her, the idea of a goddess not knowing a ceremony, but when the sunset circle on the moor was consecrated and the fire ignited, she found Abby to be right. This was not the Lams she knew.

The Wellfleet circle was as much oriented toward the male god as the female, and all were robed in sea green and tabards where deepwoods always worshiped naked. There were other sharp differences in the somber ritual, from the stately movements of the masters to the inconsistent, turbulent music that lapsed into minor when it shouldn't, that nevertheless compelled like the currents of the great ocean.

Shalane stood with Arin in a place of honor at the north of the circle, determinedly aloof from the Shortree visitors, though she found it hard to distinguish them from coven, all had the same salt-washed look.

Corian prowled the edge of the circle like a packdog, observant, curious, chatting here and there before edging in beside his friends with a gleaning of gossip.

"Shortrees heard Santee's back," he told them. "Word is to kill him on sight."

Shalane remembered the pathetic fat hunter brought by the con-stab to Karli. "Should leave him to the covens. Hoo*ee*, Arin, did you ever see so many birthing women in one place?" She hooked her arm through his. "Look, they're starting."

As the music rose from the assembled coven, the masters en-tered the purified circle from the north. Shalane opened herself to bathe in the total experience, feeling the power build steadily around her. Except that the god remained outside the circle, the opening was familiar. Abby Pettibone danced a circuit of the fire with a full, graceful revolution of her body at each cardinal point. Her arms ex-tended out and up, lowered to her stomach with each turn in a stylized caress, symbolizing Goddess Earth in late summer and ready to bear: as woman is full of child, so the earth at Lams is heavy with treasure to be harvested.

With the end of Abby's dance, the music ceased abruptly. The masters cleared a corridor and the dozen or more pregnant women filed in to stand in a tight group at the west.

Now Jon Pettibone moved forward.

As the god stepped inside the circle, a chord ripped from the singers' throats, so startling that Corian winced. Not so much a chord as a slash of dark sound, complex, unresolved, that stabbed at deep memory and flickered brief light over a picture he didn't want to remember. The sound was chaotic, frightening, yet somehow not alien; he *knew* it, and that was worse.

There was a rhythm to this music, too, but the god's movements had no relation to it at all as he swayed to the center of the circle, whirling suddenly to face the group of pregnant women. He took a menacing step toward them, arms thrust out. Another step. With each crouching move, the women backed away as if to elude him, but Pettibone again flung out his arms, spreading them wide to capture the knot of women frozen at the circle's edge. And the music was like harsh breathing, a rasping sigh in half a hundred throats.

Pettibone advanced and retreated like tide, drawing back, rushing forward, each time coming closer to the women. His outstretched hand touched the nearest, but as he paused before the final engulfing rush, goddess Abby leaped and planted herself in his path, arms crossed to barricade her breast. When she did this, the music changed again, subtly purging itself of its gloomier strains until, as the god withdrew, vanquished, it surged forth in a pure dominant resolution.

Death and the sea, Corian mused, *anchored in diminished chords.* Of all the covens that worshiped and sang of life, Wellfleet alone had a *dies irae,* the inexorable gray-green death that the sea brought to them year after year, one generation on the next. Dark, frightening, beautiful *and dammit!* what did it remind him of?

After the ceremony came the feast, rich and heavy, thick noodles inundated with fish stew and clam sauce, white and garlicky, and when they all were stuffed from that, tons of sugary cakes were served to be munched and washed down with bitter cranberry wine.

After the feast came the Wintermind Ballad.

Corian nodded to Arin as a young woman stepped into the firelight that had been replenished while the company mellowed. She waited before beginning, and a hush settled over Fleeters and guests alike. An undulation stirred the air, so gentle it was felt more than heard, but Corian recognized it.

> *In the fog,*
> *In the fog.*

Chanted over and over till, at last, the lead singer began with the verses Arin already knew. When she reached the chorus that told what little there was to say about the Wintermind, she slowed down and all the Fleeters joined in. The wail on the final repetition of the word "cries" was harrowing.

The woman has a remarkable range, Corian thought. All the way from shrill to a deep, throaty vibrato. And now she came to the verses Arin had not heard him sing.

> *Well, fifteen ships all set out to sea,*
> *And fifteen crews left the shore,*

But stormclouds blew and the gulls flew free,
And many a sailor never lived to see
The sun sail the skies once more,
The sun sail the skies once more.

And when the waters no longer rolled,
But shone in the early dawn
Like a lawn of green that is tainted gold,
Only fourteen ships could be seen, I'm told,
Cos the fifteenth ship was gone,
Yes, the fifteenth ship was gone

In the fog,
In the fog.

And that missing craft on the crashing wave
Bore four lost men from the town
Who clung to the spars, their lives for to save,
But the sea got as still as a lonely grave,
And their canvas shrouds hung down,
And their canvas shrouds hung down

In the fog,
In the fog,

Where it cries in the dark like a losted child,
A baby that y' better not find,
Cos its claws run red and its eyes are wild,
And it cries, how it cries like a losted child,
That thing called the Wintermind,
That thing called the Wintermind

In the fog,
In the fog.

Listening to the massed Fleeters sing the chorus a second time, Arin realized that nobody used quite the same melody as anyone else for the repeated, "That thing called the Wintermind." But the result was not so much a disharmony as a sort of soul-wearying sorrow, a muted wail that buried all desire, all delight.

They had no food, they were far from the Fist,
And the stars shone down pale and sad
On a glassy sea that was cloaked with mist,
And their water was low, and their homes they missed,
And all of their dreams were bad,
And all of their dreams were bad

> *In the fog,*
> *In the fog.*

> *They drifted long with their throats bone-dry*
> *Seeking land they could not find,*
> *While a thing in the fog warned them they would die,*
> *A thing in the fog they heard scream and cry,*
> *A thing called the Wintermind,*
> *A thing called the Wintermind*

> *In the fog,*
> *In the fog,*

> *Where it cries in the dark like a losted child . . .*

Even she doesn't sing it the same way twice, Corian observed to himself, but it was part of the ballad's deliberately entropic effect, that and the asymmetric recurrence of the chorus and "fog" phrase, never coming regularly, never when you'd think, and when it didn't you'd hope maybe you didn't have to hear the damn thing again, but it always came back.

> *A long time later, on a rainy spring day*
> *When the fog and the wind did drive,*
> *Sam Pettibone and his brother Ray*
> *Sailed home again into Wellfleet Bay*
> *More dead than they were alive,*
> *More dead than they were alive.*

> *And they said they were helped by a far-off race*
> *Whose name they could not recall,*
> *And they brought back maps from that far-off place,*
> *Two charts that helped them their steps retrace,*
> *And they put them in the old Town Hall,*
> *And they put them in the old Town Hall.*

> *But Sam Pettibone and his brother dear*
> *Said seamen they'd no more be,*
> *And they gave no name to their secret fear,*
> *But it cries in the fog like a child, I hear,*
> *And it comes from the East, from the sea,*
> *And it comes from the East, from the sea*

> *In the fog,*
> *In the fog,*

> *Where it cries in the dark like a losted child . . .*

Arin squeezed Shalane's hand. The song vaguely reminded him
of something his brother Singer said to him once, only a casual
remark, but now it seemed like it might be significant, he had to talk
to Jon Pettibone again. Maybe tomorrow, if he decided to go along
with what Corian had been asking him for the last week to do.

There was one more verse to the ballad, ending with an eerie
new variation which all the Fleeters sang, dying away at the close
like a foghorn growing softer as it diminished in distance.

> *And it prowls in the fog, all the Fleeters tell,*
> *And one chilly Samman eve,*
> *The old town clock rang a single bell*
> *And ten Fleeters woke to their final knell*
> *And we all went to Doane for to grieve,*
> *Yes, we all went to Doane for to grieve*
>
> > *In the fog,*
> > *In the fog.*
>
> *They were dead in bed, and we all made moan,*
> *And all ten come to last harbor at Doane,*
> > *Cos they died at sea in the fog,*
> > *Yes, they died at sea*
> > > *In the fog,*
> > > *In the fog,*
> > > *The fog,*
> > > *The fog,*
> > > *Fog.*

The logician inside Corian warred with the poet. The final verse
was clear enough, at least externally. Wellfleet had an ancient clock
that chimed ship's time. One bell would be half an hour past midnight in City. About that hour one Samman, the Wintermind came
out of the East to their covenstead and murdered ten sleeping people
who got buried in the old Fleeter cemetery near Doane Rock at
Nauset. But the last line—how they died at sea in the fog—struck him
as neither logical nor good poetry. *Damned hard to do on dry land.*

There was something else that Corian noticed. Hearing the song
again brought back the gist of the whole thing, and he realized the
girl hadn't sung it all, cut maybe two-three verses.

Corian glanced over at Jon Pettibone. He allowed as how the
Fleeter god maybe had a right not to have it all sung in public, even
at Lams.

How can the music always be sweet when life isn't? Even Goddess Earth allowed waste and pain, she'd learned that hard enough, and now the music mixed with a confusion inside that she wondered at, but it fit.

Her feelings were right, this was a place for her. Shalane saw the truth of it everywhere, in the hushed peace of Great Island, in the sad-sweet songs, their traditions that went back so much further than her own. This was a place for them all. Not always, but for now, while Mady learned the ways of her own blood, worked to concentrate the power she was born with and let time rub City out of her. Then home to Karli or Charzen, Arin could decide that, but Mady had to study with masters until she stepped into the circle and won her tabard, and yet so much should come before that, learning the forest, learning horses, out on the hill with men, feeling her body grow clean and tight as her mind.

All right, Shalane admitted, *some things are different, cowans and telephones and stores. Not all good, but maybe not all bad, either.*

She could put up with the changes in her world so long as they didn't dim the ultimate vision in Shalane's mind.

Mady, goddess of Karli.

Corian kept at Arin all the way down to the masters' hall.

"All I'm gonna do is check Jon's heart and blood pressure, maybe ask a few harmless questions, and you've got one of your own you want to put to him."

But Arin knew Cory's scheme was a breach of hospitality. "I still say it's bad manners. The worst."

"Look, you've got manners, but I'm a doctor, I've got questions. They won't be rude, won't even be direct, but they'll nudge his thinking close to what I want to know. All you've got to do is stand by, ask your own question, and stay tuned for any leak from brother god's mind."

Arin exhaled with resignation. "Cory, I'm only gonna do it because I know you've got an honest reason for it. But doing it's still dishonorable."

"If I'd been honorable at Dannyline," Corian retorted, "I would've been killing people, not healing them. *Dunesk.*"

Pettibone seemed preoccupied. He submitted absently to the stethoscope, grumbling to Arin.

"Santee's back on the Fist. Guess you never heard of him, Arin."

"Sure. Cowan hunter. My dad's looking for him."

"Ben was born up Race Point, one of the few bad Shortrees. Left when he was a boy, and nobody minded none. Been away twenty years, I guess."

Stethoscope against Pettibone's back, Corian mumbled,

"Breathe in deep. Again. Again. Good enough. Got a heart as sound as Brewster's. He back yet?"

"No, Cah-ree, he ent," his patient curtly replied.

Corian closed up his bag. "Lams begins the storm season, doesn't it?"

"Does," his patient admitted. "They start way out, nobody knows where, and they coil round and round till they move west or north."

They followed his gaze across the windowsill and out toward sea, a familiar expression that Fleeters got when they contemplated that expanse, a look compounded of fear, wonder, acceptance, but also a kind of jaw-jutting challenge.

"Nathan figured to work south, then head north toward the banks. Too good a fisherman t' let a storm catch 'im that far out."

"Sure," said Corian, "he'll get back."

Pettibone watched the window. "Might."

Corian saw the barest change in Arin's expression, a flicker of his eyes.

"Arin's got a question before we leave."

"Yes?"

"It's about the Wintermind song," Arin began, paused for a nod of acknowledgment, received none. "Are those maps it mentions still in existence?"

Pettibone thawed visibly. "That they are, though that verse come along later than the rest of the song. Truth is Sam didn't give them maps up, they were something to talk about with friends at supper. The town got them later."

"All right if me and Cory take a look at them?"

Pettibone said yes. "You go on up t' Town Hall, I'll give y' the key, and you go to the big front room on the second floor. They're in a big cedar chest. If you have any trouble finding them, just go across the way and ask Binnie Bemis t'—" He stopped in mid-sentence. His eyes widened.

"What is it, Jon?" Cory wondered.

"All of a sudden realized I said this once before." He focused on Arin. "To your brother."

Arin loped along the water's edge, worrying. "Think he made it?"

"Wait, will you?" Corian panted, jogging to keep up with Arin's long-legged strides, but his friend was too excited. Exasperated, Corian leaped on his back and hung there like a dead weight.

"HEY! WAIT UP!"

Laughing, Arin swung him around before collapsing in a happy heap. Just as abruptly, his mood reverted to anxiety. "Hope he got there safe."

"You heard Jon," Corian puffed, stretched out sideways on the shell-flecked sand. "Fleeters made Singer the best ship he could buy, and he took plenty of sail, spare parts, lots of food in the freezers, tackle, had a sun engine, wore a motherless crash helmet, God-knows-why. Now where the hell you imagine he went?"

Arin thought for a moment before answering.

I am Singer and I am alone.

More than ten years earlier, Arin read that, too, though Singer activated the Girdle of Solitude and vanished from view. He'd left the protective helmet in City, but Marian later told Arin she'd gotten it to his brother just before he dropped out of history altogether.

There'd been a time when he thought he hated his older half brother, but later he pitied the sad bastard. Now he was surprised to feel proud of Singer for finally going after the fabled island he'd been looking for ever since he was a boy. Arin hoped it really was there, and that it held peace for his brother. *And a home.*

"No doubt where he went, Cory, he wouldn't have gone through all that trouble for any place else, nothing much mattered to him after the war."

"Let me guess," Corian said. "Myudah?"

"Myudah."

While Arin and Corian walked to Town Hall, Shalane took a cup of tea with Abby and broached her request.

"Have to talk it over with the masters," Abby told the younger woman, "but I 'spect if you and Arin cared to join the Fleeter circle, Fleeters'd be glad to have you." Her eyes narrowed. "How come Arin don't speak for himself?"

"What I want, he wants," Shalane murmured and looked away.

The mean part of it, Shalane knew, was that Arin came second. This was a thing for Mady and herself.

But Arin, too. Let him want it as much as me. Let him want us all again.

Couldn't live with a man for ten years, joined to his mind and body, without learning the good and bad times for getting around

him. Rainy days, forget it. Or if he mumbled in his sleep with that
old nightmare of the dark, closed-in place, or the even older one
when he shot Holder, slamming him back and back against the tree
with the first Shando arrow ever to kill within Circle. But even on the
good days, Arin was so hard to know any more, he wanted so little,
nothing you could close your hand on.

Let him want something real again.

"Myudah."

Arin held up the two charts and recalled a moment in another
life when he opened a drawer in Lishin and found the map Singer's
mother once marked.

"They look almost new," Corian said.

Arin smoothed them out on the long table in the middle of the
room. The plastic coatings whispered and crackled, they were similar
to the type used on older City records.

The first map showed the detailed coastline of the island itself,
along with its original name. The second chart was a sophisticated
navigational aid, showing more Atlantic than Arin ever hoped to see.
It was lined with prevailing ocean currents, variably shaded with
fathom soundings. In the upper left, Corian pointed out the distinc-
tive coastline of the Fist, and from it a faint, indented line ran southeast across the plastic as if lightly scored by the point of a dull knife.
When Pettibone said, "Out there," and pointed north to the sea, it
was for convenience. The line actually followed the safer route,
southwest across the bay to the canal, out Buzzards Bay, then to the
ocean, the way Brewster was headed.

"That's the direction my brother followed."

Corian nodded absently. He'd found what he wanted, too, an
old black-and-white dappled composition book neatly inked by some
early Fleeter historian: WELLFLEET STORIES AND SONGS. He
flipped the brittle pages, paused a third of the way through to read a
line that caught his interest, flipped some more, stopped.

"Here it is." He squinted down the page and overleaf, then
slapped the book lightly. "Knew she left things out!"

Bent-backed, Arin took his time making a tracing of the two
charts. "Hm?"

Corian shoved the book under his nose. "Lams night, told you
she cut a couple verses."

"Looks about the same." Arin was preoccupied.

"Down here. One verse gone right after the part where the 'four

lost men from the town' were drifting without food or water, listening
to the Wintermind stalk their ship. . . ."

> *Poor Matthew Smith, he could not stay.*
> *Dan Baker, he died too.*
> *But Sam Pettibone knew there was one way*
> *To save himself and his brother Ray.*
> *God, forgive what a man must do,*
> *God, forgive what a man must do*
>
> > *In the fog,*
> > *In the fog.*

Corian showed where two other verses had been excised just before the final Samman tragedy stanza. "The last thing we heard at
Lams was how Sam and Ray vowed never to go to sea again. Leads
you to think they just lived out the rest of their lives on the land. But
look here, what she cut."

> *Well, the Wintermind must've followed Ray,*
> *Cos he died inside three weeks.*
> *"Best bury him deep," poor Sam did say,*
> *And he moaned and he cried and he went away*
> *And I can't forget his shrieks,*
> *No, I can't forget his shrieks*
>
> > *In the fog,*
> > *In the fog.*

> *And Sam Pettibone had two sons and a wife,*
> *And his widow weeps and sighs,*
> *Cos her husband took up his big black knife*
> *And slashed his wrists for to end his life*
> *But the Wintermind still cries,*
> *But the Wintermind still cries*
>
> > *In the fog,*
> > *In the fog,*

> *Where it cries in the dark like a losted child . . .*

Arin found it obscenely wasteful of life, the whole notion. Moss
saw suicide among the Kriss, but Sam Pettibone was Circle, perhaps
even a master. Unthinkable for him to take his own life.
As unthinkable as killing Holder.
For a second, Arin forgot to breathe. The question was a worm

in his mind. He wasn't sure whether he'd thought it himself . . . or if
it was put there by another.

He looked down at the map and calculated distances. Nine hundred to a thousand miles easy, too far to lep alone. But he bet his
brother could.

Singer? You out there?

Nothing but the distant call of gulls.

They splashed barefoot through the warm surf, Corian walking gingerly as always on his partly-cloned, part-artificial foot. They
watched small crabs scutter away from their shadows. The day was
mild, but unexpectedly chilly gusts of wind came from time to time,
ruffling Arin's unruly hair.

He said to Corian, "Read Pettibone like you asked."

"Thought so."

"Got a feeling off him like some color I never saw with my
eyes, but it's there all right."

"That all? No words?"

"Yes." Arin took a step back up onto the beach, stopped to sift
sand through his toes. "You mentioned Brewster and his boats and
said something like 'they'll get back' and Jon just answered,
'Might.'"

"Well?" Corian urged.

"What he leaked was just the opposite—like maybe they
shouldn't."

Two weeks after Lams. The first storm of the season flicked its skirts at the Fist before booming out to sea. Not much of a blow, Fleeters said, but no storm was good to be out in.

The next day, a morning of stiff breeze and brilliant sun, Shalane rose early and stopped down to pester Abby again, but this time the older woman had news for her.

"Jon and I consulted all the masters, Lane, and they give their consent."

Shalane's face lit up brighter than the blazing sun, but Abby suddenly stiffened at the first faint whisper of lep.

Weak but readable and growing clearer every minute. Shalane listened and her head lowered. She put aside her joy for later.

"Sister moon?" she asked, but Abby shook her head.

"Don't take it wrong," she said, "but best you go on home for now."

Before Lams, Shalane might have resented being told to mind her business, but she understood a little better now, so she did what Abby asked, thinking as she left, *Never be quite a Fleeter, even if—*

She halted in mid-thought. *Even when,* she corrected herself.

Alerted watchers sighted the three sails a little while after the first lep.

Brewster's ships. Coming in.

Bent under a good offshore wind, the vessels passed Yarmouth hump and cut a straight course for Wellfleet Harbor. The lep repeated at intervals, all over town coveners paused to read it. Abby and Jon turned to it with hard concentration.

Coming in. One man hurt.
?
Jordy Hawks. Need Corian.

Bounding along at big Jon's side, straining his vestigial coven senses to the limit, Corian caught a vague impression of urgency. Pettibone, tight-lipped, strode fast and said nothing, and so did every other covener as they all hurried to harborside.

Shuffling uneasily on the rough logs of the pier, the taciturn crowd seemed restless and even furtive. Nobody smiled, no greetings were exchanged, there was only premonition and waiting.

The three ships eased in and bracketed the pier. Mooring lines were secured in utter silence, save for the creak of planking. One by one, the crews tottered off the ships, men and women with faces scorched by the sea-magnified sun.

They gathered in a knot before the god and goddess and still no word was spoken. Corian rapidly scanned their faces.

"Goddess," he blurted out suddenly, "where's Nathan?"

Abby flashed him a look that would have put frost on a forest fire, but did not reply.

The dull-eyed, shaken crews stood with heads bowed before their fellow coveners. Frustrated, Corian knew their tale was being told by lep. He read as much of the leak as he could, a horror faded with the passage of time, but still palpable.

Scared blue, he realized with a shock, every damn one of them.

His eyes raked the boats for some clue, but the engines sounded good coming in, the sails were intact, the hulls no lower in the water than full hatches would account for, and all six dories were secured.

And yet eleven people stood there twitching just this side of shock, if he knew the symptoms at all.

A wiry young man stepped forward from the stricken knot of sailors, knelt before Jon Pettibone to offer his knife up to the god. Corian knew him fairly well: Jordy Hawks, one of Brewster's crew. Pettibone received the knife and broke the eerie silence.

"Doctor Corian."

Jordy rose painfully as Corian approached. "How do, Cory?" he managed whitely.

"Jordy, what's wrong?"

For answer, the fisherman unsnapped his waterproof and let it fall from his shoulders. His heavy wool shirt was slashed from right shoulder to waist, scored in four straight lines stiff with dried blood, as if from the claws of a gigantic cat.

Jordy lay morosely on Corian's examination table, stripped to his deeply lacerated skin. The doctor went on cleaning his badly infected wounds.

"Ran foul of a mess of hooked lines," Jordy claimed.

Corian knew it was ridiculous, the four furrows from shoulder to stomach were slashed with such force that the pectoral area was still bruised. The wounds were made, he speculated, by blunt spatulate claws ripping a single swipe through wool, skin, deep into muscle, dangerously close to the abdominal wall. For the time, Corian relied on antitet and antibio, plus something new of Rashevsky's, an injection that produced an abnormal amount of antibodies for short periods. If that didn't work, he'd have to open up the whole mess.

"And Nathan?" Corian asked.

"Died at sea." Jordy turned his head away.

"How?"

When Jordy didn't answer, Corian urged, "Nat was a friend of mine."

Jordy winced as the taped bandages tightened over his wounds. "Tell you what I told the god, though it ent your worry. Nets got fouled, he took a dory to clear 'em, but he got lost in the storm."

"Must've had your hands full with that blow."

"Sure did. Taking up nets, getting the catch froze down, reefing in before the wust of it caught us."

Corian pulled the tape end tight with a sudden jerk. It was deliberate, catching Jordy off his guard. "Why are you lying, Jordy?"

"What—?"

"These wounds are at least ten days old, it's a wonder they're not gangrened. The storm was yesterday. You got hurt long before that and haven't used that arm since. The pectoral's torn."

The boy bit his lip and turned away again, eyes moist. Corian pressed, not hard now, but sure of himself. "Brewster trawls with two nets strung between three craft in a line, even I know that. Night, fog or storm, he'd have to work at it to get lost."

"He got pulled away from the nets."

"In a dory?"

"Right."

Corian filled a plastic phial with antibio capsules and brought them to Jordy with a wry shrug. "So now I'm blind as well as dumb?"

"Huh?"

"You were swinging both dories when you tied up. You grow one on the way back?"

Jordy couldn't contain the torment. "Cowan, shut up!"

"What happened to Nat Brewster?"

The answer was blurred in racking sobs. "Wintermind got him." Jordy sought Corian's eyes, held them with a pleading. "Cory, don't tell the god I said that."

Corian was mystified that the Fleeters' superstition could exert such an incredible hold. "Why not?"

"Just promise, Cory."

Corian's compassion flooded back. He remembered that he was a doctor. Jordy's stertorous sobs could open the wound. "Sure. Forget it." Gentle now, Corian restrained his patient from rising. "Easy. Those muscles can't handle much yet."

"Just no more questions."

"Done." Corian pointed to the phial of pills. "Two of those when you get home, one every four hours after. They'll help you stay on top of the infection. I'll stop in to see you tomorrow, hear? I don't like the looks of that thing."

The tension faded from Jordy's white face. "Bad?"

"Bad enough. Might have to go in, but don't worry now. Just go home and take your pills, stay on your back and you'll help yourself get better. Hey! You people out there. Take him home now."

Two Fleeters answered his call, eased Jordy onto their litter. The boy squeezed Corian's hand without strength. "You're a good man, Cory."

"For a cowan, huh?"

"You know what I mean."

"Jordy, for a no-lep, I can read like hell. Carry him gentle, you people. And Jordy—watch out for fish hooks."

Alone, Corian splashed disinfectant over his hands and flopped down on a stool, reaching into a lower cabinet for a thick clay jar three-quarters full of potato gin. He took a generous belt to remind himself how good it was to be alive even when it hurt. The ferocious liquor scalded his throat and he gasped with masochistic pleasure.

Died at sea. The litany of the ballad, the emotional shortmind of a taciturn folk who accepted so much death just to live by the sea.

If that's how Jordy looked living through it, what in hell did the Wintermind do to Nathan Brewster?

She'd kept her news to herself two afternoons and evenings, but on a morning like this with sun pouring in from the east window, she could reach Arin with anything. She woke him with a bowl of blackberries and fresh milk to share in bed. After he finished and she put down the bowl, they made love like they used to, easy and slow, going on and on with no need to finish, the end itself hardly any more blissful than the getting there.

At last, satisfied, Shalane rested her head on Arin's right arm, his left lying lightly over her chest. She felt a great tenderness for the twisted limb. After love, or even during it she would stroke and kiss it as if to share that she loved all of her husband, and maybe the weakest part the most.

"Arin?"

"Mm?"

"You happy?"

"Yes." He stretched, yawned and rolled over to her. "I'm glad we came."

"We needed it." Shalane nestled into the curve of his good arm. *Now. Never be a better moment.* "I'd like to stay."

Arin sighed with contentment. "I would, too. It's a good place."

"Then why don't we? You don't like City any more'n I do."

Arin thought it over, then admitted, idly, "No. Not that much."

"We *can* stay," Shalane urged in a whisper. "I asked Jon and Abby."

"Asked what?"

"Told them I wanted to live here. They said yes."

A warning instinct washed over Arin, he sensed the long-building storm had come at last. He stared at Shalane for a moment, then sat up on the edge of the bed. "You shouldn't have done that, Lane."

"Why not?"

"You had no right, we have responsibilities."

"The crowns? Any master in City could wear mine for all the good it does there."

"And without a word to me, without even sharing—"

"Trying to share now."

"—you just up and decide."

"Arin, I can't live in that place any more. I'm dumb, far as Marian and all the city-zens are concerned, but I know Circle, and what we've had for ten years ain't it."

"It's the way things are, Lane."

Shalane stifled with the desperation till she could say it evenly. "So sick of hearing that. You just said we could be happy here, you just said it."

"But—"

"Don't tell me but. I don't want to hear any buts." Shalane bounced up on her knees. "It's hard here, sure, but they're healthy and strong, and we'll be the same, and we don't need to be gods."

Arin smiled wryly. "Oh, that doesn't bother me, I never needed that. But I still can't."

"Oh, dammit, Arin, what *can* you do? What do *you* want? Is there anything left?"

He shrugged, he didn't know, he'd forsaken easy answers for over ten years. He came out of a small dark space in Lishin and ran the Self-Gate and now he read books that dragged him on to more books, answers that held only more questions—he heard his brother say that once to Bowdeen—and now he and Lane didn't think alike any more at all. He could not just live and accept now, the way he did when he was a dumb hideshirt Charzen hunter. His father and his brother shook him loose and now he felt like Jay Kriss' old story of Adam thrown out of the garden, knocking at the gate and maybe begging, *Hey, can I come back in if I promise to be dumb again?*

"Lane," he said at last, "I can't just hold onto one handful of life and pretend it's the whole thing."

"Arin, Circle never taught you that."

"Hell it didn't." He lunged up to the window, troubled that too many things he'd kept in so long were coming out so fast. "Used to say 'cowan' like it smelled bad. Way down I'm deepwoods thick as you, Lane. The war made me grow lots, but when I see something like that water that goes on forever, all the way inside my gut I cringe and want to crawl back into Shando Forest and never come out again."

"Well, why not?" she challenged him. "Is it so bad to want to stop hurting? You're Shando, I'm Karli—" She held up two fingers pressing one another. "*That* close, Arin. Deepwoods. That's what we are."

"Deepwoods maybe, Lane, but not Circle."

She stared at him, face blank.

"Lane, I don't believe in it any more."

It was too much for her to grasp all at once. "Don't believe what? Not in Goddess Earth?"

He slowly shook his head. "No. Not Circle magic, either."

She repeated the words, still uncomprehending. "Not Goddess Earth? Not Circle magic? But that's all there is."

"No, Lane, we're all there is, the magic comes from *us*, a part of our brains. Corian thinks maybe we're a new kind of people who—"

"Who *believe!*" Shalane sternly overrode him. "But then, Arin the master, Arin the god, what *do* you believe?"

No answer to that, either. He knew the innate fear that made people whirling through space on a ball of mud and water spin elaborate webs of self-deception rather than face the possibility of solitude. Prepared to murder to show something existed beyond the void besides Self. Singing to gods that flattered their own images, yet still clutching their lies to them like blankets, jamming them against their ears so they could sleep without screaming.

He fell back against the bed, arms behind his head, not knowing how to tell her he thought the end of belief was the beginning of morning, but the first hours were bitter frost. "Lane, I don't know yet."

"Yet? When, then?"

"Maybe never."

"Well, ain't that just fine!"

"Tell you a piece of it, though. What we used to know was just a beginning for Circle."

Shalane regarded him with deep suspicion. "And what comes after?"

Arin said it evenly. "City wants to build the world higher than it was before the Jings. But they need us to do it, Lane, and we need them."

If he thought she was going to argue about City, he was wrong for once. Shalane read the confusion her question had tapped in Arin, and there was so much misery mixed in with it, too. She lay down beside him and began to stroke his hair.

"I learned some City words, too," she said. "You're my husband, I'm your wife, we have a marriage and a religion. Circle never needed words like that, but we *do* have a religion, the best that ever was. Stay here, Arin. If we have to work on those scary boats, I'll do it with you. You can find the Goddess again, I know you can, but even if you don't, even if we have to stand clear outside the circle, Arin, I love you and I'll do it, but you've got to help me."

"Lane, I can't, it won't work."

"It can," she argued desperately.

"How *can* it?" he asked, rising on one elbow, bending close over Shalane with the pain of the bleak truth he wanted to spare her, but could not avoid blurting out. "Why have we been using words, Lane? Why haven't we lepped? Why don't we share like we used to?"

She ducked her head pathetically. "Arin, don't."

"If we're really still so close—"

"*If?*" she wailed. "We are, we *are!* Oh, *da-a-amn,* why can't I find anything, not even me? You did it, Arin! You and Garick. You came and said change the world, and I was with you, *you* couldn't be wrong, so Arin and Garick and the whole goddam war must be right." She jackknifed away to sit rigid on the edge of the bed. "See my scars?"

Yes, he said, he knew them, scars on her back and arms, tiny whitish pepperings that never tanned, that came from riding through an arcade of fire at Dannyline. The claw marks on her throat where the Kriss woman gouged her before dying, part of him like his twisted arm was part of her.

"No!" she shrilled. "No, Arin, not *them,* you don't know the scars I mean. Salvation! I murdered babies for Garick. *Babies,* and I only got one and she calls me IGNORANT! Now tell me, god Arin, tell me what I won, what the war gave us so much better than what got lost? What I can't find any more." The rage ebbed from her, and she gave one dry sob. "Mady says I'm dumb, Arin, so tell me, tell me now."

He didn't know. Only there'd been an argument, but Shalane wouldn't say what. He didn't know.

He touched her, tried to console her, but she twisted around. "Arin, please, if you love me . . ."

If.

He knew then how wide the rift was. Bargaining with words and kisses, denying with the same. *If* he loved her, that was the hook, *if* he loved her, he'd give her what she wanted, and she didn't even realize what she'd said. Ten years married and they never needed that word.

But he did love her. Her pain was intolerable to him, he couldn't confront it without feeling it himself, without opening up to help her, and anyway, what difference did anything really matter, *my needs are irrelevant,* and he was used to hurting by now, that's how he knew—

He shook the thought from his mind.

"All right, Lane, we'll come here."

Shalane held her breath, afraid that any motion would change his mind. "Real?" she asked finally, her voice so small she hardly heard it herself.

"Real," he nodded.

Then the tears came. "Oh, Arin, you won't be sorry."

"Hush, Lane, don't cry, I'd go anywhere with you. For you. Anywhere you want, only don't hurt ever again."

Her head bobbed up and down eagerly. "Yes. And I promise, it won't be here for always. Someday we'll go home."

He laid a silencing finger on her lips. "Shh, don't say that again. You're home to me, Lane, ten years I've worn a crown and danced in a circle I don't believe in just for you, so I'll do it here if I have to, because I'm with you. You're part of me."

"Part of each other, Arin."

But that was not what he meant. "Hear me out, Lane, you don't understand."

Shalane sensed the thing coming, the thing she'd tried to avoid. She said nothing.

"I said you're part of me. That's true. I'll come here because that's how much I love you for myself." He took a deep breath and said it at last. "But Mady stays in City."

The flush of happiness fled from her cheeks. "Oh, no. No, Arin. No way."

"Dammit, Lane, it's not me. Even if I couldn't see a hundred reasons for saying no, Mady doesn't want to leave."

"Don't you tell me City's her home, Arin, because that ice-cold place ain't home to nothing. And if she thinks she wants it, who made our baby that way? Who let Singer woman take her?"

"I did."

"You said it first, not me."

"It was right," he argued. "We're the good, she's the better. Mady stays."

"Arin, she's young. Give me three years with her in a real covenstead—"

"So she can forget how to read, how to think? Lane, she can't go back because she won't go back. She was never Circle, not really. Accept that, why can't you? I'll go with you, but not Mady."

It's all for her. All.

No, Lane, she doesn't want it.

She will if you give me a chance, Arin. Two years.

No.

I'll take her, anyway.

"No you won't." Arin rose heavily from the bed, reached for his clothes. When she spoke, he heard a new hard tone in her voice.

"What's gonna stop me, Arin?"

The determination and challenge made him turn. For a moment, they measured one another before he spoke.

"Me."

"You'll stop me?"

"Yes," he nodded.

"Your power against mine?"

"Don't be a fool." He'd played that game once, and it was dangerous. Nobody really won it.

"I'm a fool?" she echoed. "That's right! Thick. Just like the little snot said. Thick and ignorant."

He felt the warning twinge of sickness in her middle and in his, but he was too irritated now to stop. "Yes, Lane, you *are* ignorant, and you know why?"

"'Spect you'll tell me."

"Because you want to stay ignorant, that's the reason. You refuse to change, won't learn, ten years and a whole new world in front of you and you won't look anywhere but back."

"Mady comes home with me."

"She won't." He shook his head, weary of the argument. "You'll only get hurt."

Shalane couldn't retreat. "I owe her, Arin, she has to come home. With you or without you."

There. It was finally said. A tightening of the knot in their stomachs.

"Lane, don't say that." It was a plea out of his misery.

"With you or without." She wanted to press him in her arms, but she couldn't back down and neither could he.

The agony roiled within, palpable nausea that he knew wracked Shalane, too. Together ten years and now to split apart? Hard enough on anyone who loved, even more brutal to coveners and the millioned sharings of their kind of marriage, whispered daily deep in blood and muscle and brain, a drug strengthening the bond with secrets lepped mind to mind, and a severing like this had to be as physically sickening as war itself, but the thing had to be done, there were no soothing lies left to put it off any longer. Each was intractable. Mady was more important.

"With or without you, Arin."

"All right," he bit out each syllable, "then without me."

Arin!

No, I didn't mean—

But he did, and they both knew it.

The besieged anger died from her eyes. He watched her dress with distracted speed, gathering the unbound luxury of hair into a strip and pin.

He sank down on the bed, trying to quell his growing sickness with an effort of will. "You feel bad as I do, Lane?"

"Yes." She went on dressing.

"Then don't do this."

Shalane swallowed hard against her own illness. "Don't tell me what I can't do."

"You'll get hurt. Mady'll say no."

"Not to me. Not if I say git."

"Lane, stop lying to yourself. She'll pull away from you worse than ever before."

"I'll put it in her mind, like that decon guard."

He leaped to his feet, grabbed the blackberry bowl and hurled it shattering against a wall. "Don't you *ever* do that to Mady!"

A pathetic last prize to bear away: *at least he loves me enough to still get mad.*

She stumbled down the wooden steps to the narrow bay beach, wading blindly out into the warm surf up to her calves. Awkward as a drunk, she splashed the foaming salt water over her face, dragged back to shore only to collapse on her knees with a guttural moan. Turning to the edge of the water, she retched violently. Her half-digested breakfast came up, but she couldn't stop, the brutal contractions heaved and heaved, squeezing her stomach in a cruel vise till nothing emerged but bile and then only dry, agonized cries that strained her throat raw. When it passed, she rolled weakly onto her side, lay there long before willing her body and mind to obedience again.

She stumbled a few feet to clean water, washed her face and chin, then turned and started to trot clumsily at first, then faster and faster, goading her muscles like a horse until the need for rest blotted out anything else and she toppled down on the sand, unable to think beyond the next breath.

Corian wished he could remember what he'd dreamed just before waking that morning, it seemed important to recall it, but there was no time now.

Jordy Hawks' wounds had too much start for antibio, they'd developed an abscess in the peritoneum that threatened to break inward on the greater omentum. It had to be opened and drained immediately or Jordy would be dead in a few days.

An elementary operation, but Corian's problem on this complicated day was finding an assistant who could quickly absorb the simple but precise techniques for sterile scrub. Jordy's mama wouldn't do, she was too involved, and wouldn't you just know this one time, Shalane couldn't be found, not even Arin could say where she was. And he was another problem, too, the big Shando wavering in the aid station door, white as the belly of a raw fish.

"Where's Lane, Arin? I need her."

"Don't know, Cory, I—"

Then Arin ducked outside the door, vomiting, bent with spasms that racked him so bad that Corian feared he'd rupture his stomach. He shot Arin full of tranquilizer, laid him out in the anteroom, then took the first volunteer assistant who showed up: Teesha Wilkes, a young master-elect, intelligent and willing. Pretty, too, in the Fleeter way, sun-browned so dark her wide-set light blue eyes shone out piercingly, already etched with deep lines from squinting for years at the sun-dazzled ocean.

Corian rehearsed her quickly.

"Gave Jordy a diuretic first thing. We'll do an enema for rinse. Then you shave all the hair around and below the area, wash it in this disinfectant. Anesthetic, the needle will be taped to his arm. I'll put him under, you stand by for more if I say. See these marks on the needle? I'll call the number of them I need. Push slow with your thumb, and be careful. This stuff is powerful, Teesha. I want him under, not dead."

To Teesha's fascination, he let her learn the stethoscope on his own heart. "When I tell you, count Jordy's heartbeat against that red hand on the clock. Too high or low, I'll tell you what to do."

Conscious of narrowing safety time, Corian turned to the sterile tray, ticking off the instruments. "I'll try to get them myself. If I can't, you hand them. Sponges are the most important. You keep count, hear? Nine go in, nine gotta come out. When they do, hang them over the edge of this bucket so we can tally before I put in the drain."

Corian had Teesha talk the whole procedure back to him, step by step. A definite advantage in having a master's concentration. For a one-time observer, Teesha remembered more details than he did training under Rashevsky.

"Kinda fun," she grinned.

He smiled back. "Want to learn more, come see me some time in City."

She leaned back against a chair, relaxing, pleasantly aware that he liked what he saw. And he did. He appreciated her hard, supple torso under the thin shirt. Long, thin legs, hard as wire cable in her cutoff shorts, belly flat as Jordy's. *Really ought to get next to something like her before long, I could use it.* But masters-elect stayed chaste during their pledging, and Teesha would consider him outside the bounds of respectability as far as bed was concerned. Some things didn't pay to contemplate.

Then the physician in him took over. Her flat belly reminded him of Jordy's and that the patient wouldn't have much fat stored in the omentum. Had to drain quick and right.

Teesha laid out her own prep and picked up the razor. "Never saw a man with his hook end shaved."

"Looks silly as hell," Corian chuckled. "He'll itch awhile, but it grows back. Just don't get careless. Men get shaky when you wave a knife around their cock."

"Not Jordy," she said with a mischievous twinkle. "He and me used to get around a sight on fire days."

Corian winked at her. "Then you know the territory. Won't get nervous when I cut?"

The flirtatiousness faded. Quite honestly, the scalpel palled on Teesha's religious instincts. "Just the cutting, but I won't look."

He gave her arm one impetuous squeeze, liking the way she looked at him when he did. "You'll be fine, Teesha. Go tell 'em, bring Jordy. I'll set up."

He watched her leave, enjoying how her bottom swayed as she walked. Then it was time to check on Arin. Corian opened the door to the anteroom and saw his friend prostrate on one of the two post-op beds, huge, pale and pathetic, staring dully at the ceiling.

Corian's thin smile was full of reminiscent pity. In his own hard-drinking days, he must have looked like this three times a week to the patient Ted Rashevsky. A shot of B-concentrate and five minutes on oxygen usually rendered him human again, though he doubted it would do much for Arin. Coven medicine, the physiology and psychology of a people just a bit different, but you could fill a book with the unique problems, except no one had. Maybe—

"Hey, deepwoods, how do you feel?"

"Dead." Arin sounded it.

"You took enough trank to knock out a horse. What the hell happened? Too much cranberry wine?"

"Had a fight with Lane." Arin's speech came slow and spaced, dulled by the drug. "A bad one, Cory, I don't know where she is. Been open, trying to lep, but she's closed off."

Corian eased down on the edge of the bed, premonition nibbling at his instincts. "About Mady?"

Arin nodded feebly. "Wants to take her out of City. I said no."

"You knew this was coming, didn't you?"

"Yes," Arin winced, clutching his middle. The tranquilizer hadn't quelled all the physical pain. "Didn't know it'd hurt this much."

"Then she—"

Arin read the thought before it was finished. "She does, she's sick as me, but closed off. She's never shut me out like this before, Cory. When I was in Lishin, she read me all the way over Blue Mountains, but now I can't read her not even a mile away." Arin writhed as fresh agony spiraled from his stomach. "But she can't have Mady."

"I know," said Corian, "it's too late for that. Been too late for years."

"Give me something to get me going. Pain-killer, anything. I've got to find her."

"Arin, you're under severe systemic shock. Not only nausea, but I'd say your blood sugar has dropped to nothing. You might black out if you try to ride."

"Then she could, too." Arin closed a huge hand over Corian's arm. "So you better find her, Cory, find her and help her, she's sick."

A chill of helplessness raced through Corian. "I can't now. Jordy Hawks can't wait. Got to go in soon as they bring him."

"Please, Cory, Shalane can't wait, either."

"Arin, I promise—soon as Jordy's done, I'll go, but—"

"Find her! Cory, find her! I—I know how you feel about Lane."

"Shut up. Just shut up. You don't know."

"Yes I do."

A brisk knock at the outer door saved Corian a big lie. He patted Arin's shoulder reassuringly. "Be back."

It wasn't Jordy at the door, Corian didn't recognize the dour, stocky man who peered curiously past him at the steel-and-white mysteries of City medicine.

"Yes?"

"Smith. Own the stable down to Nauset. Told I'd find the City god here."

"He can't see you now. He's sick."

"So was she," Smith scowled. "Don't matter. Got his change." He held out two five-kret gold pieces. "City goddess bought a horse and saddle. Didn't have change for her. Give it to the god, she said."

Corian jingled the coins in his hand, uneasy. "You say she wasn't well, either?"

Smith nodded. "Like she got outta fever bed too soon." The laconic Fleeter squinted at the doctor. "Heard how them Karli wore deerskin, never saw't till now. Queer."

Not to a Karli, Corian thought as his premonition darkened. When they wanted to travel far and fast, they didn't wear anything else. "Which way'd she ride?"

"South," Smith told him. "Hard as hell, like she—"

But Corian was already striding back through the operating room toward the inner door. "Arin!"

Yarmouth's single street shimmered in late afternoon heat. Inside the bar-and-store, a few farmers drowsed over their drinks and conjectured on the rain they needed, enervated voices a sleepy counterpoint to the hum of flies.

A day not to move too much or too fast. Basted in the sweat of his corpulence, the storekeeper was sourly grateful there weren't more customers, he'd be hopping like a three-leg pig. Just the handful of his regulars and that dumb kid who came in for supplies, ordered a gin and sat in a corner behind the door, slupping loud as a hog, fingering his crotch and grinning like he wasn't all there. A day to say the hell with it and just let the world go bake.

The door whined open rustily, shut again. When the storekeeper turned around, the woman stood across the bar, glaring at him.

"Left my horse in the stable," she snapped in a flat, alien twang. "Want him grained and watered."

Coven, the storekeeper guessed, but no Fleeter. He took her in with the expertise of one who observed comings and goings, from her hot, angry face to the worn buckskins and black knife at her hip. He got along all right with Circle, but he didn't like the way this woman asked for things.

"Get to it in a minute."

"Now."

Nope, he sure didn't like her. He was a courteous man; he tried to tend his customers quick enough, but on a gritty, disagreeable day like this such a manner didn't sit right with him at all.

"Got something that passes for food?" she asked.

He nodded.

"Well, get it."

He looked at her more closely, realized it wasn't just anger, she was sick, shaking, no color in her lips. The farmers at the table, even the idiot kid in the corner were staring at her.

"Be a whole garick," he announced.

It was the highest price he dared charge, but she didn't even blink, just tossed the heavy gold ten-kret piece ringing on the bar. Then she asked, "This road go to Hartford?"

"What don't?"

"I'll wait for the food. Grain the horse. And be careful, he's mean."

"That figures." The storekeeper shot a glance at the watching farmers. "Some folks know how to say please on a hot day."

"Cowan." No one else heard the word. No one else saw her eyes but him. The last he clearly remembered was that her expression changed in a way he couldn't exactly name. Her smile was suddenly easy, fetching, and the most horrible thing he'd ever felt. The woman whispered another word, and his skin began to crawl under the sweat.

"Please."

Of course. He wanted only to fill her needs. Right away. Nothing else mattered.

The boy in the corner pushed back his chair. The woman turned slightly at the sound, then back to the storekeeper as the kid slipped out the door.

In the bush between the dusty road and the marsh, the two older men listened as the boy told his tale. He capered in front of them, miming his descriptions as he spoke them, full of excitement.

"Long and lean like a big stringbean," Billy Lee chortled, immensely pleased with the joke and the rhyme. "You know what I mean?"

He felt important. For once, Ben wasn't shutting him up but listening to every word. He'd done good this time, real good.

"Oh, she was Karli, sure, Ben," he judged with exaggerated authority. "Guess I seen enough in my time." He giggled. "Guess I stuck enough in my time."

Ritt scowled around the grass stalk he was chewing, but stayed silent. Ben Santee sat on the ground, chin resting on twined fists.

"Blonde, Billy Lee?"

"Long yeller hair like a horsetail."

"Scar on her left arm near her wrist?"

"Don't know, Ben." That was something he'd missed, he hoped Ben wouldn't be mad.

"Wearing something around her neck?"

"Maybe." Billy Lee struggled to remember. Mostly her back was to him—but no, she turned around when he got up to leave. Finest woman he ever saw, moved like a shadow, looked like a dream. Just sitting there in a corner, he yearned to touch her. "May-be."

Santee drew a precise crescent moon in the dirt. "Iron thing shaped like that?"

"That's it, Ben! I remember now! Saw it when she come in, too. Big iron moon on a piece of rawhide."

Santee smiled up at the hovering boy. "You're a good man, Billy Lee. The angels won't forget you quick."

Billy Lee beamed. "Did good, Ben?"

"Real good, Billy Lee, proud of you. It's Shalane. Got to be."

"Got to be," Billy Lee aped Ben, full of love for his idol.

"She got that moon sign from Red Jenna," Santee said. "We'll send it to Garick after. I'll put your name beside mine on the letter, Billy Lee."

It was too much in one day, pleasing Ben and getting his name all lettered out, he'd never seen it. "Big and clear, huh, Ben? Billy Lee!"

"Why not all our names?" Ritt muttered with dry disgust. "How 'bout a map how to find us?"

His tone more than his words made Santee turn. "You got a piece to say?"

"Had something to say quite a while, Ben, 'spect you know what it is." Ritt spat out the dandelion stalk he was chewing. "Want to hear, anyhow?"

Ben nodded. "Go on if you've a mind. Vengeance is the Lord's and he works through my hands. It won't change nothing."

"It better," Ritt said soberly. "Won't argue you know the Lord, but I know Garick, and he's a lot closer and getting closer all the time. We ain't done much up here. We could quit and get lost. But you kill her and we can't ride or *fly* far enough to get away from Garick or the constab."

Billy Lee roared his contempt. "We killed the constab! We hung 'em!"

"There's more, kid, there's always more, and they get faster and smarter and I just get older." Ritt yanked another stalk and bit at it. "Ain't worth it, Ben. Let it go."

"Rack ent worth it?" Santee asked with deceptive softness.

"Well . . ."

"Them daughters of the Devil lured him on to where others were just waiting to kill him. I will repay tenfold, saith the Lord."

"Oh, shit."

Santee's accusing finger shot out. "Don't you badmouth the Lord, Ritt. That's your trouble, you're a blasphemous man and the gates of Heaven will be shut to you. They led my boy Rack on to be killed."

"He should of known better."

"I told him, but they were waiting."

"Sure they were, and here comes Rack with his pants down and most of his brains in his hand."

Billy Lee bit his tongue to keep from laughing, he knew better than to show Ben how much he never could stand Rack's ass.

"Tenfold!"

Santee clutched his temples, rocking back and forth with the sudden passion. "Oh, tenfold will I repay. Sodom and Gomorrah, and all the cities of the plain, all the wicked who forgot the Lord, they'll all feel His wrath. Through me. Been a long time finding what I was meant for, Ritt. Been a fool, had to lose my boy Rack, but the lesson's clear now. Vengeance for him, and vengeance for Him, and all the wicked cities shall feel it."

When Ben talked like this, Ritt only felt boredom and disgust, but Billy Lee loved it. Not so much the old-time words, he didn't understand half of them, but the way Ben's eyes got big and lit up and his voice got fast and soft, rising and falling like a song.

"Not just this woman, but all that's backslid. Kill 'em, burn them out, cut with the scythe of the Lord across the chaff 'n' tares they grown. And they will suffer that they slew Jeremiah, and they will bitterly regret Uriah's murder. Oh, yes, I feel it, I feel the hand of the Lord on my shoulder. I got some cleaning to do around here, Ritt. We just started."

Ben subsided a little, remembering the arrowhead he'd been honing on a stone. "She's just the start, Ritt. You ent gonna backslide now, are you? Now, when the Lord and me need you?"

Ritt felt hopeless. There was a time when he stood up to Santee and a time when Ben had some shrewd sense, but gradually it got easier to let Ben make the decisions, and now, when he most clearly saw the bloody end of it all, he didn't have the guts to say no. Nowadays he got tired quicker in body to match the dead weight of futility on his spirit. All the places looked alike, all his tomorrows were dead as the past. He even knew why Ben needed him in on this, why Ben was honing the arrowheads.

Well, maybe at least he could kill her clean so she wouldn't suffer, then he could split off and run, he liked to think he still could.

"Gimme." He reached for the arrows. "I can edge 'em better."

Though the last light of sunset was in her eyes, Shalane intended to ride as long as the road was still visible. The stallion was rested and fed. She had no appetite for the food set before her, but forced some of it down. Her stomach needed something to work on, or she'd feel even worse.

She wouldn't think of Arin, that hurt too much. Nothing mattered now but Mady, dragging her out of that City. It had to be, she paid so much for it, but she couldn't think of that because it brought the picture of Arin and how he looked, dead as herself—

Don't think of that.

Her mind ached from running in circles, like game caught in staymagic. She tried not to think of Arin, but it hurt so much, and *he* must hurt so much, torn loose from each other and bleeding—

Stop.

The sun dropped below the trees as the stallion put road behind them with tireless strides. An easy road through tame country, not like old times when there was danger of packdogs and cowan hunters and even plague, here she saw people almost every hour, it was no real woods at all, just trees fringing a smooth clear ribbon where her horse ran. Good enough: she needed speed now rather than caution. Speed and a fast road to Mady, and she wouldn't think about Arin or the way he looked just before she closed the door between them, no, it was he who betrayed her, betrayed everything she believed in, but he wouldn't get Mady, he wouldn't get Mady, no way.

Speed: as her mind conceived it, the body obeyed years of habit, flattening forward over the stallion's arched neck—

The horse screamed. The arrow plunged deep into its chest. At full gallop, it stumbled once and then pitched forward like a stone. By reflex, Shalane yanked her feet from the stirrups. *Not thinking, not fast enough,* streaking through her startled mind as the ground rushed up at her and her skull slammed hard against the sun-baked dirt.

Distantly, she felt her body absorb the brutal shock of her fall. Limbo for a time without time, then her mind came back and control returned, her trained master's will barked commands, but her stunned body was helpless to translate them into action. Harsh foreign voices sounded a distant warning in her ears, *get up now, get up NOW,* but she could only raise herself a little, and the absurd picture of three men running meant nothing.

Three coming toward her, three cowans, she got that much. Shalane struggled to clear the film that blurred her sight, tried to reach for her knife but nothing worked and the hilt was too far, too heavy for nerveless fingers, and the darkness was falling too fast, and then the world went away.

Ritt meant to take her clean, leading her a little in the windless twilight, but a half-breath before he loosed, she leaned flat over the horse's neck. He dropped his sight with her, but too far, he knew it was too damn low just as he let go. The horse stumbled before it fell, and that broke its speed and maybe saved the woman's life. Maybe shouldn't have, considering.

This time I don't want to watch.

The wound in her head left a trail of dark blood as Santee and Billy Lee dragged her through the bush toward the marsh. Billy Lee was so excited with what Ben promised, he was stammering and loosening his pants even as they pulled her along.

Once in the bush, Santee moved with merciless determination, untying her cord belt, yanking down the deerskin trousers into a clump about her thin ankles. His breath hissed as he undid his own belt.

"Now, by God, we get our own back." Then he paused, stayed by an odd notion of justice. "Ritt brought her down," Santee said. "He can go first."

Ritt wanted no part of it, though he couldn't say why. He'd taken women before, boys, too, no better than Ben that way, but he was a hunter before all else, there was a wordless kinship with the game, as close to a belief as anything Ritt ever felt. The woman in the saddle flowed like a deer and she looked like she could make the horse fly, you'd think that to see her ride, she and that stallion, god-dam, they were fine, fast game. You missed or you brought it down, but you didn't shit on it after. All right, it was a queer notion, but it just didn't seem right.

"You go first, Ben," he stalled. "Left a good arrow in that horse, gonna get it back."

He strode away toward the road before Ben could argue. Of course, Billy Lee didn't mind, that meant he got her sooner. The dumb bastard already couldn't wait, drooling and crooning and feel-ing the woman where she lay. She looked dead, anyhow Ritt hoped so.

"You gonna do it, Ritt," Santee rasped after him. "Maybe you don't want her, but you gonna do it one time just for good old Garick."

"Yeah, hell, why not?" Nothing mattered now, from here on it'd be one village, one town after another, Arin, too, probably, and Ben'd end up standing over the corpses with a torch in one hand and singing a hymn when Garick caught up and cut him down.

Ritt guessed that didn't matter much to him, either. He concen-trated on digging out the arrow.

She floated up like a swimmer rising from deep water into a crimson tide that crackled with electricity and shocked her again and again. She groaned. Goddess Earth wouldn't allow agony like this. She tried to open her eyes, but they were stuck shut and sticky around the lids. Then, gradually, distantly, she became aware of her body being jolted back and forth and another pain lower down, not part of her yet but growing.

Still closer to the surface and the shocks were even worse, they split her apart, cut across her throbbing skull, and she was on her back with a weight pressing her down and she felt a stabbing between her legs, in and out of her dry body, that wasn't like Arin when she wasn't ready and hurt so bad.

Closer, higher, almost awake, and she couldn't believe there could be so much cruel pain in her head, it kept mounting and mounting.

Goddess, am I born again?

But if this was a waking into death, it betrayed her like every-thing and everyone else. The weight on her wasn't Arin, it had a cowan stink, and now she could open her eyes just enough to see the looming animal face.

All things betrayed her, all things fled from her. Arin, Mady, home, Goddess Earth even, nothing was real but this leering, vicious mouth close to hers, the empty rat-eyes, and the brutal member ripping deep into her so that nothing was left untaken, undirtied, unbetrayed.

Her mouth opened and she heard her last cry to the Goddess who would not help her, all gone, all run away, and she was alone, and she was dying, but as the cowan shuddered to a finish inside her, she heard, dimly, a snarling voice above.

"God's own vengeance, black knife for a coven whore! Roll off, Billy Lee, gonna cut her while she can still feel."

And then there was no more earth or air or water or fire, but only endless agony and screaming, and her eyes filled with blood and Shalane descended into night.

WINTERMIND

With the brooding precision of a deeply wronged man trying to hide his anger, Corian shuffled his notes into an orderly stack, stabbed the RECORD button and began to speak.

Tape memo, Corian to Spitt for transmit Garick STAT. Goddess Shalane is dead. Murdered. Ben Santee must've done it. Enclosed map marks where. West of Yarmouth. She was . . . she was on her way home.

I'm reading this from notes because I can't make much sense right now. Just that . . . that . . .

Just that we were too late because Jordy had to come first, even before Lane, and by the time me and Arin got the boat clear of the bay harbor, she had over two and a half hours' headstart. Burned up the battery crossbay to Dennis, but Lane could push a good horse farther and faster than that.

She and Arin had a bad fight over . . . a number of things. We were worried. . . .

—worried about her, not about murder. Who thought?

She must've been riding out of Yarmouth when we docked and got the horses. Missed her by less than an hour. We . . . we found her horse in the road after sundown. Arrow-shot.

Still enough light left to see it all happened right there. They even dug the arrow out of the horse.

I smelled the death myself, it must've been unbearable to Arin. I said something stupid like we didn't know it was Shalane's horse, but he shut me up with a look. "It was," he said. "She was here, I can still read her."

We stayed at Yarmouth and went back to the site early. Arin read it all like a page. They hit her on the road, then dragged her through the grass to a spot near the marsh. An awful lot of dried blood, obviously a struggle.

Insane amount of blood, even bits of flesh, they tore her apart. Arin read the place where they threw her on the ground, three of them at least. He didn't say, didn't have to say how bad she had to be wounded, maybe already dead, it wouldn't matter to them, but let it be that she was dead by then—

She's in the marsh now. Arin wouldn't let me get what was left of her body out, it's the coven thing about being buried where they fall, not disturbing them, and Arin said it'd be done the way Shalane believed, no City magic.

It's how Santee works, Garick. He's been seen on the Fist. Arin spent hours going over the area for tracks, but the road's got too many. Old ones, new ones. Arin picked up a faint trace, but that motherless cowan knows how to cover himself. Wandered a lot, then headed west and vanished over rocky ground.

We're all feeling . . . pretty bad.

—'cause it had to be me said, Come on Lane take a trip with me and Arin, gonna love the Fist—

Hell with that. Garick, this is a crime, but it'll be a lot bigger one if you don't bring every constab you've got to ride Santee down and finish him on sight. I've told you all I know. Along with the map I'm sending with this tape. Hope it's enough.

Spitt, don't try to call me because I'm gonna get very drunk.

Corian drank carefully at first, keeping the violence reined tight in the fist of his will, thinking in deliberate sentences, measuring them out with slow sips of gin. With the first few swallows he thought *got to help Arin, it's like he died, too, having to look at that place and read what happened, and I ought to be able to say something to Mady, but I can't handle it myself yet.*

He took another drink, felt it spread in a burning aura from his stomach and throat. He began to feel darkly cosmic.

We tell ourselves in sunlight and good times that there's a reason and a pattern to life, and we need to believe it so much we codify it into systems. But then death comes out of entropic dark and makes a lie of religion, shows us just how little a bag of subjective flesh and bone can understand of such an obscene enormity. Sing me parables of mortality, and try to make me believe it's good and necessary when death comes like a crude thief and steals and leaves a loss too agonizing for comprehension.

Then Corian drank more and thought more.

Fine words. Self-conscious, yes, overblown, but I'm beginning to have a feel for them, see them measured out on a piece of paper. But all they mean is, I can't think of her dead without wanting to kill someone, destroy something, and I'm sorrier for me than Arin or Mady. I wish just once I'd told her. But then, she always knew. They both did. It's better this way.

"THE HELL IT IS!" he roared, smashing the empty jug to the floor, realizing even as he did, the childish futility of the gesture, playing his Great Anguish for an audience of no one but himself. Corian lurched over to the cabinet, took out another pot of potato gin and stopped measuring his drinks or words. He guzzled and sobbed till he couldn't see the bottle or hold his head up, as he snarled aloud at his old enemy.

"You dirty, ugly bastard! You let me be born alive but you took my ma, you took Sayna'n the baby'n shit knows how many others I mighta saved 'cause you're always better at taking than I am at saving. And you couldn't get Jordy Hawks, so you took *her.* That make you proud? I'll get you f'good someday, you motherless goddam thief. I'll outlive you. I'll be as old as Marian Singer and save 'em all . . . I'll kill *you!*"

He'd crossed a line too well known and carefully avoided for years, drowning his mind in gin until the oldest, deepest anger ignited and flared, the anger of memory, of dragging his crutch through the iron towns where he grew up and seeing the flushed, hopeless faces of men who baked all day in the heat of the furnaces and soaked all night in turnip gin; smelling the sour sweat-and-food stink of the drab women, coveners long since robbed of Circle by poverty and the nearness of Mrikan money and the hot iron. Haunted by coven memories and faint feelings, borderline cases like himself, the music of coven instinct heard too faintly for dancing.

click

He should have rolled unconscious on the floor, but as he staggered up to heave the second empty jug away, something palpable turned on in Corian's mind like the sudden rush of blood to the head before sleep that blinks the eyes open with a start.

In the middle of his white quarters, Corian staggered, shutting his eyes against the unbearable light. He felt off balance, falling endlessly down a long, dark hole, yet always still at the top; he grew nauseous, but that passed and he was seized by a destructive rage so sudden and savage that, in his need to express it, he hurled the recorder against a wall, glaring at the mark it left as the pieces scattered on the floor.

Squares. White squares. Orderly, straight lines boxing him in, cages that imprisoned the giant he really was. Conspiring. Straight lines that should be bent, ached for bending, rending. Cramped. Too small. As he wobbled and gasped, his body seemed as much against him as the room, a tyrannical geometry whose angles, numbers, flesh warred against the shapeless, beautiful, terrible freedom that was captured by all the things that moved in straight lines and ought to be torn apart so he could remember, oh remember how it was for a while before the—

Colors—wild, primordial, jagged, hurting. The thing welling inside turned to energy in his throat, began too low for sound, but grew as he hunched forward, clutching out at the imprisoning rectangles and the square shapes that were walls, door, windows.

Yet even as he ripped himself free of it, there was something more than scream, but the darkness blotted out his mind, and the last sober molecule of his sleep-starved brain heard a different sound, something not altogether new, but unconsciousness wiped it away.

**GARICK TO MARIAN SINGER.
EFFECTIVE RECEIPT, URGENT REQUEST MAKE
FASTRAMP AVAILABLE TO CONSTAB/OTHERS
WHO WILL BOARD AT BALMER/FILSBERG FOR
WHITESTONE.**

By horse, boat and fastramp, they assembled at Old Hartford to search out and destroy Ben Santee. There were constab and volunteers from every circle in Uhia. There were Mosters from Yarmouth, Wellfleets and even Shortree Kriss. There were Mrikan bounty hunters to whom Santee was pure moneymeat with a kill-price that would set them after their own mothers. And there were men Shalane had touched personally, men like Jay Kriss from Charzen, and a young Karli named Janny whose knife Shalane purified after the hell that was Salvation.

Even Bowdeen, the black Wengen, would have left Sidele and Poke to manage his store, bar and crib girls, and immediately saddle his seldom-used horse. But Garick said no.

"You're too old, Bow. And you don't need the money."

The words froze in the air like icicles. Fat Poke, the bartender, stopped washing mugs.

"You don't want me, all right," Bowdeen said with soft emphasis, "but don't insult me. I rode with her at Dannyline."

"No insult meant, Bow, but it's still no."

The grizzled bartender, a lot paunchier than when he'd been a merk serving border duty at the Gate, leaned his belly against the counter. "Garick," Poke grunted, "you never had no respect for folks' feelings. I recollect a time when I give you a drink outta pity, 'cause you was hurt bad, and goddam if you didn't try to pay me for it." He swept Garick's mug off the bar and into the washtub. "Now *this* drink's on me, man, and I don't even wanna *see* your money!"

It eased the tension. Garick and Bowdeen had heard Poke's same complaint at least fifty times in the past ten years. Garick often drank free when Poke was at the bar.

They gathered at the east end of the Whitestone passage, some for money, some out of love, some just to finish the last of a dirty job. All knew Garick's name, but to many he was a remote legend seen now for the first time: a man six and a half feet tall with a leonine shock of graying chestnut hair, dressed in Mrikan clothes, but with a master's cord belt and thammay about his middle. He moved around the patch of cleared earth on which a rough map was etched. Still agile for his fifty-eight years, Garick was too slender for his huge frame. Eyes more watchful than stern; a man who seldom relaxed.

Garick pointed to the map with the tip of a sheddy sword. The more observant of his audience noted he rarely used one arm, even though it appeared perfectly healthy. Garick frankly preferred the prosthetic with which Rashevsky first replaced the arm incinerated at Dannyline. The new one, though grown from his own flesh, perturbed him with its unmarred, unscarred perfection.

He jabbed the sheddy at the dirt map.

"We'll lock him up this side of City. He can't get through or around it. Then we comb east and north through Wengen and the Fist. Don't worry about fresh horses, money or anything else, you'll have them, no matter how long it takes. There's lots of sand on the Fist. I don't care if we have to sift every last handful, but we're going to end this. Santee is the last. When you find him, leave him to the masters. They'll do it clean."

ARIN,

Son, I've been where you are now and it's a place beyond words. But there's so much of her in Mady, as there was so much of Jenna in you. Born again.

                                                                GARICK

"Ted."

Rashevsky looked over at his screen. The bloated, bloodshot image on it was pathetic and desperate.

"Help me," Corian croaked. "Sober me up. I gotta work."

Rashevsky sighed with irritation and pity. Someday he'd have to clone a liver for Corian. "How long this time?"

"Three days."

"Sleep?"

"Who sleeps?"

Rashevsky believed it. "You'd better. Sedate, quarter-ounce MV, shoot some B, go to bed."

"I gotta work." Corian clawed a hand through his disheveled hair.

"Inefficient. Go to bed."

Corian made a face between a scowl and a snarl. "You don't understand," he said impatiently. "It's Arin, he's sicker than me."

Rashevsky signed ?

"His dreams," Corian answered. "They wake him up. Look, I know what Arin's going through conscious, he should at least be able to sleep. She was part of him, Ted, that's not just a figure of speech, it's a physical fact." Corian's voice began to break. "And if I—if I don't help him now, I'm not, I've never been a doctor. I hate it, Ted, I *hate* it. Help me!"

Rashevsky nodded. By City measure, twenty-nine-year-old Corian was a brilliant embryo, but there was a new thing growing in him, and it was important and deserved to be assisted. Rashevsky regarded his infant colleague with far more understanding than

Corian needed as he held his aching forehead and brooded, ready to commit science, art or murder.

The little house in the park was still and hot as the day outside. Arin had all the electrical systems shut off except the air conditioning in Mady's empty room. When Corian labored in, he found the big Shando sprawled in a contour chair, unshaven and gritty with fatigue.

"Where's Mady, Arin?"

"With Marian."

Corian dropped onto a couch. "Yes, that's best. How's she taking it?"

"Numb," said Arin. "She won't even lep."

Corian dropped his medbag and rubbed his eyes.

"Cory, you look as bad as me."

"Just a hangover." He wondered how much his friend could read in him.

Arin's head moved in wan recognition. "You drink too much. Never learn."

"You're the patient. You said you can't sleep?"

"Not that so much. Dreams. They keep waking me up."

Which was unfortunate, Corian thought to himself. *Yes, I've studied sleep patterns, but there's too much that City doesn't know yet about the coven mind. The old data is only roughly applicable.* Like the time Arin's brother almost ran the Self-Gate because it never had been programmed for a mind quite like his. Then, even as Marian tried to prevent a recurrence of such an incident, along came Arin with still another new kind of coven brain, and he actually broke through the electronic barrier.

Nevertheless, Corian told Arin to talk about his disturbing dreams. He was familiar enough with Arin's normal innocuous dream patterns. Arin could barely remember most of them except the old Holder and Lishin nightmares, and they recurred less and less as time went by. Listening now, Corian postulated a possible unexpressed guilt over Shalane causing Arin so much torment and lack of sleep, maybe a general anxiety which might indicate a stronger emotion, but no, that was too facile. *Listen, don't judge.*

Sure enough, Arin described a dream unlike any of the patterns with which Corian was familiar. No real fantasy action at all, only colors: violent splashes and daubs, abstract bodies that changed jaggedly, and the hues and shapes grew progressively more insane and under it all, like a growing sound that wasn't really a sound—

"What?" Corian urged. "What's under it?"

"I don't know," Arin confessed. "But I wake suddenly, and when I fall back to sleep, it comes again and I wake again. Haven't had much rest."

Corian rubbed his forehead, prodded his gin-ravaged mind to work. "This undertone, can you describe it?"

Arin couldn't, only the feeling it brought. A desperate fear, a need to get away, protect himself. Then waking.

It could mean anything from repressed hysteria to severe exhaustion. Corian considered, then opted for the latter. Tomorrow he could think better himself. For now, Arin had to sleep like a stone. Corian went to the antiseptic white kitchen, remembering how alien Shalane always felt in it, and mixed C-concentrate with enough strong sedative to blow Arin out of the world for at least ten hours.

As he gave it to Arin, he noticed how the man smelled of his own rank sweat under the rumpled City worksuit.

"Take a good hot shower. It'll help the sedative." Corian shepherded the sagging Shando through the shower, into a clean robe and bed. Arin's eyes were already closing as he lay down.

"Thanks, Cory."

"Going to do the same myself," the other promised.

"Drink too much."

"Right. Call me when you wake."

"Drink way too much . . ."

"So hang me," Corian said with gentle affection at the door. "I'm a weak character."

Before administering the same formidable sedative to himself, Corian studied the notes he'd scribbled while Arin described the anomalous dreams.

Need to protect himself, get away.

A snatch of Wellfleet music echoed in his memory, a short indeterminate rag of melody. *Typical.* His mind was always a garbage can of unsorted trivia.

A desperate fear.

Of what?

The mournful little fragment of Fleeter music lulled him with its falling cadence as Corian sank gratefully into drugged sleep.

The solitary rider dashed through the sleepy town of Ponaug, night at his heels. On the far side of the village, Ritt took the left fork and pushed his horse hard for another dusty mile before reining in at the small farmstead he hadn't seen in over seven years. Angry sunset etched him stark against the darkling sky as he dismounted and walked his horse to the watering trough.

Upstairs in the nearby farmhouse, a boy of ten heard the horse and sat up in his sickbed. Tom's fever broke the night before, and now he was feeling better and more restless by the minute. He shielded his eyes against the dying glare and peeked out the window at the newcomer. The man looked vaguely familiar, but the child couldn't say why. Ritt was his uncle on his mother's side, but Tom only saw him once before, when he was not much more than three years old.

The boy's father—a stocky, grizzle-bearded Moster named Bare —emerged from the barn and started toward the stranger. But when he got close enough to see the man's face in the twilight, the farmer stopped dead.

Young Tom pressed his nose against the windowpane and wondered why his dad suddenly seemed so mad.

Staring at the scuffed brown patch of earth in front of his feet, Ritt gruffly asked, "Where's Jeanie?"

Bare ignored his question. "You know you ain't welcome. Dam'f I'll help you or that trash you ride with."

"I'm riding alone. Didn't come for help."

The farmer snorted his contempt. "Guess I heard Santee's been on the Fist awhile. Guess I heard what you done to Garick's kin."

Ritt winced as he remembered her screams when Ben began to cut her. He'd forked his horse and ridden out, done with it then and there, not looking back when Santee howled his name.

He put one hand to his forehead and tried to wipe away the memory. "Bare, I had no part in it. Made me so sick, I left Ben. Now I'm headin' north."

"Best make it *way* north, Ritt. Half of Uhia's on the way here to fry your ass."

"I know. Should've kept runnin', but I had to come warn you and Jeanie to watch out for Santee."

"He's Garick's problem, not ours."

"Oh, shit, man, for once will you *try* to think past your goddam sheep?" Ritt gave him a disgusted glance before lowering his eyes again. "Ben's growing crazier every day. He might come round here lookin' for me."

"Hope he does." Bare turned his head and spat. "Got a hound I'd like that bastard t' meet."

From his second-story vantage, Tom saw the man get back on his horse and ride away. The child was disappointed. He was bored from lying around all day in bed and wished something would happen.

Outside, darkness closed in on the little farm. It brought with it the first ghostly tendrils of fog from the East, from the sea.

GARICK TO MARIAN SINGER.
THANKS YOUR HELP ON FASTRAMP.
STRONGLY ADVISE PARTIAL GATE
REACTIVATION TO DETECT/ISOLATE ANY
INTRUDER. SANTEE MAY THINK CITY THE
ONLY PLACE WE WON'T LOOK.

The so-called Self-Gate, inoperant for ten years, was originally conceived as a defensive function of the synergizer at a time when political instability outside the City demanded it. The electronic barrier ringed the City's perimeter with a web of sensors able to determine the precise mental pattern of an intruder and bombard him with waves of negative energy that precisely complemented his electrochemical makeup—paranoid, schizoid, cycloid, etc.—until the intruder's brain activity was reduced to a single computer symbol: ∼.

The Gate was a tremendous drain on energy needed for vital research projects. These took a quantum leap when Marian Singer deactivated the barrier in the era of peace and cooperation that followed Dannyline.

Now Garick wanted a partial reactivation, enough to sense and find anyone prowling the edge of the City. Even without full, lethal power, compliance would entail a considerable allocation of energy as well as work-hours.

Characteristically, Marian reached her decision in seconds. She fed the problem to the synergizer, which reported immediately on current major projects, time and energy requirements and personnel involved in each. Scanning the synopsis, she made two rapid preliminary determinations. (A) Partial reactivation could be accomplished in the northern sector without critical neglect of priority power requirements. (B) No commitment seemed necessary for at least twelve hours.

Marian was grateful she had some time for another more immediate problem, a personal one she couldn't solve with her customary efficiency or detachment.

Mady.

Rashevsky was right. Mady was linked too tightly in her mind with Judith, and even though she'd finally admitted the irreconcilable differences on an intellectual level, her own ambivalent feelings toward Shalane's death complicated what ought to be a pure matter of policy.

That morning, Arin's precocious daughter slashed a smear of red crayon up and down the white walls of her room in the student dormitory. An hour later, a livid Jakov Levitt called up Marian. His fingers signaled the entire story in nine seconds: during a morning tutoring session, Mady flared from inattentive silence to shrieking rebellion, and when he tried to quiet her, Mady actually struck him.

Marian grew pale. Physical violence was absolutely forbidden in the City, it was the sole crime for which a citizen could be expelled. In all the long centuries, Marian could not remember such a thing ever happening before.

"Bring her to me," she curtly told Levitt.

There was an angry red spot on his cheek when he arrived with a sullen Mady in tow, but otherwise Levitt seemed less querulous than usual. He took Marian aside and spoke in shortmind: how it was his fault he hadn't ever properly evaluated the child's emotional state, how she was obviously in trauma over Shalane's death and, in his opinion, required careful therapy.

She noticed the slight hesitation in his fingers before he brought up therapy. Marian realized he must know her own precarious situation when it came to dealing with Mady. Nevertheless, she signed: "I'll speak to her. You're behind schedule." She was instantly sorry for the latter observation; the old bitterness flickered in his eyes at mention of his personal timetable. But he let it go and left the room.

Alone with Mady, Marian studied the child carefully. Lack of sleep, yes; that was obvious. Crouched against the wall, shocked and frightened at what she'd done, Mady looked like she wanted to run away. One leg was twisted over the other and she rubbed at her eyes, on the verge of tears.

Marian recognized the signs of emotional exhaustion, but hadn't dealt with a cranky child in centuries. Though she pitied the worn-out, disoriented little girl, she had to fight her impatience and irritation at time passing without result while the City's vital work hung in abeyance. She considered calling Mady's father, but remembered he was as helpless with grief as his daughter.

Mady whined about the way Levitt always treated her, how she hated the pedant. She spoke in fragments of sentences, partly in shortmind, partly in English that sometimes slurred into her parents' dialect.

Marian's mind raced over probabilities, alternatives, long- and short-term goals, mutually exclusive solutions. Garick's recent request concerning the Self-Gate triggered a memory, and a choice suddenly clicked into place.

Temporary external focus. Lever: compassion.

She signed for Mady to sit. The child dropped sideways into a chair, worming about, whimpering.

"Mady," she said, "be quiet now. I'm going to tell a secret you mustn't repeat, not even to your father."

The child raised her small head, sniffling, pathetic, yet—as always—intensely curious.

The Great Schism, Marian reminded Mady, was the period in the City's early history when nearly half the population ultimately decided to abandon the experiment and go elsewhere to live. Many issues sharply divided the citizens, but the critical one was whether to establish an electronic barrier that would shut off the City from the rest of the world. Jakov Levitt, opposition leader, damned the proposed defense system for several reasons, but his chief objection was ethical: the Self-Gate was repugnant because it would kill trespassers, and that was a violation of the City's cornerstone principle that human life is precious and must be preserved.

Marian shifted from shortmind to English, sensing that the child would derive a degree of comfort from the soothing cadence of a familiar voice. "It came to a vote. The measure carried, but the rift was irreparable. Jakov's faction entered voluntary exile. Only he remained behind. Do you want to know why?"

Mady nodded, interested in spite of her personal misery. Anyone who studied the schism and subsequent Myudan pilgrimage had to puzzle over Levitt's seemingly perverse role in those events.

"Here's the secret, Mady. You must never divulge it to anyone. Jakov's system can't properly assimilate metabolic-adjustment medication. It slows the aging process for him, but can't eliminate it.

That's why he looks middle-aged. Had he emigrated with his adherents, he'd be long dead by now. Here, at least, we've retarded his disease. Perhaps someday Dr. Rashevsky may discover how to cure
him. Meanwhile, Jakov must live with people whose philosophy, civil
policy and very appearance deeply agitate him."

She paused. No need to draw morals. The child realized the rev-
elation of Levitt's secret was an enormous breach of etiquette on
Marian's part. The fact had its impact.

"All right," Marian said gently, "the incident's closed. Return
to class and apologize."

Mady rose, but did not go.

"Yes?" the woman asked in shortmind. "Else?"

"P-please . . ." She stopped, looking as if she wanted to draw
closer, but was afraid to.

"Come closer," Marian told her. "Tell me what's wrong."

"I . . . I want you to explain like you used to. About my
dreams."

Something stirred in its old grave in Marian's heart. *Ted's right.
Helping Mady won't atone for Judith. But—*

"State."

Mady's small hand began to move, then paused, at a loss how
to describe her nightmares.

"What happens in your dreams?" Marian asked in shortmind.
"List components."

"Colors. Numbers. Shapes."

"What shapes?"

The little fingers flew. "No shape. Colors. Numbers. Digits repeated. Sound."

?

Again Mady's fingers hesitated. "Underneath," she whispered.
"Behind the numbers. A sound."

"What kind of sound?"

"I don't know."

"State."

"I don't know, I don't *know*." Mady raised her voice in anguish. "I'm scared to sleep and . . ." Emotion overcame her. Burst-
ing into tears, she stumbled to Marian and buried her small head
in the woman's lap. Only for an instant did Marian's habitual sense
of isolation prompt her to draw back. Forcing herself into exercis-
ing iron control over her own will, she clasped Mady in her arms

and gently rocked her. *Ted can be right for the next two hundred years, but so's this. It's a crossroads.*

Even as she held the child tight, she realized the City never was going to be quite the same again. What was that term the ancient philosopher employed? *Revaluation of values.* But there was no time to extrapolate tomorrow's trends, the only important thing now was Mady. *What words? Can't tell her what she is, three decades before she'll realize she's everything Judith wanted. Not the Girdle. Not Garick. Not even Singer. It's you, Mady, but I can't explain you yet to yourself: City mind, coven spirit.* And meanwhile, the ganglylegged bundle of grief needed comforting with simple truth fashioned with complex subtlety. Even shortmind was insufficient.

Sitting down, Marian lifted Mady into her lap and, cradling her head against her bosom, spoke softly to her. "Mady, what you feel starts when we're very little. Perhaps before birth. Part of mama's body. Even cut away from her, we're still tied. The bond's there; we think we're the center, and all good and bad things somehow come from us. If you're coven, it's even closer. Mama was always there in your mind, or you in hers, just a thought away whenever you needed to touch. Except you grew one way and mama went another. And that hurt, didn't it?"

The little head bobbed up and down on Marian's breast.

"Then mama went away and never came back. So we feel somehow that we sent her away."

"I was mean to her," Mady whimpered. "I said bad things."

"No, Mady. What you were was yourself." Marian paused. The child didn't realize how taxing prolonged speaking was to citizens. Language was so slow, *all* language. Marian envied coveners their lightning-swift sharing. But she put the irrelevant emotion aside and continued. "I think that's what your dreams are trying to say, that you're a distinct entity, Mady. It's life's most painful lesson. Some never learn it. I think it hurts you so much that even your dreams can't say it plain, but have to hide it behind colors and shapes. One night—"

"Sound," Mady murmured, starting to relax for the first time in long weeks. "It's like it's trying to talk."

"One night it will. You'll have a dream where you'll say you're sorry mama died. You'll cry. Afterwards, you won't feel half so much it was your fault. Because it wasn't, Mady, believe me."

Mady nodded, trusting her. The child's eyes misted over. She drowsed.

Marian held her close. All the complex strands of the great
City's interwoven purposes hung slack on the loom while the chief
weaver rocked a sleeping child and actually neglected to heed the
clock.

The communicator buzzed softly. Turning her chair slowly so as
not to waken Mady, Marian answered the call. It was Corian Trevanni.

He took in the picture of her and the child in her lap for a moment without speaking. Marian signed *?* but still he hesitated.

"State."

"Oh. Right. Just you look so fine holding her."

She brushed it aside, oddly embarrassed. "Matter?"

"Will state soon. *?* Problem with Mady *?*"

Marian had intended a sedative for Mady, an examination by
Rashevsky, perhaps further therapy. But looking at Corian, she realized he was instinctively a better internist. Rapidly she signed the
child's symptoms: lack of sleep, the disruptive weirdly abstract
dreams. Corian listened, head cocked to one side.

"Abstract?"

"Color/shape. Near-subliminal sound. Numbers."

Abruptly, he lapsed into English. "Marian, do you trust me?
Medically?"

Irritating time-wasting question. "Re coven, implicit. State."

His fingers shaped the request: EEG for Arin/Mady, all sleep
periods.

She nodded.

"Thanks. Suggest Ted for sedative. On my way out of City. Urgent. Request status your decision Garick's reactivation of Self-
Gate."

"Considered. Compliance in twelve hours."

To Marian's annoyance, Corian burst again into Wengen-ac-
cented English. "Negative, Marian, negative! Santee hit a farm near
Ponaug. That's a Moster village, check it on your readout maps.
Only an hour or two away from the nearest City boundary line.
Turn on the Gate *now*."

"Will consider," she signed.

"Consider, hell!" he shouted. "If Santee slips through the City
and west, he could be gone forever."

"How are you relevant to that? You're a doctor, not constabulary."

His head drooped and she could only see his mop of black hair on her screen. "I want Santee," he said quietly. "I want to nail him good. Don't tell Arin about this, he's sick enough and Mady needs him. But no one needs me, so I'm going. Do what you have to with power priorities, but *turn on that motherless Gate.*"

Her screen went dark. Corian was gone.

Marian sat still, enjoying the child's small warmth and soft breathing against her chest. Out of habit, her mind began to work again, shortening her twelve-hour estimate to one or two. She'd need at least six citizens, divided in shifts of two each, to monitor the electronic web. Necessary because she wasn't going to restore the Gate to lethal force. Who could she spare? Clavell and Kemp, of course. A charmingly irresponsible duo who could use the discipline.

Decision made, she reached to the console board to punch a conference call. Randall must be advised, also Rashevsky. *Levitt? Perhaps—*

Mady writhed suddenly with a low wail that grew into an anguished cry of fear as she twisted in Marian's arms. The sound went from a slurred frightened mumble into sharp, clear speech.

"Uh . . . UH! 3 2 6 5 9 7 UH 2 3 6 3 . . . Mama . . . mama!"

Marian pressed her tight while she shivered, her eyes still unseeing, still turned in on the dream and the unbearable shapes she fled from, but maybe this time she'd be able to deal with it.

Marian acted with gratifying despatch. When Corian's battery-driven cart rolled off the ramp at Old Hartford, the constabulary guard told him the Gate would be sensor-operational within the hour.

Corian felt a grim satisfaction as he turned east into the Passage road. North, south and west now were shut off to Santee. Not that the outlaw was operating with any sane kind of plan. To raid for food and horses at least made some logistical sense, but to turn back toward City and commit the kind of slaughter Jay Kriss said happened at Ponaug was an act of red madness.

When Jay phoned Corian about it, his voice was thick with horror and bafflement. "Indescribable," he choked.

Out of his own frustration, Corian snapped, "Nothing's indescribable."

"Then come look yourself."

"Dammit, I will."

"Fine!" Jay shot back. "I'll be there. It'll all be there. Nothing's going to move."

As the cart bounced at top speed along the dusty, heat-shimmering road, Corian's thoughts jolted and rattled about his mind. Jay had sounded as bad as he felt himself. There was a closeness between Jay and Shalane that went back to the old days, you could always hear the tenderness when they spoke of one another. *Enough of that.* EEGs. They'd be useful. Maybe not much, and he didn't really know how, except there was a disturbing similarity in the dreams of Mady and Arin. Perhaps father and daughter were lep/sharing unconsciously in their sleep. *Damn, so much I don't know about coven minds.* At least EEGs were tangible.

Corian gagged as a cloud of grit went down his windpipe.

"Shit!"

The cart hummed through the tiny center of Ponaug, all the "town" a farming community needed: a stable and the bar-and-store typical of most City-bordering settlements. Jay had called him a mile or two up the line where Garick's telephone poles were marching inexorably down the Passage road toward the Fist, drawing Uhia too tight-close for men like Santee.

He cruised past the town center to a fork Jay mentioned and followed it to the left. He raised sight of the first farm, rode by it. A quarter mile ahead where a farm trail intersected the road he was on, two riders wheeled suddenly and galloped toward him along the road edge, avoiding its center. One waved him to a halt; when Corian ignored him, the man wheeled his horse directly in front of the cart. Corian skidded to a cloudy stop.

"Hey, I'm Corian from City. I gotta get up there."

They were Suffec constab, a boy and girl no more than fifteen. For all their youth, they had the mean, peculiarly feral look of the back-bayou Suffec.

"You walk," one ordered tersely. "Stay clear the road."

"Man, that's half a mile—" Corian stopped. The other rider edged in on his off side, her sheddy drawn. Corian spread his hands in philosophic defeat. "Walk."

No sense trying to reason with Suffec, it couldn't be done. Most had a vocabulary of three hundred words and only needed half of that. As Corian pulled the cart off the road, another rider galloped across country toward him. It was a white-haired man who sat the huge stallion as if he needed no bridle to control him. Horse and man took a board fence in one effortless jump and reined in at the road's edge.

"Hey, Cory."

The doctor recognized him with relief. "Moss, I'm glad to see you. How come I can't drive up to the place?"

"Come up behind, I'll ride you."

When Corian was set behind Moss, he glanced back at the Suffec, but he and his cart no longer existed for them. They paced each side of the road, concentrating on the dust, moving back the way they came.

"Looking for tracks," said Moss. "Got more searching the other side of the farm. Can't find nothing, but them Suffec, they start something, they don't quit."

He touched his heels to the stallion's flank and trotted towards the farm half a mile away. Corian wondered what he could say to Shalane's father and decided on the old Circle blessing.

"She's born again, Moss."

"To the Karli," Moss confirmed, then let it drop.

Corian slipped down from the horse, slapped Moss on the leg and strode across the farmyard with his off-balance, lunging gait. The riders assembled there, men and women, were a cross-section of all Uhia: Shando, Karli, Wengen close-ins, Moster friends of the slaughtered family already digging graves in a field nearby. Corian recognized Fleeters in the crowd and even Shortrees. The silence was striking for so many people—near fifty of them, he guessed—but he knew most of their communication was lep. He felt their suppressed fury like humidity. In the fallow field east of the barn, another detail of Suffec moved about on foot studying the ground. More of them squatted by the barn door, the wolfish, inbred set of their expressions almost comically suffused with an odd bafflement like dogs who'd buried bones and then, for the first time, forgotten where.

Corian grasped the hand offered by the handsome, bearded man in deerskin. "Hello, Jay."

"God bless, Cory. You just missed Garick. He rode out north with some Shando in case Santee headed toward City."

"Garick here?" Corian's mouth curled with the wry, ancient Wengen joke. "So who's minding the store?"

"Spitt, I guess."

Corian shrugged. "Why not? Genius is fine, but now and then the world needs a good clerk."

Their smiles faded as the reality of the day pressed in on them. "It's all here," Jay said. "If you want to see. The constab've pretty well pieced together how it happened."

"Show me." Corian bobbed along at the taller man's side as Jay tersely outlined the occurrence. As at Yarmouth, Santee showed unusual slyness in covering his tracks, but then he'd been escaping Garick's nets for a long time. The constab could find only faint traces of a trail east of the farm and always on the hardest, rockiest ground. They pinpointed the trail of a single rider approaching the house at dark, but Santee's other men presumably waited close behind.

"Maybe they've split up," Corian suggested. "How many were there?"

"They tracked four out of Karli and caught one of those, fat man name of Gosset who got ended just after Sinjin. So there's Santee and two others."

Until the single rider crossed the east field, the sparse trail could have been one horse or three in a tight line, so carefully was the ground chosen. The track did not approach the house directly, but meandered back and forth. "Probably looking for hard ground," Jay explained, "though there wasn't any, so he left the horse here." He leaned over an unpainted board fence dividing the field from the barnyard, and pointed to horse droppings. "Over twelve hours old, Suffec say. Around midnight last night. Maybe a little earlier."

With Corian following, Jay moved toward the springhouse, gently booting aside the gaggle of hens that pecked around for loose kernels of feed, supremely unconcerned with the tragedy beyond them.

It was a springhouse in name only. The small creek over which it was built had long since gone dry and the interior was ice-cold with new City refrigeration, the hams and sides of beef hung in rows, kept at a precise temperature for indefinite storage with variable-degree compartments for produce and poultry.

"Came in here for food," Jay said, "but didn't take much. Neighbor out there in the field said he sold the beef and hams to Bare last week. Bare, that was the farmer's name. His wife was called Jeanie. Hardly a thing missing from here. Maybe an egg and some cooked chicken from a cooler drawer."

Corian cocked his head. "That's a close guess."

"Suffec don't miss much. Found some eggshell and chicken shreds on the floor." Jay led Corian out of the springhouse and snapped the metal bolt on the door. "The ground's packed hard between here and the barn, but they picked up a track or two. See? Here. And here."

The two barely discernible marks in the hard barnyard earth looked like mere toe impressions. Corian noted the long distance between them.

"All right, Cory, over here." Jay stopped outside the closed barn door. Two Suffec sprawled to either side looked up at him inscrutably. In the heat, Corian could smell their unwashed bodies. "The dog must have heard sounds outside," said Jay, "and the howl-

ing wakened Bare and his wife and . . ." He broke off with a vague
gesture. "You can go in, Cory. I've seen it."

"Bad?"

Jay pulled the door open, but said nothing else. Corian's nose
immediately detected the faint odor of early decomposition. The interior was a shadowed contrast to the brilliant sunlight; it was airless
and stifling. In their stalls, two mares snorted and stamped restlessly,
made nervous by the smell of death. Corian appraised the horses before turning to the covered things on the scarlet straw. Good, clean-
limbed animals, neither more than two years old. *Odd.*

The stench of decay overrode the barn smells of straw, dust,
hay and rosemary. Corian got to work, starting with the dog, which
no one had bothered to cover. Bare must've run a few sheep; this
was the kind of animal bred to herd them, a huge cross-strain of two
or three of the largest breeds still domesticated. Corian guessed its
weight over a hundred pounds; not a mofo to mess with. Those jaws
could snap a forearm like tinder. But the animal, now no more than
a shapeless mass of blood and coarse gray-brown hair, never got a
chance. Its upper and lower jaws, both filled with powerful teeth, lay
open at impossible angles to the rest of the battered skull. Literally
forced apart till they ripped back to the ears. There was a huge cavity over the broad rib cage. Corian felt at it gingerly. It gave, sicken-
ingly soft.

He tried to reconstruct the logic. The dog must have come after
the intruder who was quick enough to grab the savage jaws and prize
them open. Then he slammed the beast down on its side and stove in
the ribs with one brutal blow of a fist. The fractured ribs punctured a
lung; hence the blood in its mouth.

The dog must have barked, then screamed while it had time. By
now, Bare and his wife had to be awake and striding towards the
barn while the horses snorted and kicked at their stalls, and then the
farmer loomed at the door.

Corian moved to the two blanket-covered mounds in the center
of the straw-littered floor. He pulled the concealing cloth away from
the first.

Hanging on the door sill, Corian swung his head and shoulders
out into the fresh air, breathing deep. Close by, Jay silently watched
him as Corian took several deep gulps of air. He was pale.

"Finished, Cory?"

"No, I—no. Had to get away from it for a second. The dog was bad enough, but—"

Jay looked off across the field where four Moster men dug with sure, unhurried movements. He exchanged a glance with Corian, a knowledge that needed no words. Both of them hated violence and wasteful death; both of them knew too much of it all their lives. But even at Dannyline and before, when bodies were mutilated by the merks for profit, things like this were not done. Santee's insanity was beyond description.

Jay indicated the diggers. "They'll want to bury them soon."

"I won't be long."

Back in the airless heat of the barn, Corian again uncovered the two bodies. Not squeamishness, but the lunatic extent of the butchery made him wince. He thought of Jordy Hawks' wounds, tried to shove it from his mind, but couldn't. *Stop wasting time and face the truth. Shalane died this way. Now behave like a doctor.*

He checked Bare's muscular limbs. They felt supple. Rigor mortis came and went quickly in the summer heat. Decomposition already was palpable. There was a large bruise on the jaw; under it, the bone was broken. He was totally eviscerated, the abdominal cavity torn open in one upsweeping slash from left hip to lower right rib: the killer was right-handed. The fact hovered disconnected in Corian's mind before he dismissed it for another observation. Bare's wound was forced open by hand, and the rest was carnage. Heart, intestines and other vital organs had been hauled out like the stuffing of a rag doll despoiled by a destructive child. Corian was glad to pull the blanket back over the corpse.

By comparison, the woman suffered very little. Her severed head lay beside the shoulder of her lean, unmarked body. Corian scrutinized the neatness of the cut. It was almost surgically clean. One swipe sliced through skin, flesh, jugular, esophagus, ganglia, cartilage and spinal cord. A sheddy could manage it, provided it was sharp enough and driven with sufficiently concentrated force. Left to right this time, back-handed, the whole arm, shoulder and weight behind it.

The head came off clean, no other mark on it. The eyes were wide open and held a peculiar lack of expression, but then dead muscles tend to relax and lose whatever emotion raged through the victim at the moment of death.

Jay called in. "Cory, they're ready to bury them now."

Corian stepped out into the light, bemused, fumbling in a

pocket for pad and pen. "Nathan," he mumbled, writing slowly. Then he paused. "What, Jay?"

"I said there's another one in the house. A boy."

The same maniacal fury that killed Bare and Jeanie spent itself on the farmhouse. From the battered-in door through the main room and on upstairs to the boy's small chamber, Corian followed a swath of furious destruction. Broken dishes. Overturned table, splintered chairs. The boy's door was hit so hard it hung at an angle, one hinge torn halfway loose.

The child still sat upright in bed, a sturdy, sunburned youth of nine or ten, mouth as slack as his mother's, eyes open wide. There was no mark on him.

Corian realized the boy must have died of fright. Shock, or maybe a defective heart that gave out when the child heard the screams, the smashing progress through the yard and downstairs, the shattering of the door to his own room.

Near the bed was a wide-open window. *He should've gone through it, and never the hell mind about the drop.*

Corian stared at the dead child in the fly-crawling bed for a long time before pulling the sheet up over him.

He stepped back into the yard, squinting in the sun. The crowd was starting to thin out. Riders were busy cinching their saddles, watering their mounts, getting ready to move, but the Suffec still hovered about with that worried-hound look. Corian walked to the well where Jay Kriss was taking a drink. When Jay saw him, he offered the dipper to the physician.

Corian absently accepted it, drank, then poured cool water over his sweaty head.

Jay mused, "Know what bothers me about this?"

"Everything about it bothers me."

"First, why's Santee running back west when his only chance is east?"

"By now, Jay, his actions defy rational analysis."

"Second, he kills a whole family, tears the place apart, but hardly takes a thing."

"He's not interested in taking any more, Jay. Just killing."

"But why Mosters? They're not deepwoods. And that reminds me, how about them?" He pointed to the sour-faced Suffec. "Those constab can track fish through muddy water, but Santee's trail comes here and just stops."

Corian nodded, no longer paying much attention, lost in his own tangled snarl of thought. Jay persisted in worrying at unanswerable questions, but he couldn't help himself, he was a Kriss.

Then something Jay said brought Cory up short.

"*What?*"

"I said Moss caught a leaked thought between two of the Fleeters over there." Jay indicated the field where the three wrapped bodies were just being lowered into the earth. "Moss asked me, but I said I never heard of the word. Why, Cory? You know what's a 'wintermind'?"

Diane studied her students for eight years before devising special intelligence tests for coveners. By all known standards, she planned them correctly and administered them properly, yet the overall IQ surveys stubbornly refused to correlate with the high aptitudes she knew most of her pupils had.

Frustrated, she called Corian the day before, but the one time she really needed his advice, he was off rummaging the hinterland for some irrelevant outlaw. She left a message for him to come as soon as he got back.

Her bell rang. It was Corian. She pushed the door button, braced herself to quash his usual spate of flirtatiousness. But he just wandered in, silent, preoccupied and oblivious. Incongruous behavior for a man who normally exploded into a room like a meteorite.

"What, Raddy?" No more than that. Astonishing.

She signed: "IQ tests don't show projected scores."

"Oh." He gave her a vague look. "Told you not to set 'em up that way."

She recognized the flicker of an urge to vindicate herself, but thrust the tedious atavism aside. "Method fallacy?"

"Uh-huh. They're too verbal, Raddy."

Diane dropped into a contour chair and spoke aloud. "But, Cory, I administered them verbally."

"Doesn't matter. Still too verbal. I scored like a moron till I learned how to read. How'd Arin and Bern score?"

"High."

"Sure. They've both been thinking in words for years."

"Intelligence is intelligence," she argued, impatient with his foggy lack of concern. It was obvious that little of his attention bore on her problem. She returned to shortmind. "Thought=concept."

"Yes and no, Raddy. You've never shared the way coveners do."

"Produce practical answer."

"Just like that?" Corian responded from a great distance. "Give me a day to think about it." He drifted to Diane's painting of the mountain with its disconcerting red slash. She watched curiously as he studied the canvas.

"What's wrong with you?" she asked aloud, since his back was turned. "Normally you're as remote as a toothache."

He didn't appear to have heard. "Whole new set of parameters."

"Fine. Procedure?"

"Don't crowd me, Raddy," he said, turning away from the painting. "Just as an interim measure, you could ask Arin or Bern to give the existing tests."

Diane considered the possibility. It might work. A bridge between verbal and non-verbal. She signed: "How long to indoctrinate them?"

"Two weeks. Bern first. Arin's got troubles just now."

She nodded. "Else?"

His unfocused gaze rested on Diane's dusty, long-unused camera lying on a storage table. "Pictures," he muttered. Then his casual slouch suddenly snapped straight with purpose. He fumbled in his pocket for a scrap of paper, glanced at it. "I was going to look at pictures."

"What *are* you talking about?"

"Raddy," Corian said, shaking his head, "I know I'm not making any sense. Not to you, not much to me, either. I'm shaking an apple tree and pears are falling down. See you later."

Before she could protest, he was gone.

He found the photographs in his cluttered quarters under a stack of music tapes. He'd taken them several years earlier on the visit to the Fist when he delivered Nat Brewster's son. While the proud father invited him to empty a few jugs in celebration, Corian took pictures with Diane's borrowed camera.

Yes.

There was Nathan settled back in the best chair at Brewster's Fancy, his sea-weathered visage suffused with his first heady taste of parenthood. Caught in a moment of contentment, the clay pipe in his right hand, one calloused finger of the left tamping dried bearberry tobacco into the blackened bowl.

Corian stared at the photo, then at another of the fisherman with the pipe still in his hand while the other raised a mug to his newborn son, the boy who would succumb to the erythro-fetalis condition that afflicted many Fleeter infants.

> *Where it cries in the dark like a losted child,*
> *A baby that y' better not find . . .*

Fleeter music = swamp fever = ?

Corian stared and stared at the photo while pears continued to fall from the apple tree.

All sectors negative. Supremely bored, Peter Clavell punched up the record entry with two fingers.

1:25– ~.

On his screen he saw his shift partner, Austin Kemp, sign: "Dreary."

"Dull," Clavell responded with one hand.

"Degrading."

Clavell topped him in the alliterative game: "Dirty."

"Dogged. Disgusting. Dilatory."

Clavell nodded, but noted: "Duty."

Sitting far north at Old Hartford, Kemp said, "Delirious delight." South, Clavell yawned and mumbled into his headset, "Stand by new sweep."

They both considered the Gate detail an egregious waste of their potential and time. In that order. Which partly accounted for Marian's immediate choice of the pair for the assignment. They had their priorities confused and she meant to make them realize it. Someday both would be excellent electronic researchers. Together they designed Garick's new phone equipment. But each had his counterproductive streak, and Marian felt that since they were both senior to Diane Radclif, who seemed to be settling well into her work, it was about time they began to evince signs of doing the same.

Austin Kemp possessed an arrogant pride in his own talents, a sense of self-importance that led him to hop from one research project to another without any real focus or insight. Inefficient. Without hesitation, Marian punched his name at the top of the Gate duty roster.

Peter Clavell was a bit more mature, though hardly fired with motivation. He was too young to have any personal knowledge of death, having been born long after the first establishment of the Gate. He and Kemp and perhaps even Diane seemed convinced that they alone would escape their statistically inevitable accidents and live forever, and in that case, how could a little time-wasting *really* hurt? Clavell had Diane's flair for the composition and play of forms, but where it expressed itself in paintings and photographic art with Diane, his talent ran to the hyperbole of cartooning. Deft at carica-ture, Clavell completely forgot in a recent synergizer conference with Marian that she had a clear view of his latest computer drawing affixed to the wall behind his console chair: a close likeness of Marian lying supine with a stopwatch in her hand while, scythe for-gotten and beard flying in goatish abandon, Father Time redis-covered his youth between her wide-spread, willing thighs.

Privately his irreverence amused Marian. But programming pic-tures on the synergizer stole City-allocated power and could not be countenanced. Perhaps he'd revaluate some of his values while spending a few unrecapturable hours monitoring the Gate.

Clavell and Kemp began another sweep of the five latitudinal sectors that Marian chose for sensor-reactivation. Sector 1 began at Filsberg checkpoint. Sector 5 ended at the City's northern extremity, just beyond the Old Boston limit. The five areas together comprised a little more than half of the City's 500-mile length.

Scanning one sector at a time wasted power, so they worked from opposite ends 1–2, 5–4, overlapping in Sector 3, then 4–5, 2–1 to complete the sweep. The readout screens flashed a green Gate gridding beneath a blue overlay representing the subject sector con-tour, with red dots for the various checkpoints: Filsberg, Whitestone, Old Hartford, Old Boston, and the smaller guard and decon stations in between. Each console had a red button marked NP; neither man could unlock its lethal negative probe without the other. A safety measure, guarding against an accidental slip of a finger; once nega-tive probe was engaged, the Gate's full, deadly power became opera-tive, beamable to whichever designated coordinates the sensors pin-pointed.

Clavell and Kemp worked in darkened rooms to conserve power and also for comfort, since the circuitry raised the temperature considerably in their scanning stations. Though they partly com-municated via shortmind over their viewscreens, the readouts claimed most of their attention and, as a result, much of their mike-chatter lapsed into English or mere punchup symbols.

Clavell signed: commence Sector 1.

Commence 5.

On the screen, two white horizontal lines began moving towards each other.

Negative 1.

Negative 5.

"Negative 2," Clavell said.

"Negative 4," Kemp replied.

Clavell watched the two lines fuse, cross and halt. "Negative 3."

"Confirm."

"Continue. Negative 4."

"Negative 2."

Clavell: "Negative 5."

Kemp: "Negative 1."

"Recording."

1:34– ~.

"Depressing," Kemp grumbled.

"Dastardly."

"Can't understand why Marian picked us. She could have assigned one of the infants. What brains does it take to punch buttons and stare at lines?"

Clavell shrugged philosophically. "Like the mudminds say . . . *dunesk*. Maybe she saw my stopwatch caricature."

"Teach you to compudoodle. But what about me?"

Clavell thought he had a pretty good idea why Marian picked his shift partner. The light of Kemp's genius ought to be gratefully discovered by those who groped in ignorance, rather than be proclaimed by the lamp itself.

"Commence new sweep."

Clavell nodded. Again the white beams inched toward one another. "Negative 1."

Negative 5.

Negative 2.

Kemp: "Negative–hold. Got a blip." He made a quick fine-tune adjustment, resolving the signal from amber fuzz to a sharp dot on his own screen.

"Affirm."

With a concrete task to do, Kemp's slim hands moved like a musician's over the console, lighting the auxiliary screen, keying memory banks, eyes riveted to the readout forming in clear green symbols as sensors scanned the intruder's mind.

$$22279477/0919-76482$$

V

"Bread and butter," Kemp yawned, bored. In their arch slang, developed during their first monitoring shift, "bread and butter" indicated a mental pattern so normal it was soporific. This one exhibited a wholly containable problem with ego integration and a slight tendency toward cyclic depression. "Bread and butter" was at least a step up from "mudmind," a pattern so unaccented, they wondered how the owner was able to get dressed without help.

Studying the "bread and butter" symbol, Clavell said, "Probably a checkpoint guard. Sic 'im, Kemp."

His partner flicked a switch. "Attention. Attention. You are being monitored on our sensors. There's a checkpoint near you. Please call 611 for voice-ident."

Within five minutes, the phone rang next to Kemp. He spoke into it. "Sensor probe. Name?"

"Ma-Mason." The guard didn't sound young. He was panting from his quick sprint to the checkpoint.

"Stand by." Kemp punched up M's from the memory bank, found the name, keyed another bank. "Please repeat name, then count from one to five."

"Uh . . . Mason. One two three four five."

"Stand by." Quickly Kemp overlaid the voice pattern with the projected bank pattern. They matched.

"They're digging us a new latrine," Mason gratuitously explained. "Old one's full. Came out into the field."

"Acknowledge," Kemp responded with ironic courtesy. "If you're quite finished, clear the zone."

The blip vanished.

So it went. At 2:19, a mudmind guard blundered into Sector 1 at Filsberg. At 2:47, there was a flurry of interest near the same point: two fairly complex bread and butters, a boy and girl who giggled and stammered that they'd just come out for a walk.

"Good night, Rosalind. Orlando, farewell," Clavell saluted them gallantly. "To thy sylvan pleasures, go—but a little to the west, please."

Their blip vanished from Clavell's life and Kemp characterized them with the beginning of a new round of alliterative banter.

"Nincompoops."

"Nebulous," Clavell replied.

"Nonentities."

"Nebbishes."

?

Clavell: "Early Wengen. Look it up."

Kemp would not be vanquished. "Niddering."

?

"Late Anglo-Saxon. Look it up."

"I think you win."

"Nay," quoth Kemp, "an thou'lt deviously digress, I'll delve as diligently as *du*."

"Heady, Hedda. Shall we sweep?"

"Commence."

"Negative 1," said Clavell, as the lines once more began to converge.

"Negative 5."

"Negative 2."

"Negative—wait."

?

"Had something," Kemp muttered. "Gone now."

?

"Sector 4, Plot A. There, see him?"

"Copy. Right in your neighborhood."

The amber blip was large and clear, needing no resolution. Kemp squinted at it, his eyes already strained from three hours of peering at electronic colors. The large dot pulsed slightly, its very presence defiant and vital, but even as he moved to engage the pattern banks, the blip vanished again.

They waited. Nothing. They conducted another complete double-sweep. Nothing.

3:04— ~. SPORADIC BLIP SECTOR 4, DISCONTINUED, UNIDENT.

The green and blue hues cast from the screen lit Kemp's sharp features eerily. He watched the point where the blip vanished. The thing bothered him. Too big, too strong. His kinetic instincts registered a hairline distinction between something actually wrong and something uniquely un-right. Clearing his throat, he spoke into the headset. "Stand by, Pete. Running a line check."

"Malfunction?"

"Shh. Running." It took Kemp a few practiced seconds to scan all operating circuits for any possible problem; an easy task, since the synergizer was totally self-analytic. The screen glowed its reply. 2975. Negative. All circuits operational at optimum.

Kemp engaged the auxiliary screen and the memory banks; then, as an afterthought, keyed in the printout. The paper began to unroll.

At 3:07, the blip reappeared, pulsed, hovered, disappeared again.

"Mudmind's playing with us," Clavell frowned.

"But I recorded. Stand by." Kemp pinpointed the intruder somewhere northeast of Old Hartford, between him and the nearest decon station. The analysis leaped onto the auxiliary screen.

$$\frac{6427}{I\text{--}II} \cdot \frac{09707}{\ldots\ldots} \longleftarrow$$

Incomplete. Also: *impossible.*

"That's no mudmind," Kemp murmured. Even as he spoke, the amber blip again lit up. He jabbed a button. In the zone where the intruder was, powerful speakers hissed. "Attention. Attention. You're being tracked on our sensors. There's a phone near you. Call 611 and—"

He faltered into silence as the matchup sprayed across the auxiliary screen in green symbols that fluctuated as if the synergizer couldn't decide.

"—611 and voice-ident." He glanced at Clavell's image. "See that pattern? Can't be!"

"Circuitry check?"

"Affirm, neg/mal."

Clavell gaped at the symbols fluttering back and forth between two alternatives with inconstant dips into yet a third while Kemp urgently repeated his request. And then, yet again the blip vanished. Kemp patched the open phone into his own speakers and Clavell's. They waited. The paper rustled from the printout, curling on the floor.

One minute. Two. Three stretching to five.

"Better record," Kemp said finally. "What should we call that crazy matchup?"

"Checking." Clavell consulted his matchup codebook while Kemp reran the blip tape.

The pattern fluttered and changed. Kemp tried to follow. "Para/schiz. Failure to override . . . *damn!*" He reran it again, hoping to catch the fleeting fragment. "There! Superego can't override. Unfactored variants."

Clavell looked up. "No compensation. It's a lunatic."

Kemp shook his head. "No, not exactly."

"Did you read compensation?"

"No."

"Then it's a mental basket case. Ought to be howling on the ground."

"*Not,* Pete. Confirm aberration, but . . ."

?

"Unsure, brain scan's not my specialty. But the condition seems to be its *own* compensation."

Clavell exhaled noisily. "Then there's only one way to record."

Kemp agreed.

3:09—231 SECTOR 4.

231=anomaly.

Clavell shuddered. It all reduced to one fact: somewhere near the Old Hartford checkpoint, a murderous lunatic, totally adjusted within madness *by* madness, was prowling the summer night. Abruptly, he reached a decision.

"Kemp, if he blips again, be ready to NP."

"Pete, should we? Without contacting Marian?"

"Can't spare time away from monitoring." Clavell jerked a thumb at his own chest. "My responsibility." It was a heavy one; ten years ago, a checkpoint guard, practically an infant, got caught in the zone when the full force of the Gate was turned back on. But Clavell still didn't want that lurking amber blip moving inside the City limits. Grimly, he turned the key under the red button two full revolutions to the right. "Unlocking."

At his console, Kemp repeated the process. "Unlocked."

"Full lock Sectors 1—5, excluding 4."

"Done."

Clavell nodded. Kemp keyed a button that flowered Sector 4 into four smaller plots of yellow, violet, orange and gray-white. There was the intruder, a pulsing blip—practically breathing, Kemp thought—just inside the yellow line. He pressed a bank of four white buttons just below the NP control.

"Plots B, C, D full lock."

Kemp turned the key under each two revolutions. "B, C, D locked full."

"All ready," Clavell rasped. "Sector 4, Plot A."

Kemp swallowed hard. *Whoever you are,* he thought desperately, *get out now!* Clavell once held Gate duty, but this was the first time for Kemp. He was beginning to sweat. *Now! Please!*

He pushed the loudspeaker button again. "Attention. Intruder near Old Hartford checkpoint. The Gate is armed. The Gate is armed. Voice-ident immediately, or we activate."

The blip vanished. Kemp found he'd forgotten to breathe. He let it out with tentative relief, stabbed the decon checkpoint intercom. "Checkpoint, do you read?"

Thirty seconds, then his phone rang. The decon guard grumped into his pickup: "Whassamatta? You people all over that talk-box tonight."

Kemp ignored the question. "You see or hear anyone near you?"

"Nah."

"Are you armed?"

"Right."

"Stay that way," Kemp advised. "There's an unidentified intruder in your area." An insight suddenly occurred to him. "May be two of them, close together. Consider them extremely dangerous."

"Ain't seen nothin'." The guard hung up.

"Think that's the answer?" Clavell asked over the synergizer screen.

"Could be. Covener talk is there's a psycho named Santee out there. May have a few men with him."

Clavell said nothing. The synergizer was used to dealing with more than one trespasser at a time. He doubted Kemp was right.

The two listened in silence. Seconds crawled by. Kemp's skin prickled. Then, suddenly crisp and urgent: "Pete, turn up your gain *quick.*"

Clavell thumbed a dial. His speakers hissed and crackled with the night sounds of summer: insects stridulating, a frog's guttural croak, the myriad rustle of nocturnal creatures. That was all.

"Keep listening," Kemp urged.

Clavell strained to hear. If there was a sound, it was buried under the aural mush pouring from his speakers. Maybe he *did* notice something, a faint unidentifiable murmur out of the night, but not part of it.

"Recording," Kemp reported. "Too weak, might not get anything."

The tape rolled. The alien murmur wavered back and forth on the threshold of audibility. Neither of them could be certain when it faded out altogether.

Silence. Kemp pressed rewind, stopped the tape, played it back. Summer night reviewed, and yes, just on the edge of hearing, the faint undulation that their nerves more than their ears told them was *wrong*.

Half an hour to go before relief. Kemp muttered, "They say Santee's a killer."

Clavell nodded, lost in his own somber thoughts. Better not to think about the madman out there. Do something positive.

"Austin . . . stand by to sweep."

Diane knew Corian was right about the intelligence factors. Arin alone went from illiteracy to writing letters in two months under the telepathic tutelage of Garick, whose IQ (measured during his brief stay in the City) was 155+. Arin lep-taught Bern in three months; it was like one computer passing data to another. Not quite that simple or direct, but close enough. A new test method clearly must be designed.

"You were right," she told Corian, seated across from her at Diane's littered work table. "Procedure?"

He smiled crookedly at her tacit self-criticism. He knew her mistake didn't bother her half so much as the expense of time invested in a wrong choice. "Raddy, how long ago did you assimilate the major works of social anthropology? A hundred years, two hundred? In two centuries, you've been right enough to be wrong for once without City falling apart."

"Irrelevant," she said softly, and yet it was decent of him to say it. No, she thought, decent is incorrect diction. It was—*idiom?*—yes: *sweet* of him to say it. A whim welled up to touch him; she swiftly pigeonholed it. "Procedure?" she insisted.

Corian idly riffled through an old sheaf of papers near his end of the table. "I see you haven't programmed these phys/psych profiles of the test groups yet."

"Relevant?"

"Maybe. How come?"

"Marian curtailed my synergizer time last year. It's restored, but I've got an input backlog."

He nodded. "Okay, Raddy. I've got a theory. First off, feed these profiles into the synergizer *stat*. Also the intelligence tests."

"Purpose?"

"Ask why the tests are inappropriate."

She shook her head. "Your oververbalization hypothesis accepted."

"Forget that. I'm going for something a whole lot bigger."

Diane made a lightning-swift choice. Rising, she took the first batch of profiles to the feed-tray.

They both stared, hypnotized, at the glowing symbols on the screen.

952: 2/06-0680 [3/0620]–*60%*——→031/0361.

Diane's tongue darted between her lips. She spoke in an awed whisper. "Cory. The coveners don't fit basic parameters of *homo sapiens*. They could be a whole new evolutionary subspecies."

He nodded. "Something a whole lot bigger."

The turn of a wheel larger than history itself.

With sudden urgency, Corian said, "Raddy, I want to see those EEGs."

—shapes without logic, shapes without reason, shapes springing up in Mady's path as she fled, an asymmetric forest of giant sick things like toadstools to escape—seven-sided, nine-sided, daubed by a mad painter in primal riots of yellow, blue and red that stabbed her eyes.

She ran desperately but slowly, so slowly, so hard, moving only inches for all the frightened churning of her legs. The sound pursued her as it always did *where it cries in the dark like a losted child* hurt, heartbroken, wrenching, but with no sorrow in it that could be salved *and it cries and it cries* and if it caught Mady, it would grow and grow and *its eyes are wild* and she'd see its unbearable shape, the ultimate terror-shape that could not be faced but must—

And it was gaining. Stalking swiftly after her through the abstract shapes. Close behind now, filling her mind, filling the world. No, it wouldn't get her, because she knew thinking would keep it at bay, any thought, numbers even, it couldn't get through that.

"1 *2* 4 8 16 *32* 11 *22* 17 19 21 23 25 27 29 *31* 30 31 *32*—"

"—and that's when she wakes." Corian bent over the electroencephalogram with its two inked lines of peaks, plateaus and valleys.

"Eight seconds," Diane observed. She looked from Mady's graph to Arin's. "From their descriptions, they're dreaming almost the same thing."

"Except for the way the cortex resolves it," Corian said. "They start the same—rems, an increase in theta wave."

Diane's eye followed, tracing the lower of the two lines. Theta wave, the ramp function in coveners called lep. The disturbance began quite palpably in theta; immediately, Mady's alpha wave, her cortex activity, rose in response.

"But alpha *is* the dream center," she pondered, "not a compensation."

"If we're talking about a new subspecies, Raddy, that may be irrelevant. Your coven sleep studies often show theta a significant part of dreams. How much?" He shrugged. "Without evidence, I'd say a lot more than *homo sapiens*. Look, see how Mady's alpha rises almost immediately after the incline in the theta."

The jagged peaks shot up and fell along the graph. In several places, they almost fused together, but the alpha always outstripped the theta, rising feverishly at the end of the dream-cycle, leaping into consciousness.

Diane shook her head. No wonder the child was a wreck, literally dreaming herself into exhaustion. She signed to Corian: "Deduce? Lepping with Arin in their sleep?"

"No evidence in studies," Corian responded. "Postulate shut-off mechanism. We never isolated one, but in a culture based on group-consciousness, it's the ego's safety valve."

"Induce?"

"*Dunesk*." He pointed to Arin's graph. "See how he resolves it."

—shapes that hurt his eyes, colors barely registered before they changed, warps and bulges as the contours mushroomed out of one another, now straight, now angled impossibly. Try to retreat, but *how* when they were the whole cosmos? No escape, only hiding from the rats, find a closet, find Lishin, but no closet, no Lishin, nobody over his shoulder pulling strings, in his mind like a worm, and now the thing was just behind him and *its claws run red* and he turned, screaming, and—

The dream changed.

Hot sun, a dusty street.

I remember this, Arin knew, relieved. *It's Lorl. It's over. End of that long nightmare.*

Lorl on that day ten years ago when Lane came from Dannyline and he from City and neither really expected to be alive this long. He walked out of Korbin's and sat down on the wooden sidewalk, released from bondage at last, and after all that he'd undergone, he'd forgotten that Lane might be there, and then he saw her coming across the dusty road toward him. *Hair chopped short, holes in her old hide shirt where the thrower burned through, but she walked proud and she was beautiful.*

The dream was sweet and sad. Shalane came and slipped down beside him, her dream-face young as it was then and yet the way he remembered her last in Wellfleet.

"You cut your hair," he said.

"It'll grow."

He held her, and they tried to share, but it was hard, and there were no tears left, but she cried in his arms, though Lane's eyes were dry and then along came Diane with her camera and took their picture while they glared suspiciously at the little black box. . . .

"—and then he wakes." Corian traced the alpha line with a finger. "When theta rises beyond a certain point, he just cuts it off. The last few seconds of alpha activity is totally different, a normal dream, maybe an old one."

Diane blinked, suddenly aware that she was rudely inattentive. Corian was bent forward toward her, his sunbrown hands on the graph paper on the table, and she'd been staring at the small scar on his chin, paler than the stubbly skin around it. She'd never before noticed it.

"Raddy?"

"Oh, I—excuse me."

?

"Nothing."

"You looked like—"

"*Nothing.*" She felt embarrassed; first inattentive, then too much verbal emphasis. "Just that scar on your chin. I never really saw it before."

"This?" He brushed his finger against the small mark. A long time ago, another world; he had to think for a moment. "In Korbin's, that bar in Lorl that Bowdeen bought. Just before Dannyline. Put the badmouth on some merk twice my size. He laid me out cold." Unconsciously, Corian lapsed into his singsong native accent. "Man, they say every crib girl in the place land on that mofo. Bust his motherless head so bad, he had to think in sections." He grinned reminiscently. "Forgot all about that."

Standing close to him, Diane thought it was a good chin, even with the scar. Another hundred years of education, and Corian might even be attractive, *and so what?* she asked herself sharply, silently snapping back to relevance.

Corian was staring with jealous hunger at the console. He wasn't City, the synergizer's immeasurable capacity was rarely at his disposal. "Time on this mother," he murmured. "That's what I need."

"Purpose?"

"Need to run a few empiricals on this subspecies thing."

She shook her head. "Insufficient technique. No time allocation. Power priorities."

"Sooner or later," he pleaded, "Marian's got to let me try."

"Not with the Gate drawing so much power now. Irrelevant."

He threw up his hands. That again, the ultimate stonewall City answer. "*M'shugah!* Mady's not relevant? Arin's not? Look at those EEGs! Don't you care?"

She signed: "Concern irrelevant."

"Damn it, Raddy, it *is!* Ten minutes."

"No."

Corian sensed the uncertainty in the way she shook her head. Mady was a good shot, Diane cared about the child.

"Five minutes. You helping. Only a few rough answers."

"Can't expect answers. Just—"

"Raddy, no lectures! Five minutes!"

Diane hesitated, darting a glance at the digital clock. She expected a routine call from Marian any time now, and certainly she must report the cataclysmic new possibility re coven phys/psych profile, but she'd lost so much syn/time because of Marian—

"All right," she signed, wanting to see for herself what the synergizer did with the problem. "Five minutes by the clock. Parameters ready?"

He nodded.

"Punch up."

Corian kissed her impulsively. "Raddy, I could love you."

"Four minutes, fifty-five. Learn about time, child! *Punch!*"

He sprang at the console, activating simultaneous readout/

printout: Ready all coven parameters, selective studies. Breakdown subspecies hypothesis.

47. The synergizer was ready with the exception of minor Gate data relegated to an auxiliary bank, though it ran a memo for Corian, in case he wanted that, too. But he had no time for digression, even though the 231 included in the footnotish readout momentarily piqued his curiosity. His fingers darted over the keyboard, occasionally hesitating while Diane gave him procedural advice.

"How do you tell it to factor?"

She reached over his shoulder and punched: 5974. "What?"

"Phys/psych profiles," he replied. "Test results. Sexual determinants. Mean longevity."

It took her longer to enter it than for the machine to respond: 47.

Corian had it by now. He pressed 5974 and a code to factor cerebral code by mass.

2947(90)—*83%*. 1369—*11%*. 4-642—6%.

Diane stopped watching the clock and concentrated on the screen. Eleven per cent limbic was an interesting figure in brain mass. The seat of deep emotion and aggressive potential so heightened in a determinedly nonaggressive culture like Circle. No wonder they won at Dannyline against superior military strength.

"Interesting, Cory. Hurry!"

His fingers danced: Factor from selective studies, % of children born with effective lep potential.

93%.

Factor, ibid., % born without basic primate survival fears of dark, falling.

98%: 031/0361.∴.2929105.

"That's not reliable," Diane said. "Sample too small."

"Shush! *My* time!"

She smiled. He had possibilities.

Factor, ibid., observed % born without normal vestigial organs.

60457: *60%*.

Diane was drawn by the implications. "Looks good, but—"

The synergizer finished it for her, again qualifying the high percentile with the warning that samples were small and inconclusive.

He punched angrily. He'd taken the samples himself during long years as a doctor delivering children, doing emergency calls for snakebite. 02480/643740.

Two minutes left. This was crucial—projection based on the

subspecies hypothesis. Any interpretation would only be marginally indicative without an ocean of data, but there was just barely time to get a rough estimate of why he kept getting pears from the apple tree. Tapes whirred in the distant bowels of the synergizer. Electronic intelligence surveyed the scanty data. The machine couldn't give the logical human answer: *Synergize with just this to go on? You're out of your Wengen mind!* Being what it was, it finally answered the question posed, as well as it could.

Diane helped Corian translate the response: FROM DOMINANT TRAITS ENHANCED THROUGH ENFORCED INBREEDING, EXTRAPOLATE ACCELERATED CHANGE IN NEOCORTEX. CEREBRAL/CULTURAL TENDENCY TOWARD NONVERBAL COMMUNICATION WILL ACCELERATE VARIATIONS IN DEVELOPMENT OF R-BRAIN AND LIMBIC SYSTEM WITHOUT SIGNIFICANT CHANGE IN MASS RATIO. SEE THEORIES OF ALLOPLASTIC EVOLUTION.

Diane's statistical over-sense, developed over twenty decades in her field, read more into the answer than Corian could. Involved now, tongue protruding slightly between small white teeth, she nudged herself close to the console. "Let me."

?

"Time's short," she murmured. "I think—"

She cut off the seconds-wasting explanation, punched in a query: 07/590: 547(8)4/952/077.

"What the hell you doing? It's my five minutes."

She signed: Look.

He followed her glance to the screen where the green symbols formed a fat 80%.

"What?"

Diane said, "I asked it to project the efficacy of further coven study along these lines. That 80% will buy you more synergizer time from Marian."

Corian swallowed, nervous, elated and simultaneously depressed, and he didn't know why. His mind ran swiftly. 80% was virtually unavoidable, Marian couldn't argue. But *why* was it so high a percentage on such scanty data?

"Raddy," he said, "whatever this means, you're pure gold."

She nodded acknowledged thanks for the compliment, but observed: "Forty seconds remaining."

Time for one more question: why the synergizer predicated 80% on such a meager sampling. The clock scissored off his remaining seconds while the screen glowed with what seemed to be a long irrelevant corollary.

"Raddy, what the hell's a sabertooth tiger?"

"Extinct mammal. Thirty seconds."

At last, the synergizer was drawing to its point: FROM DATA, SUBSPECIES 10% VULNERABILITY TO MENTAL ILLNESS CF. HOMO SAPIENS—

"Impossible!" Diane exclaimed. "They're still human. No one's that well adjusted."

Corian's fingers flew furiously: How significant?

"Fifteen seconds, Cory."

"Shut *up*."

FROM DATA, POTENTIAL EXISTS FAILURE OF NEOCORTEX TO OVERRIDE LIMBIC AND—

The communication light glowed. "It's Marian," Diane warned.

"Wait!"

But her hand came down on the console, wiping the screen blank. Corian writhed with silent frustration as Diane turned with sprightly, efficient innocence to greet Marian.

Furiously, he ripped the printout from the roll, devouring its last, incomplete symbols.

—OVERRIDE LIMBIC AND R-BRAIN SYSTEMS THROUGH CHRONIC DIETARY LACK STRESS VIT—

Fragmentary, marginally reliable, but at least it held a practical suggestion that might benefit Arin and Mady, *and dammit, what did it remind him of?*

He scribbled a note to the now preoccupied Diane to keep running EEGs on both exhausted sleepers, then left to inject B complex into Arin and Mady.

He went to bed early, mind deeply troubled. He twisted and thrashed his way into feverish slumber.

He sat in Nat Brewster's living room. His friend was in the chair opposite, tamping bearberry tobacco into his pipe. Outside, the sea murmured and the night sky throbbed with the pathetic cries of the Wintermind.

"Evening, Cah-ree," the fisherman acknowledged. "Still shaking apple trees and pears falling down, right?"

Yes, Nat.

"Damfool," Brewster said, gesturing with his pipe. "How long you gonna pretend you ent shaking a pear tree?"

He couldn't answer. Suddenly he stood on the shore of Nauset Beach, looking into the mist looming over the moon-shot sea. The Wintermind drew closer and closer, he could hear its whimpering, didn't want to see its familiar staring eyes and crimson claws.

"Evening, Cah-ree."

The fog drifted away. Nat Brewster hovered a few feet above the choppy surf, blood spilling from the long diagonal slash that gutted him from shoulder to hip.

"Let one of *these* romp down your gullet," Nathan said. "Wellfleet oysters. The rest can go home." He held out his black knife, expecting Corian to take it, and they were back again in Brewster's home, yet at the same time they faced each other over the red glow of the burning sea and Nathan reached for the salt and let it pour over the sharp forged edge of his coven knife before he held it out again to Corian and the Wintermind howled louder and louder until Corian bolted up in bed, throat raw from the wail of anguish and rage torn out of his own soul.

Once before he'd uttered such a cry, a long time ago in the southern swamps.

brrrinnnggggg

The phone dragged the fat man from sleep. Spitt hawked viscidly, spat, groped one-handed for the jangling instrument.

". . . uh?"

"Spitt!" The voice was young, powerful, obscenely awake for the time of day.

"Corian, you know how early it is?"

"Listen, Spitt—"

The bald little man winced. "Don't yell."

Corian sailed on with barely diminished volume. "Garick still up north?"

". . . uh."

"If that's a yes, then I'm speaking to the Uhian government."

Spitt squinted blearily at the digital clock. "It's 6:13. You want a law passed?"

"No. Any new word on Santee?"

Spitt groaned. "So now I'm a newsreel?" Before that shattering voice could stab his eardrums again, he answered the question. "Late last night, the Gate monitors picked up a bad blip at Old Hartford. No ident, very strange pattern. Could be Santee. They wanted Garick to know."

"Hartford?"

"Uh-huh. Garick's right, figured Santee would try to get west through City."

A long silence. Then Corian asked a favor.

"Spitt, can you ask Bowdeen to call me?"

"You woke me up for that?"

"If Bow had a phone—"

"You woke me up just to—"

"It's important!"

"Don't yell," Spitt groaned. "When should he call?"

"Now. In an hour. As soon as you can get him."

"Right." Spitt yawned. "Mind if I get a little more sleep first? I'm not that young any more."

"Who is? Spitt, it can't wait."

Spitt rumbled his begrudging acquiescence and hung up.

Corian made a note to call the Gate monitors after he was finished talking to Bowdeen.

The Wengen music drawled out of Corian's phone, a duskier sound than his own, tones like dark honey.

"Cory? Old Spitt said you want me."

"Hey, Bow. Thanks for getting right back. How's Sidele?"

"Gettin' fat."

"And my girls?"

"They say, when'zat old Cory coming back to check us up?" Bowdeen chuckled. "Bossy retired. Didn't think that ass of hers'd *ever* wear out."

"Bossy-girl." Corian remembered her with a smile: Bossy who did the work of three the day he limped in from Dannyline. "Crib Street won't be the same. Listen, Bow, Spitt can't hear you now, can he?"

"Naw, he's snorin' in the other room."

"That's how he used t' spy for Garick during the war. Keep your voice down, just in case."

"Will do, Cory. What's up?"

"Got a job for you. Is Cabonna around Lorl?"

"I can find him."

"Good. Do that, and find five others like him. Ten krets for your trouble, ten to each of them."

Bowdeen whistled. "On you?"

"On me. Cash in gold."

"You must be serious, boy. Gotta be a busy night for me to take in seventy krets at the bar."

"I am serious, Bow. Can you do it?"

"No problem, man."

"Part of your ten buys a short memory. Not a word to anyone, not even Sidele."

Bowdeen asked cautiously, "You gonna break some law?"

"Not break. Maybe bend."

"Man, you better say what."

"I have to drag that marsh for Shalane's body." He heard a sharp intake of breath at the other end, but before Bowdeen could react, Corian rapid-fired the rest. As he did, Bowdeen realized it would cost the doctor a lot more than seventy krets to meet Cabonna and five others and go up-Sound in a Moster ship to Yarmouth. The vessel was to continue to Wellfleet with specific requests to Jon and Abby Pettibone, then, after two days, return to pick them up. "Two days ought to be enough," Corian observed. "No current in that marsh, we won't have to look long."

"Boy, they can find her the first day. You'n me was never real Circle, Cory, but—"

"I know."

"Where they fall, that's where they bury Circle folks."

Corian was only too aware of it. It was so deep a tradition, even disbelieving Arin felt its force. By coven standards, what Corian proposed was unthinkable. Arin would never consent.

"It's too big a thing with them, Cory," Bowdeen judged. "They find out, you be walkin' around with a raw bone where your ass used t' be. No, man. I do business with them folks—"

"Fifteen krets. I'll do it, anyway. You'll just save me time."

"It ain't the money," Bowdeen objected with failing conviction. "I'da gone after Santee for free if Garick woulda let me."

"Bow, this is important."

A silence, then: "Twenty krets' worth of important?"

Corian had to laugh. "All right, twenty, but that buys a lot of quiet."

"Man, I already forgot what we're talkin' about."

"Like you said, Bow, I'm glad it's not just the money."

Dark-honey laughter rolled over the wire. "Hell, Cory, you could always buy me. That's why I'm still alive. But look, boy . . ."

Corian endured the poignant pause.

"Cory," Bowdeen at last asked softly, "you really need to see that?"

"Yeah." His own voice sounded flat and too old. "Yeah, I need to see that."

After Corian hung up, he talked to the Gate monitors. When he was through with them, he ran a tape memo for Rashevsky.

**Ted, I'm heading north. Be back ASAP. Keep shooting Arin
and Mady full of B complex. All they can assimilate and then
some, it ought to help them sleep, trust me. Make sure Diane
continues monitoring EEGs, but please, Ted, don't ask questions, not yet. Trust me. I'm sure I'm right.**

He was almost positive he was right and the righter he got, the
less he wanted to be. As the ramp purred north through early morning sunlight, the shapeless inconceivable network of circumstance
gathered itself into a lunatic logic that could not be denied or
avoided. The thing the Fleeters sang about at Lams was not some
distant legend, some long-gone myth.

The Wintermind was real.

The black Wengen named Cabonna was glad of a ten-kret job, but he'd work for Cory, anyway, any day. That little mofo kept him alive on the long road back from Dannyline.

Ten krets, but they were earning their money. Old swamp stank in the humid weather. With freezer boxes in the two small skiffs, they poked and probed in and out of the marshweed and cattails, sweating and batting mosquitos, and everything in the world—animal, weed or goddam bird—seemed to pick this marsh to die in. Cory saw there was plenty of good food along for the workers, but after a day of the marsh, appetite dropped off. Then they found the crab-chewed leg and, later, the bloated, headless torso with its arms about to fall off. Nobody ate then, forget it.

"Get that thing in the *box*, man!"

Like overcooked meat dropping off a soupbone, Cabonna thought. The pieces had to be frozen stiff before Corian could deal with them. A long leg. The goddess was all legs, Cabonna dimly remembered her around Lorl. One proud-walking woman.

They all worked with cloth masks rubbed with herbs, probing for more pieces. The others preferred the boats to being around Corian just now. They wanted to quit, and Cabonna couldn't blame them. Not that he was soft. He was a big-shouldered man, black as Bowdeen, but he'd stayed hard and Bow hadn't. Life wasn't that good to him. His eyes were bitter from thirty years of fighting and anger, their whites pinkish with tiny burst blood vessels.

He watched the little medic from a discreet distance. In his own time, he'd done things that took a strong stomach, but Cory had him beat by a long mile.

The frozen leg was propped with obscene jauntiness against the inner edge of its open freezer, the headless torso upright in its own, the swollen arms stuck out at an angle from the body as if frozen in mid-gesture. The stuff came mucky black out of the sucking mud. Washed with clean water and alcohol, it came up to a gray-white under the rotted deerskin shirt. With the bloat and the jelly clumps of fish eggs clinging to it, you wouldn't know it was human at first. Man, Cabonna winced, you didn't want to know it was human once. And Cory could work at that thing and eat at the same time?

He could. Totally engrossed, the doctor nibbled a sandwich as he scraped bits of decay from the severed neck. He finished the snack and wiped his mouth on a sweaty forearm, glancing up at Cabonna. He didn't look sick, Cabonna judged, just troubled; a quick flash of some unidentifiable emotion before Corian stuffed another sandwich into his mouth.

Slicing stiff folds of deerhide so expertly that nothing else came away with it, precisely delineating between human flesh, clothing and clustered marine organisms, Corian sponged the cleared area with alcohol until the patch of skin emerged with its four small lacerations that looked like deep fingernail scratches. Corian studied them closely in silence, gave the warped chest another swipe or two before returning his full attention to the neck.

Cabonna couldn't understand the maddening deliberation with which Corian labored over the neck, oblivious to the mosquitos lunching off his own naked back. He did neat work, Cabonna gave him that. When Cory finally was finished, the neck-stump looked clean as fresh-butchered pork.

Cabonna remembered his errand. "We dragged up everything for hunnerd yards around," he stated, anxious as the other men to be gone.

The physician kept on working.

Cabonna tried again. "Everything else is crab-et or sunk down in that mud. Lotta quicksand in there." Mosquitos whined past his ear. Cabonna smelled his own sweat, the marsh and the faint odor the freezer box couldn't quite kill. "Boat be waiting soon, Cory."

"Yeah," Corian finally answered. He made one more pass over the neck, then dropped his scraper in the tray of alcohol. "We're done, Cab. Call them in."

Cabonna relaxed, allowing himself to breathe deeper, despite the subtly sickening odor. "That's good. We can—*hey*."

It took some doing to shock Cabonna, but Corian did when he

picked up the leg and tossed it in the other box, shoving the torso un-gently down on top of it.

"Don't do that, Cory."

Corian didn't even look at him.

"It ain't my place," Cabonna said with a dignity that surprised him. "But she was a goddess. Ain't no way to do her."

Corian's back stiffened, but he said nothing. He slammed the box shut and slumped down on the lid. Staring inscrutably at his hands, the doctor stripped off the surgical gloves and dropped them on the ground. Suddenly, Corian glared up at the black man. "We're done," he said in a flat, querulous tone. "Pack up, Cab."

Cabonna nodded and turned away from Corian. He hadn't real-ized how much the doctor's professional detachment had cost him. Now Cory looked plain sick.

Lorl's Crib Street was officially closed for the day. All its girls, dressed in their best robes, stood, reclined or paced about in front of Bowdeen's bar and store. Once Korbin's till he retired, the place was neater now for regular painting, more frequent scrubbing and a sharp upturn in cash flow since canny Sidele organized the crib girls into a monopoly.

"You gotta spend money to make it," she reasoned.

Corian once told her that selling box was illegal in old Mrika, and so was pretending to read the future. Sidele didn't believe him; she never met a man who didn't want (a) a woman when he needed one and (b) some edge on tomorrow. She was glad to be living in a more enlightened age.

"Give 'em what they want. You can't help making money."

With Corian's help, she cleaned up the girls, dressed them decently, got them better food, even set aside the old storeroom for Corian's clinic. He took payment in trade more out of affection now than anything else. To the girls, Cory belonged to Crib Street, its one enduring hero. And he was due any minute.

"There he is!"

"Oh, Siddy, Siddy, look. Here he comes!"

Sidele leaned into Bowdeen's shoulder as he rested against the porch rail, letting the tide of chattering women flow past into the street. She grinned sourly at Bowdeen. "Just another man. Better'n most, but just a man."

The road-grimed battery cart bounced down the rutted street and pulled up, girls clambering on and over it before the vehicle came to a halt. Sidele and Bowdeen waited; no one could get close to

Corian until the girls hugged and tugged and screamed and sloppy-kissed him to total dishevelment.

"Yay, Cory!"

"What's in the box?"

"Nothing."

"Presents?"

"No, leave it alone—leggo my *head,* Doosie."

Corian's arm fought out of a tangle of tussling limbs to beckon Bowdeen. "Hey, help me with the box." He struggled up to sit on the seatback. "Hey—hey, everybody—SHUDDUP!"

"Quiet, Cory's tryin' t' talk."

"QWY-YUT!"

"We're gonna have a good visit," Corian managed finally, a crib girl on each arm. "Want to see all of you in the exam room. Check you out, then we'll have fun."

"Ya-ay!"

"So let's go, let's movemove*move*. Line up and gimme a smile."

The girls rushed in past the bar in a laughing flood, jostling the late afternoon customers nursing their drinks, queueing up raucously at the door of Corian's clinic.

"Hey, Cory, come on!"

"We're ready."

"Gotta work tonight."

"Hell yes, wanna die rich as Garick. Even if it's tomorrow."

"Specially if it's tomorrow!"

Outside, Bowdeen hauled the freezer box from the cart while Sidele hugged Corian, feeling his heartiness vanish with the last of the girls. "What is it?" she asked with narrowed eyes. "You look like a shit sandwich."

"I should feel that good. Bring a drink to the room, okay?"

As they carried the box between them, Bowdeen's eyes flicked down to it and thought he understood. *It's her.*

Corian's gaze was in the dust as he carefully watched his feet shuffle into the bar. "Siddy," he said, "don't forget my drink."

Corian examined his girls with escapist relish. If there were questions, they were all in the freezer box. Here in his kingdom, with its microscope, stains, swabs and slides, there were none he could not decide with authority and despatch. Three cc's of blood from each girl, a vaginal smear and a few moments' chat with an old friend. He enjoyed it, he savored them. His money was no good at the bar and Poke saw to it that his drink had no bottom. It was part party, part examination, those not immediately summoned by Corian passing out drinks or calling for them. Someone brought in sandwiches— "made it myself just for you"—and the women collected like grounded birds on chairs, on every table, in the doorway, perched atop the freezer box. Corian moved quickly about his rounds, taking smears, drawing and labeling blood—

"I wish just one of you women could write."

—while they roared and squealed to each other the finer points of the ritual.

"Make a fist, you won't bleed to death. . . ."

". . . *spread* that thing, Doosie. Give Cory a great big smile."

Small questions, quick answers, large and gusty affection as he checked out Sidele's stock in trade. No pears from apple trees, only the slide under the microscope, healthy albumen and its variants or the sluggish, crescent-shaped gonococci. No problem with blood; the spirochete was there, corkscrewing under your eye, or it was not. And crabs were easy.

"Hate that powder, Cory."

"Use it. Shave yourself clean and use it."

"Itches."

"All those little bugs dying. Damn right it itches."

"Use it!" sang the chorus to the afflicted. "Cory says. And it works."

"Gotta shoot you, Minny."

The wail of frustration. "Not *again?*"

"You got it. Lean over the table. . . ."

No questions without answers. Part of Corian wished he'd never left Lorl. "Where's my drink? Next!"

Marian's face appeared on Rashevsky's viewscreen. He signaled: *?*

Her fingers swiftly expressed her ongoing concern for Mady's erratic behavior. "Last week she slapped Levitt. Today she grabbed him, kissed his cheek."

"Upset?" the doctor asked, referring to Levitt.

"Flustered."

"Her emotional equilibrium's shattered. Agitated sleep/dreams aggravating condition."

"Remedy?"

"Injecting Mady/Arin massive B complex, Corian suggestion."

"Effect?" Marian asked.

"Ameliorative. Insufficient."

"Other treatment?"

"Await Corian's return."

That triggered something in her memory. "Subspecies predication suggests Corian syn/time."

"Affirmative," Rashevsky signed. "Give him plenty."

?

"Suspect crucial situation. Anyway, he needs syn/experience."

"*Why?*" She actually mouthed the word.

The uncharacteristic emphasis amused the doctor; he was well aware that Marian had a blind spot when it came to Corian's potential.

"Because," he answered, "someday I suspect he'll be one of us."

The girls were gone, dinner done, and Sidele only needed a hint of the freezer's contents to ensure them privacy. Bowdeen didn't wince when Corian opened the box, but his tone altered. "What you want me to see?"

Corian fitted small hands into surgical gloves while the chemical frost steamed out into the warm air. He propped the torso, back outward, against the side of the box. "Look at the neck, Bow."

Bowdeen leaned over the specimen with a professional interest. "One cut, real clean."

"Like the woman at Ponaug." Corian glanced up at the black man. "If anybody knows what a blade can do, it's Bowdeen. Could a razor do that?"

"No," Bowdeen decided without hesitation. "Too light."

"Say he's stronger than most men."

"*I* was stronger than most men, Cory. I couldn't do it. The bone'd stop it."

"A sheddy, then?"

Bowdeen looked dubiously at the severed neck. "Maybe. But that's awful clean for a sheddy." He moved away from the box, nostrils repelled by the tinge of decay beneath the chemical smell. "What's the difference, Cory?"

Corian persisted. "Sheddy, yes or no?"

"I don't know, man."

"Look again."

Reluctantly, Bowdeen returned to the box, squatted on heavy haunches, eyes level with the sliced neck. "Maybe."

"Held in the right hand."

"Aw, how can you tell that?"

"The Ponaug woman was killed by a back-handed stroke, left to right. A left-handed blow would back-hand right to left. She was fairly tall; the blow had to travel up."

Bowdeen wagged his head, still doubtful. "You could sideswing that—" He narrowed his eyes at the stump. "Right hand? You sure of that?"

"Positive."

Bowdeen carried a sheddy for years when he was in the merks— fought with it, dug with it, chopped underbrush and firewood. The use and balance of the weapon was second-nature to him. "Wouldn't back-hand a sheddy 'less you missed the first swing. You'd come *down,* then left to right. The tilt's all wrong."

"The angle, yes." Corian bent close, brushing the frozen stump with a gloved finger. "This wound goes *up,* see? Left to right, front to back. Clean as a scalpel at entry, less clean in the back where it's been slowed by the bone. Actually, the blade went through this section of vertebrae where it was joined by cartilage."

Bowdeen had to move away from the thing again. Its smell was stronger and he wondered how Corian could stand it. He poured himself a sida. "Not a sheddy."

"Or a razor. Well, Bow?"

Bowdeen still couldn't read that cloudy expression. "Well, what?"

"You've used a coven knife."

"Still do. Best blade in the place."

"In two thousand miles," Corian agreed. "I've been that far to see. Carve hickory all day and still shave close with it. I've done surgery with them when I had to. Ten years ago, they were the best, and even better now that the iron works use City fuel."

Bowdeen agreed carefully. "Ye-es. Coven knife'd do it that clean. Man'd got to be strong. Santee have one?"

Corian nodded darkly. "Santee stripped those Suffec he hung."

"I heard."

"Took their knives. Sheddy. Coven blade. Maybe more than one."

"Sure, Cory."

"Damn right he did." He said it angrily, Bowdeen thought, like daring you to argue.

To Bowdeen's tacit relief, Corian shoved the carrion back down into the box, closed it and reached for the sida jug. He drank deep without the nicety of a mug and sagged down on his cot, staring at the floor, the jug ear dangling from a forefinger.

"You done, Cory?"

"Yeah." Corian drank again, shuddering as the liquor burned down. "Real done."

"You always pushing," his friend said with compassion, "always driving, Cory. You never go easy."

"Have to be the big man with all the answers. No time, Bow."

"Hey," Bowdeen grinned, "Siddy thought maybe you'd at least have time for a little company. We heard them City women don't believe in it." He sat beside the hunched little doctor, burying Corian's shoulder in a big, fatherly hug. "You like that?"

Corian only shrugged.

"What's wrong, boy?"

"Dunesk. Two days in the hot sun."

"You look bad, Cory. Get some rest, then Siddy'll send one of the girls."

But not just any girl, Bowdeen told himself as he left the room, leaving Corian to lapse into an exhausted slumber. Cory needed a special friend to talk with, and a mean box to wring his cock six ways from Sinjin and tuck him in comfy afterwards. And didn't Sidele know just the woman for that.

"Cory?"

The slightly cracked voice called several times before he lifted his head and focused on the woman in the doorway. Short and going to comfortable plumpness, she still had the remnants of a strong, well-defined figure: broad hips and heavy breasts that she now let lounge in an attitude of sensual indolence that once kept her crib moving like a fastramp.

Corian grinned blearily. "Hey, Bossy-girl."

"Bow said you was hanging low."

"Real low. Come in."

Bossy strolled behind his chair, working over his shoulders with an expert touch.

"That's good. So damn tired. Heard you quit."

"Did." Bossy kneaded his shoulders with affectionate skill.

"You with somebody?" Corian asked.

"Couple of them, when I want," she allowed. "One's a trader, gone to Karli this week. The other ain't around much. I sort of like having that whole bed to myself." She kissed the sunburned nape of his neck. "We all missed you."

Poor damn little Cory, she thought. Sunburned and run down and grubby and he drank too much and took care of everyone but himself.

"Drink, Bossy?"

He measured a double drink for them to share and held her hand in silence. Bossy who couldn't read or write or add much beyond twenty looked at her old friend with bottomless wisdom. Cory was real City now: his green suit had pockets closed with those weird things he called zippers, and they were full of shiny pencils and other City things. But a lot of the old, wild, slambang Cory was gone.

"What you doing in that damn place, boy?"

"I wanted to get smart, Bossy. Just get dumber."

Her hand slid up the brown skin of his arm. "They find that old Santee?"

"No." Corian nestled his stubbly cheek in Bossy's warm, square hand.

"Garick and the constab and everybody up there looking. Where else can that mofo run?"

"Where, indeed." Corian reared up precariously from the table, weaving a little, smiling muzzily at his friend. He embraced Bossy from behind, cupping the familiar weight of her breasts. "Do a favor?"

"Ten of 'em."

"Wouldn't ask just anyone. How'd you like to take my virginity?"

Bossy tilted her head back in a cracked, raucous laugh and nipped his ear. "Love to. Where'd you leave it?"

The sun was just up when he woke to share biscuits and pungent tea with Bowdeen and Sidele. He hugged them both and kissed Bossy goodbye. Before climbing in his cart, he told Bowdeen privately to bury the contents of the box. Then he drove to Lorl checkpoint, voice-identified with the Gate monitors and bounced over the road to the fastramp, hoping he hadn't taken too long, cursing the whole concept of time that ran always away and away.

7:14—SPORADIC STRONG CONTACT SECTOR 2/DISCONTINUED/NO IDENT.

At about the moment Corian got on the fastramp, the tail end of the night shift of Gate monitors detected a powerful blip on the edge of Sector 2, pulsing briefly on their screens before it vanished again. There was no time to scan, barely enough to record its position approximately fifteen miles north of the Whitestone passage. They thought it might be a guard.

7:28—The slightly built, sandy-haired citizen sat down at his desk, yawning. Peter Clavell fervently wished he could find some way to get out of the irksome Gate detail, but Marian was still adamant. Today he had the morning shift, and it was almost time to relieve Pearson.

Clavell's desk was piled with scribbled papers and reference volumes relating to tardy projects, but he really didn't feel like working on his own tasks, let alone the Gate. It was a beautiful day outside his west-facing window. There was a hint of coolness in the air, and the shore across the river looked green, lazy and inviting. . . .

Enough; he *did* waste time, his worst habit.

7:30—Clavell punched up all Gate sensors, matchup and voice-ident files, then flashed Pearson. The owlish little historian was sourly glad to see him prompt.

"Scan on Sectors 1–5," Clavell signed. "Anything unusual?"

Pearson responded tacitly, punching a précis of the morning's recorded sweeps on Clavell's screen as he pointedly declared himself off the unloved detail for the day. Before opening communications with Hartford, Clavell took a few seconds to skim the morning contacts. Not much. By now most of the guards knew enough to stay out of the zone and avoid the bother of voice-ident. All sweeps negative until 7:14. Fifteen miles north of Whitestone.

"Shall we dance?" Kemp asked, winking at him from the screen. "Late, sorry. Theory work on new print-circuitry. Scan on, ready?"

Clavell signaled to wait, patched Pearson's contact record into the Hartford line. Kemp rapidly digested it.

"Very strong."

"You know those mudminds up there. Could this be our anomaly?"

"Could be."

Clavell prepared for the first sweep with an apprehensive glance at Pearson's laconic entry. "Ready 1–5."

They swept the five northern sectors back and forth again and again as the sun slowly mounted the morning sky. Once Kemp suggested a round of Abbott's Ultima to pass the time, but Clavell's attention was riveted to the blue sensor lines. Purely emotional, but he could *feel* that anomalous blip lurking off-screen, expected it to show up suddenly every time the indicator line swept over Sector 2.

11:03—"Contact, Sector 2!" Clavell's hands streaked over the console for a location fix, activating the pattern banks while Kemp blurted through his headset, "It's him, Peter, I know it!"

The intruder disappeared before the banks could even begin a definition, but they had a close fix: nine miles north of Whitestone. Moving south.

The sun hovered at meridian, then inched west into afternoon.

12:57—As Clavell's indicator swept over Sector 2, Plot D, the blip was there again.

"That's him," Kemp worried. "Still moving south."

Clavell's fingers stabbed several keys in rapid succession: sensors, pattern bank, location fix, and at the same time, a call to Spitt at Lorl.

"Hello, Spitt? Gate again. I think we've got a fix on the intruder. Has Garick got phone monitors along the line?"

"Sure," Spitt rumbled in his phlegmy voice. "From Whitestone up. Where's Santee?"

Clavell paused a second before answering to watch the symbols spray the now familiar lunacy across the screen, followed by the 231 code for anomaly, a classic understatement.

"We've got him, Spitt. Six or seven miles north of Whitestone check. Where's Garick?"

"Guess he's near Hartford," the gravelly voice replied.

"Call him there." Another glance at the mathematical madness on the screen. Clavell realized the intruder ought to be approached only with extreme caution. The factors overriding that strange mind would kill detachedly and very likely not even remember it. "Tell Garick to collect his men at the south fastramp, but—and this is important—don't start south until he has loudspeaker clearance from us. If we have to negative probe, it's going to be tight choking it down to one or two plots. Those fastramps do about a hundred and fifty miles an hour. If any of Garick's people are in that plot while the probe's on—"

"I've got the picture, son," Spitt said gently. This from a Mrikan centuries younger. Any other time, Clavell would have been amused, but now he was only aware of a mounting tension, and his throat already hurt from the strain of speech.

"Spitt, impress Garick that he *must* wait for clearance. Call you back. . . ."

The huge man swung up the line of waiting riders with a coven master's gliding movement, only slightly marred by his unconscious habit of favoring the leg arrow-shot at Dannyline.

The bloody fact that was Santee ran before Garick like a mocking ghost. He'd hoped to box him in at Old Hartford, but again Garick's best Suffec trackers were baffled. Once more the trail, always over the rockiest ground, began just short of any given spot and ended not far off.

Garick's men were dismounted, waiting for ramp clearance. A half mile away, in the Gate zone, the southbound ramps sparkled in the sun, motionless till activated. As Garick moved up the line, the lep reached him from a dozen minds.

Move soon?

Once he would have trapped Santee as impersonally as a marauding fox, but the outlaw hit too close. There was already little enough left that Garick could call a life. As his visions of a revitalized country expanded, his own horizons shriveled. Jenna—fine, raw-souled Jenna, full of a love he never returned—was gone. City was a place to avoid; Marian's face and form too vividly recalled his first wife, Judith, now no more than a sunken grave under a tree in Shando Forest, a tree carved deep by his vindictive first son, Singer.

Singer, whose mental powers far outstripped even the most potent
coven masters. Singer, who idled his way through the war while his
people died; Singer, who let his own brother Arin run the horrors of
the Gate. Garick knew he was right to banish Singer, and yet . . .

Though he never spoke of his first son, he thought about him
more and more as the years passed. Beneath the anger and, yes, the
jealousy—because Singer was with Judith when she died, and he
wasn't—there was still a dark knot of unpaid love that Garick
couldn't untangle.

For a man who changed history, Garick took few treasures for
himself. The only ones remaining in the last private chamber of his
heart were Arin and Mady. Shalane had been cut away.

He felt a blood hatred for Santee that he never knew before, not
even when he faced the dying Kriss leader, Uriah, at Salvation. But
the whole pattern of Santee's latest atrocities bothered him. There
was the family at Ponaug, little food taken, the parents butchered,
the young boy apparently untouched, but dead as a log.

And at Old Hartford, Garick's men found a hermit farmer dead
under similar circumstances: a small amount of food stolen, the man
lying in the maniacally scattered rubble of his dirty house, but no
mark on him.

The dead horse bothered Garick more than all the rest. His
Suffec remembered the peculiarities of the unshod hoof: one of Santee's for sure. But as he ran his hand over the saddle and stirrups,
Garick received totally unsettling psychic impressions. And there was
a neat square cut high on the scrawny rump where perhaps a half-
pound of flesh had been sliced from the animal. Cowan hunters
might neglect a horse, ride it to death as this one clearly was, but no
one in Garick's memory had carved a horse for eating since Karli
Forest.

Santee was making no move that made sense. Even his overall
route was insane, trying to get back across City to the west. For all
his elusiveness, he had now boxed himself between City and the
water at Whitestone. It would end today, for sure.

Garick reached his destination. Swinging out of the saddle, he
strode to the phone kiosk and punched through his call to the Gate
monitors.

Diane frowned as Corian entered. "You're sunburned."

"No health lectures, Raddy, I'm in a hurry." Out of breath, he said, "I heard the Gate monitors picked up a bad blip the other night at Old Hartford. Need to see."

"How relevant?" she shortminded.

He replied likewise: "No City games. Time's urgent."

"Haven't *I* mentioned that?" But she made an immediate decision and turned to her console. In a few seconds, they watched a rerun of the anomaly scanned by Clavell and Kemp.

"Pretty messy," Diane observed. "Value fluctuations."

Messy it was, Corian saw. Insanely nonsequential with sudden leaping changes, value-wipes, as if the synergizer couldn't make up its electronic mind.

"Order up a printout." Diane punched in the demand; the paper began unrolling. Corian tore it off, studied it. "What are these red underlines? They weren't on the playback."

She peered over his shoulder. "That's Clavell's initials. He apparently worked it up, found some consistencies in the disorder."

"Yes," Corian agreed, scanning the annotated printout. "Patterns weaving in and out of chaos."

Diane smiled inwardly. Corian's pattern, she was sure, was manic-depressive. Bouncing with energy one day, somber the next. She wondered whether Ted was right, that Cory had the makings of a City researcher. She couldn't imagine anything taming his unbridled temperament, not even two hundred mirror-imaged years of work.

"What's this?" He stabbed his finger at a short series of symbols not underlined by Clavell.

She examined the code. "The synergizer couldn't classify the pattern, except as anomalous. The referent's to related material stored in an auxiliary bank."

Staring at the 231, Corian snapped his fingers. "Right! I came across it when we were running the subspecies thing. No time then to look at it."

There was no need for him to ask it, Diane already was busy keying in the call. Corian continued to study the symbols on the printout.

The first set, hard to fathom because of the constant disconcerting wipes, seemed to represent a paranoid pattern of unbelievable severity directed against all outside stimuli: neurosis tipped over into the pathological. Offset by brief but recurring traces of an equally severe schizoid pattern. A third pattern also pulsed ineffectually, futile attempts by higher neocortical centers to override certain unclassified variants. And repeat. Over and over down the page, like a magnetized needle darting among three powerful currents. A pathology in such constant flux that the synergizer read the condition as its own compensation.

"Here's the auxiliary," Diane said. "About eleven years old. A power burnout at the Gate."

"What?"

"Yes, it was quite a shock to everyone here."

"Details," he signaled.

She punched in the order, then translated. "New brain pattern, so powerful and anomalous that the synergizer had to drain power away from other sources to deal with it."

"Eleven years?" Corian calculated. About the time that Singer, Arin's half brother, tried to run the Gate alone. A year later, Arin succeeded where Singer failed and changed history. It was the only passing reference to his first son that Garick occasionally tolerated hearing.

"More data on burnout," Corian demanded. "Specifics."

She entered it and the symbols danced: location of the major power cells damaged, and the mental pattern of the intruder. Singer, the only person to fail at the Gate and live through it—a classic paranoid pattern, though compensated in a fashion that the City never anticipated when first programming the Gate. Following was a crossref to Arin's successful entry into City a year later. No power failure then; Marlan couldn't risk a second burnout. She shut off the Gate, instead.

"You need Arin's mental set?" Diane asked.

"Yes."

The numbers came up. There were similarities to Singer, yet Arin's précis held a linkup that made no sense. It was intriguing, but Corian had no time for an eleven-year-old mystery. The important and startling parallel was the similarity between the patterns of both brothers and the blip Clavell monitored. All had the same delicate equilibrium, the same potential, but only the Hartford anomaly's balance was tipped off center.

"Cory," Diane suddenly said, "there's a note at the bottom of Peter's printout."

"What?"

"He taped the intruder."

"Play it!"

"He hasn't entered it into the synergizer."

"Is he on Gate now?"

"Yes."

"Call and ask him to patch it over the line."

She did so. Soon Diane's office was filled with the sounds of night near Old Hartford. They strained to hear.

Corian took over at the console. "Pete, it's too faint. Play it again. Gonna make a copy."

During the rerecording, the doctor adjusted the amplification. Then he rewound the dub and punched playback. "Brace yourself, Raddy, I'm stepping up the gain."

A moment of anticipation, then the silence was broken by the noise of stridulating crickets, loud as giant fingers scraping slate. A frog croaked like a hoarse lion. The magnified thrashings of tiny nocturnal animals.

"Cory, listen!"

"*Shhh!*"

Even now, the other night sounds muffled it, but there was no mistaking the muted rise and fall of inconsolable sobbing.

"What *is* it?" Diane whispered, blood draining from her cheeks. "Surely that's not the man Garick's chasing."

"No," Corian replied, shaking his head. "Fleeters call it the Wintermind. . . ."

The anomaly was now practically at the Whitestone checkpoint. Clavell was barely finished with Corian when Kemp snapped over the audio: "Pete, we've got a second blip. No. Make that *three*."

Clavell flicked his glance to the plot screen, conscious of rising tension. Two new blips, and much too close to the dangerous intruder, practically crowding him.

"Who are they?"

Kemp replied, "One of them is a checkpoint guard. Got his pattern from the banks."

Clavell indulged in a rare fit of swearing and snatched up his phone. "Whitestone check, do you read?"

To his relief, the checkpoint immediately answered. "Whitestone here. You people pick up that whatzis in the zone?"

"Yes."

"The other guard went in to see with one of Garick's men. You probably got them, too, on your whaddayacallit."

Clavell's throat was raw and dry. He swallowed hard. "Call them back. We may negative-probe."

The guard's voice, sloppy with a Mrikan remnant of English,

began to sound as apprehensive as Clavell felt. "I can't now. They're too far away."

"Stand by." Wheeling around, Clavell saw the three blips so close together they resembled an amber cluster of fireflies. "Whitestone, I'll warn them. Can they hear the speakers?"

"Hell, yes. Those goddam things can be heard for a mile. But it's just someone hurt in the zone. We heard 'im—"

Clavell closed his eyes, his heart beating fast. *So have I.*

"Heard 'im cryin'," the guard said. "Cryin' bad."

The two men trotted out of the checkpoint, down the path and then across a field, drawn by the quavering, undulating cries from the thick bush on the other side. Halfway across, they slowed to a walk. They were in the zone now, a decayed part of the City long before Jing times. The field was treacherous with unexpected holes and outcroppings of rubbled concrete. The Mrikan guard stayed upwind of Garick's constab. He couldn't guess where the man was from, but he obviously hadn't been near a house or had a bath in weeks. A long, mean constab with a black knife and sheddy banging against the legs of his worn hide trousers.

When they'd almost reached the patch of bush from which the crying emerged, the loudspeakers near the zone sign barked into life with a clipped City accent.

"Attention. Whitestone guard, Garick's man. Get out of the zone now. Get—out—of—the—zone. You're in danger."

The warning was repeated, each syllable clearly enunciated. In the ensuing silence, the puzzled pair became aware that the sobs from the underbrush had subtly altered: lower now, softer, a crooning.

The checkpoint guard raised his voice. "Hey! Whoever you are in there, look, we all gotta get out. That's City talking—"

The guard shut up when he saw his companion stiffen and begin to draw his sheddy. Even as the constab backed away and turned to retreat, he rasped a warning whisper to the Mrikan guard. "Move *quick*. Run!"

"Attention! You two in the zone. CLEAR IT! *You are in danger—*"

The guard was momentarily transfixed between the loudspeaker's urgent warning and the naked fear in the covener's face. Once more he yelled to the bushes, "Hey, you hurt in there?"

He froze midstep. The bushes thrashed suddenly and parted. He blinked, thought for an instant his eyes were going bad. The patch of bush blurred red. Behind him, a sharp cry as the constab buckled to his knees. Whirling, scared, he still saw nothing definite, only a crimson wash that he did not so much perceive as sense, and it cried and it cried as it rushed at him with lethal speed—

On Clavell's screen, the two normal patterns grew momentarily brighter, then began to fade, element by element as the electrochemical systems winked out, trailing a trace from the lower motor centers, then nothing.

Kemp whispered it. "Pete, are they out of the zone or—?"

The intruder blip pulsed alone and virulent before it, too, vanished. Clavell put his hand over the phone and spoke softly into the headset. "Death expressed as equation." He gulped a lungful of air. "Austin, stand by." He called Whitestone again, the phone slippery with the sweat from his palm.

"Whitestone, you people have gone off the screen. Whitestone, do you read?"

No answer but the *bonk-bonk* of the dangling phone knocking against the wall of the guard shack.

At Hartford, Kemp almost fell out of his chair when the phone buzzed.

He picked it up. "Gate."

"This is Garick." The granite authority floated easily on the surface of his soft drawl. "We're at the ramps and we want to get this done. How about clearance?"

Kemp was at a loss. He signaled his shift partner over the screen: "Garick wants clearance. Patching to you."

"Why me?" Clavell signed wearily.

"You know how to deal with royalty."

Swallowing some water, Clavell opened his line to Garick. "Gate. You have ramp clearance to decon station 3. Don't pass 3 till you receive further clearance."

"Why the delay?" Garick demanded.

"The intruder's south of Whitestone and in the zone. I think we're going to have to probe."

"Don't think about it! *Burn the bastard!*"

When Arin opened the door, Corian saw that the big Shando seemed more rested. The B shots obviously helped some. He wondered how his friend would look once they were done talking.

"How's Mady?"

"Not feeling good." Arin lowered his voice as Corian entered the living room. "She's in her room. I kept her home from lessons today. How long will we have to sleep hooked up to that eejee?"

"No more, Arin." Corian noticed the rarely used desk piled with Diane's IQ surveys. Arin evidently had been working on them when he rang the bell.

"I have to start living again," Arin said in a tone poignant for its simple acceptance. "I'll try to do a good job on this. We're intelligent people. Time we knew it."

"Time you knew a lot of things." Corian sat in an oversized chair, dropped his medbag at his feet. He shrugged bleakly. "Things you and Mady and I have known all along in our sleep. Or when I was drunk, wouldn't you know?"

He spoke slowly, softly and reluctantly. Arin waited with mild curiosity. He didn't follow Corian's eliding drift, but the Wengen's rudimentary lep-center leaked sadness and possibly fear. And something connected with Corian's medbag . . .

"What, Cory?"

"I'm talking about the Wintermind, Arin."

No sooner was Clavell finished with Garick than another phone buzzed, a rarely used terminal at a decon station not far south of Whitestone.

"Gate," he husked through his strained throat. "Hello? Hello?"

For a moment, he heard nothing but labored breathing. Then a man spoke. "T-turn on the Gate. Full power!"

"Who is this?"

"Bates. I was at Whitestone, we was just on the line. Turn on that Gate! All the way!"

Clavell recognized the voice. Bates must have been sprinting, terrified, to save his life. Clavell gulped water and mouthed a medicated lozenge to salve his inflamed throat. "What's the matter?"

"You got that goddam thing on your screen?"

"Not at the moment."

"I been running," Bates panted. "Scared. I dunno what happened to the others, but out in the field—"

"What?" Clavell urged. "What?"

"Dunno. I thought I was going blind or something. Just a funny kind of blur, sort of, and the crying but not sad like we first heard, but angry, like no kinda sound I can describe, and it's like red when there's anything at all, red and black 'n' then I couldn't see nothing, just this blur comin' across the field, and I ran and didn't stop till I got here." Bates paused to suck in more air, pathetic in his fear. "Look, man, I—I dunno what I saw, but I ain't crazy, and I don't care what the pay is, man, 'cause I'm *gone*. Just turn on that Gate."

And he was off the line. Clavell could only stare at the phone and the severed half of an enigmatic conversation.

"Pete," Kemp's voice shrilled over the speaker, "we've got him again! Look where he is!"

His eyes sought the screen. The intruder now was southwest of Whitestone passage, where the converging waters define the northern end of the City's heart. The distance between the waters and the eastern ramps was less than half a mile.

Kemp reminded the other that Garick wanted them to probe. Clavell nodded. With the anomaly so close to Marian's headquarters, he felt it improper to make the decision on his own authority. But if it was going to be made at all, it had to be within minutes.

"That Fleeter thing, Cory? The ballad?"

"Yes. I should've figured it out when Nathan Brewster's ships came back late, and I saw Jordy Hawks on the pier with Jon Pettibone. Or later, when I examined Jordy's wound."

"What are you talking about?"

"A tendency. It's what the ballad's all about. It's what the illogical, random element in Fleeter music expresses." Corian's voice held a weariness more of the spirit than the body. "The Wintermind isn't a thing, Arin, it's a metaphor for murder. And worse."

"Still don't see what you're getting at."

"No? Remember that bad storm Brewster's ships got caught in? That's when Jordy had to finish Nathan to save the rest of the fishing crew."

Arin sat up. "Hold on! Brewster was lost at sea."

"Sure. Buried where he fell. The day Nat's boats returned to Wellfleet Harbor—"

The three ships eased in and bracketed the pier. Mooring lines were secured in utter silence, save for the creak of the planking. One by one, the crews tottered off the ships, men and women with faces scorched by the sea-magnified sun. They gathered in a knot before the god and goddess and still no word was spoken. The dull-eyed, shaken crews stood with heads bowed before their fellow coveners. Scared blue, every one of them. A wiry young man stepped forward from the stricken knot of sailors, knelt before Jon Pettibone to offer up his knife to be purified with the ritual salt, water and fire.

"Bad as he was hurt," Corian said, "Jordy couldn't bear to carry an unclean knife any longer, not after killing Nathan with it."

"You weren't there," Arin said doubtfully, "you can't know what really happened in that storm."

"Can't I? I examined that wound, Arin. Made by four blunt claws. Jordy was torn open from right shoulder to waist by a human hand. Had to be a *left* hand, the way the rip traveled diagonally downward. Nathan was left-handed. I've got a photograph that proves it."

"One-handed? Where'd Brewster get that kind of strength, Cory?"

"From the Wintermind. From the tendency of all order to disintegrate. Entropy. Even Raddy has it, she was my first clue. She painted a marvelously economical picture of a mountain, then put one stupid red slash down its side. Mady did practically the same, I heard, in her dormitory room. *Homo sapiens* has the tendency, but—but you coveners are probably a whole new subspecies. Did Diane tell you?"

"She mentioned the possibility of it."

"Maybe not a subspecies, not yet, but sure headed that way. After the Jings left the land or became part of it, coven folk hit on an old answer, made it their new one. Group consciousness as salvation from Self. Over the centuries, Nature replaced instinctive primate defenses in coveners with a telepathic brain capable of projecting thoughts, emotions, hallucination, or even death, just by willing it to happen. Think about that, Arin. Maybe the tremendous aversion in Circle to taking life stems from an unconscious group horror at possessing so much power."

"You're not talking about a tendency," Arin observed. "You're describing insanity."

"Yes and no. Like I said, the tendency's there in *sapiens,* too, but it's a working part of the coven mind, a quirk in the genes. If you're talking insanity, call Nature crazy. Sickness is just a word . . . a sound. I heard a sound in my own head after Yarmouth, before I blacked out so drunk I couldn't stand up. A wailing yearning towards violence. *That's* what I heard in Fleeter music, Arin, something familiar because years ago down south, looking for Garick's gold, I got so fever-sick I howled like that. You see?" Corian looked at the bigger man with a sad smile. "There's that much coven in me, anyway. Isolate me, take me away from all the known referents, and the fire starts. And I'm only a no-lep Wengen."

But Corian was also a doctor. Factors unstated by the synergizer nevertheless were obvious to him. The Fleeters in the ballad had to be sent home by Myudan doctors with enough B vitamins to control the stress that could bring on the condition called Wintermind. Since then, Fleeters alone of all the covens crammed their diet with as much B as they could ingest. They ate enormous quantities of bread and meal and cake.

Corian also could see that a physiology linked to the tendency, simultaneously detesting it, could shoot abnormal amounts of adrenaline through muscles and heart, producing for short periods the demon strength needed to rip open Jordy Hawks from shoulder to belly with one bare hand. Or—

"Cory," Arin argued, "how can you be so sure this is reality? Nobody but the Fleeters ever heard of this sickness."

"Deepwoods life, up to recently, anyway, was a peaceful one. Flareups of Wintermind, I'd guess, were culturally, statistically improbable. But change the conditions and the tendency becomes a weapon, Arin. Fleeters felt it first because they live by the sea. The ocean means both life and death to them, death just to keep living.

Out on their ships, totally isolated from their world, they must be painfully aware of the paradox. That's the trigger, Arin. Isolation. The one thing coveners can't take. You've told me about Lishin."

Bleakly, Arin admitted that much of the truth to himself. He went mad in Lishin, would have stayed that way if there hadn't been a will strong enough to clamp over the insanity and force him to accept the awful, innocent horror of a world without guarantees or answers, only questions. But as he mused on what Cory was telling him, he sensed there was one answer, at least, something just beyond memory, whispering in darkness.

"Shando and Karli are as old as Wellfleet," Arin protested with failing conviction. "How come I never heard of anything like Wintermind happening in either place?"

"Arin, we don't know it hasn't. All covens have a song-story tradition, but only Fleeters have a sense of historical continuity. Wintermind may have flared up among your people, but it had to be rare, isolated cases. You deepwoods folk don't speak of bad things or pass them on from one generation to another. Till Dannyline, forest covens were pretty much closed boxes to the rest of the world. Tight, secure, self-enclosed. Stagnant."

"I know," Arin said soberly.

Corian couldn't sit any more, the urgency of his truth made him rise and pace the room. "Nature never gives, Arin. It trades. You don't get something for nothing. Coveners drew apart, deliberately bred for lep till most of you had it. You started to look alike—tall country people who grew even taller, so much that the elasticity of your bones couldn't keep up with the length. Childbirth became a danger. So inbred you were unable to stamp out genetic weaknesses. So group-centered that eventually separation from the collective self also became an actual danger."

"Tell me about it," Arin mused.

"And stress vitamins? Forget it! Up on the Fist, you and Shalane never ate bread or cake, you don't even like it. Once a year, maybe, at Samman. A little corn meal in pone, tiny amount of B in meat—mostly beef and pork, and deepwoods are only just now getting that in any significant amount. And covenmasters don't eat much of anything, anyway, too much food just dulls lep capabilities."

Arin shifted uneasily in his chair. Corian noted it, pressed on more relentlessly. "Look, Arin, I've been into your dreams like a rat rooting garbage, charted them, even free-associated with your descriptions. Mady knows the answer, but stops just short; *you* know, but it's a sum you won't total—"

"Your bag," Arin suddenly interrupted, bending forward.

"Uh?"

"Since you came in, you've been leaking something about your medbag. It hurts you. You're afraid of it."

"Yes." Corian looked down at his hands. "There's some synergizer printout I just ran off with Diane. And . . . something else."

"What?"

Without answering, Corian opened the bag and removed the roll of paper. He put it in Arin's hands.

Arin scanned the symbols, translating them with only minimal difficulty into English.

SUBSPECIES POSSESSES IMMENSE POTENTIAL FOR DESTRUCTIVE DEFENSIVE PARANOIA WITH NO NORMAL COMPENSATION. ABERRATION BECOMES ITS OWN BALANCE. FAILURE OF SUPEREGO TO OVERRIDE AGGRESSIVE/DEFENSIVE TENDENCIES IN LIMBIC SYSTEM. HEIGHTENED POTENTIAL ENERGY-MATTER TRANSMUTATION. SEE: "WHITEBRAIN," ALSO PHYS/CHEM OF INDUCED HALLUCINATION, SYN/REF—

And still Arin refused to look at the total. Slowly, wincing as if the effort of bending down hurt him, Corian leaned over and again put his hand in his medbag. He withdrew the copy he'd made of Clavell's tape.

"Hope you forgive me for this someday," the doctor murmured.

"Forgive you what, Cory?"

He snapped the cassette into Arin's tape player. "For being right."

"Garick's loading on the ramps," Kemp reported as the cluster blip blossomed under his indicator.

Clavell signed: "Activate all speakers, Sector 3, Plot A. Last he can safely cross. Start warning when he enters 3, Plot B."

"Acknowledge."

"Back soon." Clavell wiped Kemp from his screen, watched the intruder blip as it crawled south, millimeter by millimeter on his scanner: not yet on the ramps. It'd move lots faster then.

The blip was not far from another decon station, but Clavell had taken the precaution of telling its guards to vacate immediately. Clavell intended to scare them, so they wouldn't dawdle. He succeeded better than expected; the guard he was speaking to quit the conversation in mid-sentence, not even bothering to hang up the field phone.

On impulse, Clavell patched the line over his speakers and boosted the signal just short of feedback howl.

As the blip drew closer to the decon post, Clavell heard the thing again. *Yes, near the phone and getting nearer,* the same chilling sound that rose and fell faintly on the tape he'd made, the crying—

—that keened out of the speakers. Corian recopied Clavell's tape with 500 watts amplification and high gain to get a frequency spread on the signal, retaped with a noise reduction adaptor and narrow crystal. The result was a bloated, soupy sound, half-aspirated by the crystal's leveling effect. For all that, the sound now was painfully recognizable, cries throbbing out of a constant agony, breaking in sobs, ebbing, exploding again into murderous fury.

Arin listened twice through, silent, the printout clutched in one huge hand, tears streaking his face like slow blood from a wound.

"You were there, Cory. You saw what Santee did to her."

"No, Arin. We saw the aftermath of a massacre, that's all. And for all your enlightened ways, god Arin, neither you nor Garick would do the logical thing." Corian took a breath. "So I did it."

"Did what?"

"Dragged the marsh for her body."

When Arin turned on him, Corian felt the disapproval as a physical force, a thrill of fear skittering through his stomach. The loathing in that look could close every circle in Uhia to Corian. "You went into her natural grave—"

"*You* wouldn't!"

Arin said it quietly, but it had a cutting edge. "You couldn't do it alone, and no covener would help. You hired cowans like yourself."

"That's right," Corian agreed. "Cowans like me. None of that born-again song for us, man. Wengens get born owing money. That teaches you reality, Arin. Don't look at me like something to be stepped on. You heard the tape, now hear me out."

Arin shook his head, inarticulate with the desecration, but more because he couldn't dodge the fact that Corian was right.

"It wasn't Shalane that we pulled out of that marsh."

"What does that prove?"

"That I found one of Santee's men. It was a *man's* body, Arin.

Mosters don't wear deerskins, but cowan hunters do. Garick's hunting Santee with how many coveners? Vengeance on a goddess' murder." Corian vented a short bark of a laugh. "Shit, you want to know where's Santee? You *saw* him—parts, anyway. He's been decorating the Yarmouth landscape for days."

Arin tried to reject the figures, to erase from his memory the disturbed but recognizable keening on the tape. He couldn't. Not guilt, but sober hindsight said: *if this is true, then I did as much as anyone to make it so. Day by day, moment by moment. Total attack. Ten years of it, hating this City every day, reaching for me while I drifted further and further away, feeling useless, wanting one thing enough to try to steal Mady from City. And then those last few minutes by the marsh . . . total attack. Me as much as Santee. More.*

But not Mady. Not then. Not now. Not ever.

He turned to Corian. The doctor saw in the grave hazel eyes that *other*-light that Corian noted so often in coveners from Suffec swampers to Garick. Eerie to recognize it now for what it was. Neanderthal must have seen that look in Cro-Magnon.

"What can you do for her, Cory?"

"Nothing. Maybe you and Mady can, though. I want you to link minds with her."

"I can't do that."

"You've got to."

"No. Mady's never shared, not even with Shalane."

"Especially not with Shalane," Corian said dully. "But you'll do it now, Arin, because those dreams are tearing Mady apart. She can't override them like you. The first coven child born and raised in City, her mind a fine and private place. She's not a master, she can only cover the dreams with random thought. You've got to end it, Arin, because you love—"

The buzzer made both men jump. Arin impatiently stabbed the respond button. Diane appeared on the screen. She anxiously asked for Corian.

"What, Raddy? You haven't said anything yet to Marian, have you?"

"No. But I can't wait much longer. The Gate reports two casualties at Whitestone. The intruder's south of there, nearing the ramps. In the zone."

Arin exploded. "They're not going to turn on the Gate, are they? Do they know, Cory?"

"Only that they've got a killer in range for negative probe," the doctor replied. "This is it, Arin. You know why she's come all the way from Yarmouth. You've got to link now with Mady. To save her."

"Yes." Cory was right: right enough for Arin to break the old rule of respect and love never encroached upon before. That—and lies—no longer could be held onto. He turned towards the hall, seeing the white door of Mady's bedroom in his mind, feeling beyond it. *Mady?*

Clavell's throat felt like sandpaper. He punched in a call to Marian Singer, heartily sick of the lozenge taste, spitting the last fragments in a disposal as the chief administrator's image filled the screen.

She raised her eyebrows, signaling *question.*

He signed: "Dangerous zone intruder. Sensor scan follows."

Marian quickly digested the information, then told him to proceed.

"Advise. Full Gate power?" he asked.

"NP?"

Clavell nodded.

Mady?

Arin lepped his daughter, waiting for her clear little flute-like reply. When it didn't come, he first supposed she'd drifted into the sleep she needed so much. He felt for her presence delicately. *Mady?*

Nothing. A void.

"Where is she?" Corian wondered, reading the sudden concern in Arin's face.

"No answer, Cory."

"Could she have slipped off to school?"

In four long strides, Arin was down the hall and at her door. The white room was empty. He grew more apprehensive, remembering how he'd had to lep to her twice to come to breakfast. When she appeared, his daughter had been red-eyed, abstracted and cranky.

"Arin," Corian said tightly, "she's going to meet her."

"*Shh!*"

Arin opened himself to Mady's essence, unlocking that small silent area where things too dear and private or painful are kept unspoken. Holder was there, and Kon and Magill and the part of him that died called Elin, and there was his mother, Jenna, and sharp-edged Singer, and especially the joy and sorrow of Shalane. Finally, the tiny treasure of his daughter. Arin felt for Mady's mind, sifting the other impressions—*Mady, it's daddy*—and then he had her. He winced at the splintered contact, Mady's small, useless struggle against the powerful tide that drew her on.

"She's running," Arin whispered. *Mady, answer me.*

The lepped reply was only part Mady, part the force that pulled her brutally on, staggering ahead on weary child-legs. *1 2 4 8 16 32 come home come home hurt so bad help Mady 8 10 20 30 31 32 help Mady*

"Sharing, Cory, she's being forced to share, forced to run. She's trying to block it with random numbers, always stopping at 32."

"Sure. Translate 33 to syn/language and you've got 'mama.' Arin, you've got to stop her. Do it now!"

"Trying." Arin's mind pushed gently at a door already thrown wide by the other lethal force, the Wintermind. He shrank back from the murderous rage in that darkness. He shared Mady's terror.

2 4 8 16 32 32 don't please don't DADDY

I'm coming, punkin! Where are you?

Make her stop.

Impossible now to separate Mady's frantic lep from the red wash shadowing, filling it in, but Arin read a fleeting impression of thinning trees, the beginning of a street, a meadow beyond. "East through the park, Cory. Almost at the edge."

"Knock her out," Corian begged. "You know what's happening. Knock her out."

"I can't, I could hurt her."

"Arin, all the way from Yarmouth, killing without even remembering, and now she's below Whitestone and you know what for. Give us a chance to stop her. Knock Mady out!"

"I'm going after her, Cory," Arin said with a kind of frozen calm.

"Arin, *no!*"

But in one unbroken movement, Arin grabbed Corian and literally carried him through the front door across the grass towards the cart.

"Hey—" Corian's feet dangled and kicked uselessly as the big Shando lifted him into the driver's seat, vaulting in beside him.

"Drive. I'll tell you where."

"But Marian has to be told."

Arin wasn't listening. Eyes closed, his mind felt again for his daughter. For the moment, he had forgotten about the Gate.

Through the park, northeast across the meadow that used to be ancient concrete City blocks, Mady sprinted on, headed towards the river, coiled and stretched like a new steel spring, closer and closer to the beginning of the zone, her mind finally and totally surrendered to the will that summoned her, that sweet, forgiving voice that pulled her ever forward.

—oh the reeeal pretty girl I'll show . . . at Samman. We'll be together yes we will, Mady, never find us in deepwoods Mady I hurt so bad come quick. . . .

Yet, as Mady ran, a part of her mind recognized the strangeness in mama's voice as it battered at her, powerful yet limping, incomplete, no longer pure but refracted like dim light through cloudy water.

Mady sprang high over an outcrop of old concrete, knowing at last how good it was to feel like mama, to *be* like mama. She didn't pause at the Gate zone sign but ran faster, enchanted by that familiar/strange voice she'd ignored so long in her dreams but now opened up to as it called in her mind, conjuring fear in one breath that the next overrode with love, forgiveness and promise. Mama held her mind now, hugging her close and warm as when they built houses in bed, invading more of her than Mady ever permitted before, but it was all right now, they'd get away, mama said, they'd go now and not look back, except where was—

NO! the voice warned. *DON'T THINK OF HIM NOT HIM HE LET ME GO, KILL HIM IF HE COMES!*

Mady lurched off balance as the force that pulled her was checked by a jolt of an equal counterforce. A shadow passed over her mind and sight. The child wobbled and dropped clumsily to her knees, blinking as the darkness gently covered her like a warm blanket. *Just a little sleep, punkin.* Her daddy's mind hugged her close; but not too far off, mama was crying and as Mady sank into fresh grass, she vaguely wondered how anyone could make a sound like that.

"Where is she?" Corian asked, driving the cart.

"In the zone."

"Arin, we've got to warn Marian. She might NP. There's a field phone at the barrier. Let me use it."

"Got to get to Mady before Shalane does," Arin protested, shaking his head. "She's not far off. If she hits the ramps, she'll be here even faster."

"Takes even less time to press a button," Corian argued.

Marian faced Peter Clavell.

She signed: "Bioscan shows presence of dangerous bacteria. Stand by to NP. Where's intruder?"

"Getting on the eastern fastramp."

"Halt ramps. Standard warn, then activate NP."

He acknowledged, and she switched off. Her buzzer sounded at the same time. Diane's face swam onto her screen.

?

"Marian, don't probe! Intruder's not Santee."

"Irrelevant. Unacceptable bioscan. Pattern reveals murderous instincts."

"I know," Diane acknowledged.

?

"Corian just ran syn/inq. The intruder is Shalane."

Marian's knees buckled, a sensation so unfamiliar she almost lost her balance. Forcing her will to override her feelings, she demanded details. Diane outlined it as fast as shortmind allowed.

When the young woman signed off, Marian's mind raced to analyze alternatives. No matter who the intruder was, she couldn't permit her into the City, she was contaminated, deadly. But she was Arin's wife, Mady's mother. *Salvageable?*

Her fingers attacked the console keys. Rashevsky answered. She told the story in the compacted, continuous flow of advanced shortmind, referencing whole concepts in mutually familiar ellipses.

The physician nodded. "Suspected Corian evolving subspecies pathology, particular ref: Arin/Mady. Never considered Shalane= anomaly."

"Advise."

"Marian, how can I? No therapeutic data, decades of study needed. Cryonic storage?"

She shook her head. "Hideous bioscan."

"Then," Rashevsky said sadly, abandoning shortmind, "it's your decision."

A rare, sad sight, Rashevsky thought as her image faded. The City's chief administrator—frozen, bleak, helpless. Usually Marian wore her mask better.

"Authority to NP," Clavell signed to Kemp. "Stand by."

The straight-handled switch, rarely used, squeaked in its slot as the eastern ramps slowed to a halt. Clavell tried to think only of procedure, precise and bloodless. Someone was going to die because he and Kemp pressed buttons. For that thing out there, the two-minute warning would be a lost formality. He measured the intruder's present position and signed to Kemp: "Acknowledge all sectors locked."

"Full locked," Kemp signed.

Clavell wet dry lips with a sip of water. "Unlock Plots C and D, Sector—"

It only took an instant to prepare the zone areas for death.

"Take the scan, Austin. Two-minute warn."

Clavell opened the relevant bank of speakers, conscious of the ache in his throat as he tried to disregard the other agony he felt. "Attention. The Gate is armed. There's a phone near you. Call 611. Voice-ident or clear the zone. You have two minutes."

On his other screen, the sensor pattern shimmered green in diseased solitude as its remaining seconds bled away.

"Oh, no!"

Kemp wished he were mistaken, but there it was, a sleep-pattern, registering only trace activity on sensors well inside the zone. No matter how many times they warned the guards, there was always someone careless enough to doze off in the sunny meadow.

"Pete, got a trace in Plot C."

"Acknowledge," Clavell signed, boosting power in his loudspeakers, one eye on the clock.

"Attention! One-minute warn. Gate activates in one minute. Clear the zone. *Clear the zone.*" He hardly had any voice left to repeat the warning.

"Wake up!" Kemp pleaded helplessly to the trace pattern. "Please wake *up.* . . ."

Clavell punched Marian's call code, but received no answer.

Marian gazed at the bright amber spot oozing down her screen like an aneurism along a vein.

Go away, she pleaded, ignoring the buzz of her phone, *go away, don't make us kill you, don't do this to Mady.*

She couldn't stop the negative probe, it was necessary, justified. The mad woman's contamination might destroy more citizens than her insane killer instincts. *I have to,* Marian told herself, *I shut out Judith, my own daughter, because she was contaminated, and Singer knows and Arin knows how much it cost. Irrelevant.*

The buzzer wouldn't shut up. With a sigh, Marian depressed the button, nodded to Clavell.

"Marian, Austin detected someone else in the zone."

?

"Unidentified. Probably a sleeping guard. Advise."

No choice. "Proceed with NP."

He looked shocked, but said nothing. Her screen went dark. Marian pitied Clavell for the responsibility she'd just given him. Though at least for him the intruder and the guard were faceless. Not Mady's mother. Not Marian's own daughter. *Judith.*

Arin and Corian heard the speakers just as the cart jolted them to the edge of the park with no sign of Mady.

"Beyond here's all meadow," Corian said. "The zone starts halfway across."

Arin didn't need to be told. He'd stopped Mady, put her to sleep, but perhaps too late. A clammy fear wrapped around his heart as he tried to calculate the remaining seconds.

"Cory, how far's the phone?"

"Tell you when I get back," Corian shouted over his shoulder, pushing the cart to top speed, swerving the wheels south.

"Attention! One-minute warn. Gate activates in one minute. Clear the zone. *Clear the zone!*"

Mady, wake! Wake up! Run to me, home on me, it's dad. WAKE. RUN!

Part of him wondered whether Corian would reach Marian in time, and whether she'd let it happen, anyway.

Mady, wake up! RUN!

"Trace waking," Kemp noted hopefully. "Coming up fast. Must've heard the speakers. Come on, get out. Get out!"

"Fifty seconds," Clavell rasped hoarsely.

"Can't we . . . ?" Kemp stopped the useless question. No way; the intruder blip was so close now to the trace blip that delay for the latter would certainly set the other free inside the City.

"Forty seconds," Clavell signed.

"I hate this, Peter."

"Ditto. Thirty-second warn."

"Thirty-second warn!" the speaker brayed. "Clear the zone . . . *please!*"

Arin's powerful lep more than the noise of the announcement

lifted Mady out of induced sleep. The brazen roar of the speaker drowned the other cry. Suddenly, with a stab of fear, she realized exactly what was happening. *Mama, go back! The Gate! Go back!*

But mama couldn't; her only hope was this way. And then Mady was afraid for herself, and she started to run for the zone sign that was far, never-reach-it-in-time far away. The last thing she saw was the cart at the edge of the meadow, but it was rolling in the wrong direction and she tried to go even faster, straining so hard her ribs hurt.

"Twenty seconds," Clavell signed.

"The second blip's moving!" Kemp exclaimed. "Just a little—"

Clavell shook his head. "Ten seconds. Standby NP."

The last seconds revolved on their digital clocks. Clavell set one sweat-moist finger on the negative probe button. Kemp did the same.

Their eyes met in misery on their viewscreens. Clavell began the countdown.

"Five. Four. Three. Two. One. Engage probe."

Mady's mind grew fever-bright. In an instant, all the interlocking, warring facets that made up what she was—Marian's teaching, the deeper mama-gift of life and early warmth/love—all stood out, apart, over a huge rift like an earth-fault that widened while a force even greater than mamadad pried at her with merciless electronic fingers.

The sign was much nearer now, but her legs moved slower, her tortured brain spun faster and faster like a flywheel loosed from its throttle. Her rubbery legs failed her. Mady weaved drunkenly, sprawled in the grass, clutching at her head. It throbbed with an agonized wail that matched her own keening.

Over the phone, Corian yelled, "Marian, it's Shalane, don't probe!"

"No choice."

"But Mady's in the zone, too!"

Marian spun around and looked at the scan, saw the second smaller blip that Clavell warned her about. It was moving, but still too far from safety. *Mady!*

Judith's back, Marian.
Where, Ted?
Lorl. Border town. She wants readmittance.

Marian heard Peter's raw voice husking the final countdown. ". . . Two. One. Engage probe."

One trembling fist against her mouth, Marian shook in a tidal wave of emotion she never knew still lived within her heart. She wanted to burn with Mady. The City was endangered, she'd been willing to sacrifice the second blip when she thought it was just a Mrikan border guard, yet *all* life was precious, and how could she make an exception for Mady when her sick and lethal mother would break through?

She watched both amber spots brighten unnaturally as the probe impersonally, indiscriminately shredded mother and daughter alike.

> *Judith's back, Marian . . . wants readmittance.*
> *Bioscan?*
> *Bad. Skin/lungs carry multiple bacterial infection.*
> *Quarantinable?*
> *Negative. She built antibodies. Maybe we wouldn't.*

That simple. Exclusion meant death within years instead of life for centuries. But there was no choice.

> *Judith, you can't come back inside.*
> *Mama, no! Please.*
> *You were warned not to leave.*
> *Please, mama . . .*
> *Judith, there's no choice. The answer's—*

"NO!" The raw scream tore from her throat. Marian's balled fist clubbed down on the OVERRIDE button.

In the ensuing silence, her body shook with wracking sobs. "Judith. My baby . . ."

Clavell's skin was paper-white and glistening with perspiration. He watched the unnatural brightness fade, leaving the two blips pulsing irregularly—*but alive*. He heard Kemp's long sigh of relief in Old Hartford.

He punched Marian's call code. It took a moment for her to respond, and when she did, he was stunned to see her face streaming with tears.

"Did you override?" he signed.

She nodded once, listlessly. "Gate off."

?

"Arin will handle it. It's his wife and child, Peter."

Her reply filled him with bafflement and the beginnings of a horrified understanding. Then he remembered, and signed: "Garick's reached Sector 3. Requests clearance to continue."

Marian ignored the irrelevancy. She was busy calculating the number of seconds Mady was exposed to the Gate. The bright little spot throbbed on her screen, and so did Shalane's, quite close by. As she watched, she saw two new blips appear.

Clavell verbally repeated his request. "Garick?"

Marian shrugged. "He's too far away to help. But let him come."

He nodded acknowledgment. Business completed; he ought to sign off, but he had to ask. "Marian, are you all right?"

Time-wasting question, but she tolerated it with surprising patience. "Yes, Peter. I've survived this long, I can weather a little irrelevant emotion. Your voice is badly strained. Conserve it."

Clavell and Kemp, her two bad boys. She wondered how much they could possibly learn about responsibility when she'd just thrown hers away. "Peter—you've handled this all rather well. Austin, too. All the monitors. Please tell them for me."

Clavell sucked a deep, ragged breath as Marian's face vanished. The Priestess of Solitude: that's what Judy Singer used to call her mother, something like that, but right or wrong, she'd taken death out of his hands, and he was grateful. With unexpected insight, Clavell thought he saw the reason why he dawdled away so much time, daring Marian to punish him. Like the bawdy compudoodle he'd made of her, hung in such a ridiculously obvious place she couldn't help but notice it.

What was the old word? Quixotic. Clavell felt embarrassed that he was still young enough to want a woman at all, let alone one he never could have.

Though Marian's stature was slight and her figure trim, her body felt heavier than lead. She pressed Rashevsky's call code sluggishly, one digit at a time.

?

She signed the story in brief. "I'm going out there, Ted." Then she hung up before he could argue.

On the Gate scan, she saw the four blips clustered close together and wondered fearfully what was going on in the meadow.

She couldn't remember feeling so tired. But Marian dragged

herself out of her chair and started towards the elevator. She supposed Ted would be downstairs, waiting for her.

Mady lay only a little way past the zone sign. Before Corian skidded to a halt, Arin was already running. Corian bobbed and panted after him, his heart a block of ice. Mady might already be dead, or past the point where living was a mercy. Only when he saw Arin scoop up his daughter and start back toward the sign did Corian realize the Gate was off.

Once past the sign, Corian gently pried the child away from her father. Mady's eyes were half open, pupils rolled back, her breathing rapid and shallow. That much was shock; the rest only Arin could tell, but at the moment, he was no help at all trying to hug her again. Corian fended him off.

"No, she's in bad shock. Get the blanket from my cart." When Arin brought it, Corian ordered him to feel for Mady's mind.

Bowed over his daughter, shaking, Arin locked away his fear and probed delicately at the bruised, barely fluttering intelligence that he knew so well. "Maybe . . . maybe they turned it off in time. Yes. It's like a punch in the stomach, I know. You can't breathe at first. I think she's all right. I think she's still herself."

Fingers at Mady's throat, counting the feeble pulse, Corian let out a long breath. *Poor Marian. Eight hundred years old at least, and a terminal case of involvement. She'll never forgive herself.*

Arin stiffened. His head came up like a wolf smelling danger. "Cory, get her out of here quick."

Corian, in the act of elevating Mady's legs, couldn't believe Arin. *"Now?* This is shock."

But Arin's tone brooked no argument.

"Out. Now. Quick!"

Corian still tried to resist. If Mady's mind was intact, her condition remained critical. From her motor centers, the shock reached down into every part of her. The doctor didn't have his medkit, Arin carried him out of the house without it.

"Go, Cory! Lane's coming."

The Wengen gaped. "That's imposs— she couldn't."

"No? What did the printout say? 'Incorporate the aberration into the working mind.' It didn't stop Singer, it didn't stop me." Arin rose, alert for a voice only he could hear. "I read her now. The Gate hurt her. Bad. But she's coming, Cory. She reads us, too. Put Mady in the cart and get the hell out of here."

It was one danger measured against a greater. Corian lifted Mady, tried to obey Arin, but as soon as he picked up the child, he felt a sudden numbing fear from nowhere. His stomach turned over. His legs stopped working. He tried to force them to move, but as he did he heard the harrowing wail begin just over the eastern horizon. He twisted towards it, awkward and off balance. There, at the top of the rise, like a cataract blurring his vision, a crimson optical impossibility shimmered against the sharp division of sky and earth. And it was moving down on them.

"Arin, I can't walk!"

"Tight it."

He tried, but his legs went out from under him. That was how she took them all, he guessed, even Santee. A vicious power that deluded sight and drained the very marrow from the will. Clumsily, Mady against his chest, Corian thrashed and struggled like the cripple he once was, rolling by inches over the ground towards the cart.

"Can you see her, Arin?"

"Better than you."

Arin stalked forward as the shadow came at him in a limping crouch like a spider with a missing leg. Behind all his pity, knotted love and horror, Arin saw his wife and read her pain.

Your power against mine.

"No, Lane."

Your power against mine.

The challenge thrown at him in Wellfleet. She couldn't let it go, though she was now long past the purpose. Only monomaniacal determination dragged her this far. The brief exposure to the Gate was the last of a thousand blows, not the worst, merely the deadliest. She reeled, unable to stand erect. Arin realized she was dying. And yet she drew all her ebbing energy up again, channeling her diseased but disciplined master's power into a flowing tide.

Your power against mine.

The chimera halted, swayed. Her force concentrated and flicked out at Arin's defenses. Not like his old contest with Singer, reined and blunted of its killing power. Shalane couldn't afford that, she must spend what she had left to prize Mady away from him.

She aimed her first javelin of power at paralyzing his motor centers. Arin never expected so much strength. As he met the spear with a deflecting shield of will, she struck again, battering through the wall of his force, coiling about his mind, not trying to whitebrain him, but rather to shatter Arin physically. Already he felt cold tendrils reaching for his heart to stifle its beating, but even as he concentrated to rip them free, Shalane found another opening and thrust through with numbing force.

Arin projected lines of power, feinting to draw her away. He only wanted to fend her off, play out her strength without fighting back. He didn't want to end her, but it was impossible to survive without attacking, she was too strong and edged with madness.

Her mind flailed at him like a whip, each separate lash a threat that must be met. Hunched behind his will, Arin husbanded his own power, coiling it loop upon loop, ready to spring, hating the necessity that gave him no choice.

He felt at Shalane gingerly. She was spending some of her power in holding Cory on the ground. The idea was repugnant to Arin, but he had to do it, risk an opening that would cut him free. . . .

The numbness ebbed from Corian's legs as suddenly as it came. Clutching Mady, he scrambled to rise, but as soon as he did, the dark smudge hovering over Arin paused, then turned on Corian.

"Stay!"

His legs went rubbery again. In helpless fear, Corian huddled in a ball around Mady as the storm that was the Wintermind swept over him. He threw out a futile hand to ward her off.

"Goddess, no!"

In the fluctuating optical spiral surrounding her, Corian caught a distorted vision of wild, hollow eyes and the shifting illusion of a face, changing before his mind could register a single impression.

"Give me her."

Not even her own voice. Fragments of words tossed like flotsam on an ocean of fury and pain. Her hands ripped at his grip; they felt like steel pincers. He rolled over, trying to cover the child completely with his body, but the first blow of her fist hammered him flat against the earth. With a guttural snarl, Shalane flipped Corian over on his back and tore the child from his grasp. Desperately, Corian propelled himself into the whirlwind's center, flailing at anything solid. She might trick his sight with illusion, but not the sense of touch. Corian's arms closed around bony emaciation covered with torn, stinking deerhide. His head exploded with light as another blow landed, this time between eye and ear, but he hung on until the next smashing impact in the same spot loosened his hold and he slipped,

WINTERMIND 279

half-conscious, to the ground—only to be yanked back up again by his neck, her claw-nails penetrating skin, piercing tissue beneath.

Drifting into darkness, Corian thought, *she'll break my neck and not even remember.*

A dangerous trick, and contemptible, but the only thing he could try. Her longing for Mady was too strong, wouldn't allow Corian to try to take the child away.

The ruse gave Arin the time he needed to recover and marshal all his master's power behind one lethal arrow of force.

Shalane's grip faltered. Corian fell heavily to the ground. Mady folded down beside him. The doctor's arm automatically went around the child as he shook his head to clear it, wondering why he wasn't dead. Then he saw Arin up on one knee, gaze bent on Shalane with the merciless expression of a blind god sitting in judgment.

Shalane recoiled, still only a suggestion of form within the flickering remnants of illusion. A smeared watercolor edged with harsh sunlight. Ghost hands floated up to a smudge that must be her head. Shalane's indistinct silhouette wavered in the sun as Arin's gathered power broke upon her in full force.

Shalane was growing clearer and clearer now in Corian's sight. Twisting, writhing, falling, trying to rise again, she at last abandoned the fight and began to crawl towards Corian and what he held in his arms.

"M—M—"

Clearer and clearer. How could anyone hurt her like that? Not even Santee . . .

"M—M—Mady."

Like a patina of dust wiped away from a picture, the blur resolved and cleared. Shalane lay in the grass, limp and still.

Arin moved now. He tottered slowly to his wife. He knelt, lips twitching silently. He turned her over as Corian heaved himself to his feet.

"Cory, don't look."

But he couldn't help himself.

Hollow eyes stared fixedly from a starved, scarred face. Someone had cut a deep X over her mouth, the loose, infected flesh shriveling back from teeth and gums in a parody of a grin, framed by the wisps of hair that hung about her cheeks in clotted strings.

Shalane was emaciated and insect-bitten, her frame shrunken to bone and the last ropes of muscle, legs swollen by the miles from her knees down to blackened, scabby feet. Her deerskin clothes were dark with filth and dried blood. Under the torn shirt, Corian saw a wide lateral slash across the top of her left breast. It was abscessed, and there were similar wounds caked along her thighs. Two hundred miles, butchering and butchered, dying from the start. All for Mady and a dream she couldn't bury.

Funny how you never thought of Lane as beautiful till she moved or rode. Like the gulls at Wellfleet, clumsy on their web feet, but when they float on the wind, you know what they were born for. The way she flew out of a saddle before the horse was barely slowed from a gallop, flying through the air, long legs balanced under her, ready for the ground when it came, laughing as she landed.

Arin caught some of it leaking from Corian, but said nothing. He moved to take up his daughter in her blanket. Cradling her close to his chest, whispering to the child, he knelt again by Shalane. He bent low, kissed the torn mouth.

Beautiful is just a word. Like my brother, I've only learned to spell it in time to carve it over a grave.

Corian was becoming aware of his own pain, the continued throbbing of his contused head, his bruised, bleeding neck, probably infected where her fingers dug in. His back protested every movement. X-rays for sure. Something felt broken. He winced when Arin passed the blanketed child to him again.

"Arin . . . what are you doing?"

Slipping the black knife from Shalane's hip sheath, Arin held the blade high before his eyes, as if concentrating all his loss in it, everything that brought them all to this moment of parting. Then he sank the knife hilt-deep in the soft earth. Again and again he lifted and struck, scooping out great clods. With each swing, dry sounds hacked out of his throat, as if the knife were also hollowing him.

"Born again," he said. "Born again. Say it, Cory."

"Born again."

Arin flailed at the flying brown earth. "Born again. To the Karli. Say it!"

"To the Karli." Corian could only mouth the words that neither of them believed. He watched Arin digging Shalane's grave with an unutterable compassion that yet held something strangely remote in it. *When all the agony is shrouded with ash—*

"Born again." Arin warred at Goddess Earth with his dead wife's blade. "Born again."

—when all the words have been tried and found useless—

"To the Karli." Arin repeated the litany over the threshing knife.

—when there's no word or even a thought big enough for the smallest part of it—

"Born again."

—and only the cold flame of dead tenderness remains in your memory—

"Born again."

—that's when you write of love.

Corian heard the cart jouncing toward them over the meadow, Marian at the wheel, Rashevsky beside her, clutching his medbag. With an effort, Corian rose with Mady.

Digging furiously, Arin didn't look up. "They can't take her yet."

Marian braked the cart and hurried to Mady, Rashevsky close behind. She cast one look at Shalane, then averted her eyes.

"Oh, no." It was a mew of pity. "We didn't do that."

"No," Corian said.

"We turned the Gate off. *I* turned it off."

"I know," Corian said. "Ted, did you bring oxygen?"

"In the cart," Rashevsky assured him, anxiously examining the pallid child. "Oxygen, stimulants. But let's get her on a table for a scan. You, too, Cory. You're hurt."

"Not yet," Arin said dully, tearing at the earth. "Mady's not finished here."

"*Now,* Arin!" Rashevsky said. "Her condition's serious."

"I said wait," the soft voice contradicted.

In the act of reaching out for Mady, Rashevsky found it was the last thing he could, or even wanted to do. The legs under him could stand, but they'd forgotten how to move. He waited, transfixed, while Arin lifted Shalane's head and removed the moon-sigil from her neck. He laid her head back with the same reverent care and brought the sigil to Mady and placed it around her neck.

"Lane would want this," Arin said quietly. "She ought to have at least one thing she came for. You can take her now, Ted."

After they were gone, Arin offered his own knife to Corian.

"Can you cut a circle right?"

The answer was flinty. "I got enough coven in me for that."

Arin went back to the body and began to unwind Shalane's cord belt, passing it over and under her, moving her as little as possible.

At last the entire length was free. He brought the belt with its precisely spaced knots to Corian.

"You know the way. Measure it right and dig."

Corian knew the ritual as well as any deepwoods covener. Starting from Shalane's head, he stretched the six-foot belt three times to a radius of eighteen feet; four times he measured north, south, east, west, then four more between the cardinal points, marking each with a turned sod until Shalane lay within a pocked wheel. Corian began again at the north, cutting a neat trench to connect the holes, working meticulously, not scooping but carving out the turf in precise sections, placing the loose clods in a lip around the shallow trench.

Not till he was almost done did it strike him that he'd carved from the outside, the trench between himself and Shalane.

Well enough. She would have killed me. She was going to kill me.

The funeral circle was closing under Corian's knife when the riders led by Garick, Moss and Jay topped the eastern rise. Corian knew who would be called into the circle and who would stand outside, and he knew what words they'd speak . . . *this is the belly of Goddess Earth and Shalane goes home to her now* and now the circle was done, all except for a small opening left at the north end, which someone else could close from the inside.

"Finished, Arin."

Corian raised the knife and sank it upright in the earth. Then he wobbled to his feet and left the circle, got in his cart and drove away before the funeral began.

Corian sat in his book-piled, tape-littered living room with the lights off. The pillow propped behind him and the special brace for his hairline-cracked vertebrae forced him to sit unnaturally erect in his chair. Between the brace and the ice bag clamped against the swollen side of his face, he was altogether uncomfortable. With care he might manage to put on some lights or play a tape, but darkness and silence were better company now.

She would have killed me. Hold onto that. She was going to kill me. He kept the thought up front like a medical caustic to stop the tears and curdle the grief.

Always outside, looking in. Not really a cowan, but not Circle either, so what was he? He could—he did—waste a lot of years in anger and sorrow over the way coveners excluded him. But now it occurred to Corian, sharp as the pain in his back, that sometimes the deepest layers of the mind were wiser than the spirit that all the coveners talked about and Kriss called the soul. Or maybe they were one and the same. He'd never be Circle, but delving deep below feeling, he realized he could define and encompass coveners in a view never before seen, not even by Rashevsky. And in defining their strength and weakness, he finally purged himself of the need to be one of them.

He'd carved his last circle for Shalane. Now he could write his own signature: not part of them, only himself, content to be other. If he belonged anywhere, it was in the City where he ultimately wanted to be. Maybe, in a hundred years or so of growing up, against all odds, he would belong there.

Corian raised his glass and sipped a fiery concoction of C-concentrate and turnip gin. Together with the pain pill he'd taken, the drink kept his complex misery at a foggy distance.

"Cory?" A sudden voice in the doorway, startling him.

"Hey?"

"The door's open. How are you?"

"Fine, Raddy."

"Sure you are." Diane threaded her way through books and clutter to find a seat on the floor beside his chair. She placed a paper in his lap. Whatever, it wasn't worth turning on the lights for. After all his carnal invitations, he was vaguely curious why she'd come this evening. Probably because he couldn't do much about it.

"It's a note from Marian," she told him. "Your official clearance for full syn/time. As much as you need."

In spite of his condition, Corian was impressed. "Imagine Ted had something to do with this."

"Oh, Marian didn't need much persuading. Though Ted did say something about your having no scruples as a researcher. That's a compliment."

He fingered the paper, then just let it rest in his lap. Diane shifted closer.

"I can save you time, teach you technique. I'd like to."

He swigged from his glass. "Thanks, Raddy."

"If you won't explode every time I suggest."

"No." The ice bag canted a little towards her. "All help appreciated. When I'm ready." His tone suggested that event was nowhere in the near future.

"So," she said with strained brightness, "how does one say congratulations in Wengen?"

"Look, I don't feel too good right now."

"No wonder. Ever see a chem/scan on what you're drinking?"

"Yeah, yeah, yeah."

"*Well,*" she said, smiling coolly in the dark. "Old come-close-go-away Cory. 'Gimme your ass, Raddy, but don't get too close along the way.'"

"Dammit, shut up."

"*And* shut up, Raddy, the child says." She couldn't suppress a giggle, chin on her knees. "You're so afraid someone'll really know you. Well, I do. Without your permission, I seem to have developed a preposterous affection for you."

"So?"

"So. It must be horrible to be thirty. I've forgotten."

EPILOGUE

(from Spitt's Diary)

There's less mystery to me than one might expect in Arin's disappearance from City. From the moment his father forced him into mastership, Arin's gaze turned outward to new things, rather than the unchanging rhythms of Circle. In the end, he took some of what both Circle and City have to offer and, like Singer, went away to seek his own answers.

I'm sure Shalane's death was a catalyst to his actions. For several years, he remained in City to help Mady get over the death of her mother. She came to depend more and more on Marian's heartfelt care and during that time, father and daughter were seldom apart.

But one day, Arin handed me a sealed letter for his father, and then he simply was gone. Later I found out he was last seen taking a southbound trading boat for Balmer.

The letter was a thick one. Garick read it, then said to me, "Arin's looking for Singer."

That part was understandable. I always sensed something unfinished between Arin and Singer, between Singer and Garick. The two boys were at such poles of Garick's and the world's opinion. Hero and outcast. For my money, Singer never valued anything so much as his father's love, but Arin seemed done with all that. No love left unspoken or ungiven. When he buried Shalane, a door closed forever and another opened.

The remarkable thing that still sticks in my memory is how, for the first time in well over a decade, Garick spoke Singer's name with a warmth I thought he no longer had in him.

But I never got to read Arin's letter.

#

Full grown, Mady looks more like Garick than either of her parents. For a while after the Gate incident, she suffered partial memory loss, and she'll always have to deal with some impairment of motor centers, but like most City women, she's only concerned with her body as a vehicle for work.

She's much taller than Shalane, but has none of her mother's physical awareness, let alone her grace. Though her personal charm more than makes up for it. If Mady breaks a glass or stumbles for lack of coordination, there's something about her that makes you eager to collect the pieces or gently steady her before she falls.

Mady's earned her reputation as a theorist in lep learning, and though she identifies more with City than Circle, she's become a master, too. But I've never seen her wear any badge of rank other than her mother's moon-sigil.

She works closely now with Jakov Levitt. Surprising at first, considering how cranky he is. But he actually seems fond of her.

I mentioned it to Ted. He said someday he might be able to tell me about Levitt, but not then. I pestered him about it, but the only other thing he said didn't help much.

"City people have to learn to die a little, too," Ted murmured.

#

When I was sixty and already viewing death as an imminent reality, Ted plugged me in for a few more free decades, and I'm glad I let him. Age has given me an unusual sense of the arch of changing times. But there are drawbacks, too. I was talking to Bern's mathematician grandson the other day. He just took a Mrikan as his cohabitor. Coven and cowan mingle more freely now, and if older deep-woods grumble about it over their pone (eaten off new, fine-glazed dishes), their disapproval no longer holds a gasp of religious horror. Not like Shalane who thought cowans untouchable except for Jay Kriss and Corian.

Well, I showed Bern's grandson an old photograph that Diane took—was it *that* long ago?—when the covens came to Lorl after Dannyline. Shalane—there she sits, frozen in the past, on Korbin's old plank porch in deerskin and tabard with the black knife at her hip and her hair chopped short. Wild and wary as a forest creature thrust from timelessness into a cage ticking with numbered minutes, days, months and years that had no meaning for her.

I've contemplated that picture many times. With a magnifier, you can see something in her eyes, an expression both vital and alien

—a woman born to live, hear and see differently from me or any Mrikan. But Bern's grandson—the great-grandson of a Karli goddess —smiled at the picture and said it was *quaint*.

Kids. Know so little and think they know so much. I found it hard to be polite to him. But after a drink or two, I tacitly forgave him. He couldn't help it. No one wears deerskin or tabards now, and he's never been to Karli.

Little by little, the old ways are fading out everywhere . . . and people forget so fast. . . .